FIREBOLT

THE DRAGONIAN SERIES

ADRIENNE WOODS

DEDICATION

To my Heinrich, Maddison, and Jamie-Leigh: I've loved you since the first time I saw you, and without you this wouldn't have been possible.

ACKNOWLEDGEMENTS

First and the most important, thanks go to our Father in Heaven, for blessing me every day. Without Your guidance, I wouldn't have done or finished with this if You were not involved in this every day. You are my purpose of life and I will love You till the end of time.

Then I would like to thank my extraordinary beta readers, Cloey, Lasse Moller, Ken and Esmerelda Lourens, for your valuable input, patience and willingness to delve into another world head first.

To the lovely people of my writing group: Claire my GG, Lucy, Amanda, Kelly and Rodney. Your input and compliments pushed me through the tough and difficult times when I wanted to give up.

For the endless support of my family; I would be lost without your loving support and your ability to keep me pursuing this project when I didn't want to carry on.

To Vinique; for devouring an endless pile of query letters without a word of complaint. Love you to bits and thank you for being such a significant person in my life.

To Graeme, with your unique personality, and for the back flip of this novel. You are a jewel and a genius when it comes to words.

A special thanks to my wonderful editors: Hillery, you are a true Paegeian and your love for beautiful words has given *Firebolt* the wings it needed to soar. Monique and Zoe, your insight to the words on these pages made Elena and all her friends so much more entertaining, and a big thank you for polishing my work to perfection.

To my cover artist Joemel. Your grace and elegance with lines, shadows and colors has made my novel cover truly spectacular. You were able to reach into my imagination, capture, and re-imagine a world I thought only I would ever see. Because of your passion and skill I truly hope my book will be judged by its cover.

You are all unique, inspiring and gifted. I'm truly blessed to have each and every one of you in my life. Without each of your gifts and support, *Firebolt* would still be a dream. Thank you for weaving my dream into reality.

.

"Man must rise above the Earth—to the top of the atmosphere and beyond—for only thus will he fully understand the world in which he lives."

Socrates

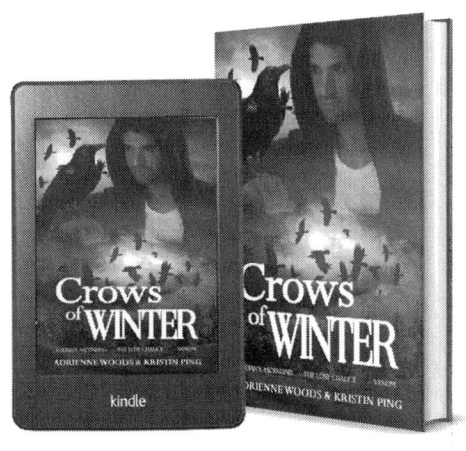

FREE READ AT THE END OF THE BOOK AND
INTRODUCING KRISTIN PING

SERIES ORDER

FIREBOLT
THUNDERLIGHT
FROSTBITE
MOONBREEZE
STARLIGHT

NOVELLAS
VENOM (1.5)
POISON(3.5)

SPIN-OFF
MOONBEAM
DARKBEAM PART I-III
STARBEAM
FIREBEAM
BLAKE'S JOURNAL
THE WORLD OF PAEGEIA
(please note that not all the spin-off's are published)

1

A Girl singing out her heart out about a miracle boomed inside my ear. A miracle would get me what I needed: a chance at a semi-normal life.

The bedroom door hitting the wall expelled the thought from my mind. With his hand tangled up in his copper hair, and with huge brown eyes, dad's figure filled the entire doorway. "Pack your bags." He had that set to his jaw, the one that meant there was no way out of this. He bolted out of the room just as suddenly as he had appeared.

I ground my teeth, hard. A sharp pain behind my eyes, I guessed from the lack of sleep, grew stronger. Every fiber of my being wanted to explode.

Ever since I could remember my name, dad and I had been on the run. From what? *Beats me.*

For the past two weeks, I'd been pacing through the house, struggling to fall asleep at night, waiting for this day.

For the love of blueberries, no sixteen-year-old should live this way!

I climbed off my bed, and the first step I took left my toe tangled in the wide leg of my jeans. I tried to regain my balance as the closet inched closer, but with wildly flailing arms, I came crashing down. The thud reverberated across the wooden floor, and it sounded as if I'd broken something.

Dad darted back into my room. "Are you okay?" He lifted me back onto my feet as if I weighed nothing.

Tears lurked in the corners of my eyes, as I stared up at him.

"Don't give me that look, Elena. Please, we need to hurry." He pulled my suitcase from the top shelf and chucked it haphazardly onto my bed. "We need to go. Now."

"Dad..."

He started to grab my clothes from the shelf and tossed them messily inside my small suitcase. Then he paused, sighed, and looked up with soft eyes. He stroked the side of my cheek. "This..." He looked past me. "...wasn't the right place, Bear. Please, you've got to trust me."

He reached back to pull everything off my shelf, while I curled my hands into balls of fury. My heart pounded fast as those two words bounced inside my skull. "Trust you?"

"Elena, we don't have much time," he yelled. "Pack your bags! You can ask questions later." He left, and the hollow *thump* from his stomping footsteps rang loudly as he made his way into the hall.

Ask questions? Yeah right! I'll only get answers that don't reveal why we are on the run for the gazillionth time. "Trust me" and "I'll tell you when the time is right" were the only two answers dad gave. *Guess the time with him will never be right.*

It was no use arguing with him anyway. Once, he had

thrown me over his shoulder and carried me out without any of my things.

So I grabbed the stuff I needed: my MP3 player, a photo of Mom and me on my first birthday that dad didn't know I had, and my journal from underneath my bed. I tossed them into my backpack. It wasn't much, but it was the stuff that made my miserable life feel less pathetic. I zipped up my suitcase and took a deep breath. Looking around my bedroom for the last time, I said goodbye to my sixtieth-something room.

Dad almost ran me over in the hall, his army bag slung over his shoulder. He grumbled, which I assumed was an apology, took my suitcase, and ran downstairs. He always rented these huge old houses, pre-furnished and near the countryside, and we always left after three months.

The pickup's horn honked as I shut the front door. I closed my eyes and took another deep breath. *Just two more years, then I'll be eighteen and free from this freak show.* Huge raindrops fell hard onto the ground. The smell of wet dirt filled the air. It was my favorite smell.

The water that pooled on the ground covered all the gaps in the driveway, forcing me to hopscotch around all of them. My shoe got caught in one of the gaps and I smacked down hard in a huge puddle. By the time I reached the truck, my jeans and shoes dripped with water.

Warm heat from the vents inside the truck hit me full blast as I jumped in; a million goosebumps erupted across my skin. As soon as I shut the rusty door, dad floored the gas pedal. Tires screeched and the truck spun away as if the devil were chasing us. My lower lip quivered softly as he swerved onto the road. The streetlights flew by in a blur, and I plugged in my earphones. The same stupid song about a miracle boomed from my MP3 player, drowning the sound of the engine and the hard dribbles on the roof, a percussion that became the perpetual soundtrack to my misery.

A feeling of utter loneliness consumed my heart while I stared out the window. Homes with white picket fences and a convenience store whizzed by in a flash. A tear rolled down my cheek. Saying a silent goodbye, I released my breath and watched as it created a foggy condensation on the glass. With my index finger, I reached out and drew a small heart. These were the reasons why Mom had left. She couldn't handle his paranoia, but why she'd left her two-year-old daughter to deal with it was a mystery. Dad constantly reminded me of the latter; that was the only time he ever spoke of her. If he ever discovered I had that picture, he would kill me. That was how much he hated her for leaving us.

The lights of a vehicle in the upcoming lane shone directly into my face. I shut my eyes, waiting for it to disappear. When I was little, I used to watch dad as we drove away from yet another house. He would glare into his rearview mirror every five seconds, all the muscles in his face clenched, and his knuckles white on the steering wheel. I hadn't been able to force myself to peek out the window then, as it used to scare the living crap out of me to consider the possible reasons why he was fleeing, or who might be following us. Now, I didn't look at him or care much about what he was going through. He'd created this problem, with me becoming the luggage. It was a ritual I endured every three months, and nothing during the past sixteen years had ever changed that.

The "Interstate 40" sign flew by in a whirl, and the pickup slowly moved onto the turnoff lane.

My eyes started to burn as I stared at the rain running sideways against my window. Each rivet resembled another town, another place I could never again call home. Exhaustion consumed me and my eyelids felt heavy. I laid my head against the window and struggled to stay awake.

Suddenly, a huge figure flew past me. Dad swerved to the left, which made me crash into his side. My entire body pumped with adrenaline. I jumped straight in my seat and tore out my earphones as I wrenched the seatbelt over my shoulder to buckle myself in, while trying to process what had just happened.

"What was that?" I looked at dad.

His eyes huge, he kept checking his rearview mirror every five seconds. Beads of sweat rolled from his hairline down to the side of his temple. Sure, he was paranoid, but I'd never seen dad this scared in my entire life. This was something more than his usual paranoia.

"Dad!"

"Did you see where it went?" he asked, attempting to

inject calm into his voice, but I could hear the fear lacing each syllable.

"See where what went? Dad, what was that?"

"You wouldn't believe me if I told you."

"For once in your life, just tell me!" I screamed. Sixteen years of frustration exploded from my lungs. I couldn't take the unknown anymore.

"Fine." He mumbled something else that I didn't catch. "Do you remember the stories I used to tell you?"

"Stories? What stories?"

"The stories about Paegeia, Elena." He looked in his rearview mirror again.

Vaguely, but I didn't tell him that. "What does that have to do with this?"

"They're real."

I froze and stared at him.

"All of it, it's real. The dragons, the magic, the Wall, everything is real."

"Dragons!" I couldn't believe this. "Is this why we've been on the run my whole life? That's your reason?" I took a deep breath.

"You can believe what you want, it doesn't change the fact that they are real, and somewhere out there." He looked over his shoulder.

A figure with huge paws and talons flew in front of the truck. Tires screeched at the same time as I shrieked. The truck spun around a couple of times and came to a standstill on the dark stretch of road. My heart jumped at a great speed. My throat and lips became dry from my deep, heavy breathing.

My face pushed against the cool glass of the passenger window, I searched the horizon for any sign of life. Apart from the pickup's headlights, not a single light peeked through the blanketed darkness, and the rain crushing down made me see figures, but I couldn't tell if they were real. *Dragons don't exist.*

"You okay?" my dad yelled.

"I'm fine." I tore my gaze away from the window.

His hands were on the door's handle. "Elena, I need to get out—"

"No, no, please don't leave me here!" I grabbed his jacket. I could feel the fear beginning to rise again, and my vision became blurry. *Why am I afraid? Dragons aren't real.*

He cupped my face and made me look at him. I only noticed now how his hands trembled. "Listen to me, Elena. Listen!"

I tried to swallow my tears, but it was no use. They were caught in the back of my throat, silencing me.

He hugged me tightly and kissed me on my forehead. I could feel the love he had for me behind that kiss. "You drive like hell, you hear me? Don't slow down for anybody. There's a motel on Interstate Forty. Just stay on this road, you can't miss it. Someone named Matt will meet you there."

"Dad, it's pouring outside. I can't leave you here with whatever..." *We can sort this out rationally.*

Dad cringed and stared at his jeans When he looked at me again, that set to his jaw was back. My words hadn't made any impact on him whatsoever. He had already made up his mind for the both of us.

My strength returned as I slowly came to terms with what I had to do.

A man appeared in the middle of the road. We both stared at him for a few seconds. I squinted, as the rain made it hard for me to see him, but the headlights of the truck outlined his figure. I looked back at dad and could tell from the look on dad's face that this guy was no stranger.

My gaze turned back to the guy in the rain. He was tall with long black hair; wet strands clung to his face. He wore a pair of pants, no T-shirt, and it looked like no shoes either. He stared at the pickup and it made my heart pound faster. He began to walk slowly toward us.

"Dad?" I slapped his shoulder, trying to expel the fear from my body.

"Elena." He grabbed my wrist. "I'll be fine. You need to go. Now. And, Bear, I'm so sorry. Whatever happens, don't stop for anything."

"Dad?" My lower lip quivered again. He kissed me one more time on my forehead and wiped away my tears gently with his thumbs.

"I'll meet you there." He sounded stern, climbed out of the truck and slammed the door. My gaze switched back to

8

this macho loon making his way toward dad, who stood right next to the pickup. I quickly moved into the driver's seat, took a deep breath, and buckled up.

With my hands trembling on the steering wheel, I took another deep breath.

You can do this, the voice in my head rambled a few times. The key sat lazily in the ignition, and I jerked it to the right. The pickup sputtered and died. The guy disappeared into the darkness, and a new fear pumped through my veins.

"No, no, no, no! Please don't die on me now," I mumbled as I tried to restart the engine. The man appeared again in the faint glow of the headlights. He was getting closer.

"Start you stupid piece of crap!" I yelled over the roar of the blood pumping in my ears.

The engine came to life and I screamed as the man leaped toward the pickup. Dad jumped and tackled him in midair. "Go, Elena!" he shouted over the pounding rain.

I floored the gas pedal and the pickup's tires screeched as I drove past dad, who'd wrestled the guy onto the road. Tears blurred my sight.

I can't just leave him back there. I struggled to come to terms with what was going on.

My father and the other man quickly disappeared into the horizon of my rearview mirror. I wiped away my tears with the back of my hand and lowered the mirror so that I could see dad, but they had vanished into the night.

Don't stop for anything, his voice replayed inside my head.

My hands trembled on the shift as I found third gear. A strong force hit the pickup on the passenger's side. The impact of the blow jolted through my body as the truck rolled a few times then came to a halt on its roof, leaving me suspended in the air. My head and body throbbed, and my hand went automatically to the ache on my head. It was warm and wet, and when I brought back my hand, it was smeared with dark blood. My head began to buzz and my vision started to slip away.

Lightning struck, and the road was instantly engulfed in flames, leaving me wide awake. Something to the left grabbed my attention as the fire slowly began to creep toward the overturned truck. Something lifted the truck, righting it on the asphalt once again, and a shrill sound left my lips.

The belly of a huge, blue beast on four legs the size of tree stumps stood in front of the pickup. The sight left me breathless and my entire body froze. *Dragons don't exist.*

A part of its head popped in front of me. Huge horns on the top of his nose lingered inches from the windshield, leaving a foggy condensation on the glass as he breathed. One of his frilly ears lay flat against his head, like a cat's when sensing danger.

He placed a front leg on top of the hood, and my body trembled as the truck started to crumple. A part of his wing came into sight. It appeared to be shredded, with a sharp talon located at the end. Oval-shaped blue scales fanned over its entire body, glistening in the flames on the side of the road. Maybe it only looked that way through the tears blinding my sight. Beady eyes, sunken deeply into its skull, locked with mine. The picture in front of me just became my nightmare. I yelped as the dragon's weight shifted, forcing the pickup to crumple even more.

Another dragon sank its jaws into the one in front of me. Two huge copper horns lay flat on top of its copper head. The blue dragon growled, and snapped with gaping jaws at the copper one attacking it. With powerful force the blue dragon was dragged off the pickup's hood and thankfully away from me. The truck shook slightly and groaned, while my heart pounded as if I'd just run a mile.

A bolt of fire came from the sky and lit up the entire scene in front of me.

More dragons landed with thuds in the middle of the road. One seemed to be green with a long neck and a fin-like mane running from the top of its head to its tail. A cloud of dark fog emerged slightly from its nostrils. Another was red and oddly beautiful, but something evil derived from its aura. They attacked the copper dragon with startling savagery.

Get the hell away from here, my inner voice shrilled. Quickly, I tried to unbuckle my seatbelt, but the clip wouldn't release. The earth shook with bolts of fire, and lightning flew through the air, while I tried to free myself.

My father wouldn't just leave me here! As each second ticked by, I worried more about dad.

The dragons came close to the truck a number of times, but the copper one kept driving them back, as if it was trying to protect me. I shook my head, trying to expel that thought. *Dragons don't exist. Wake up.* The tips of my fingers felt raw as I hammered endlessly on the buckle of the safety belt. My face was soaked with sweat and blood, and I knew that I had to get out of the truck, quickly. With trembling hands, I pounded on the buckle with my fist until it unlocked. Throwing the restraint from around me, I watched in horror as the copper dragon bit fiercely into the blue's neck. Blood squirted everywhere and pooled in thick puddles on the road. The blue dragon staggered and dropped down to the ground. Electricity still sparked off its body, but soon died away. The green and red dragons jumped on top of the copper, but it knocked the red one onto the ground forcefully and crushed the green dragon with its huge front legs. The sound of flesh ripping was sickening, and I had to lean over as tremors wracked my stomach, but for some reason I couldn't look away. The picture of the copper dragon shredding the green dragon's wing sent a stab of new fear deep into me.

"Dad, where the hell are you?" I pleaded into the darkness.

The red dragon got back up and flew away just as the copper one moved from the green's wing to his neck. I flinched and finally looked away as more blood squirted out of where the green dragon's neck used to be. When I looked again, the copper dragon had turned its gaze to me.

I started to kick at the windshield with my newly freed legs. A new sense of urgency punctuated every kick.

C'mon! I kicked three, four times, but it only left long cracks in the glass. Watching the copper dragon trudge toward the pickup through the jagged cracks made the scene before me even more terrifying. The dragon stopped right in front of the pickup, our eyes locked, and I could see the vertical pupils inside a pair of dark, rich brown irises. My heart thumped wildly as it hooked one of its talons gently into the windshield and ripped it off.

It paused, stared at me for what seemed like an eternity, took a few steps back, and nodded in my direction.

It wants me to get out? You're imagining things, Elena. Dragon's aren't real.

I didn't act. I couldn't. The dragon started to shrink. Its wings and legs dwindled into a smaller size until they disappeared. Its big head and horns shrank into nothing. I watched as the dragon's huge shape melted away, and the heap transformed into a low-crouching figure. He lifted his head, and huge cuts seeping with blood became visible. It felt as if somebody had squeezed all the air out of my lungs. I'd finally found my father—without a shred of clothing.

2

"DAD? WHAT THE—" I couldn't find a way to put into words of what I'd just seen.

He staggered toward the pickup and I closed my eyes. I would be scarred for the rest of my life after seeing him naked. My mind went crazy with words like "dragon," and "Dad," and "dragon" again—thoughts that would land me in the nuthouse if spoken out loud.

The zip of his army bag pierced the silence. I could hear him struggling to get into his pants. I pinched myself with shaky fingers. *How did I not know any of this? Is this actually happening? No, it's a dream. I'm going to wake up soon and—*

"You can open your eyes, Elena." His voice interrupted my string of thoughts and I knew I wasn't dreaming.

I opened my eyes and stared at him. "Dad, why didn't—"

"I didn't want you to find out this way. I'm so sorry." He cleaned the cuts on his face with another t-shirt. Our eyes met, and he looked at me with a clenched jaw. All traces of the copper beast were gone, not one scale in sight.

He held out his hand for mine, his other raised, as if to signal surrender. Trembling, I accepted and he helped me get out through the opening where the windshield should've been. My entire body shook now, and the cut on my head stung fiercely.

My hoody and jeans hooked and tore on pieces of broken glass as I placed my shoes on the crumpled bonnet, but my gaze didn't leave Dad as I climbed through the jagged gap. When I was free from the truck, I watched him pour clean water from a bottle onto a shirt that he pressed to my head.

"Ow!" I pulled away my head.

"Hold still," he said, and patted my forehead softly with the cool, wet shirt.

I ground my teeth. It felt as if someone had hit me with a baseball bat.

I didn't know what to say, and a horrible silence filled the air between us while he put a Band-Aid on my face.

"I need to make a call."

"Dad?" I grabbed his arm, and he turned back around to face me. "Are more dragons coming for us?"

"I don't know, Bear." He caressed my cheek gently with his thumb. He dialed a number and held the phone carefully to his ear. His eyes searched everywhere, his face illuminated by the soft glow of the phone. "Matt, Herbert here. We got attacked by dragons." Dad spoke fast and listened for a few seconds. He walked away from me, facing away from the truck. "No...I told you, not over the phone." He spoke softly. "We are stuck on Interstate Forty, just meet us and please hurry...I don't know if more are coming." Dad switched off the phone, returned it to the pocket of his pants then faced me again.

"Elena, I need to tell you something. Believe me when I say this wasn't how I planned on doing this." He sniffed hard and wiped his nose with his index finger and thumb. His eyes searched the horizon before they fell back onto mine. "I wanted to take you out for a nice dinner and maybe ease into things." The corner of his lips curved softly, and then the smile disappeared just as fast. "But..." He sighed, blinked a few times, and looked away. "Bear." His gaze found mine again with tears in his eyes. "I love you more than life itself, and I would never let anything happen to you. You need to understand that."

I nodded more than once, but struggled to wrap my head around the fact that my Dad could morph into a dragon.

He swallowed hard and lowered his gaze.

What is he not telling me?

A screech that pierced the darkness made both of us jump.

"Elena, just run," Dad hissed and pushed me gently in the direction I needed to follow. "As fast as you can. Matt is on his way, go, now!"

I heard the sound of ripping jeans, and when I looked back, a huge dragon stood in the place where my father had been seconds ago. I didn't even have time to say goodbye or "I love you." All I could do was what he asked, and I started to run.

Tears blurred my vision, and I wiped them away vigorously. Not that it helped; everything was pitch-dark and I couldn't see a thing in front of me. I fell down hard but got back up and kept running. I didn't look back as I silently prayed for the motel to come into sight. Another screech made me stumble again. This time fire lit up the entire road. I looked at the sky and saw the outline of the dragon, the one with the beautiful face. A shiver ran up my spine as I remembered the evil emanating from him.

Where is my father? I'm going to die. Don't give up, Elena. Get up! I kept running, while the dragon, lurking in the darkness, followed my trail. A predator that I could not see was stalking me, but each new shiver told me it was there.

I shrieked as something hard pressed into my rib cage. I hadn't even heard it coming. One moment my feet were touching the ground, the next, I was soaring through the air. Its talons pressed hard into my flesh. If it pressed any harder, it would snap me in two.

The flapping of its wings was loud and it reeked of sulfur. I started to cough uncontrollably as the strong smell crept into my lungs. My eyes started to burn, and it felt as if my head were going to explode.

My whole body shook when the dragon collided with something hard. The dragon's weight was thrown back, and his grip around my torso vanished.

I tumbled through the air. A vague vision of another dragon snapping at the red dragon came into view. The red dragon breathed fire that lit up the sky. The two dragons became smaller as I descended. My heart beat so fast. Then everything went black and all became silent.

～

DULL VOICES SPOKE quietly in the background. At first, I couldn't make out what was being said. It sounded hollow, as if they were speaking into a tin can. One question dwelled in my mind: *Was Dad okay?*

Sight returned in shadows, first the light, then a bit of gray. Four figures stood over me, but I couldn't tell whether they were male or female.

"Constance?" A man with a strong Asian accent spoke clearly.

"Not now, Master Longwei," a woman admonished in a British accent.

I tried to lift my hands from my sides. I couldn't move.

Why can't I move?

The British woman barked a breakdown of medical stuff to someone, and one of the figures disappeared.

"There's something else you need to know," a man who sounded vaguely American said to my right. "She has the mark. It's a dark one too."

Mark? What does that mean? Am I dangerous? Will I be okay?

My heart rate rose again, something heavy sat on my chest.

"But you said that her father was a dragon," the Asian man said, sounding confused.

"How is this possible, Matt?" the British woman asked.

"I don't know, Constance. I told you everything I know."

Matt? Where's my Dad?

The three figures lean over me. The British woman wore a long, white lab coat and had a stethoscope draped around her neck. She had the strangest silver glow in her hair, and she exuded confidence. The Asian man was short, middle-aged, and wore the ugliest Hawaiian shirt I had ever seen. The American, who I assumed was Matt, appeared to be in his fifties, with golden blond hair and a huge nose.

"You did well, Matt." The Asian man patted him on the shoulder

"I just wish that I'd gotten there sooner," Matt said with a darkness returning to his eyes. My heart beat faster.

The doctor turned her attention to me. "Do you know her name?"

"I think he said it was Eloise, or Elena. I think it is Elena," Matt said.

"Elena, can you hear me?" she asked, shining a light into my eyes. Dark spots danced across my sight.

I hate that.

The woman repeated my name. Each time she became more anxious.

The Asian man touched the woman's shoulder gently. "Constance?"

Her gaze snapped back to him. "No, Master Longwei," she said in a firm tone. "I'm not giving up. She's too young and she has barely lived. I will—"

"You can't save them, Constance. Their minds don't perceive our reality. She needs—"

"No! I won't give her the serum. Her mark is dark; we should try to get her back!" Her gaze fell on mine again. "Elena, please!" She had tears in her eyes as she pleaded with my immobile body. "Just blink once. It's all you have to do."

Blink, Elena, blink, the voice in my head demanded. I didn't want any serum, but I couldn't blink.

She waited a few seconds. "Elena!" she yelled.

The Asian gawked at her, stunned by the sudden outburst.

I finally blinked. I did it multiple times, afraid they hadn't seen.

A hysterical laugh mixed with relief escaped from the doctor's lips as she wiped the tears from her face with the back of her hand.

Matt took a deep breath.

"What can I do, Constance?" asked the Asian, I assumed was Master Long-something.

"Nothing at the moment, just let her rest. She's been through enough for one day."

MY EYES OPENED, and I found myself lying on a small bed in an infirmary. Each limb worked again, except my arms. They did their own crazy thing and moved without my control. My one hand clawed and pulled at the IV bulging from under my skin. Liquid squirted everywhere and the machine connected to the syringe made a crazy high-pitched sound.

The rest of the beds were empty and I pushed myself up straight while I desperately searched for Dad.

Haven't they found him?

"Everything is going to be okay." The doctor's voice came from right next to me. It made me jerk. I hadn't even seen her.

Our eyes met, and I ended up staring like an idiot. Her light gray eyes, with dark spots inside the irises, started to calm my nerves.

With warm hands she pressed gently against my jaw.

I felt the cold metal disk of her stethoscope on my back. Goosebumps blossomed everywhere on my skin, as she moved the metal disk around.

"Breathe," she ordered, authority filling her voice.

I took a deep breath. The question of my father's fate scorched the tip of my tongue as I struggled to take another breath. Tears lurked in the corners of my eyes as different scenarios played around The stethoscope went back around her neck when she finished.

"Where's...my dad?"

The corners of her mouth dropped and her eyes became soft.

I knew with what had happened last night that the chances of him being alive were slim. "Is he...dead?" It scarcely came out as my chest contracted with barely contained emotion.

She nodded.

"No," I said in a soft whisper, and a tear rolled down my cheek and landed on the white linens of my bed. My throat closed up, and I struggled to breathe. She carefully helped me dangle my bare feet over the edge of the bed then placed an oxygen mask over my face. Air filled my lungs once more as she ordered me to take deep breaths.

An image of Dad in our last moments before that dragon came back played in my mind. He had wanted to tell me something, but had never gotten the chance.

A shattering pain went through my heart, breaking it into a million pieces. I couldn't hold back the tears anymore, and I let them run angrily across my flushed face.

"Sweetheart?" The doctor cupped my face in her hands and crouched in front of me. She pressed me tightly against her chest, and her arms curled around my shoulders, while she waited for me to calm down. It was only when my sobs turned into heaves that she spoke again. "My name is Constance. You came to us two days ago. Do you remember?"

Two days ago? I nodded as my teeth dented the inside of my mouth. My jaw muscles tightened. "How did he die?"

"The dragons killed him," Constance said.

I bit hard on my lip as I tried to force back more tears.

She told me about Matt catching me right before I hit the ground. Matt must have been the other dragon that collided with the red one. He was part of the FBI and one of his co-workers who worked with him on the scene had gone to look for any survivors, but they had found none.

She told me how every dragon was registered, except for us. Her explanation raised more questions than it gave answers—questions I couldn't answer.

She poured a glass of water. "Elena, why were the dragons after your father?"

"I don't know. I didn't even know he was a dragon!" I said as I took the glass from her hand.

"When did you find out?" she asked.

"The night on Interstate Forty." It sounded like the title of a bad love song.

The conversation in the pickup before the accident suddenly jumped into my head.

"Where am I?" I asked.

"You're inside Paegeia. It's a world—"

"I know about Paegeia." I didn't know what to make of it.

"He told you about our world?"

I nodded as deeply as my bruised neck would allow.

"Then I'm sure that you know that no human can leave after going past the Wall."

I sighed. The stories were foggy. 'The Bermuda Triangle' were the only words that occupied my mind. I struggled to remember more details. Tears welled up in my eyes again. I succumbed, buried my face in my palms, and sobbed.

She held me close against her chest and murmured words of comfort into my hair. When my crying reduced to dry heaves yet again, Constance spoke cautiously. "I'm sorry to ask you this, Elena, but did your father ever mention the mark of the Dragonians?"

I snapped up my head and stared at her. "The what?"

"Your mark is of true significance on this side," she continued. "One as dark as yours, well, let's just say that dragon children don't bear something that special."

I remembered them speaking about the mark earlier, but I still didn't know what it meant for me. I shook my head.

Everything twirled inside my mind, making me dizzy. Touching my cheeks, and sliding my hands to the back of my neck, I leaned against the pillow. I stared at the ceiling, watching a fan spin really fast until it blurred out, into nothing.

Dad's gone. I'll never see him again. "I shouldn't have left him that night." I spoke to the ceiling until I broke down again. *I didn't even say goodbye.*

"Don't blame yourself, Elena," Constance said, offering me only comfort; no words could erase the pain and guilt.

She caressed my arm and waited patiently for me to finish processing.

"Wait, if Dad was a dragon, am I—" I said in a panic, attempting to push myself back up to a sitting position.

"No." She giggled, and helped me back down onto the bed. *Sorry*, Constance mouthed and took a deep breath. "You would've known by now if you were a dragon." She pulled the blankets back over me. "I think that's enough for one night, don't you?"

I glanced at the clock on the wall. The arms showed three o'clock, and by the silence, I guessed it was a.m.

I nodded slowly, positioning my head back onto the soft pillow. Our conversation had ended.

3

I PRESSED THE GREEN button near my head and warm, soft pink water came splashing from the metal nozzle. It smelled like roses, and a sense of calm washed over me.

I had never been in a shower quite like this one, until a few days ago. Grecian marble seats lined the walls with mosaic tiles placed in delicate and intricate patterns on the floor. The water cleared and rinsed my body mentally and physically. The flow, softer than before, caressed my skin, creating small waves across my still-bruised flesh. My skin had begun to flush in the heat, making my now greenish-yellow bruises darker and more pronounced.

The tension in my muscles and the pounding inside my head started to evaporate as the heat and smells enveloped me. At the moment, these showers were the highlight of every day.

I got lost in the string of thoughts swirling inside my head like an unrelenting vortex.

I'd always wondered about Dad's stories and if Paegeia was really located inside the Bermuda Triangle. A part of me always felt that it could be real. I just never imagined it was. I still couldn't remember the details, just that he used to tell them to me. The only thing I could recall was that

Paegeia was a realm hidden from the human world behind an enchanted wall, a realm where dragons and magic existed.

During the past few days, Constance had tried to help me make peace with whatever was going on outside. She was beautiful, tall, skinny, and had that kind of smile that made you feel you could do anything, take on anything, even if it involved scaly beasts soaring through the sky. She also explained that the people of Paegeia had had to conjure the Wall nine hundred years ago to protect magic from other people—dark, selfish ones who wanted to harness and abuse the magic for themselves. Only after the Wall was erected had they realized that just the dragons could cross it. Once a human entered Paegeia, they could never leave. I looked at it like buying a one-way ticket to Neverland.

Still, Dad must have told me about this, but why I couldn't remember it raised more questions.

The water continued to wash over me. I really struggled to accept Dad's death. I felt responsible for it. No matter how many times that scene of him yelling at me to run played in my mind, and how many times I tried to tell myself it was what he wanted, I felt the opposite. I should've stayed. I could've helped, not knowing how; I should've been there to try. Matt wasn't that far and, if I could've distracted the dragon, just maybe Dad might still have been alive.

His death, and the fact that dragons were real, were the

reasons I had spent nearly five days sequestered inside this infirmary.

I hated hospitals, more than I hated moving, but Constance and Julia were really kind. Julia helped her with nursing duties. She was beautiful with big doe eyes and thick waves of black hair. She was funny too, and made me giggle more than once with her dry sense of humor. For some reason I imagined her as a goth chick on her days off, with dark makeup and wearing black clothes with lace-up boots and a nose ring or two.

The two of them had been my only company since I arrived here, other than Master Longwei. He was the head-master of Dragonia, where this infirmary was located. He too popped in from time to time to check on my recovery.

We would have these long conversations of making peace with the past and focusing on the future crap that ended up making me feel more guilty.

His number one piece of advice: if I wanted to keep my sanity, I had to face whatever was out there. Today, I reluctantly decided to take that step.

I didn't want to end up in the loony bin just because I couldn't accept what was real, even though magic and dragons belonged only in fairy tales.

Fortunately, there was a silver lining around this dark cloud: my birthmark.

Back home, a mark like mine was common. Doctors diagnosed these marks as pigment defects.

My version was an ugly, dark splat above my knee that

kept me from wearing shorts even during the height of summer. In Paegeia, it was something significant. The people saw it as an honor and, according to Julia, most humans would kill for one as dark as mine. I still hadn't figured out what it really meant, but it was my ticket straight into Dragonia Academy.

I took a deep breath and climbed out of the shower. Goosebumps broke out over my flesh as the cool air made contact with my warm body. I quickly grabbed a large, white towel positioned on a hook next to the shower and tried to retain some of the shower's warmth.

Then the doubt came as it always did just as I thought I would be okay with whatever was going on outside of these four walls.

What if I was already crazy and stuck in the loony bin they warned me of if I didn't accept this? What if this was my mind's way of dealing with Dad's death? What if all of this was made up and I was really sitting in some white room, eating Checker chips and drooling on everything?

I closed my eyes and pinched myself. No, it was real, and knowing that also meant that Longwei was right. I must accept this. It was my life now, and unfortunately, my surroundings appeared quite corporeal.

"Elena, you okay?" Constance knocked softly on the door.

"Just give me a minute," I yelled as I towel-dried my long hair. The shower had felt great and the clothes Master Longwei had given me fit perfectly.

A quick glance at the price tags before I ripped them off revealed the name "Twigs" written in big bold letters. Master Longwei had dropped them off last night when he'd come to check on me. The jeans were the kind I had always wanted. They had the effect of being washed too many times that made them look really old. The emerald-green tee went well with the color of my eyes, and the flip-flops were the perfect size.

How had he known what size to get? With his fashion sense, I considered myself lucky to receive an outfit this ordinary.

Dad had never bought me the things I really wanted. It was always in and out of stores with him, too quickly to try anything on, so my clothes always ended up being too small or too large. My throat tightened up at the memory. I swallowed my tears, pushing him to the back of my mind. There was no more time for crying. I had to be strong now.

I pulled my almost dry hair back into a high ponytail, and took another deep breath before opening the door.

"Don't you look beautiful?" Constance's echo bounced off the walls around me. Julia stood next to her and gasped.

I knew I looked pretty good considering the circumstances of my arrival and, of course, the bruises.

"Are you ready?" Constance asked.

"As ready as I'll ever be," I mused. "Besides, I'll go nuts if I have to stay here another day."

Constance pulled me into a tight hug, crushing me against her stethoscope. "If you need anything, I'm right here," she whispered softly into my ear. "Please don't be a stranger."

"And she doesn't mean by breaking a leg," Julia said with a mischievous glint in her eye.

"I could still end up losing my mind, and then you'll be stuck with me forever," I countered.

"Nonsense, you're a tough cookie." Constance smiled warmly.

"I'm going to miss you," I said, feeling the emotions beginning to clog in my throat. Both these women had become something familiar and provided a sense of security. Leaving them behind to face the unknown—which in my head was my worst nightmare—pained me.

Julia leaned closer and grabbed me around the neck too. I was bowled over as I never imagined her being someone that was fond of close contact. "Believe it or not," she said dryly, "I'm going to miss you too. It's too quiet here sometimes."

I couldn't help but smile.

A soft knock came from the door and we all turned to find Master Longwei waiting patiently.

Constance nodded once and he joined our small gathering.

They nodded back and forth a few times. It was as if he asked her for permission or something. Then the clothes popped into my head. "Thank you, Master, the clothes fit perfectly."

"You're welcome, Elena." He had a huge grin plastered on his face. "Tomorrow we can go to Elm and buy more."

"Elm?"

"A city close by that the students would call '*awesome*.'"

We laughed at the way his nose wrinkled when he said it. He even got the rock and roll sign right; I had to give him credit for that.

"You ready?" he asked timidly.

I assumed that he didn't want to tear me away from the familiar too quickly.

The corners of my mouth twitched slightly upwards, and I played with my ponytail as I moved slowly toward the door. Constance looked at me with anticipation. She was probably scared a dragon would swoop down and fly away with me to its nest or something. Julia's expression, on the other hand, suggested she was waiting for a prank to happen.

Master Longwei whispered something. I hoped he alleviated Constance's worries, but it only made me more nervous.

The first step I took was blinding. When my eyes finally adjusted, I found myself standing on a huge wooden deck. The smell of fresh paint burned my nostrils.

A part of me was still waiting for something to jump out of thin air.

I turned back and waved to the two women as I tried to process my surroundings.

Taking the first step off the porch made my throat dry and I swallowed hard. *Please don't let me see any dragons soaring through the sky!*

"Are you all right, Elena?" Master Longwei stood next to me with his arms folded behind his back.

I felt unsure. Forcing myself to look away from the sky, I saw a big brass statue of a man. It stood right in the middle of a courtyard surrounded by cobblestone pathways that formed a wagon wheel with many intersections. We followed the paths through a small grove of oak trees, and a gigantic castle rose majestically in the distance.

Master Longwei stopped in front of the statue, launching into teaching mode. "This statue is of the founder of Dragonia and the greatest king that ever lived, King Albert. Who knows where we would be if it wasn't for him." He tapped the feet of the statue a few times.

We turned off the main path and took one of the smaller trails that led toward the entrance of the castle. As we walked, birds chirped from high up in the branches. The grass was a bright green; unlike any I had ever seen. It made me think of magic again. I had never believed in its existence until now.

I finally came face to face with the hulking castle rising on the horizon. It was built out of a dark gray stone that looked weathered with age. The entrance to the Academy reminded me of a painting I had once seen of a sixteenth-century castle: three towers were connected to the main building, soaring into the sky like New York skyscrapers.

Two of them had a million windows right to the top. The third one reminded me of Rapunzel's tower, except this one had an entrance at the bottom. Climbing up the walls were bright green vines, providing a touch of color with small violet blooms.

The Academy definitely looked elite, the kind that probably had board members and a few sororities. A bird launched itself from a branch above my head, flapped its wings in my direction before it flew away. I jerked my head up, searching the sky once more. Still no dragons. I breathed a sigh of relief at this small comfort.

I looked back down, catching Master Longwei searching the skies too. He grinned broadly as he caught me staring at him. I looked away and I locked onto a giant gate to our far left. Rooted in place, I stared at it for a brief second. The metal vines curling around the beams moved. Metal flowers blossomed, and I narrowed my eyes. They were definitely metal. Then I saw what was behind those gates.

I closed my eyes and prayed that they were playing tricks on me. When I opened them, it was still there. *So much for that.* "Is the school built on air?"

Master Longwei roared with laughter. "Sorry Elena. The look on your face is priceless. Yes, and we're safe up here."

"What's holding it up?" I whispered, afraid that, if I spoke any louder, the entire Academy would drop to the surface.

"Magic," he said with a soft voice.

"Magic?" My right eyebrow arched slightly and I took a

deep breath. Sometimes it was easy to believe, but at other times, logical thinking took hold and I struggled to believe any of this was real.

"This is Paegeia, Elena. You are going to learn strange things here that science cannot explain. You need to have an open mind, and try to accept it."

I glared at the gate again. The roses and vines still moved around the beams, but didn't hide that clouds were gliding by. The effect made it impossible to think of any plausible reason for an entire Academy to rise above the air.

"What if we fall?" I asked, fear lacing my words.

"We haven't for the past hundred years."

I took a deep breath, trying to move my thoughts away from the academy-stuck-in-the-sky thing. I looked up one last time just to make sure that there were still no dragons.

Master Longwei glanced at his watch. "Elena, we need to get going. Class will start soon." He took bigger strides and I had to run to keep pace with him as we entered a door three times my height.

We picked up my schedule from the woman seated at the reception desk. Horn-rimmed glasses rested haphazardly on the tip of her nose. She greeted me with a welcoming tone, encouraging me with words meant to instill confidence. *Yeah right, she's probably never been to the other side where things are normal. What does she know?*

I had to run to keep up with Master Longwei as he hurried down a long passage. The narrowed hall held that old dusty smell often found in basements. A golden statue of a dragon with its head bowed stood sentry at the end of the passage.

We walked into a spacious lobby, with two sets of staircases leading to what I assumed were separate wings of the castle. Dragon paintings and armored statues were stacked meticulously against the wall. The students who passed us greeted Master Longwei with chirpy "hi's," followed by soft whispers and pointing fingers as they laid their eyes on me. It was the first day of school all over again, and heaven knew I'd had my fair share of those.

I almost lost Master Longwei in the throng of students as he ran up the staircase to the left and came to a sudden stop in front of a row of doorways.

We entered a wooden door with a woman embracing a dragon engraved on it that led to another set of stairs.

"This place is really big," I mumbled, annoyed, knowing I would never learn my way around all the staircases and passages.

"It has to be. Where do you think everybody stays?" Master Longwei said. "These are the girls' dormitories. Boys are on the right."

We entered the new space and climbed three separate staircases. By the time we reached the fourth set, my lungs felt ready to burst. He finally stopped at the door with a gold '4' woven in an intricate braided design, while I silently suggested the construction of an elevator.

Placing his hand against the door, he pushed and it

opened slowly into a cul-de-sac with three doors. He knocked to the first one and we waited.

The door eventually opened.

"Good morning, Master Longwei," a girl said in a chirpy tone, her toothbrush still in her hand. Her cropped black hair and big brown eyes lit up when she saw me.

"Good morning, Becky, may we come in?" he asked politely.

"Yeah sure, where are my manners?" She took a step back, encouraging us to enter.

We entered a room with three gigantic poster beds, two on the right wall facing another positioned across the room. They were stunning, with white lace hanging from the top that cascaded down wooden beams and pooled onto the floor.

The carpet had plain, dark brown shag so lush my flip-flops almost disappeared. A fancy chandelier cast a majestic glow. I was sure now that magic existed, and it was somehow responsible for this magnificent bedroom.

"Becky? I want you to meet Elena," Master Longwei said as he began the introductions.

"Hi, Elena, welcome to Dragonia." She sounded as if she'd drunk ten Red Bulls for breakfast.

I smiled at her nervously and my greeting came out barely louder than a squeak.

"Just show her around, and please don't let her get lost. There are still many things she doesn't know. Try to tell her as much as you can," he explained.

"Master Longwei," Becky intoned. "You always do this to me." A slowly emerging whine replaced her overwhelming hyperactivity.

"I thought talking to someone her age would help her to understand our world better. I'm much too old for this, and don't know how to be cool about stuff. You two speak the same language, Becky," Master Longwei replied.

"Fine, I'll try." She raised both her eyebrows and took a long, deep breath. "Thank heavens she knows about the dragons."

Master Longwei ignored Becky's comment as he turned to me. "Good luck, Elena, and if you need anything, don't hesitate to come and see me. I'll see you tomorrow morning for some shopping."

Becky gasped. "Are you going to Elm?"

"Yes, and if you manage not to freak her out today, you can come too," he said.

She bounced up and down, barely able to contain her excitement.

I really liked her. She had an air of a pixie rushing on adrenaline. "This is your room, Elena, I hope you like it. Enjoy your day, girls." Master Longwei disappeared back through the door we had just come through.

This is my room.

I repeated the thought over in my head a million times and waited for it to finally sink in. Becky closed the door, and my eye caught the small lounge with a big-screen TV hidden in the corner.

She led me toward the empty bed. "Here's your bed. I will help you with the linen." She gave me a soft smile. "I know they're huge, but there's a reason for that."

"Where's the other girl?" I referred to the other bed that was obviously already occupied.

"Sammy is an early riser and you've got Vicky's spot. She's on a self-discovery quest," she said, as if I was supposed to know what that meant. "I have a bit of a problem with the first, second and third time my alarm goes off. I love the snooze button way too much." Her nose wrinkled up. "So, I bet you have a lot of questions, huh?"

"I did, but my mind has gone blank."

"Yeah, I know the feeling."

I was glad that she offered to help with the bed. I didn't know how I would've managed it all by myself.

"I heard that you have a very dark mark." She lifted up her sleeve, showing me the light brown stain on her arm. "You can barely see mine." She promptly waited for me to show her mine.

"Mine is above my knee." I gestured to my newly acquired jeans.

Her smile dropped instantly.

"Can I show you tonight?"

She nodded, and her smile went all the way up to her eyes. "So, your dad was really a Copper-Horn?"

"Yes," I said in a soft whisper.

She gave me a one-sided smile. "I'm sorry that he died,

Copper-Horns are extremely lovable. I can't imagine who would want to hurt one, not to mention kill one."

Tears formed in my eyes, and I wiped them away quickly before she could see. "Did you know my dad?"

"No, he must have left when King Albert died. Many dragons left when he died," she explained sadly.

"King Albert...he's the guy who built this school, right?" I tucked one of the corners of the linen underneath the heavy mattress.

"Yes, he was also the true ruler of Paegeia, and the greatest king that ever lived. He was betrayed by his best friend but nobody likes to talk about it."

We finished and fell breathless on top of the freshly made bed.

She looked at her watch and jumped up. "Yikes, is that the time?" She grabbed her backpack with one hand and my arm with the other.

I practically flew out the room, through the main door and down the stairs. My feet skidded off the steps as she dragged me behind her and I prayed that I wouldn't fall on my face, or worse, break my neck.

"We are so late. Master Longwei is going to kill me," she said, panting with exertion.

We ran into the reception area, and I gave her a hand with the door.

We managed to open it wide enough for both of us to squeeze through. More buildings appeared on the other side, which made the castle begin to look more like a school.

She darted around the first corner, down another hallway and stopped. She turned around. "You ready?" She opened the door and ushered me into a hall filled with other students. I felt as if I was drowning. Good thing I was a fast swimmer.

4

THE HALL WE entered was filled with students and the lecture had already begun. Becky and I crouched and walked to the second row, while the teacher scribbled on the blackboard back turned to the rows of students. As soon as we could, we slipped into the only two empty chairs next to each other.

The other students chuckled softly at our stealthy plan.

"Late again, Ms. Johnson?" the teacher asked in a brisk Irish accent.

"Thanks, you guys," Becky said to the chortling students. Turning to look at me, she rolled her eyes dramatically.

"Welcome, Elena," the teacher said, and turned around with a grin not meant to be ignored. I gave him a small smile back. "My name is Sir Edward. In this class you will learn Paegeia's mysteries," he said excitedly, and the whole class sighed. It felt as if the entire room was deflating with their obvious displeasure.

The teacher appeared much too young to be a professor, with honey-colored eyes and golden blond hair. He wore a pair of faded jeans and a black t-shirt with a tribal print design covering his chest. "Now, where were we?"

"You were telling us about the King of Lion Sword," a boy with bulgy eyes and dark brown hair reminded him.

"Thank you, Trevor," Sir Edward said. "The King of Lion Sword is the only sword that can slay evil too strong for non-magical weapons, especially dragons."

I gasped.

"Not all dragons are good," Becky whispered at my apparent discomfort.

"Why is this sword the only capable sword, Becky?" Sir Edward asked, and she shrank into her chair.

"It's the only sword blessed by King William, a thousand years ago." She'd clearly sucked the answer out of her thumb.

"Yes, and how did the sword get blessed?" he asked.

"Holy water," she answered, and everyone laughed. Sir Edward smiled.

"No. Try to pay more attention, Ms. Johnson. Riley," he called on a girl in the third row whose hand reached the highest.

She flipped her hair and gave Becky an I'm-smarter-than-you-are smile. "No one knows for sure, but there are plenty of ideas."

"She's a big know-it-all. A real toothache, if you ask me," Becky whispered as Riley gave a breakdown of a million possibilities.

"Correct, Riley," Sir Edward said.

"So we shouldn't rule out holy water," Becky chirped and the class broke out in laughter again.

"No, Becky, that one has been tested," he said, ignoring her curled lip. "Who can tell me what the Japanese call it?"

The know-it-all, Riley, was the only one who knew the answer this time.

"Riley?"

"Shishiwo," she said.

While she was answering, Becky was doing an accurate impersonation of Riley, and I had to suppress my laughter in order to not draw any more attention to us.

"Here, you deserve it." Sir Edward tossed Riley a chocolate bar.

"Who can tell me how many King of Lion weapons we have?" he asked. This time everyone's hands went up, except for mine.

"Charlie?" He pointed to a boy in the first row.

"One," the boy said. "Now where's my candy?"

Sir Edward chuckled and tossed him one too.

"So if something happens to the King of Lion, we're basically screwed?" another boy asked.

"Don't think of it that way. Hope is always near to those who believe. Besides, the sword is well protected in the city of Elm." Turning from the front of the room Sir Edward started to walk my way. As he passed our row, he dropped a handbook on my desk. "Please, if you can open to page sixty-seven."

On the page was a picture of a sword with the King of Lion written in small letters at the bottom.

An image of Excalibur popped in my head as I looked

over the page. It had a golden hilt that curled up the divine blade with a lion's head emblazoned on the hilt. The text below the image explained that Richard the Lion Heart once possessed the sword.

"The story we're going to cover is the recovering of the King of Lion. The year 1320 BTW."

I looked at Becky. "Before the Wall," she whispered without taking her gaze from the book.

"A Japanese folk tale of danger, love, sacrifice, and adventure in the Daki islands," Sir Edward began. "Around 1320, a samurai named Kalibi Shima was banished by a chieftain called Hio Tukituki. They exiled him to a small island called Yamasaki, of the Oki islands. Kalibi had an eighteen-year-old daughter, Kayatan, whom he loved very much."

I became lost in his tale of a brave Kayatan who saved her father and slayed a dragon that was torturing the villagers. In return, the town gave her the King of Lion Sword. The story reminded me of the stories Dad used to tell me, but I just couldn't seem to recall the details. Then my thoughts shifted to Dad saving my life. I could never have done what Kayatan had. My eyes welled up again. *I should never have left him.*

I jumped out of my seat as the bell rang and the students began packing up their books. Becky left her backpack open for my handbook and I gently placed it in with the rest of hers.

"On Monday, we'll discuss the other Japanese legend,

Yorimasa the Dragon Slayer." Sir Edward's voice echoed over the racket the students made as they exited the lecture hall.

"Come on, it's time for Art of War," Becky said, gripping my arm. Thank heavens she didn't make a big fuss over my vanishing tears.

Back out in the hallway, students jostled in the narrow space, rushing and pushing against one another to get to their next class. On our way, we passed the cafeteria and ran to another door.

I squeezed through quickly as Becky struggled to keep the door open. Instead of more lecturing halls, in front of me stood acres of land with mountains rising in the distance. The view was breathtaking. My awe only lasted a minute, however, before I remembered the dragons and looked frantically to the skies. Becky's gaze followed mine, with a confused expression on her face.

I sighed. *So what if I found a dragon soaring through the sky? The faster I accept that dragons exist the better off I'll be.*

Lowering my gaze, I caught sight of students walking toward a coliseum similar to that in Rome—except this one hadn't been left in ruins. Becky grabbed my arm and pulled me in the opposite direction toward a smaller, domed building.

Two huge stone dragons stood guard at the entrance as we walked through the door. A low grumble came from the one, and my head snapped to it. I glimpsed scales moving and closed my eyes quickly. It stopped. My mind was seriously starting to play games with me.

Then the stone dragon moved, and I watched with huge eyes as its stone head bowed down to mine and it took a big sniff. I froze.

"Grimdoe, stop it," Becky said in a teasing tone. She laid her hands on his body and spoke words that sounded like Greek, and the statue moved back into its original place.

Becky laughed as she saw my expression then pulled me into the building.

"Some of the stone figures like to mess with the first years' minds," she said, as if it was the most natural thing in the world for a statue to move.

I took another huge breath and waited for my heart to start beating again.

My eyes grew as I found a room similar to a sports arena, but instead of a basketball court or a running track, there were rows and rows of targets, with shields stacked against the right wall. In the corner of the room was a big wooden oak cupboard and bleachers stacked near the back.

The left wall held rows and rows of giant axes and spears, taller than I was, with thousands of helmets stacked underneath. Something Becky had said suddenly hit me. It made the stone dragon disappear from my mind within a millisecond and my heartbeat went crazy again. "When you said Art of War, you didn't mean it literally, did you?"

She looked at me, confused. "Did you think I was referring to theories?" The one side of her lip arched slightly over her teeth. "That's so boring!"

"We're going to fight? I can't fight!" The last part barely came out, but my feet finally did what I had wanted to do ever since I had come to Paegeia, and I scrambled toward the door, trying to exit the building as quickly as possible.

She pulled me back by my arm. "Relax Elena. It's just practice."

"The closest I've ever come to wielding a weapon is a steak knife at the dinner table." My hands trembled, and I folded my arms to hide them from Becky.

She laughed. "You're funny."

I looked up again, still thinking of dragons, as we waited for our practice session to begin.

"What are you looking at?" Becky looked up at the ceiling too.

"Nothing," I whispered, feeling like an idiot for always staring up at the sky.

"You're so weird. Let's go." She led me to a small group of students huddled around a young woman.

"Elena," a young girl greeted me.

"Hi, Professor Mia." Becky said to the girl, who couldn't have been much older than her students. She was stunning, with auburn hair and big blue eyes. Her smile seemed to light up the room, but I froze when I saw her swinging a real sword in her left hand. She looked so much like Xena, the Warrior Princess.

"Elena has a bit of stage fright. I don't think they have classes like this on the other side," Becky explained.

"You think?" the professor said in a sarcastic tone. "Not to worry, Elena. We're not going to throw you into the deep end just yet. We'll just take it one step at a time, okay?"

The corner of my mouth twitched as I tried desperately to hide my doubts that anything good was going to come out of me holding a weapon. Silently, I resigned myself to the reality that I was going to suck with a sword and would probably fail this class.

"Becky," Professor Mia said, "go and get her some armor. We'll take it from there."

Becky gripped my arm again and pulled me over to the cupboard. We found an old safety vest that I barely caught when Becky tossed the thing to me. It reeked of old sweat, and I made involuntary gagging sounds. It smelled even worse when I tried to pull it over my head. When I finally surfaced I found Becky leaning against the cupboard with crisscrossed legs, laughing in total hysterics.

Standing up she regained control of herself and wiped away her tears. "Don't worry, we'll find you one tomorrow in Elm that will fit," she said, without looking at me.

The thing was double my size, and I knew I looked ridiculous. So much for first impressions.

Now I know how a stuffed animal feels.

"Becky, is it going to be today?" Professor Mia yelled, irritation lacing her voice.

Becky burst into laughter again, which was starting to

annoy me. It got even worse when the class joined her.

"Comedy hour is finished. Get back to practice," Professor Mia ordered, and Becky stopped.

I trembled as I listened to steel slamming against steel. It looked like total war out there.

I'm so not cut out for this.

I didn't even have to try it once; I was going to be absolutely terrible.

"Is there any way I can drop this class?" I whispered to Becky, pleading with my eyes for any way out of this situation.

She snorted and tried desperately not to break out into laughter again. "Sorry." She worked hard to keep a straight face. "No, it's mandatory. Besides, how are you going to protect yourself, Elena?"

"From what?" I asked, but before Becky could burst out laughing again, I realized the answer. They were huge, had wings, and breathed fire. A typical David and Goliath story, only ten times worse.

"Give it a try. Who knows? You might love it," she suggested, as if there were an alternative.

We reached Professor Mia slowly, who methodically made her way around the small room, wielding her sword with unbelievable precision. After a short and not very informative lesson from Becky, she placed a sword in my hand. It made me tip over like a bowling pin. Once I'd righted myself, I stared at it like an idiot and I could feel my eyes grow larger as I took in the metal blade.

"Becky, go spar with Collin," Professor Mia ordered.

Becky left my side for the first time since we'd met.

"Elena, here." Professor Mia touched my chin and turned my face to look into hers. "The first rule of combat is never to take your eyes off your opponent."

CLASS WAS EXCRUCIATING. In ten minutes, every muscle and joint in my body was inflamed. Right before I thought I was going to pass out, Professor Mia mercifully stopped. She had made a mistake when she said that I would get better. I knew it, she knew it, and the unrelenting laughter emanating from the class indicated that the other students knew it. The second half of class, I rested on the bleachers. I was so exhausted I hardly had the strength to take off my vest.

Sitting alone, I watched the other students as they trained around the room. Becky was good. I felt sorry for her opponent. She even threw in a kick or two between the fierce blows of her sword. I now understood why they called wielding a weapon the art of dueling.

Thankfully, a bell rang in the distance and everyone stopped on Professor Mia's command. The students walked with high spirits toward the wall to return their equipment. I tried to get up, but my body ached, and I fell back onto the bleachers in a huff.

I'm going to regret this in the morning.

Becky put her shield and helmet against the wall, and walked over to the cupboard to put away her sword. When she was finished, she ran over to me. "Are you okay?"

"I'll live," I said sulkily.

"You'll see. It's going to be your favorite class too. I don't think there's a student here who hates Art of War." She gave me a hand up.

"Well, then I'm going to be the first. I'm definitely a lover, not a fighter," I said, honesty coating every syllable.

She giggled, and pulled me toward the exit. We cleared the field back on our way to the main building.

"Can I ask you something?"

She nodded, carrying her sweaty vest over her shoulder.

"What happens if someone gets hurt?"

"Swallow Annexes are good at healing cuts and bruises," Becky said simply, as if that offered any real explanation.

Swallow Annex? The term sounded Greek and dangerous, and I decided against asking for a translation. My legs burned as I started to climb the stairs that led to the big wooden door we had exited an hour ago. Each step sent a biting pain into my knees. To make matters worse, they didn't want to bend properly, turning my balance into a big fat zero.

My gaze caught the huge structure straight out of ancient Rome on our far left. "What's that?"

"It's the coliseum."

"Do they fight there too?"

She huffed. "You could say that."

"What do they call the one we were just in?"

"The Parthenon Dome."

"Does everything in this country start with a P?"

She snorted and hit me playfully with her sweaty vest.

We went up to the room, so I could take a quick shower before lunch. Once I'd slipped off my sweaty clothes, I tried to enjoy the sanctuary of the shower, but the grumbling in my stomach hastened my usual routine. Finishing quickly, I joined Becky in the main bedroom and we made our way to the cafeteria.

When I entered the outdoor lunch area, the first thing I noticed was more magic. One of the boys played with real fire in his hands. It was in the form of a small animal that ran through his fingers, underneath another and slipped over the next. Another boy zapped a girl's ass with a bolt of soft lightning. She cried out softly, jumped around and slapped him as hard as she could, which made his friends laugh. Becky pulled my arm again, and I had to look twice as we passed another girl who frosted some berries with her breath. I couldn't stop gawking at all these people and I got a few glares back as if I was invading their privacy.

I got dragged behind Becky like a star-struck idiot as we made our way to the buffet line stationed below huge oak trees. I regained myself as I kept saying over in my head that I had to deal with this like a normal person, even though nothing about what I had just seen was normal.

Behind the buffet line stood a man with a huge stomach

who was dressed in a chef's uniform. Dad had always said nobody trusts a skinny chef, and I laughed to myself. His hair had the same copper glint as Dad's had and the smell of his food made my mouth water.

"Chef, this is the new girl, Elena," Becky introduced.

"Elena, I was wondering when you were going to join the living," he teased.

"So, what are we having today?" she asked.

"Rice and fresh vegetables with a lovely roast beef." He sighed in satisfaction. I giggled as he somehow reminded me of my dad, and for a short second I forgot what it was I had seen a few minutes ago.

"Urgh! Nobody got the riddle yesterday?" Becky mumbled.

"No, have you seen today's?" he asked playfully.

She waved it away. "It's too difficult anyway."

He laughed at her apparent frustration and turned his gaze onto me. "Are you good at riddles, Elena?"

I shook my head. "Sorry." Dad used to ask me riddles almost daily as well, and I never knew any of their answers.

"Not to worry, Riley will have to choose your menu then."

"Miss-know-it-all gets most of the riddles right, and then we get pasta, pasta, and oh, what's that other thing she likes so much?" Becky asked the chef.

"Pasta!" they both replied in unison. I smiled at their bickering, and started to miss Dad horribly.

After we dished up, we waved goodbye and made our

way to a group of tables teeming with students. I could still see some playing with fire and other elements out of the corner of my eye, but decided to make peace with this reality as soon as possible and focus my energy on familiar things, like conversation.

"Let me get this straight. Whoever solves the riddle can choose what we have to eat?" I asked Becky, as she was looking over the heads of other students for an open table.

"Yeah, every day a new one gets posted on the board," she said, without taking her gaze from the search. "Occasionally, one of the other kids guesses right, and then we get burgers and fries, or hot dogs and pizza."

Awesome! I tried to imagine what kind of pizza this chef could create. My mouth started watering just thinking about it, and I couldn't wait to dig in.

To our left, two guys suddenly stood up from a table, and Becky made a run for it.

As we slipped into the chairs, my eyes locked on a guy sitting four tables away from us. Something inside my stomach twirled as I gawked at him playing absentmindedly with a soda can. He sat with a group of six other guys, though he clearly stood out. His raven black hair was in perfect accord with his sun-kissed skin. A strange feeling that I had never felt before began to boil inside my gut. I would soon learn that staring at him would be the biggest mistake of my life.

5

CAREFULLY, I RELEASED my lower lip when I realized I was chewing on it.

The mysterious guy looked up, spoke to the guy opposite him and then smiled. My heart beat faster. He had the same smile as Dad, a smile that lit up his face and reached all the way to his eyes, creating vertical dimples in his cheeks. The smile I loved and missed so much. His peacock blue eyes made me feel as if I were falling straight into a rabbit hole—one that I could never find my way out of, not that I would want to.

Suddenly, a middle finger jumped right in front of his face, blocking my view. It belonged to a girl with short, snow-white hair. She was a stunner with light blue eyes and a long, oval face. It was no miracle how they had ended up together.

Becky laughed when she saw who I was staring at. "Don't pay her any attention, she's a bitch. You're not the only one who stares at him with googly eyes and a drooling mouth."

"Who's he?"

"His name is Blake Leaf." She let out a small, lustful sigh. "He's *verautiful*, but such a dick." She started picking at her vegetables again.

"Verautiful?"

"Combination of very and beautiful."

I giggled.

"The bitchy girl is Tabitha. She's always had a thing for Blake. I'm still not sure if they're an item or not. Blake has this phobia of being spoken for," she explained.

"He doesn't want a girlfriend?" I asked, stunned.

She shrugged. "Something like that."

I looked up at the sky once more. I must have done it a million times today and saw Becky following my gaze.

"Elena, what is with you? Why do you keep looking up at the sky?"

"It's stupid, you'll laugh." I nervously tried to make her drop the subject.

"I might, but I can't help it. You're hilarious."

"I keep waiting to see...a dragon."

She looked at me with a raised eyebrow as if I was crazy.

"Forget it," I said when an extremely loud laugh pierced my ears. I glanced over my shoulder. A girl with long auburn hair and hazelnut eyes plummeted onto the seat right next to me. "She's hilarious!"

"I know, right?" Becky said, in an agreeing tone.

I wished for the earth to open up and swallow me whole.

"How many times has she looked up today?"

"Like a million."

I felt stupid as they made jokes.

"Elena, this is Sammy." Becky said.

"Short for Samantha." She reached out her hand for a shake. "I'm one of the roomies." She was a tiny thing, even more petite than I was, and her dimples were definitely her main attraction.

I took her hand and shook it gently.

"She really doesn't know?"

"I don't think so. Master Longwei asked me to give her the crash course."

"May I?" she pleaded.

Becky nodded and looked at me with a huge smile.

"What are you doing?" My heart thumped painfully. The last time I felt like this, Dad had transformed into a dragon.

"Relax, Elena. Sammy just wants to introduce you to a dragon."

"A dragon? Where?" I yelled, and everyone outside fell into an utter silence. This was so not cool. A number of students laughed, while others shook their heads in disgust. I covered my face with my palms. In one millisecond I had killed my only chance of ever finding a social life.

"Oh, shut up," Becky said loudly. "Eat your food."

"Sammy, you should take her to Constance for the serum, before she goes mental," the girl with the white hair sang, and everyone, including Blake, laughed.

Sammy flipped up the middle finger Tabitha had thrown me a few minutes ago. "Suck on that biatch."

Looking incredibly pissed off, Tabitha jumped up from her chair, ready to attack.

Appearing uninterested in witnessing a full-on girl-fight,

Blake carefully pushed her back into her seat. I heard her protesting and he leaned in closer to her to whisper something into her ear. Her sweet smile appeared, revealing perfect white pearls.

"You're going to get your ass kicked one day, Sammy," Becky warned her.

"By Tabitha? She wishes," Sammy said.

I tried to picture this tiny girl with a sword and wondered what damage she could do with one.

"We need to tell her, Becky."

"Go ahead. You were busy anyway."

"Elena, promise you won't freak out." Sammy took my hand between her small ones.

I closed my eyes and cringed.

"Promise!" she said in an ordering tone.

"Fine, I promise."

"My name is Sammy Leaf."

I looked at Becky, who arched her left eyebrow with a slight twitch in the corner of her mouth.

"Are you related to Blake?"

"She's hardly started her first day, and she already knows who my brother is?" Sammy said.

Becky laughed.

"Sammy, everyone knows your brother," someone said. Another dreamy guy walked over to our table. He was the total opposite of Blake, although their eyes were the same color. He was tall and slender, with blond, cropped hair and fair skin. His smile made my heart skip a beat.

"Lucian, Elena. Elena, Lucian, the prince of every girl's heart and of Tith." Becky gave him one of her million-dollar smiles.

Lucian shook his head, faintly smiling back. "Nice to meet you, Elena." He held out his hand for a shake.

"You're a prince for real?" The words slipped out while I shook his hand.

He replied with a quick nod and a huge smile that lit up his blue eyes. Then he took the seat next to Becky.

"Lucian is the other frat boy." Becky carried on teasing him, bumping him with her shoulder.

"I'm not the other frat boy, okay. Blake is way above me."

"My brother is a dick, Lucian, which makes him lose a thousand points and you gain a thousand just by having that cute smile," Sammy said.

He lowered his eyes, embarrassed, and complained in a playful manner, which made the three of us laugh.

I had to admit he was kind of hot, but after seeing Blake, it was going to be impossible to find anyone else sharing that kind of beauty.

"So did you tell her yet?" he asked.

Sammy gave him the eye. "I'm trying to, but every time I get rudely interrupted."

They turned to me. "For heaven's sake just tell me."

"She can be feisty, I love it," Sammy said in a singsong tone and took my hand in hers again.

"Elena, darling," she said. "As I was busy introducing

myself—and don't interrupt me again—my name is Sammy Leaf, and I'm a Fire-Tail."

I stared at her for a few seconds, blankly. It took a while for me to process what she was trying to tell me. "Please tell me you're not a dragon," I spoke in a shaky voice.

Everyone at the table kept quiet, waiting for my next reaction.

"Oh shit." I heard Becky's voice as I turned into a pillar.

Sammy still held a death grip on my hand.

"Elena, don't do this please. I need to go to Elm."

"Wait, Elm is on the line?" Sammy shouted.

"Maybe this was too soon." Lucian's voice sounded far off.

"Yes, but if she freaks out, we don't go with them," Becky answered Sammy.

"Elena!" Sammy yelled. "You promised!" She slapped me across my face. Hard.

"Sammy!" Becky and Lucian cried together, but the slap worked. She'd brought me back.

I lifted my hand, motioning that I needed a minute to regain myself. Resting my head on my arms, I took deep breaths and absorbed this new information. I should've seen that one coming. Dad had been a dragon hiding among humans. I chided my denseness as the students nearby snickered.

"Just breathe, okay? I promise I won't eat you," Sammy said in a soft voice while gently stroking my back.

"Sammy!" Becky and Lucian said together again.

"What! She might think that."

I lifted my head and untangled my tongue. "So, basically your everyday form is human?"

"Except for class when I need to morph into a big, ugly dragon," she said with a raised lip.

Becky and Lucian released their collective breath.

"You're not ugly," Lucian said in an admiring tone.

"Maybe not to you, but to Elena I might be."

"So no dragons are soaring through the sky?" I looked at Becky.

"No, Elena. The dragons are all around you."

I looked at the other tables. Everyone had gone back to chatting and enjoying their meals, my little outburst from earlier already forgotten.

I sighed. "I don't care what you are as long as you promise me you'll stay in this form."

She smiled and her dimples dented deep, just underneath her cheeks.

"She's back," Becky sang.

"Welcome to Dragonia," Lucian said as he picked up his tray from our table. Turning with a short wave goodbye, he joined another table crowded with boys.

"You're a dragon, for real?" I asked, and she nodded.

"Can I come with tomorrow?" she begged both of us.

"Well, you broke it to her, so I guess you're in," Becky said.

Sammy clapped her hands excitedly.

"So, you're a dragon too?" I asked Becky.

"No, Elena, I have the mark."

In my panic I had completely forgotten about the mark thing. "Who else are dragons?"

"Easy. You can tell by the hair or the color of their eyes. We have a mark too," Sammy explained, and pulled down the back of her shirt to show me a mark on her shoulder. The sign curled up into flames and the ink was red, exquisite, and similar to a tribal sign. "Every species has a different one."

Constance's eyes popped into my head. "Wait, you said eyes."

"Yes, they're extraordinarily freaky."

"So Constance is a dragon?" It was weird thinking it, not to mention saying it out loud.

"Julia too," Becky chirped.

"The nurse?"

"Unless you know another Julia," she said.

I'd spent a week with two dragons in disguise. They must have thought I was an idiot with the way I had behaved. I looked at the girl with the snowy blond hair. Becky and Sammy followed my gaze as I stared at her smiling and flirting with Blake.

"Tabitha's a Snow dragon. They're white and the smallest of all the dragons," Sammy said. "The one next to her is a Moon-Bolt, his name is George. Do you see how blue his eyes are?"

"Wait, he's a blue dragon?" The dragon that had

attacked us the night Dad had died had been sort of a bluish color.

"Yes, do you get what I'm saying?"

I looked at all the boys at Blake's table. One of them had red hair, the kind you'd dye for a carnival. Another one had bright green stripes mixed throughout his jet black hair. Basically, everyone at that table had either vibrant color patterns in their hair or extraordinary eyes.

"So this school is basically for dragons?" I asked, as the name "Dragonia" popped into my head.

"More or less," Sammy said.

"Then why are humans here with you guys?" I remembered what Constance told me, but what the hell did being special have to do with dragons?

"We belong with them, Elena. Everyone who bears the mark is likely to become a Dragonian," Becky explained. "And one day when I ascend, I'll make one of these bitches my own."

"You need to work harder on your fighting skills if that is ever going to happen." Sammy smirked.

"Wait, what do you mean making one of these bitches your own? You're not talking about a dragon, are you?"

"That's what Dragonians do, Elena, we ride them."

My stomach swirled now as I finally understood what Constance had meant. Images of humans on top of dragons popped into my head, but I pushed them away when skies and clouds appeared. I hadn't thought for one second that being a Dragonian meant riding a dragon.

"Oh shit, Master Longwei didn't mention it?" Becky asked.

I shook my head.

"Urgh! He better make this trip to Elm so worth it."

"Elena, just breathe, okay? It's not an obligation," Sammy said.

I took another breath.

"Unless you're part of a dent," Becky replied, which brought back the worry.

"Becky—"

"What? She could be. Master Longwei said her mark is really dark, Sammy."

"What does that mean?" I asked.

"The darker the mark, the more you'll do," Sammy answered cryptically.

I shook my head again. It wasn't what I wanted to hear.

"Relax, deep breaths." Sammy tried to calm me again. "You mean being part of a dent?"

"Yes."

"If you're part of one you don't have a choice. You need to claim the dragon you belong with."

"They'll force you to," Becky said.

Are they nuts?

"Why?" I sounded hysterical.

"Because a dent is more than just a rider and a dragon, they are soul mates," Sammy explained.

"I don't understand."

"If they're the same sex, they're called a brother or a

sisterhood, which is the most common one. If they're of the opposite gender, they become partners for life. The bond is unexplainable, but strong, and lasts forever. Dents are extremely rare."

"You mean as husband and wife?" My mind locked on the phrase "partners for life."

"Lovers," Becky said in a singing voice.

Somehow, I managed to blush scarlet in the face of all this craziness.

They both gasped in shock.

"Elena, are you still a virgin?"

"I'm only sixteen, what do you think?"

They looked around nervously.

Becky leaned in to whisper. "Just watch out for Brian. He's a Sun-Blast."

I looked at her; she might as well have spoken French, because I had no idea what a Sun-Blast was, or who Brian was.

"There, the guy with the red hair. If he knows you're still intact, he'll do whatever he needs to deflower you." Becky pointed awkwardly at someone who looked like a younger version of George Clooney. *Why were they all so damn gorgeous?*

"Why would he do that?"

"Sun-Blasts are obsessed with virgins. Humans used to sacrifice maidens to them just so they wouldn't eat the villagers."

"What?"

"It doesn't happen anymore. Besides, Master Longwei will cut off his balls if he even thinks about it," Sammy assured me.

"But he might try to charm your panties off, if you know what I mean." The picture Becky put into my mind turned my face scarlet once again.

What was it with this girl? She acted as if she was the bearer of bad news and enjoyed it. I got the picture, though.

"So basically what you're saying is my life is in danger unless I get laid?"

They looked at me, before bursting into laughter once again at my expense.

"Lucky for you, Brian is the only Sun-Blast here," Becky reassured me.

"So I take it the Sun-Blast is red." I remembered the red dragon, and shuddered as the same eerie feeling crept up my spine.

They both nodded.

"They're fire breathers, like moi." Sammy pointed at herself and puffed out her chest. "But we're nothing alike. Sun-Blasts can live in volcanoes, and my dad said they're able to handle the sun's heat. They also make their Dragonians rich, making them roll in it, if you get what I'm saying. I think it's the only reason the Dragonians go for a Sun-Blast before claiming a Fire-Tail. Sun-Blasts have built-in radars that constantly track and search for objects of value," Sammy babbled. "The only problem is, they're extremely vile and have bad tempers. It's a bitch to claim one too."

"What do you mean by 'claim one?'"

"Claiming is a term we use for the event where a Dragonian tries to break in a dragon. If the Dragonian can't beat the dragon he or she faces, the Dragonian can try again at a later stage. It's better to wait until you've ascended."

"Ascended?"

"The humans with the mark will gain an extra ability around their seventeenth birthday. Some manifest later while others could ascend much earlier than expected."

"But it's not likely," Sammy interrupted.

I guessed she saw the terrified look on my face again.

Becky gave her the eye and carried on as if Sammy hadn't spoken a word. "Whether you can handle a fire's heat or toxic gas, no one knows. Only then will you know which dragon you can claim."

I sighed. "Is your brother a dragon too?"

"Oh no, girl, erase him from your mind," Becky said.

Before I could protest, Sammy said, "Yes, my brother's a dragon too, but he's the only one of his kind. He's called a Rubicon. Only one lives at a time otherwise they'd annihilate this world. He's both Metallic and Chromatic, which causes a lot of problems. The last Rubicon died a thousand years ago and Blake was born nine hundred and eighty-one years later."

"Wait, a metal and chrome what?" I asked, clearly confused again. It would take me forever to get this all straight. I wasn't sure I even wanted to. None of this seemed real, and then there was Dad. How could I sit here acting like everything was fine, when I'd been thrown into a foreign land with the knowledge that I would never see my father again?

Becky started to explain. She clearly didn't pick up my escaping-this-world thoughts. I took a deep breath and listened. The Chromatics were the basic evil dragon, bent on destruction and that sort of thing, but this dark side could be overcome once they were a part of a dent. There were five classes in total; I would have to remind her to write those down so I could steer clear. The Metallic dragons, like Sammy, were not overcome by their darker desires, and stayed pure. They were generally friendly, helpful, and kind toward humans, making them much more welcome.

"But how can he be a Rubicon and you a Fire-Tail?" I thought that was what she had called herself.

"Um, it's hard to explain."

Okay? I tried another route. "What can he do?"

"He can do everything from healing broken bones to spitting acid. We'll learn about his anatomy in the second year."

"So his rider—"

"Blake doesn't have one," Becky interrupted.

"Why not?"

"Because his true Dragonian doesn't exist. Another long story and one we'll tell you about later," Becky said.

"Elena, you're going to be fine." Sammy saw right

through me. "The only things you need to know are that magic and dragons exist."

"And that Sammy talks way too much," Becky chirped.

"Oh, shut your trap," Sammy snapped back playfully.

"You must see her pucker when she's a dragon."

"This pucker can light your ass on fire, missy."

I laughed at their playful bickering. It reminded me of Dad, at least the times when he had been normal. Thinking of him again, a horrible emptiness filled my heart once more.

"Hey," Becky said. "Don't worry, we'll help you."

I smiled. Tears lurked behind my eyelids.

Looking around at the emptying tables, Becky glanced at her watch and slowly got up from our table.

Sammy followed closely behind and took my tray, along with her empty one.

My hands placed on the table, I braced myself as I got up. My legs felt as if I had pushed tree stumps. Glancing at my full tray I hated that I hadn't eaten any of my food and it was going to land up in the bin.

Sammy dropped our trays at the drop-off zone, just as the bell rang. "See you later," she said, and disappeared around the corner.

Becky started to laugh as she saw me walking like a stick figure and she pulled me along by my arm.

"Is Sammy really a dragon?" I asked as we made our way down an unfamiliar hallway.

"Yeah, Fire-Tails are babblers, but they're also the kind of dragon you can ask to incinerate a body when in need."

As we turned the corner to make our way to our next class I walked straight into something hard. It was he.

I froze.

6

HOW HAD THE dragon found me? Matt said they were all dead. I should've run but my feet were rooted to the ground. My heart pounded painfully as the warmth of the dragon's fishy breath blew over my skin. Goosebumps rippled across my flesh. I strained at my frozen legs with my last ounce of strength and lurched into a retreat, stumbled, and landed flat on my ass.

As much as I wanted to look away, I couldn't. My eyes were locked in terror on the scaly blue beast standing before me. I tried to scream, but nothing came out. The dragon roared while stomping its feet. The ground rumbled, shaking me violently in the quake.

A tear rolled down my cheek as I couldn't look away from its beady eyes. They were dark, like rippling pools of onyx. As I stared deeper and deeper into their murky depths, I could feel myself drowning.

"Dammit, George, this isn't funny!" Becky screamed right next to me, bringing me sharply back to reality. Everything began to move again slowly, as if in that moment time had stood still. Someone whistled loudly in the distance, and the blue dragon looming in front of me turned around and lumbered away in the opposite direction. Laughter echoed off the walls and I couldn't tell if it had just started or was just dying out. Regardless, I could feel my face blush a harsh crimson in my embarrassment.

I coughed again as the strong antiseptic smell so commonly found in hospitals burned my nose. Humid air clung to my face, making my flushed skin feel hot and sticky. Beads of sweat rolled lazily down my spine, making me shiver.

"I'm so sorry, Elena," Becky said, sounding terrified as she crouched beside me.

"What happened?" Lucian had reached us and helped Becky get me back onto my feet, shaky as they were.

"Elena, are you okay?" Becky asked, concern filling her voice.

"What happened?" Lucian demanded this time and shook Becky.

"It was George!"

He grunted with agitation. "Which way, Becky?" he asked, determination punctuating every syllable.

She pointed in the direction George had run. I watched Lucian disappear through the mass of people gawking in the hall, until I could no longer see the broad lines of his back.

"Elena, please snap out of it," she begged, while some students stood there staring and chattering to each other as if I had lost my marbles. "There's nothing to see! Go to your classes!" she yelled.

"Why did George do that?" I managed to say, my voice breaking.

She grabbed my neck and pulled me into a tight hug, stemming the tears threatening to expose my fear to the entire hallway.

"It was a stupid prank, Elena. I told you those guys are jerks!" She led me back toward the cafeteria, slowing her stride to match my hesitant steps.

"Where are you taking me?"

"To Master Longwei."

"No, please, Becky. I'll be fine."

"Are you sure?" she asked with reservation in her voice.

"Yes, can we just go to our room please?"

The second we crossed the threshold, bile rose in my throat and I made a run for the bathroom. I barely made it to the toilet before I hurled. My body was wracked with painful dry heaves as it tried to expel the adrenaline that had been pumping through my veins. This was so stupid. I wiped my mouth gently with the back of my hand. Rising, clumsily, from the porcelain bowl, I got up, walked over to the basin, and turned on the tap full blast. The girl looking back at me in the mirror looked terrified. Strands of blond hair shielded her face from the harsh glare of the lights. Hints of fear still remained in her light green eyes, and she trembled slightly. I closed my eyes and the horrified expression on the face in the mirror disappeared, replaced with the image of the blue dragon.

"Elena, are you okay?" Becky's voice came from the other side of the door as she knocked softly.

"Yeah," I yelled back, and splashed cold water over my face before I opened the door.

Reaching out, she hugged me again. "I'm so sorry about what happened."

I took a few deep breathes to compose myself, as Becky piloted me to the couch. "Here, sit." She ran over to the fridge.

I buried my face in between my legs and took another long, deep breath.

"The sugar will help," she said, and thrust a soda into my hands.

I frowned at the word Coca-Cola twirled in white letters all over the can.

"How's this possible?" I asked, perplexed.

"Oh, they're so fast in between morphing. They need five seconds at the most," she explained with a Coke clutched in her hand as well.

"Not that Becky. This?" I held the Coke can out for her inspection.

She frowned.

"Apart from the dragons and inexplicable things like a school built on air, you guys live a normal life with things I'm familiar with from the other side. How is it possible that you guys have Coke and know about stuff like pizza and burgers?"

A small grin played around the corners of her mouth. "We have cell phones too." She took out a phone. It looked like a smart phone, but was slightly smaller "They're way more advanced, or so I've heard." She settled herself in the chair next to me, sliding the cover of the phone open. "It is called a Cam-phone."

The top didn't have a screen, just a small, red, blinking button.

"Watch this!" She turned the phone upside down and spoke with a soft voice to the rubber part on the back corner of the cell. "Lucian McKenzie." She turned the phone back again. After the tenth beeping sound she started to tap her thumbs impatiently. A hologram in the shape of Lucian's face appeared before us.

"I'm not losing another Cammy, Becky," he whisper.

"Sorry, I'm showing Elena our cool toys," she said, putting the phone on her lap.

"She okay?" he asked quietly.

"She's a tough girl; I don't think she's going to the wacky-bin."

Lucian shook his head. "Bye." The hologram disappeared with a small flash.

"You can send text messages too, but we don't type. We say what we want to, and the phone transforms the voice recording into writing. Then you can send it by speaking the person's name. They'll read the text the same way Lucian's face appeared. It comes with so many apps, like silent mode, and a homework app, but you have to be careful of it. Sometimes it gives you the wrong answers. My favorite is the What-looks-good-on-me-app. Just to mention a few. Cool, huh?"

I nodded, still impressed by the talking hologram.

"The dragons still do business on the other side. We have the currencies of every country in the world right here in the bank of Paegeia." She took a sip of her Coke. "I mean honestly, Elena, who do you think invents most of the technology?"

"Dragons?" I asked tentatively.

She nodded, touching the bottom of my can and lifting it to my mouth.

I took a few more gulps. The sugar helped, and the knots in my stomach start to loosen. "Why didn't I see any of the dragons?" I was still trying to take it all in.

"You couldn't. They're very good at disguising themselves. But, if the Council thinks they won't be able to contain their true form, especially the Chromatic dragons, they won't grant them a pass. They're not allowed to invent anything on the other side of the Wall, because they could draw too much attention to themselves. On that side they're only allowed to give the humans ideas, and it's usually enough for the humans to fill in the missing pieces."

"Why does the law forbid them?"

"They're filled with the essence of life, which means they age differently than humans. Most of the Metallic dragons can live up to twelve thousand years."

"Twelve thousand years?" I exclaimed, stunned.

"The coolest part is that, if their bond with their Dragonians is strong, they can grant them a part of their essence."

"How?"

"I'm not a hundred percent sure. Dragons and their riders are very secretive about it. It's rare, the same as the dent thing. A normal dragon bond isn't that strong, but King Albert had the essence from his dragon. King Albert celebrated his two-hundred-and-fiftieth birthday the year he died."

"Wow. How do you know if you're part of a dent?" I asked.

"We have a Viden. She's a Moon-Bolt dragon. They have the ability to foretell the future, but they don't always predict it in a way we can understand. Our Viden lives in the tower behind the boys' dormitories and everyone is required to see her at least once a month. You will too. If she picks up a Dragonian in one of the sessions she has with a dragon, they mostly end up in a brother-hood or sisterhood. She even feels something when it's time for one of her predictions to be fulfilled. That part is amazing, but most of the time she sucks predictions out of her thumb." She laughed. "Sammy's version is easy; she says the Viden speaks a lot of shit."

"How will I know whether she speaks the truth then?"

"Believe me, you'll know. It's best to wait until you see her."

All this new information swirled around in my head and the intricacies of ascending were on my mind once again. "So do you know what ability you'll get?" I asked, hoping one day I wouldn't have to be constantly asking questions.

"No, but I have a feeling I'm a fire wielder. When that happens, Sammy and I will team up."

"You're going to claim Sammy?"

"No, the Metallic dragons don't throw tantrums the same way as the Chromatic ones. They usually decide they want to be your dragon and surrender, but there is still a lot of paperwork that is just as painful. You need to register with the Council and give them a statement of intent. Lately, we have to ask the Council permission for everything. That's why I envy Blake. He gets away with everything, especially when it comes to the Council. I think it's because he has so many abilities," she said.

"Wait, if he's both, why doesn't he just surrender?" I placed my empty soda can on the coffee table. "I mean, if he needs a Dragonian, and he's half Metallic, why doesn't he choose?"

"Elena, not every story ends with good overcoming evil. In Blake's case, only his Dragonian can keep him from turning."

"But you said his Dragonian doesn't exist."

She inhaled deeply.

"I'm asking way too—"

"It's not that. Blake can get claimed, but whoever is going to claim him needs a miracle. Arianna, the princess of Areeth, has tried once and Lucian twice now. He almost had him the last time, but he got a surprise blow from an ability none of us knew Blake had. The problem with a claim like his, and this might sound crazy to you...," she said nervously and put her feet on the couch, hugging her knees to her chest. "There are ways to keep the Chromatic dragons, that don't dent, from becoming evil—"

"What ways?" I asked, intrigued.

"Beating the evil out of them," she said and shrank into the chair.

"What?" Disgust laced my tone.

"I know, it sounds pretty awful, but it's the only thing that works."

"So whoever claims Blake has to beat the living crap out of him so he won't become evil?" I said skeptically.

"Pretty much."

"Lucian knows this?" I asked, though I still couldn't believe it.

"Yes, Elena. He says it's a sacrifice he is willing to make in order to not lose the Rubicon this time."

I struggled to wrap my mind around the whole beating thing, while simultaneously processing the fact that Lucian was okay with doing that. Any attraction I had once felt disappeared in a flash.

"Told you it sounds nuts, but I take my hat off to the ones who want to claim a Chromatic dragon if they're not dents. They say when the Chromatic is good they'll do anything for their Dragonian. No matter how crazy the task is."

"So basically they let their Dragonians abuse them and then let them take advantage of them after the fact. Sounds like a match made in heaven."

"Elena, you make it sound so...evil."

"Becky, it is!" I could feel my voice rising, though I wasn't really upset with her.

"No, it's not. Look, they don't get beaten on a daily basis. Only when they really need to control their evil selves, and on this side we grow up knowing that Dragonians don't always get the ability they want. If fate messed up and we get the ability that matches one of the Chromatic dragons, we know what needs to be done. They'll let their Dragonian know when the dark in them becomes too much to control." She was trying to get me to understand the situation from her point of view, but it wasn't working.

"I don't understand," I said solemnly, refusing even to consider the situation as anything other than abuse.

"Dragons know what it takes to stay good. Why do you think Sammy has different classes than us? She learns other stuff."

"So the dragons want their Dragonians to beat them?"

"Only the Chromatic dragons, and yes, they truly love their Dragonians for helping them stay good. It's not a cruel game, nor do we enjoy it. So please, don't go start a group against dragon abuse."

"They really beg their Dragonians?"

"It's not that difficult to grasp, Elena, believe me, the Dragonian hurts more than the dragon."

"The Dragonians don't like beating them?"

"Not unless they're psychos."

I still couldn't come to terms with the abuse, but I

decided I would do as Becky asked. I told her I wouldn't say anything bad about the beatings or bring them up ever again.

Suddenly, the bell rang and we both jerked. "You ready to go back to class, or do you want to stay here?"

"No, let's go back," I said, thinking my current problems weren't as bad in comparison to some of the others I would have to confront in this new world. I would even face another dragon if I had to, because running away was part of my past now. Heaven knows I'd had enough of it.

7

I TOOK A DEEP breath, let it out slowly, and opened the classroom door an inch so I could peer inside. Becky came up behind me and opened the door wide, nudging me softly in the back to go in. I expected the stares, but a boy in the third row had the nerve to snicker audibly. Becky gave him a sharp glare as she dragged me to the last row. We slipped into the only two chairs available and I sank inside my seat, wishing I could disappear.

The tutor at the front of the room paged through his textbook. His youthful appearance reminded me of Professor Mia and Sir Edward.

Becky leaned in to whisper. "Professor Gregory graduated a couple of years ago from Dragonia. He's one of the smartest humans ever."

"Welcome to Anatomy, Elena," Professor Gregory said. *Are you okay?* he mouthed, and I nodded carefully, not appreciating the extra attention he directed my way.

"If I ever catch anyone pulling the stunt George did earlier this afternoon, I swear, you'll wish you'd never hatched."

The air was sucked from the room as the class went silent.

Hatched? I frowned at his word choice.

"Open your books to page three hundred and fifteen," he said.

The sound of pages turning carried on for ten seconds as the class did as he asked. A picture of a dragon standing next to a human took up the whole page. For the love of blueberries, the ratio between them was way off and it looked terribly unrealistic.

Run, Forrest, run. I bit the inside of my mouth and stifled a laugh.

"Dragons come in different sizes and colors. They start out as eggs, which can be anywhere between one to four feet in length." Professor Gregory picked up a huge egg with a gritty, rocky surface. The harsh lights of the hall cast an eerie glow, creating a funny greenish shine. He handed it to the blond girl in the front row to pass around when she'd finished with her inspection. I didn't want to be anywhere near that thing.

"Sammy came from an egg?" I asked Becky in a whisper.

"Yup."

"A dragon's wingspan can reach up to a hundred and seventy feet," Professor Gregory's voice echoed through the lecture hall. "A dragon's eye has a large iris and a vertical pupil, just like a cat's eye. Can anyone tell me why?"

"I'm sure Riley knows," Becky whispered.

I knew cats because I had fed a lot of strays during our life on the run; it was easier than making friends I would just have to keep leaving. I lifted my hand tentatively. Becky and Professor Gregory looked surprised.

"Elena?"

The entire class turned around and stared at me.

"Well, if it's the same as cat's eyes, then the pupils can open wider to admit more light," I said, not quite sure of my answer.

He smiled. "You're right. Well done." He threw a candy bar in my direction.

"He's lecturing with chocolate bars too," Becky said.

"The white of a human's eye is often a different color than a dragon's. It can be yellow, gold, green, orange, red or even silver. It's protected by a leathery outer eyelid and three smooth inner eyelids. The innermost membrane is crystal clear and protects the eye from damage while the dragon flies." He drew a picture of an eye on the blackboard and pointed to the various parts. "The other two eyelids mainly serve to keep the eye clean. They're not as thick or clear as the innermost membrane. A dragon can use these inner lids to protect its eyes from sudden flashes of bright light."

The chalk made a screeching noise on the blackboard, and everybody cringed.

Professor Gregory chucked the chalk into the trashcan and grabbed another one. "Sorry," he said, and pulled a face.

The class laughed.

We covered dragon eyes over the next hour. I had never enjoyed a class this much before. Sure, everything was still completely unbelievable and I wasn't sure about my life anymore, but this class sure beat Trig. Whenever I gave Becky the '*huh?*' look, her whispered answer got me back on track again.

Too soon, the bell rang and everyone jumped out of their chairs. Becky grabbed my books and put them in her backpack. "The first thing we're going to get you tomorrow is a backpack." She threw the strap over her shoulder.

"Sorry, do you want me to carry that?" I asked, seeing her struggle slightly under the weight.

She waved me off. "I don't want you to pull another muscle."

Everything in my body still ached from earlier and I complained as I looked at the steps that led to the dorms.

She laughed and started to push me up one step at a time. If I thought Becky hadn't noticed my soreness, I was sure she had by the time we got to our room.

As we entered, we found Sammy lying on her bed. She had a sour pout.

I fell on top of my bed in a heap, while Becky headed for the bathroom. I wasn't very good at starting conversations, other than bickering with Dad. *He must have missed Paegeia so much.* I stared at the patterns on the ceiling until Sammy finally broke the silence.

"Elena, I'm so sorry about what George did." Sammy got up from her bed and came over to mine. She looked at me and sighed. The guilt weighed heavily on her shoulders.

I nodded the way Constance did with Master Longwei.

She sat softly on my bed.

"Hey, don't blame yourself, Sammy," I said.

She shook her head, looking at the pillow clutched tightly in her arms. "He gives us dragons a crappy name. Not all of us are like him, honest."

"I know and I'm fine. I have to admit, I came close to a heart attack, but Becky made me feel better."

"Do you understand now why we call my brother a jerk?"

"Wait, your brother asked him to do that?" I remembered someone had whistled before the dragon ran away.

"I heard Toby, a boy in my class, giving Blake the credit. He's so mean and I'm terrified of what's going to happen to him if nobody claims him." Tears welled up in her eyes.

"Hey, I only learned about all this dragon stuff today but I know you need to have faith. Everything will work out the way it's supposed to happen." I wasn't sure what else to say so I gave her Dad's advice; I only wished it had worked out better for him.

The corner of her mouth curved slightly, and then she grabbed me around my neck, pulling me to her chest. When she released me her dimples showed. "We can be BFFs, but Becky comes with the package, no exceptions."

"I like Becky, and thank you for trying to tell me everything in an hour. The two of you give a mean crash course."

She giggled. "We just wanted to get you up to date with

everything in Paegeia. I'm sure you'll learn more tomorrow. The city of Elm is full of stories," she said.

Becky came out of the bathroom and sat on the bed next to us. "Are you ready? Sammy and I want to show you a special spot."

I was reluctant to leave my room again, but my curiosity won out. They took me back to the steps, which took us a decade to descend because of my stiff knees.

A dozen students carrying suitcases chatted loudly with each other in the lobby.

"Spoiled brats," Sammy said. "I don't think they've ever spent a weekend at Dragonia."

"They're going home?"

"Only for the weekend."

Becky struggled with the wooden door again. "A little help, please."

"Hold on, drama queen, before you end up losing an arm," Sammy said, and pulled the door open without effort.

She's strong. Must be a dragon thing. My conscience shrugged internally, but it still bothered me. Sammy was really nice and everything, but there were still other dragons out there that were not nice. I'd seen it first-hand, and it was the reason my dad was gone.

We slipped through the opening and entered the school grounds.

As we walked, Sammy went back to being playful and bumped Becky softly. I was glad she didn't feel bad anymore and a small part of me wished I could put things behind me as easily as she seemed to do.

Coming around a sharp corner, we ran into Blake next to the stairs. He was making out with Tabitha, and they made no effort to hide what they were doing.

Sammy turned into a ferocious beast, well figuratively, when she saw them together, stalked up to her brother, and pushed him away, interrupting their make-out session. "You're such an asshole, Blake."

He laughed and my knees went weak.

Why does he have to be so damn gorgeous? I pulled on the collar of my t-shirt in a rhythmic beat, hoping the pathetic excuse for a breeze would make the hot flashes Blake brought on disappear.

"Dad will hear about this," she said.

His smile vanished. "It was a joke, Samantha!"

She spun around to face him. "A joke? Larry and Brent went to the bar is a joke, Blake, not what you and George pulled off this afternoon."

His eyes twitched and he glared at me.

Great, now the hottest guy in school thinks I'm a loser.

"Didn't you hear what Master Longwei said about Elena the other night? I guess not, you were probably too busy thinking about Medusa's naked body."

Tabitha's eyes narrowed and she lunged at Sammy, but Blake pinned her against the wall with one strong arm.

"I'm going to kill you, Samantha. Your mouth is way too big."

"She's not worth it, babes, calm down," Blake said. He whispered something in her ear, and her smile returned.

"At least I'm not a coward," Sammy chirped.

"Sammy," Becky said through clenched teeth.

Tabitha's jaw muscles tightened viciously as we turned and walked away.

"Oh c'mon, Becky, she deserved that. Isn't it enough that I have to be nice to her whenever we go home?"

"Tabitha goes with you guys?"

Sammy curled up her lip and rolled her eyes. "He only wants her for one thing."

"They're an item now?" Becky's eyebrow arched.

"Who cares?" said Sammy.

"You didn't have to do that, Sammy." I felt terrible about the way he'd looked at me, and for his father finding out what he had done.

"Yes, I did," she said. "The day my brother forgets what consequences mean, is the day it's too late."

Becky gave her a one-armed hug. "I'll try to claim him too if you want me to?"

"Honey, you're good with a sword and a shield, but your skills are nowhere near good enough to tame my brother."

"I said try, but by the tone of your voice you can forget about my offer."

Sammy kicked Becky's butt playfully and bumped her softly. "I love you, thanks for trying to make me feel better."

The two girls acted as if they already shared a sisterhood.

"Why did you call Tabitha a coward?" I asked, still confused about what I had just encountered.

Well, except for the part when Blake got me all hot and bothered.

She sighed. "I'm probably going to hear it from my mom. 'Metallic dragons are better than backbiting, Samantha Leaf'," she mimicked in a strong British accent.

We laughed.

"Snow dragons are the biggest cowards," Becky said, answering my earlier question. "When the going gets tough, well, they usually go poof, but I have to give it to her, she's one smart cookie. She does Blake's homework for him on a daily basis."

"Urgh! My brother is just lazy."

"Did Master Longwei really tell you guys about me?" I asked quietly.

"Oh, Elena, your arrival is the biggest excitement this school has had in years. Master Longwei had to say something," Sammy said.

Great, just what I needed.

We exited the doors that led to the dome, and I cringed as I caught sight of more steps.

"Hop on my back." Sammy crouched in front of me.

"Sammy, no, it's fine," I said, looking at her ridiculous posture.

"C'mon, Elena, I won't let you fall. Promise."

"Fine." I gave in and climbed onto her back.

Maybe it was a good thing Sammy carried me down the

stairs, otherwise, I would have probably ended up breaking a leg or something.

When she reached the bottom, she released me.

"So, Elena, what's happening on the other side?" Sammy asked quizzically.

I figured after they had told me so much, it was only fair to tell them everything. We spoke about Dad, even though the tears still lurked in the corner of my eyes and my heart still felt raw every time I thought of him. They gasped when I mentioned how many times I had to move because of Dad's paranoia. They didn't understand why, and I didn't have the answers to make them.

In return, Sammy explained more about the dragons, with Becky's skillful interruptions whenever she felt Sammy's explanations lacked color.

Sammy disliked every single one of Becky's interjections and glared at her constantly. I didn't care. My ears were glued to what both of them had to say. The Night Villain was black and breathed acid; even his saliva could burn a hole right through a shield. I met the Sun-Blast, and they called the green dragon a Green-Vapor. They had the ability to lie through their teeth and owned the gift of persuasion. They were also chlorine breathers.

Reaching a fork in the road, we took the path that wound past the Parthenon Dome and walked to a forest with rocky mountains in the distance. I laughed when Sammy said a young Moon-Bolt, like George, would get banned from casinos, because Moon-Bolts could predict the dealers' cards. Her hands moved wildly through the air as she spoke and I wondered if she'd still be able to talk if they were tied up. Nevertheless, I couldn't take my eyes off of her.

Suddenly, I slammed into Becky, who had stopped walking in front of us.

"Sorry, Elena. I didn't think anyone would be here," Becky apologized.

I looked at what she was staring at and saw two dragons. They were big. One of them had a bronze shimmer to his skin, and the other one had a silver glow with huge swallow-shaped wings.

"It's a Crown-Tail and a Swallow Annex," Becky whispered.

The dragons stared back at us and the silver one bowed its head in my direction. My heart thumped again.

"What are they doing here?" I asked nervously.

"They come here to be in their true form." Becky grabbed my arm and pulled me back the way we had come.

"Are they students?" I asked.

Both nodded.

"It's Becky's and my sanctuary. We love the trees, and there's a nice spot by the lake where you can clear your mind. Sometimes I help Becky to improve her fighting skills," she explained.

"What do you mean?"

"Fight, Elena. Sometimes Sammy is my sparring partner."

"In my dragon form," Sammy added, which gave it a whole different meaning.

"Are you insane?" I shouted.

Becky laughed. "C'mon, what do you think Sammy's going to do? She can't even hurt a fly."

"Oh, yeah? Remember that when I light your ass on fire next time," she warned.

We turned around and followed the same path we had taken all the way back to our room.

When I got inside the room once again, I couldn't stop staring at my bed. "So, what's going to happen if the other girl comes back?" I asked, scared Master Longwei might chuck me out of Dragonia Academy. I had nowhere else to go.

"Vicky?" Sammy fell on the couch. "I don't think she will be back any time soon. Sometimes a quest takes up to a year in order to figure out what your destiny is."

"Especially the way the Viden predicts them." Becky opened the fridge door.

Sammy gave her the glare she'd been giving Becky all day whenever she interrupted her. "She's a Crown-Tail, and on a self-discovery quest."

"What's a self-discovery quest?

Becky had mentioned that term earlier, while I sat on one of the other couches.

"Sometimes the Viden sees something that leads to a self-discovery quest. She'll see something that you must find. Whether it's something emotional or hidden, we can't choose. I don't know what she has seen with Vicky, but I remember the state she was in when she came back," Sammy said.

"Vicky disliked the Viden very much. She hated her even more after the day she got her foretelling, but we're obligated to see her at least once a month. Do you remember how obsessed she got?"

Sammy nodded.

"She spent most of her time in the library, just research-ing. When she started to miss classes, Master Longwei forced her to go on a self-discovery quest and she was ordered not to return until she found whatever she was looking for."

"They let you go on quests alone?"

Becky tossed us each a soda and sat down next to Sammy.

Sammy nodded.

I didn't like the way they forced things here, and after all these stories, I sure didn't look forward to meeting the Viden.

While we sat there sipping our sodas, Sammy explained how a self-discovery quest took weeks to plan. You had to do a whole statement, explaining the reasons you wanted to go. The members of the Academy board arranged a meeting and decided if the reasons were valid enough for a full fund and whether you absolutely needed to go.

After this started to border on tiresome, the conversation switched over to dragons again. I listened in awe as Sammy explained, in detail, the rest of the Metallic dragons. The Crown-Tail had bronze colored skin, and most of them went into law; they hated cruelty and loved the human race. She said that a lot of them disappeared the night of King Albert's death. The Copper-Horns, like Dad, loved telling jokes and riddles, and pulling pranks, but the good clean kind, not what George had earlier. The best part of what she told me was that Chef was a Copper-Horn too. They were also one of the Big Three, the largest of all the dragons. The Night Villain and Sun-Blast were the others. The Swallow Annex was silver and loved to fly. They had the biggest wings of all the dragon species. I felt proud remembering the wings were the first thing I noticed when we found them this afternoon. They had the ability to heal human injuries.

I was told this was why Constance had gone into medicine. She was the best of Paegeia's doctors, which made her the head of the Health Association and a Council member, but she devoted her time to the Academy. Becoming a member of the Council was Becky's biggest dream.

"Can I ask you something, Sammy?"

"Shoot."

"How's it that you are a Fire-Tail, but your brother is a Rubicon?"

They both giggled, but I was used to that by now.

"Let me think." She frowned while staring at the carpet as if the answer were written in the kinky fibers.

"Use cats, they have cats on the other side," Becky said, looking for a way to explain it so I would understand.

"Cats can work. You know when a litter of kittens is born, not one looks the same? It's the same with dragons. You never know what you might get until they're hatched."

"I still can't believe that you were born out of an egg."

She giggled. "Dragons only shift into humans when they're about five years old."

"Why do you have two forms?" I asked.

"Well, to blend in, I guess, like your dad."

"You know, most of the teachers here are dragons too," Becky said, changing the topic of our conversation away from Dad.

"Really? Like who?"

"Sir Edward and Professor Gregory teamed up a couple of years ago. They're not a dent, but you would think they were if you saw the two of them together."

"Who's the dragon?"

"Sir Edward. He and Master Longwei are both Fin-Tails. The only two left, I think."

"Master Longwei is a dragon?" I hadn't seen that one coming.

"C'mon, Elena, you can see that he is from a mile away. His eyes?"

I remembered the golden glint in them, but had thought it was my imagination playing tricks.

"What's the time?" Sammy sulked after her stomach growled loudly, interrupting us.

"It's time to go."

8

THE TABLES INSIDE the cafeteria had big fluffy pillows lined up on either side instead of chairs. Each table had a square sky lantern on top that was lit from the inside and glowed with a majestic light. Chinese balloon lanterns floated from the ceiling, illuminating the room. We quickly went through the buffet line at the back. Fresh fruit, milk, root beer, and other major soda brands, with chicken, fish, beef, and pork served with steamed vegetables and rice made my choice difficult. They even had a pudding section, which had a huge sign in front hanging from a golden chain that read CLOSED.

Becky pulled up her nose and made an unpleasant sound while she eyed the food.

I didn't care what we ate; I was starving.

"Good evening ladies," Chef said. His beard had a red-brown shimmer underneath the bright lights that gleamed over the buffet line.

"You've outdone yourself tonight," Sammy praised as she grabbed a plate and a tray. She poured orange juice into her glass.

"It's Friday. I want junk food," Becky whined.

"Then answer my riddle, and you can choose whatever your little heart desires," Chef countered.

"Fine, I'll see what the stupid riddle says," Becky mumbled the last part.

I laughed, remembering how much I also hated riddles. I would give up this meal, though, if it meant hearing one from Dad's lips again.

Sammy and I sat at the nearest table with our trays. Becky went over to look at the riddle posted on the board in the corner of the cafeteria.

She wrote it down on a napkin and walked back to our table.

"Anyone have it yet?" Sammy asked, curious.

She raised the corner of her upper lip and read the riddle out loud. "I never was, am always to be. No one ever saw me, nor ever will, and yet I am the confidence of all, to live and breathe on this terrestrial ball. What am I?"

"Come again?" Sammy asked, clearly confused.

"That's my point. Guess we're going to have cooked meals for the next two months," she said, and chucked the napkin aside.

"Anybody got the riddle's answer yet?" Lucian's voice made me jump as he approached us.

He apologized for the scare, giving me one of his super smiles, and plopped onto the empty pillow next to me.

"What are you still doing here?" Becky's mood changed in a flash.

"My dad had to leave this afternoon for the meeting in Areeth. He'll swing by tomorrow to come and fetch me."

"Meetings of the Royal Council," Sammy whispered.

Becky recited the riddle to him and he frowned.

"C'mon Lucian, you're good at this crap."

"Sorry Becky, the riddle sounds like French," he said, and gave a sexy chuckle. A million goosebumps broke out across my skin. *Weird. Guess the image of him being okay with beating Blake half to death wasn't as much of a turn-off as I'd thought.*

"Oh please, I don't know where Chef gets them. I wonder if he even knows the answers himself," Becky said with a pout.

The answer popped into my head. "It's tomorrow."

"What?"

"The answer is tomorrow. I think."

The three of them stared at me with wide eyes.

Becky recited the riddle softly. She left out an excited squeal and jumped from her pillow. "Oh my word, Elena, you're right."

"You're good at riddles?" Lucian asked.

"It's the first one I got right. I usually suck at them."

"Wicked," he said.

Becky reached the buffet line. She leaned over to speak to Chef. He smiled, went over to a big bell, and rang it twice.

She did a happy dance, which made the entire cafeteria laugh.

Lucian leaned closer to me. "You're going to be her favorite person," he said breathily in my ear, which made my skin tingle all over.

"Hey everyone, what about pizza for breakfast?" Becky announced.

Some boys cheered, with loud whistles.

"It's hardly a food group," Sammy whined

Becky returned with a tray of food and a big smile. "Why didn't you tell me that you were good at riddles?"

"I didn't know I was. Please, don't make this a daily thing."

"You're at least going to try, Elena," she said, completely serious.

"So what's on the menu for tomorrow?" Lucian asked.

"Pizza for breakfast, hot dogs for lunch, and hamburgers for dinner." She sounded pleased. Lucian reached his hand in the air and Becky slapped it playfully in a high-five.

"I might just stay for that."

"And give up a weekend of freedom? You'll leave and go with your dad tomorrow, Lucian, even if I have to push you onto Emanuel myself."

"Emanuel is King Helmut's dragon," Sammy whispered again.

Riley entered the cafeteria and went first to the buffet line. Chef nodded in the direction of our table and she turned around to look at us. Disappointment was written over her face as she stalked to our table. Riley wasn't pretty, but not ugly either. She had a strong body and I wondered who would win between her and Becky in the Parthenon Dome.

Without saying hello she asked, "You got the riddle?"

I kicked Becky's shin underneath the table and begged her with my eyes not to tell Riley it was me.

"Yes, you have a problem with that?" she challenged.

Riley huffed, arched her eyebrows and stormed away to a table filled with girls who couldn't stop glaring our way. She dropped into a pillow and huddled in with the girls there.

"Why don't you want to let them in on the fact that you're good at solving riddles?" Lucian's question broke my gaze from their table.

"I'm not good at dealing with confrontations the way Becky is." I nodded toward her. She made brushing people off look so easy.

He looked at his plate again and smiled. A gentle crease formed on his forehead. I could feel myself getting warm again; this had to stop happening in public.

The food was great, just like the company. I listened to Lucian talk with admiration about his father's kingdom, Tith, and how he wanted to make his biggest dream, to claim Blake, a reality. He spun his empty glass in circles on his plate as he talked. He sounded so brave when speaking of swords, shields, and fighting. He hardly made eye contact with me, but the few times our gazes met, I could feel the electricity passing through us. Maybe it was just my imagination running wild, but the picture of Lucian the dragon abuser vanished, leaving behind the image of Lucian—the hottest guy ever.

By the end of the night, a number of girls had either

scolded or murdered me with their eyes. I tried to ignore them, but I could feel their glares burning straight through to my soul.

When the bell chimed nine times, we returned to our dorms. We said goodbye to Lucian by the stairs and I wished him a lovely weekend. I had a different view of things after our talk. A fuzzy feeling rose inside my chest whenever he popped into my mind, especially his brilliant smile.

I still had one lingering question on my mind as the three of us sat down on Sammy's bed. "Do any of the humans ever get hurt during a claim?"

"Oh yes, the Chromatic dragons don't give up easily," Sammy said.

"Then claiming a dragon can kill you?" I was suddenly afraid for Lucian, since he had just explained to me that he was planning a third attempt to claim Blake.

"There's always one of the professors nearby, Elena," Becky said in an assuring tone. "So when it gets too rough they jump in."

I was just glad they didn't go 'poof.'

The subject soon changed away from the claiming to their capital city, Etan. Sammy said that creepers had consumed the entire city, along with the nearby villages and farms, on the night of King Albert's and Queen Catherine's deaths. For the past fifteen years, brave Dragonians had tried to find a way through the creepers, but when they got too close, the creepers became wild and alive, tearing apart everything in their reach. Every year, scientists checked the creepers to measure their growth, but they had yet to find a single one dead. The way the two of them explained it made me think about Sleeping Beauty and how the prince had to hack his way through to get to her. Becky had her own opinion and believed the Council was wasting their time with science. She believed only Blake and his true Dragonian would be able to pass, like the Viden had prophesied when Blake's egg hatched. But since his true Dragonian didn't exist, Etan was lost forever.

When Blake's egg hatched, the Viden had also predicted that his Dragonian would be from King Albert and Queen Catherine's bloodline.

"They died before producing an heir and, with that, my brother's only chance at getting claimed."

"Oh, Sammy, you can't say that," Becky said, giving her a side hug as Sammy's eyes sparkled with tears.

She sighed and wiped her eyes with the back of her hand.

"When the Viden makes a true calling, she has never been wrong, Becky," she said in a soft, sad tone.

In an attempt to lighten the mood, we changed our conversation to the Viden. She was three hundred years old, but her human body was still relatively young. The boys attending Dragonia Academy drooled over her. Sammy explained to me how vain she was and how the Viden had a fondness for only her famous foretellings, like Blake. He saw her at least twice a week.

We kept talking until the clock chimed eleven, then we called it a night.

I struggled to go to sleep even though I was so exhausted my brain cells hurt. I wasn't sure if it was all the information my mind was trying to process or the new bed. I shivered, thinking of what the other side would do if they discovered dragons were real. Humans had the tendency to destroy everything they didn't understand. They wouldn't even consider a truce.

I hoped Constance was right about the Wall and that it would never lose its power, otherwise Paegeia could be in serious danger. I said a small prayer to keep us safe as I drifted off to sleep.

9

THE NEXT DAY I had the pleasure of discovering just how much Becky loved her alarm clock. She hit the snooze button at least a million times until the device fell off the nightstand and crashed to the floor.

Sammy jumped on Becky. "Wake up sleepy head, or else we're leaving without you!"

Becky growled, but reluctantly got out of bed. I laughed as she struggled to wake even as we were leaving our room.

We found Master Longwei at the main entrance, where we came to a silent halt. He was unlocking the gate and didn't notice our arrival.

The gate I love and hate all at the same time.

"He really needs help with his fashion choices. Those ankle shorts are so last season. Not to mention his ancient Hawaiian shirt," Becky said, as if she were the fifth member of Fashion Police.

"It's not so bad," Sammy said.

Becky rolled her eyes. "Sammy, no offense, but if I didn't tell you what to wear every day, you'd be dressed like a circus clown."

"My choices aren't that bad. I just love color."

I smiled, feeling at home with these girls. Dad jumped

into my mind again, and a lump rose in my throat as I thought about how many of their mannerisms aligned with his.

"Good morning girls." Master Longwei swung the gate open and turned to face us. "How did your first day go, Elena?"

"Well, I'm still alive." I swallowed hard, and tried to hide my fear of heights behind a shaky smile. I looked around and found the sky and clouds where buildings and trees should've been.

"I heard about George. I'm deeply sorry about his behavior and I assure you it will never happen again."

"No hassle," I said, brushing it off with a wave of my hand, hoping to change the subject. "Why didn't you tell me you're a dragon?"

His expression told me he hadn't expected that question. "I should have known Becky would enlighten you as to what I am."

"See it as a little payback. Do you have any idea how hard we had to work to keep Elena from running away?" Becky chirped.

We all laughed.

"Are you comfortable with having a dragon for a head-master?" he asked hesitantly.

"It's okay. If it's not too personal, can I ask you another question? How old are you?"

He grinned. "I'm scared you'll run away screaming. But

Elm with all the historical buildings and museums is a good place to stumble onto something like that."

"Screaming my head off while running away is so yesterday's news," I said, injecting more confidence into my voice than I felt.

He chuckled and watched me carefully as he spoke. "I will be celebrating my four thousand, three hundred, and sixteenth birthday next month."

To my surprise, running for the hills didn't pop into my head. I guess the girls' crash course had worked.

"That young?" A smile turned up the corners of my mouth.

My smile soon vanished, however, as I remembered why he was unlocking the gate. My heart started to thump inside my throat and my knees trembled softly as the edge, just a few feet past the gate, caught my eye.

"Close your eyes, Elena," he said.

I did as he told me and an image of him transforming into a dragon flashed into my mind.

My eyes flew open when my feet bumped against a small step.

"You are such a wuss," Becky said, already in her seat.

I found myself standing on the step of a modern carriage with leather couches. A strong lemon aroma hung in the air around us.

I felt like a twenty-first-century Cinderella. The windows were tinted—not that I had an urge to look outside anyway. I took a seat next to Sammy as I struggled to tear my gaze away from the carriage's finer details. Someone had hand-stitched the black couches, and the soft, dark brown velvet that bedecked the walls gave the carriage a warm ambience.

Master Longwei took a seat right next to Becky. Our eyes met as my attention wandered to the ceiling.

"So, I heard that you solved the chef's riddle last night."

I nodded and let out a tiny shriek as the carriage lifted off the ground. I grabbed the safety belt and buckled up.

"Do you like riddles?"

"Not really," I spoke fast as the carriage started to stabilize itself once again.

I took a deep breath but didn't unclench my fists.

"She got the answer on the first try. We were complaining about the horrible food when she just blurted out the answer," Becky said.

"Speak for yourself, I like Chef's cooking," Sammy snapped.

"You mean those disgusting leaves you're always eating?"

"Vegetarianism is a life choice."

"Sammy, you're the first dragon I've met that's a vegetarian."

Sammy stuck out her tongue at Becky.

"My intuition tells me Chef is going to make a lot of junk food," Master Longwei said.

I just smiled nervously.

As the turbulence returned I began to wish the ride

would end and closed my eyes tightly. Elm had better be worth this horrible ride. A soft nudge in my rib cage made my eyes fly open. I saw Sammy nodding earnestly toward the exit.

Becky crouched in front of me and shook her head as she prepared to disembark.

We landed in the woods near a narrow path. I automatically searched for what had pulled the carriage. I should've known what I would find: two big-ass dragons.

I quickly followed the others down the path to a small village. We didn't have to wait long before a tram came into sight. "You have normal transport too?" I asked half mockingly.

Sammy giggled, and Becky ushered me onto the tram. The conductor greeted Master Longwei with a firm handshake, and they started to talk. For the first ten minutes I tried to figure out whether the conductor was a dragon, but curiosity vanished the minute we entered the city.

It reminded me of New York mixed with Venice. People walked on the sidewalks with dogs, and a few even drove around in little mobile carts. We passed a fountain where a couple was tossing in loose coins. Next to the fountain, an artist worked his magic on an easel, reproducing the beautiful scenes around him.

Shops started flashing by, and the streets buzzed with more and more people. As the road narrowed, I was surprised to see more conventional transport: bicycles and motorcycles. A touch of home but there were also some things out of this world. Some people were standing on a sort of skateboard contraption, flying a few inches above the air. A flame of blue steam came from the back of the board. Their riders were really good and zoomed in between the people.

"What is that?"

"It's called a raider," Sammy said. "Your side doesn't have them yet?"

I shook my head without taking my gaze off one.

Sammy started to laugh and looked at Becky. "Becky's tried like fifty odd times to get hers."

"Hahaha," Becky said sarcastically. Sammy and I laughed. "It's not fifty yet."

"Okay, then let me rephrase: the next time will be your fiftieth."

Becky glared at her, but a small smile appeared and I knew she took Sammy's comment as a joke.

The tram came to a halt in front of a big mall with coffee shops dominating the area around it. People were drinking coffee and reading newspapers at the sidewalk tables.

Sammy pulled me out of the way and a raider just missed my head. It was followed by two other raiders and the guys who rode them all wore goggles and laughed.

Everywhere we went, people greeted Master Longwei. He simply nodded and smiled back politely.

"Give," Becky said, hand open and her palm facing up.

"Oh no, I am not going to be fooled this time, young

lady. Here is money. My credit card isn't safe between the two of you," he said. I sensed this wasn't the first time he'd asked Becky to run errands for him. He gave her paper money that had horizontal patterns printed on it. "I will meet you by the carriage at three o'clock. Three o'clock, Rebecca." He gave her a knowing stare with his eyebrow arched, letting us know he meant it. "Good luck, Elena." He smiled then went to one of the coffee shops.

Becky grabbed my wrist and pulled me toward the store with the same name that was on the label of my jeans: Twiggs.

"If you buy from Twiggs you will never be out of fashion," Sammy explained excitedly. "Lucky for you, Becky has a good eye for what goes together and what doesn't."

"Thank you, girl." Becky beamed at Sammy's compliment as we entered through a revolving door.

Inside the store was a nightmare. I had never changed so many times in one day, but I had to admit, Becky did have an eye for fashion.

As the pile of clothes on the counter grew, I began to worry whether we had enough cash, but the three bills offered to the cashier seemed to do the trick.

Sammy carried most of the bags, which looked so unnatural.

I thought we were done and intended to return to the coffee shops, when Becky pulled me into another store. "Weatherly's and Co." was written in big green letters above the door.

"This is Lucian's favorite store," Becky said, and her smile made me wonder if she didn't have a thing for him. Not that I blamed her.

Inside, the store, swords, axes, fighting hammers, whips —even the one with the long chain and ball at the end—and a variety of shields were displayed on rows of shelves. My jaw dropped.

There were uniforms in all different colors stacked in another aisle with more raiders. They all had different shapes and sizes.

Goggles and huge saddles were placed in another part of the store. I didn't know where to look.

Plenty of little boys admired the swords, with their hands tucked behind their backs. They made me smile as I realized it didn't matter where you grew up, every boy dreamed about being a knight.

We walked past two boys sparring playfully. One of the boys pretended to be a knight, the other one a dragon, and not just any dragon—the Rubicon.

Thankfully, Becky took me straight to the vest section.

"Rebecca Johnson, how is your mother doing?" the clerk asked.

While she gave me her famous eye roll, she flashed the clerk her beautiful smile. "Oh, she's fine. I'm looking for a vest for my friend. Her name is Elena."

The clerk's shoulder-to-hip scrutiny made me uncomfortable.

He turned around and disappeared into the back.

"He has a thing for my mom." Her lack of excitement was obvious.

"What does your father think about that?"

"He died when I was really little," she said.

"I'm so sorry, Becky." *I always say the wrong stuff.*

"It's cool, Elena. Besides, I never knew him."

I was glad when the bearded man returned right at that moment with a small black disk and handed it to me for inspection. I turned to Becky and scrunched up my face with confusion. Once she'd taken the small disk, she pressed the small green gem located in the center and put it back on the counter. In five seconds, the disk was gone, and in its place was an impressive black vest.

I picked it up and stared at it. The vest was light with quilted padding on the inside and a rock-hard exterior.

"What is it?" Becky asked, leaning over my shoulder.

"It's the Samurai Three Thousand. Nice, huh?"

I glided my fingers over the engravings that decorated the shell-like exterior.

Becky glanced at the price tag. "This is way too expensive." She grabbed the vest from my hands and shoved it back at the clerk.

He disappeared again and returned with another. This disk was more of an oval shape, with a delicate blue stone in the shape of a lightning bolt. I cautiously touched the gem and flinched as the new vest appeared in my arms. It didn't resemble the Samurai Three Thousand, but it still looked pretty awesome. The name "Black Bolt" and the number "5" were engraved on top of the vest's surface.

"Try it on," Becky said after she glanced at the tag.

The vest fit perfectly, covering all the important areas, and didn't smell like stale sweat, like the one in which I'd practiced the day before.

Sammy—who'd been on her own mission—found us as I was adjusting the straps. "That's really nice, Elena."

"How does it fit?" Becky asked.

"I actually feel safe."

They both giggled.

"We'll take it. Can I drop off mine in three weeks for a cleaning?" Becky asked. The clerk assured her it would be fine.

As he disappeared, something behind Becky caught my eye.

I gasped.

"Cool huh?" Becky stood right beside me.

"I'm going to check the latest gear," Sammy said, and squeezed past us.

"Is this armor for dragons?" I asked as we investigated the racks further.

"Yes," Becky said. "This section is for the Night Villains. They have to make the armor with special steel because of the acid they breathe. That one at the top is *vereautiful*. If I had a Night Villain I would buy him that." She pointed at a shiny silver torso and head armor hanging above our heads.

We were so engrossed we ended up walking the entire section.

There was gear for Moon-Bolts, Sun-Blasts and even Snow dragons. By the size of the harness, the Snow dragon was indeed not as big as the others. The gear came in all the colors of the rainbow and were a variety of different designs. We found Sammy by the Fire-Tail section purring over a black number with silver spiky studs.

"This would look freaky with my brass color, right?" Sammy looked at Becky for approval.

"For the first time you might be right, Sammy."

We paid for the vest, which was transformed back into the oval disk, and I picked up a pack of playing cards from a small basket by the register. Becky grabbed a pack, winked at me, and tossed it in with the vest.

I glanced at my watch: five to three. Jeez, time flew when you shopped with friends.

Running, we caught the tram and reached the woods shortly after three. Master Longwei was waiting for us, tapping his foot in annoyance.

"I said three, Rebecca Johnson."

"Oh, you can be glad that it's a couple of minutes and not half an hour. Six hours was hardly enough."

He grinned. "Did you enjoy your shopping?"

"Yes, thank you, Master," I said, and climbed into the carriage. Words couldn't describe how I felt at that moment. I pulled the safety belt over my shoulder slowly, feeling a bit drained from our trip, but giddy from my new purchases.

I felt sorry for Master Longwei. He had no choice but to listen to Becky babbling about shopping. She even tried to throw in some fashion tips, which meant Sammy and I had to suppress our laughter so we wouldn't cause offense.

I fell on my bed when we eventually made it back to our room, completely immobile.

Sitting next to me Becky opened the pack of cards and handed me one. "It's all the famous people throughout the years. Many of the young boys and girls collect them."

Sammy mumbled something as she picked at a packet of crisps, and dove into it as if she hadn't seen food for days.

On one card was a picture of a guy named Theodore Verona, whoever that was. I turned it around and all his stats were listed on the back, like a baseball card. He'd lived in the thirteenth century and had been a knight. They had his number of kills along with his victories at the Annual Games. He had slain one thousand and five dragons.

Becky handed me a second card that depicted a woman named Delilah. She was a Fire-Tail dragon and must've been the oldest of them all because she had celebrated her fourteen thousandth birthday nineteen years ago. It said King Albert had thrown her a huge party. A third card depicted Sir Chan Wei-Ling, also a dragon, and the General of King Albert's court.

I froze as I stared blankly at the last one and my mouth fell open. "Are you serious?" I showed Sammy a card of her brother.

"He's the Rubicon, Elena. That card is extremely rare. You can exchange it for at least ten cards."

I guess I still didn't get how famous Blake was.

"He hates going to town, it's a big mess," she explained.

"Really?"

"He's usually in disguise but always gets caught by one of the locals," Sammy said.

"At times I pity him," Becky admitted.

I looked at his picture. A strange sadness shone through his eyes. "Can I ask you guys a question? Where does Master Longwei get the money to pay for our little trips?"

"Dragonia is loaded. The parents whose children are not born with the mark pay plenty of money to get them in, which covers situations like these," Becky explained, while she helped me unpack the shopping bags.

"Master Longwei allows them inside Dragonia without the mark?"

"It's not written anywhere that you have to ascend to claim a dragon," Sammy answered.

"Just because one person has done it, doesn't mean all of them can," Becky countered.

"Wait, you actually mean somebody claimed a dragon that didn't have an extra ability?"

They only nodded since *Mystical Song*, a TV series, had started and the conversation ended there.

I lay back on my bed, too tired for another teen drama, and drifted away with Sammy's hyena laughter echoing noisily in the background. A huge emptiness filled my heart and I wished I could have shared this day with Dad. As I thought back back on the past forty-eight hours, my new reality started to kick in. I rolled over as a tear escaped and landed softly on the pillow. I would never share anything with him ever again.

10

WE FOUND THE most amazing burgers waiting for us at the buffet later that night. Becky tried her luck again with the next riddle. That girl could not get enough greasy food. To my surprise I knew the answer to this one as well. I didn't get it as fast as the last time, but I was impressed that I had gotten it at all. It was fire, but I kept the answer to myself because Sammy wasn't too fond of greasy food.

That night I felt dead tired again, but for some reason I still struggled to fall asleep. Blake had been on my mind a lot throughout the day. During dinner he had been sitting alone at a table, apparently deep in thought. There was a hard look to his face as he mixed the food on his plate methodically, as if he could find the answers to all his problems in his French fries. He'd eventually given up on the food and dismantled the lantern sitting on the table so he could play with the glowing embers. That was how I had come up with the answer to the riddle. When I finally fell asleep, I dreamed of him. I'd taken Tabitha's place next to him at the table. He had reached into my hair, pulled my face to his and given me one of those long, hard passionate kisses. I feared waking, feared leaving him. Lost as I was in the passion of the moment, I experienced a shift as my dream turned odd.

Blake disappeared, and I stood alone on top of a grassy hill. *Where the hell am I?*

I had no idea how I'd gotten there. I looked around me, perplexed because nothing seemed familiar. If this dream was an indication of my current state of mind, I was in trouble. Before me was a massive expanse of forest. Its tall trees and mass of fauna and flora, hiding who knew what, made it harder to breathe. As I started to walk across the hill, I noticed a dark-haired woman waiting for me on the other side. It felt as if it took forever to reach her. At first I thought it was Julia, but the closer I got, the more I realized it was a stranger.

She had an oval face, with fair skin and sad gray eyes. Long dark curls hung loose over her shoulders, with a few tendrils out of place being blown about by the wind. She just stared at me with a blank expression. I wanted to ask her, "What am I doing here?" No sound came from my lips.

She raised her arm, pointed to the forest, and ordered me to enter. I studied the forest quizzically before turning back to face her. Why on Earth did she want me to go in there? I refused. That was my first mistake, I thought, as she brought the forest to me. I was consumed by fear as I felt myself drowning in fifty feet of high, dense trees. I started to suffocate as if an invisible force was pressing the air out of my lungs. The woman vanished from sight as the trees pulled me deeper. My last glimpse of her before she disappeared revealed a smile playing at the corners of her lips. Just as I felt the last breath leave my lungs, I woke.

I was breathing rapidly while I tried to adjust to my surroundings. Luckily, Becky and Sammy were deep sleepers; I didn't feel like explaining myself to them at that moment. *Why the hell did I just dream that, and who was the woman?* I kept asking myself that as I tried to catch my breath.

MONDAY MORNING, I found a note pushed under the door to our room.

It was folded delicately but did not bring welcoming news. I had to go see the Viden at ten, the note explained in willowy silver script.

"The sooner the better," Sammy consoled during breakfast.

We sat outside at a table. I needed the fresh air to calm my nerves.

"Good morning, ladies." Lucian possessed the jovial tone of a real morning person. Well, I guess he couldn't be perfect.

"Hi, Lucian," we said in unison.

"When did you get in?" Becky flashed him her super smile.

"My dad was stuck yesterday with meetings and proclamations, so he asked Emanuel to drop me off last night around ten. So, how was Elm?"

"Amazing," Becky said in a singsong voice. "You must check out the new Samurai Three Thousand."

His face broke out in a playful smile.

Becky's eyes narrowed. "You already got it!"

"My dad bought it for me last week. It's really a wicked vest. You don't even feel like you're wearing it."

"It's so unfair," she said.

"Oh, Becky, I'm sure you got something out of this deal." Lucian chuckled.

"Yeah, Sammy and I each got a nice shirt," she said, perking up a bit.

"So, Elena, did you get everything you needed?" he asked.

My heart flipped a few times as I nodded.

"She's seeing the Viden today," Becky whispered.

"Good luck," Lucian said. "I was there this morning. She's not in a good mood, but it's a good day for prophecies."

"What do you mean by that?" My heart started to beat faster.

He leaned forward. "Blake was in there before me, and both of us came away with something to think about."

"You heard what she told my brother?" Sammy asked.

"No, but it was written all over his face when he came out."

"She won't, you know, turn into a dragon or something?" I asked timidly, and they all burst into laughter. Well, Sammy and Becky did. Lucian just gave this sexy chuckle that made my temperature rise slightly.

"No, Elena, the Viden doesn't like her dragon form. They lose their humanity the longer they're in their true form. She's usually in a good mood. I've no idea what went wrong this morning." He shrugged, clearly at a loss for what to say to calm my obvious nerves.

When the first bell rang, we said goodbye and parted ways. "Lucian likes you, Elena," Sammy whispered behind me.

My heart stopped. "What? No!" I stated, while butter-flies danced around in my stomach.

"Want to bet?" Becky said, and I just smiled. "Sammy's right Elena, he's never sat at our table so many times in a row."

"Will the two of you knock it off?" I looked at Becky, lifting my eyebrows so she knew I meant it. I couldn't see any trace of jealousy at the idea of Lucian and me. *She really didn't like him like that?*

Shaking off this new information, I walked quickly to my first period: Math. I had no idea where the class was, so Becky went with me to the end of the hall. She told me what direction to take and ran off to her next class in the opposite direction. It was the first class we didn't have together, not to mention how much I hated math. I was doomed.

"The name is Brian." A younger version of George

Clooney was suddenly walking beside me. His left hand awkwardly stretched out for a sideways shake. "Brian likes to go for long walks on the beach, watch movies, talk till the sun comes up, oh, and has Brian mentioned he's loaded, so he can make Elena's heart's desire come true?"

I giggled even though it was a cheesy line. "Does Brian always talk about himself in third person?"

He smiled, which would make any other girl's knees wobble, but Becky had already warned me about him. "Brian does. So what does Elena say about spending some quality time with him?" He placed his hand on the small of my back.

"Elena doesn't say anything. She knows why Brian is being so nice to her when he's away from his idiotic friends. So, sorry, but Elena isn't interested," I said, flipping my ponytail as I turned to walk away.

He squinted and dropped his smile. "Did Becky get to you?"

"No, I was raised by a dragon. I can see straight through pretty faces."

His beautiful smile appeared instantly. "So, Elena thinks Brian is pretty."

"Be careful of that ego, Brian." I turned the next corner and we parted ways.

"Brian doesn't give up so easily, Elena. He'll speak to you soon." His voice echoed through the hallway.

As I continued walking to class, I found girls staring at

me again. What was it with them? I couldn't look at Blake, talk to Lucian, or speak to Brian? I shook my head and opened the huge door with the number 125 written on the frame in golden letters. Professor Dickson was human, that was the good part. Unfortunately, my joy stopped at that. This class was nothing like the math back home. It was ten times harder. After suffering my way through the two-hour lesson I was rewarded with Latin. As I walked into the large room, I was relieved when I saw Becky sitting next to an open seat. Latin was the official language of Paegeia and was still spoken up north close to the border of Etan. I also learned that it was the language of the dragons and magic, so it was mandatory.

I started to get nervous as ten o'clock approached. I couldn't focus as I watched the hands of the clock move slowly. Each tick was painful, as my imagination kept coming up with more and more terrifying scenarios about my first session with the Viden. What if she changed today? Or worse, what if she said something I really didn't want to hear? Hearing bad news seemed to be the trend lately, so I wasn't counting on anything overly encouraging.

My mind had drifted far away from the classroom, and I started when Sir Deisenberg called my name. I thought he was a dragon, but that was just my theory. The Sirs were dragons and the professors were humans, although I didn't feel like testing my theory at that particular moment. "You may go for your appointment, Elena."

Slowly rising from my chair, I dragged my books off the

table and placed them in the new green backpack I had gotten during our shopping trip in Elm.

"Good luck," Becky whispered and I gave her a nervous smile.

The Viden's tower was easy to find. It was one that reminded me of Rapunzel's. As I entered, a stench hit me straight in the face the moment I opened the door. It smelled like a cat or some small rodent had died in there, was covered in burnt hair, and then left in the sun. So all in all, it was disgusting, and my eyes watered as I began my ascent. I stumbled a few times as I climbed the million steps rising in a spiral in front of me. When I reached the top I took a deep breath, gathered my courage, and balled my hand into a fist to knock on the door.

"Come in, Elena," she said, before I had a chance to knock. *Could she read my mind?*

How did she know I was here?

I opened the door slowly. A lovely flowery smell filled my senses. It felt as if I was inhaling a bouquet of lilies, daisies, and roses. The smell was overpowering after the stench of the staircase and I had to reach out a hand and grasp the doorpost to steady myself. Inside, I saw a gorgeous woman, young, perhaps in her late twenties, with long dark hair and golden skin, standing before me at the only window. Her eyes were bright blue, like George's, and she appeared to be glowing in the light emanating from the window. I felt as if I could look into her eyes forever.

A long robe covered her petite figure. It was hard to

imagine that she was three hundred years old. "Good morning, Elena." She threw me a smile that disappeared as fast as it had arrived. Lucian hadn't been joking about that good mood.

Wiping my sweaty palms on my jeans, I could feel my heart pounding under her gaze. The Viden gave me a look, which made my skin crawl. I rubbed my arms vigorously, trying to drive away the goosebumps that had formed.

I slumped onto a puffy pillow to which she'd gestured with a short wave of her hand then stared at a crystal ball that was in the middle of the mahogany table before me.

Seriously, a crystal ball? Just looking at it made me want to giggle, but then I remembered her foul mood and bit hard on the inside of my mouth, hoping that it would stop me from laughing out loud.

Moving from the window, she went over to a small kitchen tucked into a corner of the room. I listened as water poured from the faucet and china clinked. When she turned around, she was carrying a small silver tray with two tea cups and a large teapot, which she placed next to the crystal ball. Steam emerged from the teapot's spout, forming twisted, misty patterns above the crystal ball.

"I need some chamomile. Hope you won't mind sharing a cup. It's the only thing that calms my nerves." She spoke softly, and began to pour the first cup.

"No thank you," I said.

"Drink something!" In a flash, her entire demeanor changed, anger marring her flawless beauty.

"Okay, that would be nice," I said. I didn't want her anger to emerge again. As the seconds ticked by, it seemed as if it took an eternity to fill the small cups with the steaming liquid.

She got up from the table and returned with a round plate filled with bite-sized chocolate chip cookies. Even with all her scurrying around, the ambience of the room didn't change.

"Would you like a cookie?" She held out the plate toward me. I took one, scared she might be offended, as she had been when I declined the tea.

"So, Elena, how do you find things here in Paegeia?" she asked as she settled back into her chair.

"It's nothing like I'd expected," I spoke honestly. I did not want to upset her again.

"Mmm, I believe that your father was a dragon?" She had changed the subject to the one thing I didn't want to talk about.

"Yes."

"Did you know your mother?"

I shook my head.

"So you were raised only by him?" I couldn't tell if she was asking a question or insulting me.

Unsure, I simply nodded.

"I see," she said in a pretentious tone. "Why did she leave you? Didn't she love you?"

"I don't know why she left. I was very small, and my dad never spoke about her."

"I see. I suppose you must feel guilty for the death of your father then."

My heart stopped. She had struck a nerve and she knew it. His death was the one thing I'd feared the most.

She huffed when I didn't answer her. "I have no time for weakness or self-pity. In my honest opinion, I think Master Longwei is wasting his time with you. In fact, he's wasting both of our time." She gave me a fake smile that made me want to bash her in the head with the stupid crystal ball. "You see, your father was a dragon. Dragon offspring cannot become Dragonians. You might not appreciate my opinion, but believe me when I tell you this—you will never ascend." Her cruel words stung in more ways than one. She made me feel as if I didn't belong, and angry tears formed in my eyes. "You have something on your mind?"

I was scared, but one thing Herbert Watkins had taught me was to stand up for myself when no one would. "I don't agree with some of the things you are saying."

"Is it not true? Not knowing your mother leaves a big gap right here." She tapped the area where her heart should've been. "It is going to keep you away from the things you truly want, because you will always be searching for her."

I sighed. I hated to admit it, but there was some truth in what she said. Not knowing my mother was one of my greatest challenges. Every time I wanted to achieve something great, I couldn't help but think about my mother. It caused an inner struggle that prevented me from truly reaching my goals in life. I always wondered what she would think or what she would have wanted. "It doesn't matter. My dad raised me well," I said.

"Fine, whatever. You can leave; I don't feel anything coming from you anyway. Another thing that shows me you are not important."

Rage built up inside of me and I wanted to scream, but I wouldn't give this foul woman the satisfaction of seeing my frustrations.

"Oh, and another thing, you don't need to come back again. I only spend my time on students that are of value."

Her words hit a bit too close to home. I had always felt a bit unimportant. I opened my mouth to say something, but then thought the better of it. As I had told Lucian, I didn't handle confrontations all that well, and I was in no position to confront this woman. So instead, I yanked the door open to make my exit.

"A day will come and a day will go," she said startling me, her voice sounded like ten people speaking in unison. "A choice you will have to make, otherwise the truth will never be known."

Her eyes were a crystal white color, almost silver. She was still in her human form and her hair blew wildly around her face, as if she was in the path of a strong wind. Just as suddenly she stopped and shook her head fast, and cleared her throat as if something was stuck, like the cookie.

My heart beat wildly.

When she looked up at me, her eyes were bright blue again. "I thought I told you to leave," she snapped.

Turning, I ran as fast as I could, what the hell just happened?

11

THE VIDEN'S WORDS were imprinted on my mind, and the worst part was that I didn't under-stand any of it. *What choice must I make? What truth will be revealed?* I sighed, wondering if she even meant any of it for me. Our conversation, however, made me furious.

I went straight to my room. The more I thought about our meeting, the more I wanted to strangle her! Who did she think she was, saying something like that? I was glad that I didn't have to see her again. She must have her hands full with all her "important" students. Good riddance.

Around one o'clock, Becky and Sammy found me, still in our room.

"Oh, here you are." Sammy's smile vanished when she saw my expression. "Oh crap, what did she say?"

I wanted to punch the wall out of anger. "Just leave it. It doesn't matter."

Both girls sat on my bed, clearly interested.

"She's such a snob." I sniffed, sick of all the silence.

"I told you she was vain." Sammy's upper lip twitched in disgust.

"Look, nobody likes her very much, except those that she knows are destined to do great things," Becky said.

"She treats their sessions like they're the highlights of her day."

"What did she say?" Sammy handed me a hanky.

"She said that I don't matter, because my dad was a dragon, and dragon children are not destined to wear the mark. I still don't know what that means." I sighed and wiped off a tear that had escaped onto my cheek.

"The truth?" Becky said.

I nodded, ready to hear what she had to say.

"You're the first human that bears the mark whose father was a dragon. It has never happened before, and some of the professors here at Dragonia feel that Master Longwei is wasting his time."

"Becky!" Sammy yelled, clearly stunned at her confession.

"I didn't say I felt that way! I'm just telling her how it is."

"I still don't understand."

"Dragonians have human parents, Elena."

"Let me try." Sammy touched Becky's hand softly. "Having a dragon for a father means that you have his DNA. Although you don't have a dragon form, you still carry the gene. A part of you is a dragon, and that's the reason you can't become a Dragonian."

As I let their words sink in, it was all slowly starting to make sense.

"There are a lot of dragon offspring, Elena. When a

dragon falls in love with a human, their children are human and never bear the mark."

"There are others here who aren't born with the mark, and nobody tells them they don't belong," I said stubbornly.

"Their daddies paid a crap-load of money for them to be here. Only the students with the mark are able to attend Dragonia Academy free of charge," Becky said.

"That's why they don't think I belong here, because my father didn't pay?"

"No, Elena, it's because your father was a dragon. They feel that Master Longwei is taking a chance he shouldn't. I even overheard that some of the parents with non-gifted children, who have been on the waitlist, got really pissed when he let you in. They had this huge discussion arguing the fact you'll never ascend and that your mark is just a birth defect," Becky said.

"It's what she said too."

"Did her eyes glow when she said it?" Sammy asked.

I shook my head, lied and pretended I had no idea what she was talking about. "Her eyes glow?" I wasn't ready to share that part with them just yet. I was still trying to figure out what she'd meant.

"Yes. If not, you don't pay any attention. She talks a lot of shit."

Becky raised her eyes at Sammy's remark and I giggled, remembering our conversation about how much Sammy liked the Viden.

"Do you guys think I'm wasting my time being here?"

"Hell no!" both shouted in unison.

"Sammy's right." Becky put her hand on my shoulder. "Only pay attention to what she says when her eyes light up and when her hair blows."

I sighed. I was lucky to have roommates who understood. Both were incredibly jealous when I told them that she didn't want to see me again.

"I would give my left boob for her to say those words to me," Sammy said, "but I guess with me being the Rubicon's sister, she expects great things from me too."

We shook off the stress of the whole encounter, and went to lunch. This time we found a table inside the cafeteria. It wasn't long before Lucian plunged himself down on the remaining pillow. "So how was your first time with the Viden?"

"Shhh, we don't mention her," Sammy whispered.

His smile disappeared. "That bad?"

"It's fine, I just didn't like the way she treated me."

"Elena, if her hair didn't blow and her eyes didn't shine, then you don't pay attention to the witch," he said.

I gave him a soft smile.

When the bell rang for class, I felt better.

BEFORE I KNEW IT, my first full week was over. I went through a schedule change around Tuesday, and some of my classes got swapped around. To make matters worse, not all the classes were like Professor Gregory's and Sir Edward's. They were extremely difficult, and each one may as well have been taught in Latin, because I had no idea what they were talking about half the time.

Enchantment was a nightmare. We had a professor named Longchester who lectured for the entire duration of the class. My head ached by the time his lectures finished, and he made us recite foreign words over and over again. My stuttering made the spells backfire more times than they worked. So instead of protecting myself with a stupid shield nobody could see, I got hit with tiny stings that made me look like a crazy person hitting myself. It stopped the minute Professor Longchester snapped his fingers, but not before the entire class stopped to watch the show. The students always sniggered, and Becky would chuck a pencil or eraser at whoever laughed the hardest.

She was fairly accurate at hitting her targets, which I appreciated.

I hoped things would get better by the end of the week, but they didn't.

When the last bell of the day rang on Thursday, I wanted to jump for joy; the next day was Friday.

I soon learned that Fridays were going to be the worst day of my week, because I'd ended up with a double period of Arithmetic instead of Anatomy. When the bell rang, I dashed out of the classroom and bumped straight into Brian.

"Hello, Elena, excited to see Brian?" His jolly personality made it difficult to be rude to him. I knew he was only after my virtue, and I began to understand why Sammy said they were obsessed with hunting virgins.

"No, I—"

"Oh, c'mon, Elena, Brian isn't that bad once you get to know him." Brian laughed when I blushed. "Just hang out with Brian, and if you don't like what Brian has to offer, Brian promises he'll back off."

"Is it really making you that crazy?" I said, referring to my virtue.

He chuckled. "Brian has no idea what Elena is talking about."

I laughed. "Nice try, Brian, but you forget that I was raised by a dragon. He warned me about the Sun-Blasts," I lied.

"Elena's father would have loved Brian," he said.

"Oh, you think so?" I said, rolling my eyes at his candor.

"C'mon, Elena, Brian just wants one date."

"Elena will think about it," I said and we went our separate ways. Out of the corner of my eye, I saw him fist pump into the air.

"Elena saw that, Brian!" I yelled.

"Brian doesn't care what Elena sees. All Brian wants is that date."

If that wasn't making it clear what his intentions were, I'd have to be blind and deaf.

I felt better once I reached the room and saw Becky and Sammy already inside.

"So, Elena, are you coming with us tonight?" Becky asked, as I threw my backpack on my bed.

"Where to?"

"The lake."

"Is it safe?"

"Of course! And it's fun," Sammy chirped.

I thought about it for a few seconds. "You know what? I'm in." I was going to regret it later, but I needed a break.

They clapped their hands, sounding very excited.

"So, what's at the lake?"

"A lake," they said in unison, and laughed.

"You mean we're going to swim?"

"Unless you know of something else we could do at a lake during the night," Becky said in a sarcastic tone.

"I don't have a swim suit."

"You can borrow one of mine. No biggie." Becky skipped over to her dresser, took out the top drawer, and tipped it over onto her bed. Bikinis of different colors were scattered all over.

I picked up a plain black one and tried it on. It fit perfectly. I just didn't like my flat ass. I wanted it to be plumper.

After dinner, we slipped out of the castle and grabbed our bags that were stashed by the bushes close to the entrance and made a run to Sammy and Becky's sanctuary. It took about fifteen minutes just to get there, but I was glad I hadn't chickened out. I was even happier once we arrived, and I took in the picturesque surrounding.

The tall trees and huge boulders lining the lake and cloaked in shadows made the place look a bit creepy, but with the stars and the full moon shining on the water, it took on a life of its own. The smooth surface of the lake was completely still, and the moon reflecting off the water gave it the appearance of an enormous mirror. It was as if the lake was filled with liquid mercury. As soon as we arrived at the edge, Becky and Sammy yanked off their tops and ran straight into the lake, still wearing their shorts.

"Come on, Elena, the water is perfect!" Becky yelled back.

I looked up and noticed that the weather was starting to play up. *To hell with it.* I took off my clothes and joined the girls. The small pebbles hurt my feet as I tiptoed into the lake, but I stopped noticing as soon as I hit the water.

The water felt warm, not quite bathwater, but pretty close. We enjoyed splashing and dunking each other's heads so much that none of us paid attention to what was happening on shore. All of a sudden, the bushes near where we left our bags started to quiver. We turned into pillars, frozen in the eerie darkness. Flashes of whatever might be lurking in the bushes drove me nuts, as I tried to figure out what was stalking us.

A tall figure with blond hair emerged from the bushes with a dark-haired boy following him.

"Lucian!" Becky splashed water in his direction. "You gave me a freaking heart attack!"

My heart started to beat faster.

"Why are you scared?" he said, chuckling. "You've got Sammy here."

Hot flushes went through my entire body, and my stomach rolled around as if it was now home to a million trapped butterflies.

Slowly he walked to the edge of the lake and took off his shirt. I was going to faint. His silhouette was all lean muscles and ripped abs shining in the moonlight. The effect made him look like a Da Vinci statue.

I dipped my head under the water to cool off, hoping he hadn't noticed my stare.

When I came back up for air, his back was turned toward us. Finally able to tear my gaze away, I noticed that the dark-haired boy wasn't bad looking either.

"Hi, Dean. Long time no see," Sammy said in a flirty way.

"Hi, Sammy," the dark-haired boy with beautiful legs said in a singsong tone. She giggled in response.

Lucian jumped, cannonball-style, into the deeper part of the lake, with Dean right behind him.

Dean came up first, and I looked anxiously for Lucian. *There was no way he could stay under water that long.* A small scream left my mouth when he emerged right in front of me, sending water flying everywhere.

Lucian laughed as he stood before me, dripping water. "Hello, Elena," he said in a seductive voice.

I couldn't help but smile, thinking about what Becky

and Sammy had said. I would give anything for the girls' speculations to be true.

"Hi, Lucian. What are you doing here? I thought you were one of the spoiled brats that went home over weekends." The words had slipped out without me even thinking. I didn't know where I had gotten the guts to say that.

He bit his lower lip, which made me lose my breath.

"I'm not a spoiled brat," he said in a serious tone, and splashed me. The corner of his mouth twitched.

Dean emerged from the watery depths, like Rambo, Dean took him under the water with him. We all laughed at the two playing with each other and eventually the game dissolved into a big dunking contest.

I tried to swim away and yelled when Lucian caught hold of my foot, yanking me under. When we came up, his arms were around my waist and his face was only inches from mine.

My heart was pounding again and I wondered if he could feel it too.

He stared at me with those smoldering eyes, searching for something hidden in my gaze, and then gave me one of his million-dollar smiles.

I smiled back like an idiot. He leaned in closer. My body shivered from head to toe as our lips touched.

It felt like a dream, and I decided if it was, I needed to make that kiss last for as long as I possibly could before I woke. I opened my mouth and started to kiss him back passionately. My hands got tangled up in his wet hair as I leaned in for more. It was the most amazing and perfect first kiss a girl could ask for.

His mouth felt as if it was made to fit mine. There wasn't a nose or chin in the way, and our tongues danced in perfect rhythm. It made me want more.

He pulled away softly. With my chin cupped in his hand, he made a satisfying grunt as if he had just finished his favorite meal.

Heat jolted up to my face and I was glad that he couldn't see me blushing in the dark.

"I've wanted to do that since the first day I saw you," he whispered, and wrapped his arms tighter around me.

My legs curled around his waist. I just wanted to kiss him again, I couldn't get enough.

"I hope you don't mind."

"Oh, you would have known if I did," I said as our lips found each other again.

Lightning flashed in the distance, making us both break away and look up at the threatening sky.

"I think we should call it a night," he said.

I complained silently, as I wanted to spend more time with him. Reluctantly, I untangled myself and looked around for my friends.

Becky and the others were already busy getting out of the lake as we swam over to them. I felt insecure that I wasn't wearing shorts too, just my bikini bottom.

I made a run for my towel as lightning sliced through a

tree nearby. Red sparks shot in all directions from the impact and jumped off the branches frantically.

I shrieked, terrified, and found myself in Lucian's arms once again.

Lucian laughed, but stopped and immediately let go as something caught his attention. He darted toward the clearing behind me.

I turned around and found Becky lying flat on the ground. My hands covered my mouth in horror as electricity danced along her body. She shook violently as if she was having a seizure.

Lucian crouched beside her and started to search for something. He shouted orders to us, but they sounded hollow.

I just stared with huge, unblinking eyes at Becky lying helplessly on the ground.

Sammy reached her and fell to her knees. Her arm stretched out toward Becky.

"Don't touch her, Sammy!" Lucian smacked her hand away.

"But, Lucian!"

"Touch her and your ass gets fried too," Lucian said. "Elena, go get Constance and Master Longwei."

My feet were nailed to the ground as I tried to process the situation playing out before me.

"Elena! Now!" he roared, this time waking me from my stupor.

The fear that had consumed me disappeared and I ran as fast as I could back to the main building.

At about the halfway mark, the trees started to blur around me. I realized my tears were making it difficult to see the path and wiped them away determinedly with the back of my hand.

I found the main building and yanked the door open. Pain crawled up my legs and my lungs burned as I kept running. I was heaving like a vacuum cleaner by the time I reached Master Longwei's dorm.

"Master Longwei, come!" I shouted.

"Elena, why are you wet?" He clutched a pot of tea in his hands.

Tears streamed down my face as I tried to control my breath. "Please, there's no time to explain, just come with me."

As I looked at him, my eyes begged him not to ask questions. Realizing my urgency, he called Constance over the phone and told her to meet us down at the main entrance. With me leading the way, we ran down the stairs back to the lake and met Constance near the entrance carrying a doctor's bag.

"Elena, the lake is off limits at night!" Master Longwei roared once he realized where we were heading.

"I'm sorry, sir. Becky said..." I couldn't finish my sentence as my throat began to close with emotion.

Tears rolled down my face in torrents, and I was so scared it might already be too late.

"Becky knows the rules. She should've known better. What happened?" he asked.

I couldn't speak.

"Elena, we need to know what happened," Constance tried.

I could tell she was just as concerned. "Lightning!" I managed to squeak out.

The instant the word escaped my lips, Master Longwei and Constance found a faster speed that left me far behind.

When I finally made it back to the lake, I heard Master Longwei scolding someone.

"Becky, how could you be so irresponsible!" he said. The sound of her name lifted my spirits instantly.

I saw Becky. Where I had left her on the ground, with thousands of volts of electricity running through her, she was now standing, facing off against Master Longwei.

"March!" Master Longwei shouted, looking pissed off.

I struggled to take my eyes away from her. She looked fine, except for her hair. It was standing straight up in every direction. The smell of burnt hair lingered in the air and electricity ran from the tip of her strands to the roots, releasing a spark every once in a while. She looked petrified, with big round eyes that were forever changed by the horror of tonight.

"What happened, Lucian?" I asked when I finally found my voice.

"I don't know. One minute she was down and the next she was back on her feet shaking it off as if it was nothing," Lucian said, rambling fast. His voice broke on the last part.

"Are you okay?" I could see how shaken he was by the whole event.

He was pale and looked as if he was about to faint. "Yeah, I'm just trying to figure out what the f—"

We were all ordered to return to the castle and were escorted straight to Master Longwei's office.

"Master, I have to examine Becky," Constance said, as she led her away. Becky started to protest, but Constance hissed something in her ear that silenced her.

Lucian, Dean, Sammy, and I entered Master Longwei's office, and the look he gave the four of us was worse than the scolding.

"What happened?" he asked.

"Master Longwei, she got hit by lightning and went down. I don't know how she can still be alive. There was so much voltage running through her. I know for a fact that she should not be here." Lucian spoke fast; it must be something he did whenever he was nervous.

"Lucian, how could you go to the lake at this time of night? You of all people know better. Anything could have happened—"

"It wasn't entirely his fault, we were all there too," I said.

Master Longwei's eyebrow arched and then he turned his glare at me. That one look made me wish I'd never found Paegeia. "I don't know how things work on the other side of the Wall, young lady, but here we have rules. You risked your own life and the lives of your friends when you disobeyed them. We also do not speak out of turn when an elder is talking."

I bit the inside of my lip, keeping me from saying another word. My father had always told me to share the blame if I was a culprit too. I wasn't being disrespectful and started to become angry that he had insinuated that.

"I will have to think about what punishment to give you four. You can be glad Becky is still alive. You may go. If I ever catch you going for a midnight swim again, I promise that none of you will see the light of day until you graduate!" he roared, allowing us to make our escape.

My knees wobbled as I climbed down the stairs, and I had to catch my balance on the handrail several times.

"It's going to be fine, Elena," Lucian said soothingly, rubbing my arms to try to restore the blood that had drained from my body.

I just nodded, trying hard not to cry.

"My father is so going to kill me," Dean said, walking next to Sammy.

"Let's just hope that was a warning." Lucian took a deep breath, clearly still shaken.

Sammy didn't say anything about her father. He would probably laugh at it after having to deal with Blake's shit all of the time. Her punishment would probably be a breeze. She did seem anxious, though, as we got closer and closer to our room.

Dad would have been angry too. I silently wished he was still here to yell at me.

"Hey, are you okay?" Lucian asked, as we were about to climb the stairs to the girls' dorms.

I shook my head, not knowing if I was okay, and he pulled me closer.

His arms felt good, but somehow it didn't lessen my anger. "Everything's going to be okay, I promise. See you tomorrow."

I kissed him quickly on his lips and ran up the stairs.

"Goodnight, guys," Sammy said, and I heard their faint grunts in acknowledgment.

We reached our room and fell onto our beds. I felt as if I could have ripped my pillow into a gazillion pieces. My feelings were so messed up. A part of me felt so angry and the other part worried sick about Becky. I didn't know how to cope with it. *How could lightning strike someone and the person still be alive?*

"It's okay, Elena," Sammy said, coming over to my bed. "Becky's fine."

I laid my head on Sammy's lap and sobbed. "Becky could have died tonight, and then what?"

Sammy stroked my back softly. "It's going to be fine, you'll see."

We both started as Becky opened the door. Her hair was still fanned out in every direction but I just wanted to hug her.

"Stay away!" she ordered both of us. Her eyes were

huge and she held her hands in the air as if she was a mime trapped in a glass box.

"How is this possible?" I yelled, not quite sure what or whom I was furious with.

"Are you okay?" Sammy frowned at me and looked back at Becky with soft eyes.

"I'm fine, I have ascended!" she said.

"You have what?" I was still yelling. *What is wrong with me?*

"I have ascended." She couldn't hold her tears back anymore.

Sammy stepped closer and reached out to touch her.

She put her hands up in the air again, backing away and sobbing. "Don't touch me!"

We just stood there in silence and waited for Becky to calm down. Sammy kept cooing that it was going to be okay and it began to calm her.

Becky took a deep breath. "Constance said that I still have so much electricity running through me that I can power up the entire Academy for a whole week. She actually thought about doing that." New tears streamed down her face and left small sparks in their wake. She didn't even flinch.

I guess she was really immune to it. The image of Constance wiring Becky to draw the electricity from her formed in my mind. It made it hard not to laugh.

"They're phoning my mom as we speak," she explained.

"It's going to be okay, Becky," Sammy said again for the millionth time.

"No, it's not!" she yelled. "Don't you guys get it? I can manipulate lightning. That's my power, stupid freaking lightning."

Sammy and I looked at her as if she had fried some of her brain cells too.

"I would give my left toe for an ability like yours," I said truthfully, irritated that she was so unhappy when all I wanted was to fit in.

She threw me a glare that made me feel like I was back in Master Longwei's office. "You still don't get it, Elena. I have the power of lightning. It means my dragon is a Moon-Bolt. The only one available in this school is George.

12

EVEN THOUGH GEORGE was an idiot, the guy was in the same league as Lucian when it came to his good looks. Hot as hell with dimples like Sammy's.

"George?" Sammy asked.

Becky fell on her bed and cried.

"Okay, that sucks," I said. They were the first words that popped into my head. It was the truth, because I knew she didn't like George one bit.

She looked rather upset at the realization that he was the only Moon-Bolt available. Tears streamed down her face, and Becky wasn't a soft crier. She looked comical, and I couldn't hold my laughter back anymore.

"Elena," Sammy sang.

"I'm sorry." I snorted as the tears ran down my cheeks too. Sammy and Becky joined me after a while, and it felt good to laugh, especially in lieu of what had happened tonight.

Our laughter stopped abruptly. A minute or so of silence followed.

"Can we please just talk about something else?" Becky asked quietly.

"How was the kiss, Elena?" Sammy interjected. It worked.

Becky got all excited as I explained to them how perfect his lips felt against mine. It was nice to relive it and all of us felt better when I finished my detailed review.

"I told you he was crazy about you," Becky chirped.

"Excuse me, I told her he liked her," Sammy snapped, and we fell back into laughter.

As I let the events of the night wash over me, I tried to process everything that had happened. I went to bed wondering how Sammy felt now knowing her best friend wasn't a fire wielder

WE WOKE MONDAY morning and found Becky combing out her hair furiously. Sparks flew onto her brush as she tried to get her hair to lie flat. She didn't really succeed.

I started to laugh as her hair just kept jumping up again. Frustrated, she threw her brush at me, but missed. At least she was a good sport.

When we entered the cafeteria, everyone stopped eating, turned, and stared at Becky.

"Hell, news travels fast," Sammy said as loud as she could, and some faces ducked behind their friends and others quickly turned away.

We soon discovered that there were other Moon-Bolts at the school, because each one of them threatened her to stay away. She was instantly relieved and glad she had more options.

I was happy to see Lucian smiling at me from his table. He looked better than he had Friday night. He had left on Saturday morning for the weekend and phoned me twice on Becky's Cammy. When we reached him, he stood up, cupped my face in his hands, and kissed me. It was scary how nothing else mattered, and that all my worries and concerns just seemed to disappear whenever his lips touched mine. A lot of guys mocked Lucian for being so openly affectionate. I only wished I could brush it off as easily as he did. Becky came back from the buffet line and seeing some of her hair standing up forced me to suppress my laughter once again.

"You gave us a heart attack the other night," Lucian said, as Becky sat next to us.

I burst out laughing again.

"Elena, stop it." Sammy bumped me hard in my ribs while trying desperately to suppress her laughter too. Becky rolled her eyes and looked irritated.

Lucian just stared at me. "Am I missing something here?"

I snorted again and shook my head, indicating that I would explain everything to him later.

"Oh c'mon, Lucian. Don't tell me my hair standing in every direction is not one bit funny."

He smiled, knowing she was right.

"I've had to listen to their jokes since Friday night."

"That's so mean." He was trying to make us feel bad.

I took a deep breath. "Sorry, Becky, I'll try harder to control it."

"Whatever, Elena. If it was you I would have broken myself in two."

"Umm, you did already," I reminded her of my first Art of War lesson, and she giggled.

"Becky," A third-year boy had just walked up to our table sounding serious. He saw her hair and his lips drew in a thin line.

"It's fine, you can laugh," she said.

He smiled. "Master Longwei wants to see you in his office, pronto."

"Why?"

Our jokes became less funny.

"I don't know. He just asked me to fetch you," he said and walked away.

"You want us to come with you?" Sammy asked.

"No, you guys already took a beating on Friday. I guess it's my turn," she said and got up.

"I hope that it's nothing bad," I said.

"I guess we just have to wait and see," Lucian said, stroking my back softly. When the bell rang, we left the cafeteria hand in hand.

He said goodbye with another soft kiss as we reached my class then ran off to his down the hall. I let out a satisfied sigh, feeling like some sort of fairytale character who had just found her prince. I had, literally.

During Enchantments I became worried when Becky still hadn't returned from her meeting with Master Longwei. It was right before lunchtime, and I struggled hard to concentrate, not that I understood one word of it anyway. As I made my way to the cafeteria, I found Lucian and Sammy speaking to her at a table outside.

"What happened, what did he say?" I was upset as I plunged down next to Lucian. She tried to tell me, but she stuttered too much and then began bawling again as if somebody had died.

"The Viden told Master Longwei about a foretelling. It's about George. She told him that his Dragonian would be struck by lightning," Lucian said solemnly.

"She thinks it's you?" I asked, stunned.

They both nodded on Becky's behalf, while she blew her nose into a hanky.

"They're going to force me to claim George, Elena," she bawled again.

"You are part of a foretelling?" I finally understood what she was saying, and her lower lip quivered.

"One that means absolutely nothing. I don't know why I can't refuse," she yelled.

"Because of what it is," Lucian said.

"Wait, you guys know what this means?" I asked, and they just looked at me as if they didn't see the big picture at all. "George is your dent, Becky. It's rare, isn't it?"

"Oh my word, Elena is right. It hasn't happened for a long time." Sammy sounded excited.

"Me and George?" Becky yelped and fell onto her arms. A short buzzing sound emanating from her made us all stare.

Wicked, Lucian mouthed, and I glared at him. Okay, so maybe she had seen that one coming and it was the reason why she was so upset.

"Calm down, girl," Sammy said, almost stroking her back, but yanking her hand away just in time. "You should embrace this, Becky. Besides, he isn't that bad looking."

Becky yelled. "That's the absolute worst thing you've ever said to me. I'm not shallow!"

"I didn't mean it like that," Sammy said. "Maybe George will change."

"He's a freaking Moon-Bolt. He almost gave Elena a heart attack on her first day!" She looked at the sky. "Kill me now, please."

"Calm down, Becky. I know it's hard to see the silver lining on this one, but maybe Sammy's right. He could change," Lucian said.

"Not you too!"

"What are you so worried about anyway? The fact that it's George, or the fact that he is a Moon-Bolt?" he asked.

"The fact that he's a dickhead. And to make matters worse, he's going to want to hang with us from now on."

"It's going to be fine, Becky, if George wants to hang with us. He just better treat Elena better," Sammy said, and we all burst out laughing again.

"It's going to be okay," I said, trying to boost her ego.

"It's not the end of the world, and you rock. That dragon can count his lucky stars to have you as his Dragonian."

"Aw. I wish I could hug you both. You are the best BFs a girl could ask for." Becky snorted then wiped her eyes.

"Do you really electrify people if they come too close?" Lucian asked, pretending to poke her.

Becky giggled.

"That's so wicked," he said.

I stood, seeing it as the perfect moment to grab some lunch.

When I got back, Lucian was talking about tricks to claim George and offered to train her if she wanted.

The bell rang again, ending all our fun. I sulked all the way to Arithmetic.

"So Elena is now with Lucian, what about Brian?" a soft voice said next to me.

"Elena said she will think about Brian's offer. She did, but Lucian stole her heart, and his intentions are not like Brian's."

"Elena is making a huge mistake," he said. "Brian could have offered her so much more."

"Yeah, yeah, okay, Brian, we get it. Take a hike." Lucian spoke from behind us, and he squeezed in between Brian and me.

"Your Highness's wishes are Brian's command," he teased, and walked away.

Lucian grinding his teeth hard made a horrible sound that I couldn't stand.

"Stop doing that. Besides you are the prince of Tith and—"

"Stop that," he said, poking me playfully in the ribs. This escalated into a lot of laughter, and somehow I ended up in his arms. He kissed me softly just before our paths separated.

"Your wish is everybody's command. You need to deal with it," I joked, while he walked away.

"Yours too?" he said hopefully.

"You'll have to wait and see, Your Highness."

He roared with laughter, while the other students in the hallway were shaking their heads and twittering.

I had learned how to ignore them. The left side of my lip curled up as I saw room 125. It became an involuntary reaction right before I opened the big door to Arithmetic.

By the end of day, George had finally received the bad news and was really pissed.

He cornered Becky in the hallway and threatened, "You just stay away from me."

Becky pushed him away, hard. We could hear some electricity pass between them but George didn't flinch one bit.

"You think I wanted this. I would rather spend my life with a colony of wyverns before claiming you."

He huffed with a sideways smile, accepting her challenge. "At least you know where you stand."

"As if. Let me rephrase. I would rather die than have

you around me!" she yelled, standing inches away from his face.

George grunted, bared his teeth, and raced off cussing.

"He's such an asshole. Why did I have to be struck by lightning? I would even claim a Night Villain over George Mills!" she shouted at his retreating figure.

"It's going to be okay, Becky. In a couple of days he won't be such an arrogant bastard," Sammy said softly, but it didn't seem right without the hug.

I had to admit, a part of me did pray that I'd never ascend. I wouldn't be able to handle all of this fighting.

Racing off with Becky to her favorite class, I hoped she would cheer up. Art of War was still not my thing and I felt as if I was going backward instead of forward. I struggled to concentrate as I worried about Becky and I couldn't focus on Professor Mia's instructions. So, in short, I got my ass kicked.

FOR THE REST of the week, the glares between Becky and George grew worse. The girls who liked George kept bumping into Becky as a warning. Some even threatened her about what they'd do if she claimed George. As if she had a choice.

Classes were the same and weren't getting any better. The only thing I did look forward to was spending more time with Lucian yet I felt our time together growing less as he started to train Becky for the day she was going to have to face George. By the third day of training, I was already annoyed. They only talked about fighting, and I found it foreign as they talked about highs, lows, and aims.

During Enchantments, an announcement came over the school's speaker system. Master Longwei's voice filled the entire school. "Next Thursday at four in the afternoon, there will be a claim. Rebecca Johnston for the claiming of George Mills."

There was a lot of applause from our class, as well as a lot of good luck punches on her shoulder. She couldn't stop smiling.

As everyone began to fall into the rigor of the Academy, I found myself alone most afternoons. Sammy had started with her extra activity—who knew a dragon could be into drama classes. Lucian wanted me to come and watch how Becky and he trained, but I couldn't stand the sound of weapons slamming against each other, so I ended up spending my afternoons in the library.

I saw it as time to learn about Paegeia. Most days it was an exercise in failure, because I couldn't concentrate and was instead worrying about Becky.

I crawled into bed late, scared that I was going to dream again about the woman on the hill. She had been harassing my dreams for the past week, and I still didn't know who she was, what she wanted, or why I was dreaming of her. At least I didn't wake screaming anymore. I just wished she would tell me what the hell she wanted.

I couldn't wait for Thursday, the day Becky was going to claim George. *After that, things should go back to normal*, I hoped as I settled into bed. I turned off the light and fell asleep faster than I thought I would. As usual, I felt my dream shift as the mysterious woman made her appearance once again.

13

ON THURSDAY MORNING, the slamming of the bathroom door woke me. Sammy sat on her bed and glared vehemently in the direction of the bathroom.

"Is everything okay?" I croaked.

"Whatever you do, don't look in that one's direction." Sammy pointed to the bathroom door.

"You think it's got to do with the claim?"

"I think it's got more to do with her last session with Lucian this morning. She looked highly pissed off when she stormed in."

Becky came out of the bathroom as we were talking and yanked her dresser drawer open.

"Are you okay?" I asked. I hated to see her like this.

"Yes," she said, as if she was about to take an exam, instead of fighting a dragon. T-shirts flew out of her drawer as she searched for something.

Sammy and I just stared at each other, perplexed.

"Becky, what's wrong? You seem...upset." Sammy sounded as if she'd struggled to find the right word.

"I'm fine." She turned around and sighed. "Lucian has taught me well." Her voice changed, sliding into deep sarcasm. So, Sammy was right about Lucian being the culprit behind Becky's bad mood.

"Spill!" Sammy demanded.

Becky curled her lip. "He's a 'slave driving demon' when it comes to fighting. I mean, the guy is good with a sword in his hands, but he has no sense of when he needs to stop. He's driving me insane!"

"What?" Sammy said.

"Lucian McKenzie, my Lucian?" It felt great saying that.

"You heard me." She plunged onto her bed with a pair of socks in her hand. "You only know his sweet side, Elena. He's head over heels for you."

"Well I hope so. Since he's been training you, I hardly see him," I said, irritation filling my voice.

"I'm sure he'll spend all his time with you after today. You know, he told his parents that he won't be going home over weekends anymore," Becky said, arching her eyebrows.

"Get out of here!" Sammy screamed while my stomach was doing a back flip.

"It's the truth."

"Do you guys think he told them about me?" I asked. My gut turned into a big knot.

"Who cares? He's going to stay." Sammy sounded happy on my behalf.

I had to admit, as much as I loved to spend more time with Lucian over weekends, a part of me panicked when I thought about his parents. I mean, they were ruling a country, for crying out loud. *What if they have certain expectations of me?* I swallowed hard. *Do they know I was the girl with the dragon father? What if they didn't approve?*

Anxious, I looked for Lucian during breakfast, but he was nowhere to be seen. To make matters worse, he was constantly on my mind, so I had no idea what the professors were talking about during their lectures.

At lunch, we had pasta for the zillionth time. Riley had gotten most of the riddles lately.

"Elena, please, I'm begging you, if it's going to be pasta tomorrow again, I'm going to puke," Sammy complained.

I giggled and went over to the Chef's board to see what he had in store for us today.

"All about, but cannot be seen. Can be captured but cannot be held. Can be heard but have no throat, what am I?" I tried to think. Usually the answer just popped into my head, but today was completely different. I felt someone standing behind me. When she started to tap her foot, I assumed she wanted to see the riddle. I turned around and Arianna, princess of Areeth, was all up in my face.

Long strawberry locks curled down her back and around her face. Her lips twitched as a sly smile spread across her face, and she raised an eyebrow. To her right, a girl with a pug face glared at me, and on her left was a ginger who tried to hide her freckles with too much concealer.

"Sorry," I said, and tried to step away.

Arianna stepped in front of me, blocking my exit. "I'm

not done with you, and yes, you'll be sorry if you don't do as I say."

"Excuse me?"

"Stay away from Lucian McKenzie. He always goes through a mild crush on whoever is new."

Freckles and Pug Face sniggered.

"You see, it doesn't even matter if you two do get along. Lucian is royalty, Elena, and he can't waste his time with a commoner. So the way I see it, is that you stop whatever 'this' is before you get hurt." She emphasized "you" a little too harshly.

After all that venom, her lips turned into a perfect smile, and she turned around to leave..

Becky and Sammy were approaching us, and Arianna slammed into Becky violently. It was a miracle Becky remained standing.

"Get out of my way," Arianna spoke down to them.

"This is not Areeth, Arianna!" Sammy yelled after her.

"Are you okay?" Becky said.

I nodded and felt tears clog my throat.

"Elena, whatever she said, ignore it. She is a big biatch."

"Yeah." What she'd said had stumped me.

"What was that all about?" Sammy asked, as we sat down at the table.

"It doesn't matter." I sulked and started to eat my bowl of Alfredo pasta. I'd totally forgotten about the riddle when Chef rang the bell.

Lucian mimicked Becky with her happy dance and the entire cafeteria cheered.

Could he be sexier?

I closed my eyes and pushed away my tears. What do I do now? Arianna was right and had only said what I already knew, but how could I stop what we had?

"Hey, beautiful." Lucian sat down next to me.

"Not now, okay, I have to go," I said quickly. I rose to leave as one tear lurked in the corner of my eye.

The fact that he was royalty wasn't going to change, and having a commoner for a girlfriend was probably against the law or something. How was I supposed to get rid of my feelings for him? Ever since he'd kissed me, I'd felt as if I could fly. Now whatever had made me feel so powerful had died painfully with Arianna's words.

I tried to push Lucian to the back of my mind, but struggled as I made my way back to our room and fell onto the bed.

Sammy and Becky came into the room a little while later.

"What's up, Elena?" Becky stood with her arms folded, and I knew I wasn't getting off the hook that easily.

"It doesn't matter, Becky." I picked up my brush and pulled my hair up in my usual ponytail.

"Lucian is asking if he did something wrong." She just kept talking as if she hadn't heard my reply. "Is it about what I said this morning?"

"No, Becky, just leave it, please."

"Elena, come on, I can see something is bothering you," she said.

"It's not that, okay. Just leave it."

"Oh my word, it's Arianna, isn't it?" Sammy gave an I-don't-believe-this-crap giggle.

"It's Arianna?" Becky asked, confused. "Elena, what did she say?"

"It doesn't matter, she's right. Lucian is royalty, Becky, and I'm not." My voice broke, and my hands somehow found the top of my head. This was so wrong. *Why can't he choose who he wants to be with?*

Becky paced, her lips pressed hard in a thin line.

"Don't listen to her, Elena. She's always had a thing for Lucian and my brother. Believe me, she's been trying her luck with both of them. Don't let her get under your skin." Sammy folded her arm around my shoulder.

"He's royalty. Someone is going to get hurt in the end, and I know it's me."

"If Lucian finds out about this, she's going to see her ass." Becky fiddled with her necklace.

"Don't tell him, please." I hated confrontations.

"Fine, one condition," Becky said, and stopped pacing. "You forget what she said."

"Becky?" I sighed.

She lifted her index finger for me to stop.

"She scares the living crap out of me!" I yelled.

Both girls laughed.

"Elena, she's got a big mouth, that's it. She's just like Tabitha."

"Sammy's right." Becky came over and hugged me too.

The bell rang and we were forced to head back to class.

We still had a full hour of Arts of War left, and I wasn't in the mood to fight with a sword, pretending to be the greatest gladiator who ever lived.

Unfortunately, Professor Mia had the opposite idea and drilled me even harder. I slouched to my room, stumbled into the shower, and fell onto my bed. I'd only briefly shut my eyes when Sammy stormed in.

"Elena, what are you doing?"

"What?" I said, sleepy, and looked at the clock. Somehow, I'd dozed off until four o'clock. Becky was about to claim George. I jumped up, slipped on my flip-flops, and darted for the coliseum.

Goosebumps covered my entire body as we neared. I couldn't believe I'd almost missed it.

When I heard loud cheers and chants, I made a run for it. I gasped as I saw how packed the colosseum was. There were people sitting in the stands other than the students and professors, and I finally understood how big of an event this was. Thankfully nothing had happened yet.

George threw a show for the crowd. He ran up and down the sides where all the dragons sat, touching people's hands as he passed. Loud music boomed through the coliseum, and he ripped off his t-shirt. The girls screamed wildly.

I had to admit, he was very muscular, with an eight pack bulging from his stomach.

I still hated his arrogance. The Chromatic dragons cheered the loudest and instructed him to show Becky what he was made of.

"They're wasting their time," Sammy said in a singing tone. She led me to the side where all of the Dragonians sat.

"Why?"

"That down there is Dr. Jekyll, and Mr. Hyde will come out in a couple of minutes."

I understood that analogy and should've known that she would take me straight to Lucian's seat.

He seemed agitated as he stared over at the small entrance where Becky would emerge.

Arianna's words were still fresh in my mind, making me fidget.

"Aren't you supposed to be on the other side?" a girl with short mousy blond hair snapped at Sammy.

"Oh, bite me," she snapped back and squished through to the only two empty chairs in the row, right next to Lucian. She took the first one and forced me to sit down next to him.

I stared at the crowd, anywhere but him.

"Are you okay?" he asked, looking at me.

I gave him an assuring smile, and he gave me a quick kiss on my temple. His hand folded over my leg. He smelled amazing, but by his clenched jaw and his firm grasp around my leg, I could tell he was uptight.

"Where's Becky?" I stretched my neck to see if I could spot her somewhere.

"She's still inside going over some strategies with Mia."

"So, she helps?" I asked.

"Not really, but she gives one hell of a pep talk."

I giggled. A hint of a smile appeared on his face too. I remembered how big George was that first day when he'd stood in his dragon form in front of me, and then there had been the one that had killed my father. I didn't have faith that a pep talk would do much good.

We Will Rock You by Queen started to play, and it didn't take the crowd more than a few seconds to get up on their feet and clap their hands with the rhythm.

"What's this?" I shouted.

"It is Becky's song. We each have to choose one to be introduced by before a claim," he shouted back.

Just as the music started, George exploded into his huge dragon form which made me stare like an idiot. Again.

He looked so evil it struck fear into everything that owned a soul. I still thought the humans were crazy to even consider doing this.

The crowd went ballistic when the coliseum's walls vanished. Sand dunes appeared in the distance and the air became humid. I gawked and pulled my tee away from me to fan myself. The coliseum's floor changed into sand, and George growled.

"What's this?"

"The dragons can choose any type of scene they're

comfortable with. Moon-Bolts are desert freaks," Lucian explained. "Like their temperament isn't enough."

"Is this going to turn ugly?"

He didn't reply because Becky had appeared. The Dragonians jumped to their feet and started to cheer and whistle like mad. A traditional gladiator outfit, modified for girls, hugged her body perfectly, and the tiny metal skirt showed off her slender legs. Knee-high boots and a black tee under her vest made her look sizzling hot. The guys hooted, and I rolled my eyes. Typical.

The music stopped, and Professor Mia walked right to the middle of the arena. She had a white flag in her right hand, and when she lowered it, a big lightning bolt came shooting out of George's mouth.

Becky blocked it with her shield, but it didn't look like the wisest choice, as electricity ran through the metal. If she hadn't been immune to it, she would've been on the ground shaking like she had that night at the lake.

George kept breathing lightning bolts aimed directly at Becky. I hid behind Lucian, unable to handle seeing one of my best friends take such a beating.

"C'mon, Becky, get up!" Lucian yelled. "Use your lightning."

"Her lightning?"

He didn't answer.

I hated not getting an answer; this was so confusing. My tee crinkled up inside my fists, and my skin started to feel baked from the sun's heat. I flinched every single time the lightning zapped her shield. It sounded like thunder, and when I had finally gathered enough courage to peek, I hid again as George threw Becky to the ground. It wasn't a fair fight, and I wished somebody would help her. Sammy shouted things for Becky to watch out for, but I doubted Becky could hear it.

George blew out another thunderbolt and hit Becky directly in her gut. She flew through the air and fell on her back. My heart stopped. She just lay on the floor, lifeless.

She did a back flip, righting herself once more, and I took a deep breath. My heart started to pound heavily as the whole coliseum went crazy.

She egged him on, showing him with her index finger that she wanted more.

George growled and breathed out another lightning bolt. It bounced off her body and headed straight back at him. He released another one and repeated it over again. Every single one backfired on him. She finally took control, catching the last lightning bolts in her bare hand. The entire crowd gasped. She then threw it back at him. After that, the lightning bolts only seemed to harm George. She was so fast he couldn't block or dodge them as he was pelted with his own weapon.

"That's it, Becky!" Lucian roared with a huge grin.

George stammered as Becky went Zeus on his ass. She gained more confidence with every counterattack, or maybe she'd just realized George didn't have anything over her anymore. It wasn't natural to see such a small person like her fighting against a beast of George's size, and winning.

He flew toward the crowd, trying to escape, but smashed against the invisible force that protected us. His talons made a screeching sound as he struggled to grab onto something solid.

"Yeah, it sucks when your perfect little place bites you in the ass!" Lucian yelled, and nearby students laughed.

George landed on the sand again and gave it her best.. Becky dodged and slid just like the gladiators in the movies. She caught most of the lightning bolts, and George eventually went down. The crowds cheered and she raised both arms in triumph.

She collapsed, as if a sniper had taken her out.

I jumped up while everybody booed.

"What happened?" I shrieked. "Is she okay?"

"Relax, Elena." Lucian held me back by the arm. "He's such a coward."

"What happened?" I demanded.

"She's fine. She'll be out for a couple of hours, maybe a day," Lucian said.

Sammy cussed right next to me.

"He forced her ability on her. Our human form is too weak to carry them. That's why your dragon is the keeper or what some would call the 'carrier'," Lucian explained, not taking his eyes off Becky's motionless body. "The lightning he breathes out is actually Becky's. He was born with it, but it never belonged to him. Becky is the true possessor. He just gave her the full dosage of what it feels like to carry that kind of power, and it always knocks humans out stone cold. She'll be fine, Elena." He gave me a side hug, as I just stared at her still lying on the floor. "But it's very cowardly for a dragon to do that, and you'll see this behavior only around the Chromatic ones."

"Do all of them do that?" I asked, still shaken.

"Only when they know that the battle is lost," he said.

The Dragonian side still cheered as Constance and another student carried Becky away on a stretcher.

"So what's going to happen now?"

"George is Becky's. Doesn't matter how bad he's going to resist at first, if he's part of a dent, he'll end up as tame as a lamb. We don't know what it is they are going through, but it's some sort of transformation that makes them stay together forever."

"You mean like a couple?" I wanted to know if it was what Becky spoke about on my first day.

He chuckled. "Yes, Elena. She's part of his foretelling. It's just a matter of time before he dents. I would give my left arm to be part of a dent." He smiled. He was really nuts, but then again he had tried to claim Blake twice.

I had to admit, the term "to dent" was still confusing. I mean George hated Becky, and now they expected him to do the opposite. It didn't make sense.

"Let's go, Elena." Sammy grabbed my arm when George finally shifted back into his normal body. They had to cover him with a blanket because he was butt naked. He was carried out on a stretcher too, but he wasn't nearly in the same physical state as Becky.

"Where are we going?"

"To go and see how Becky's doing. I can't believe George just did that!"

I waved at Lucian, since Sammy didn't give me time to say goodbye with a kiss. He waved back with a gorgeous smile, which made my stomach flip again.

Sammy walked so fast I struggled to keep up. I almost had to run to maintain her pace. We squashed through the crowd while they were still chatting about Becky's moves. She was a real Dragonian now.

When we reached the infirmary, Julia asked us to wait by the door while Constance tried to stabilize Becky.

My throat tightened as I saw how Constance placed a brace around her neck.

"Can a Dragonian die from this?" I asked, biting my nails while staring at Becky's still body on the bed.

"I've never seen one die. Constance was close, but anything's possible."

I felt like crying again.

I didn't want to claim a dragon, and I started to doubt Master Longwei's theory about my dark mark too. I didn't belong here. I would never have the amount of courage to do what Becky just had.

"Stop doing that." Sammy tapped my hand with hers, and I realized that I was still nibbling on my nails. I only did it when I was really nervous.

We waited for a long time. Sammy mumbled plenty of times, and by her twentieth sigh, Julia popped her head out of the door. "You may come in, but only for a couple of minutes, okay?"

We both went in without saying a word.

We couldn't do much but watch Becky lie on the bed with a bruised-up face. It looked as if she had been beaten by a jealous boyfriend.

This made me feel anger and other emotions I didn't want to feel.

Her leg was splinted and her arms were full of scrapes. Her one eye was swollen shut and had turned a greenish purple color.

My eyes started to sting.

"She is going to be okay, Elena, and believe me; George is going to feel pretty bad about what he did soon." Constance said while making Becky as comfortable as possible.

"When will she wake up?"

"It's up to her."

"Chromatic dragons are so stupid," Sammy hissed.

"If you don't mind, Becky needs her rest. You can come and check up on her later if you want," Constance said, and smiled.

We went straight to our room, and I wondered what they had done with George. I hadn't seen him in the infirmary with Becky.

Once we were settled, Sammy took a long bath. She

always felt terrible whenever a dragon did something horrible to humans, and now that it was her best friend, she must have felt even worse.

Later that night, we went back to check up on her. This time, thankfully, she was awake. "Where is that coward?" she said.

"Becky, take it easy," Constance said as she tried to get Becky to lie back down.

"Take it easy?" she hissed. "I was out for... I don't know how long. He's a coward." She grabbed her ribs in obvious pain when she moved too fast.

"You're not healed. Just give it a couple of hours." Constance said then told us to go.

"That girl is not happy," Sammy remarked as we started to leave.

"I'm just glad she woke up." I remembered the time I had spent almost a whole week in the infirmary and shuddered.

I struggled to sleep that night and when I finally fell into a deep slumber, I was rewarded with the same dream that had haunted me since my arrival.

I woke around four a.m., hot and sweating, and opened the window to clear my head. The fresh air blew gently into our room as I reflected on all the things that had changed in such a short period. A lot of things played in my head. Becky was one, and I tried to make sense of how George was magically going to like her. My dad saving my life was something that was constantly on my mind, making everything jumbled. *What did the Moon-Bolt want from us, and why did he kill Dad? What did Dad want to tell Matt that was so important he couldn't do it over the phone? Why do I have a dark birthmark when it isn't meant for dragon children? And why do they think I am going to show them great things?* It put so much pressure on me, sometimes I just wanted to scream.

What was I going to do about Lucian? I couldn't go back to being just friends again. I loved being with him, so Arianna's words shouldn't matter. I didn't care whether I was normal, I couldn't imagine my life without Lucian in it.

Our room started to turn a bit lighter. I looked outside my window and saw the first rays of sun peek over the mountains in the distance. For a few blessed moments, I forgot about all of my unanswered questions. There was something truly amazing about how the world woke. For the first time ever I watched the sunrise and felt completely at peace.

14

TODAY WAS A nightmare. With Becky still stuck in the infirmary, classes were ten times worse. I never realized how vital her quick explanations about foreign words were to keep me on track.

In Art of War, Professor Mia gave me Colin, Becky's old sparring partner, to fight against. I was less than thrilled. He was brutal, and I saw my ass a million times in the first half hour. My arms were covered with bruises and scrapes that burned like hell and it looked as if I had fought an entire army.

Every single muscle ached and felt drained.

To make things worse, Lucian was nowhere to be found. Arianna had made me feel so insecure, and I hoped with all my heart she hadn't gotten to him too. I knew I should have stopped seeing him, but it was too late. My feelings for him had grown overnight, and I didn't know how I would possibly cope without him. I became worried, and I knew something was wrong during lunchtime when he was still MIA.

After class, I fell on my bed, completely defeated. When I woke, Becky sat on her bed chatting with Sammy. The bruises around her eyes were completely gone, and she appeared to be fine.

"What's up, girl, did you miss me?" She grabbed her side when she moved too fast trying to get up off the bed.

"Don't, just take it easy." Sammy helped Becky onto her feet.

"Can we go to dinner now?" Becky said.

"You sure you are up for it? We can bring you something back," Sammy said.

"No, Constance said the faster I get on my feet, the better."

In the cafeteria, everyone was congratulating her. She really loved all the attention, and I just shook my head. Lucian was still nowhere to be found, and by now, I was really worried.

We went to bed around ten, after Becky told us all about the fight from her point of view. She told us the minute the scene changed, the entire crowd disappeared. It was only her and George somewhere in the desert.

On Monday morning, we woke an hour earlier to give us plenty of time to help Becky get ready too. I was worried about Lucian, but kept it to myself.

"Are you sure you are ready for classes?" Sammy asked. She reminded me of a mother hen, the way she fussed over Becky.

"I better be otherwise George will get a lightning bolt against the head."

We laughed. It took a long time to dress her, leaving us less time than usual to get ready. Sammy took a shower, while I brushed my hair and tied it up in a smooth ponytail.

"So, how are things going with you and Lucian?" she asked quietly.

"I don't know, Becky," I said.

"Elena?"

"I didn't see him yesterday at all. He's clearly ignoring me. What if Arianna got through to him?" My eyes started to sting. I couldn't imagine myself without him.

"He is probably just doing the gentlemanly thing by giving you some space."

Maybe she was right. I would give it time. The bell rang loudly as Sammy emerged from the bathroom.

"Ah crap, I'm starving," Sammy complained.

"Before you know it, it will be lunch," Becky said, trying to console her.

I didn't care about food at that moment. I was just glad Becky had come back. We both helped her down the stairs.

"Shoot!" Becky said.

"What is it?" Sammy asked.

"I forgot to pick up my new schedule."

"Schedule for what?" I said.

"Classes. It's so going to suck not being able to share any with you, Elena."

"What do you mean?"

"I'm starting a new schedule now that I have claimed George. He's going to be a thorn in my butt."

"New schedule?"

"I know it sucks. At least you don't have a second shadow."

"So you're not going to be in class with me anymore."
My air pipe tightened, making it difficult to breathe.

She shook her head.

"Without you, I'm so screwed. I'm going to fail."

"You're not going to fail, Elena, we'll help you."
Sammy said..

"How, Sammy? You don't have one class with me and
everything is already sounding like Greek." I was very close
to tears.

"Look, I've got to go. It will be fine, Elena. We'll sort it
all out later. Now, we all have to get to class before the
second bell rings," Becky ordered.

I sulked as I walked to my first period. They were
wrong. I was so screwed.

I made it to my seat just in time when the second bell
rang. Sir Edward began with a new chapter, and I barely
took any notice of what he said. The pop quiz after was
hard. Mystery was one of the only classes I didn't suck at,
but I found myself struggling just the same.

Without Becky, Art of War was even more painful. My
bruises from last week hadn't even healed properly, and I
learned that Collin was now my permanent partner. He
didn't know what the word "mercy" meant. I felt as if I was
about to die when the bell rang for lunch. I barely made it to
the room to take a shower.

I winced as the hot water ran over my cuts. The water
around my feet swirled in a pinkish current as it mixed with
the blood from my wounds.

Becky and Sammy were waiting for me at one of the tables when I eventually entered the cafeteria.

They waved excitedly, but their smiles disappeared the moment they saw me. I limped toward the table as my tears threaten to spill.

"Elena, what's wrong?" Sammy asked.

I fell down on my arms and complained softly. This was so embarrassing.

"Elena?" Sammy patted me on the back.

I looked up. "I'm not cut out for any of this!" I yelled. The entire cafeteria fell silent, but I didn't care anymore. "Just look at me!" I showed them my elbows.

The girls tried to soothe my uncertainty.

I decided to leave, as their feeling-sorry-expressions just prompted tears. *Where the hell is Lucian?*

I lay on my bed when Becky and Sammy entered.

"Elena, it's going to be fine," Becky soothed.

"How, Becky? I feel so stupid."

"You're not stupid, okay. You're dealing with so much, and it's a wonder that you're still sane, Elena. Most of the people that come from the other side lose their minds in the first week." Sammy tried too.

"I can understand why."

"Come here?" Becky hugged me. "We'll help you, promise, and before you know it, everything will be a walk in the park."

"Becky, it's not that easy. I didn't grow up with dragons. No offense, Sammy."

"None taken."

"And I never had anything like this on the other side. I'm not just dealing with things I never dreamed of in a million years, but I have to deal with you guys, Lucian, and everything else that goes with it," I bawled.

"What do you mean, deal with us?"

I took a deep breath. "I already told you guys, my father made us move every three months so friends weren't really a priority. The paranoia always drove them away."

"Well, you've got some now," Becky said. "The way I see it, Paegeia should've been your birthplace, Elena. You belong here and I'll make sure that you understand everything."

"I'll help," Sammy promised.

I wiped away my tears as the bell rang for the second part of the day. Everybody in Professor Gregory's class stared at me as I walked in. The familiar new-chick's-first-day-at-school-feeling came back and it was so bad that my stomach turned.

"Good afternoon, guys," he said as the second bell rang.

"And, ladies," Riley sang annoyingly.

"Sorry, ladies. Elena, Master Longwei wants to see you in his office, please."

The feeling became even worse after his words sank in. I got up and put my books into my bag. I left as he began his lecture.

The last time I was in the headmaster's office I had

received the biggest scolding of my life. *What does he want now?*

It felt as if it took an eternity to get there. I knocked timidly.

"Enter." His voice came from inside the room. I found him sitting behind his desk busy with paperwork.

"You wanted to see me, Master."

"Yes, Elena. Sit down, please. I heard what happened today in the cafeteria," he said. "I'm going to cut to the point. You have so much to deal with, and it was wrong of me to throw you in the deep water before you were ready. You are struggling to cope with all of this, and now I'm forcing you to learn everything in such a short period of time. I know you are not doing very well in your classes, and all of your professors are worried that you started this year a little too late. What I suggest is that you take it easy, and then next year you can enroll with the first-years."

"Please don't do that, Master. I swear I'll work harder," I pleaded.

"Elena?"

"Please, sir. Don't fail me because you think I can't make it. Fail me for the right reasons. Just give me a chance," I begged. "I will even take extra classes after school. Becky and Sammy said they will help me to catch up. Please."

"Elena, it is too difficult."

"I don't care. I just want a chance." I was adamant.

Silence filled his office, and he frowned at the papers splayed out on his desk.

He sighed. "Okay, fine if you're up for it, I will see what I can do from my side."

I nodded. "Thank you, sir."

"That will be all." He spoke with a whisper.

I wiped away a tear as I exited his office.

I found Becky and Sammy sitting in our room, and everything came spilling out.

"How can he even suggest something like that?" Sammy asked.

"Maybe he's just worried about Elena. She did start late." Becky said.

"I don't care, Becky. I'm not going to be left behind."

"Okay, easy. I'm sure Lucian will help too. He has—"

"Let's just see what Master Longwei is going to come up with," I interrupted, not wanting to talk about Lucian.

"It'd better be a good plan. Face it girl, you do have a lot of catching up to do," Becky said.

"It is not impossible though." Sammy eyeballed her." Besides, that mark is really dark. I'm sure Elena can do it."

"I just have to work harder," I answered both of them and left for the library.

I had no idea where to begin, so I started searching in a section that had something to do with magic.

Lucian kept jumping into my mind, and I had to push him away in order to concentrate on my task. I found a book called *Nobody's Magic* and paged through the first few pages. It sounded like a good book about where everything started, but the way the author wrote made me wonder if he was related to William Shakespeare.

Someone spun me around, as I was going to return the book to the shelf. I found myself in a pair of arms. By the smell of his shirt, I knew it was Lucian.

"Where have you been?"

"I'm sorry, Elena, I had to do something for one of the professors. I heard what happened today. Are you okay?" He clamped both my wrists with his hands to stop my weak punches.

A tear rolled down my face, and he caught it gently with his thumb. He gave me a soft kiss, and all my doubts disappeared in an instant.

"You need a break," he whispered once we'd finally stopped.

"Lucian, I need to study."

"You can study tomorrow." He grabbed my hand and dragged me to the exit. His hands were really cold, but his touch made me boil from the inside.

My stomach did so many flips it almost made me sick again.

"Where are we going?" I didn't recognize our path.

"Have you ever been on a horse's back?"

"No," I said, nervous. Dad had loved horses, but he had never made the time to take me riding.

"Today is your lucky day." He winked.

"Won't we get into trouble?" I didn't want to upset

Master Longwei after he had offered to help me with my classes.

"It is daytime, Elena. Besides, it's why the horses are here, for our use." He chuckled.

"I don't know how to ride." I was scared *What if I fall off or worse, get dragged?* My luck usually fell more in the dangerous category.

"You won't fall, I promise," he replied, as if he could read my mind.

We reached the stables in no time, and led me to the last stall. Hot flushes washed over my body as I struggled to keep my eyes off him. I wondered how I'd ended up with a guy like him.

We stopped in front of a big yellow-beige horse with a soft creamy-orange colored mane and tail.

"This is Ginger. Her mother was a gift from King Albert to my father," he explained as he put a saddle on her back.

"She's really beautiful." I wished I had the guts to stroke her.

He crouched to buckle the girth strap underneath her. Lastly, he put her bridle on and made sure that everything was safe and secure before leading her outside.

He climbed on her back and reached out for my hand. I smiled. We were going to ride together on one horse.

I grabbed his hand, and he lifted me without any effort.

I felt a bit nervous but calmed down when I felt him right behind me. Ginger started to move and there was nowhere to hold on to, so I grabbed one of his legs.

"Sorry," I giggled nervously.

"Don't worry, Elena. I know the first time is usually nerve-wracking, but you'll get used to it before we are done." He took both reins in his left hand, while his other arm wrapped around my waist. He clicked his tongue, and she started to move forward. Her pace was extra slow, as if she sensed I was scared.

We passed the stables down to the right of the coliseum. My heart still pounded fast with every move she made.

"How are your elbows feeling?" he whispered, and kissed me on my ear.

"I'll live." I smiled. I didn't want to complain around him, but had to admit they were really stinging underneath the sleeves of my jersey.

"Collin's an idiot, Elena. One kick and he'll go down."

"He might be an idiot, but he's a 'fast' idiot. He doesn't even give me a chance to kick him," I said.

"I'll teach you the finer details about fighting," he said.

I liked the idea of spending more time with him. "I can understand why people from the other side are going mental. Subjects here are completely the opposite of what we're used to. If they knew that we fight here with swords and axes and it is mandatory, they would think I'm nuts."

He shook behind me and I heard a soft snort.

"I am glad I can't leave. I love everything about Paegeia. I can't imagine how dull it is without dragons or being able to fight without weapons."

"Thanks for offering me your help. Are you sure it's not going to be a problem?"

"Elena—" He sounded surprised. "—time with you will never be a problem." His words made me feel like one of his gems, and my one hand slid over his arm that was holding me tight.

I gasped when we reached our destination. It was on top of a hill, looking down on an immense landscape. *A perfect spot for a picnic.* The view with the mountains at the back, the clouds turning pink from a dark grey gave me an urge to start painting again developed inside my gut. I used to be good at it, but I'd lost the passion a long time ago.

He helped me down after he'd jumped off and chose the nearest flat rock for us to sit on. Gazing out over the expansive landscape, I couldn't help but wonder that it was weird how no dragons were soaring in the sky like I thought they would be.

"So, how do things look on the other side?" he asked me.

"To be honest, I didn't know what to expect on my first trip to Elm. I imagined totally the opposite, thinking I would have to shop with dragons and that I'd have to dodge poop droppings."

He sniggered. "It is forbidden."

"What, the poop droppings"

We both laughed.

"This side looks exactly the same, except for the dragons and magic."

"What did you learn in school then?" he asked.

"Almost the same as in Dragonia. Social studies and anatomy of different animal species. We had math too, but it's much easier than Paegeia's. I hate it, and you can just imagine how much I love it on this side."

"Yeah, sometimes I have to scratch my head too. What was your favorite subject back home?"

"Art, the drawing type."

He looked away, and when he turned back, a small smile was playing around the corner of his mouth.

"You're really funny. I love that part of you," he said, and gave me his million-dollar smile.

"Yeah, so Becky and Sammy keep telling me."

We started to talk about art in Tith. He told me about an amazing gallery that sold startling pieces and someday he promised he would take me there. I liked that part of someday because I knew Arianna hadn't gotten to him the way she'd gotten to me. We talked about all different kinds of things for hours.

"It made sense what you said before about the people going mental this side," he said. "I mean, when things look so normal to you guys but isn't really, I think it's easier to lose your mind."

"I guess. So have you ascended yet?"

"No, I'm still waiting for that part. To be honest, I barely qualified, otherwise I would have been known as one of the wannabes, and my father would have to pay a crap-load of money so that I could attend Dragonia. My mark is barely noticeable, and I can relate to what it is you're going through a little. I had to work extra hard to prove to them that I truly belong here too. I guess it's one of the things we have in common, sort of. I take it by now that you know that you're the only human with a dragon father that bears the mark of the Dragonians."

"That part still doesn't make sense to me. I have read so many dragon stories and all of them that are born from a dragon parent can shift into dragons."

"They're not dragons, Elena, they're shape shifters. It's a completely different thing."

"How's that different?" I asked, confused again.

"Shape shifting is a gift, just like the ones we will receive when we ascend. The only difference is that you're born a shape shifter. Turning into the form they shift into, now that is genetic."

I finally understood what he was saying.

"Are there any shape shifters in Paegeia?"

"There used to be a long time ago, but, like the dragons, most of them were hunted down and killed. I imagine the ones that are still left this side hide it because there haven't been any sightings for a long time."

I sighed. "That's just wrong." It was quiet for a while. "So what will happen if you don't ascend?"

"Nothing. You make your own future."

"But how do you know what dragon to choose then?"

"You can choose anyone. It just makes it harder without an ability. Three of the Metallic dragons don't even have abilities, and yet they are the most important dragons of war. Without them, the chances of winning are very slim."

"Most of the Metallic dragons don't have an ability?"

"Yes, it's only the Fire-Tail and the Swallow Annex that have them," he said. "The rest have to rely on their speed and strength. Their exterior is much more advanced than the Chromatic dragons. They are the attackers and not scared to fly in and take out the enemy in close contact."

"Why do you fight?"

"We fight for the same reason war starts on the other side—freedom, peace, love." He smiled on the last word and stroked my back.

He leaned in for a kiss, and I knew that it was my favorite thing in the entire world, kissing him.

"We need to go, it is almost dinnertime," he whispered as our noses touched. I looked at my watch and saw that it was half past five. I sulked, which made him laugh.

"I know I have been neglecting you this last couple of weeks, but I promise it's going to change," he said, and kissed me one more time.

The ride back was too short. We ended up talking about him trying to claim Blake again.

"Lucian, Becky told me the last time you got seriously hurt. Why do you keep on trying if he can kill you?"

"Blake won't kill me and the girls are real drama queens. They make things sound twenty times worse than they are. I barely broke a rib."

I didn't know if that was supposed to be a joke.

"It's nice that you worry about me."

"Of course I worry," I yelled, thinking what kind of a girlfriend I would be if I didn't.

"Are you ready to find out how it feels when Ginger runs?" he asked.

I left out a small yelp.

"Fine, I will keep it at a gentle gallop." He clicked his tongue again, and she started to walk a little faster and then turned into a smooth gallop.

Our ride ended when we arrived back at the stable, and I waited while he removed the saddle from Ginger's back. My head felt much lighter, and I was amazed at the effect a horse could have on a human. They were so gentle. After the ride, my problems didn't seem quite so big anymore.

"Thank you, Lucian, I really needed that." I hugged him from behind.

He turned around. "Everyone needs a break now and then. You will see everything is going to be fine."

We entered the cafeteria hand in hand, and my eyes caught Arianna's. She glared at me, clearly pissed, as if he belonged to her or something. I looked away, ignoring her, and walked with him to the buffet line.

The dinner conversation revolved around Becky complaining about George and how difficult he was making it not cooperating with her in class. I said goodnight to Lucian by the stairs and went to my room. I struggled to fall asleep, thinking about finals and Lucian. I didn't want to fail.

When I finally drifted away, I found myself standing alone in the forest once again.

~

WHEN BECKY'S ALARM woke me, my head felt stuffed, and the effects of the horse ride had vanished.

My first two periods of the day were Latin.

"Elena, Master Longwei wants to see you in his office," Sir Deisenberg said, and I packed away my books once more.

Just like yesterday, I found him sitting behind his desk, buried in a stack of papers.

"Sit, Elena. I have spoken to a couple of the staff, and each gave me a name of their best student in all the subjects that you struggle with. Here is a list. They all agreed to help you."

I looked at the piece of paper with the names, times, and who was willing to tutor me. I froze when I looked at Monday and saw the name written next to Enchantments—it was Arianna's. History was on Tuesday and someone with the name of Cheng. I smiled as I saw Lucian's name on Wednesday, right next to Art of War. My heart stopped on the name next to Latin that was on Thursday—Blake.

.

15

AFTER I LEFT Master Longwei's office, it was time for lunch. I swiftly entered the cafeteria and found Becky's table. Lucian was not there yet.

"Are you okay?" Becky asked as I sat down.

"Just don't make me think about anything. Please," I pleaded.

"Elena?"

"Hey, sweetheart, you ready for sparring classes?" Lucian plunged onto the pillow right next to me, and I couldn't help but smile at him.

"I probably don't have a choice." I sulked and he chuckled.

"It's not that bad."

"Excuse me, you are a slave-driving demon when it comes to fighting," Becky snapped at him playfully.

"It got you your dragon," he countered.

"Not the one I was hoping for."

"Sorry." I stood up. "I need to get something in my system before Professor Mia's class. Collin's probably going to kill me today."

"He's a push-over," Becky said, in a singsong tone.

"Give it a month, and he is going to be the one sulking,"

Lucian promised and was right next to me. He gave me a side hug.

~

COLLIN, ENOUGH!" I yelled as he hit me with another blow that landed me flat on my butt. He laughed. Now I was sure that Lucian would deliver, because I was determined to kick Collin's ass.

"Elena, go to Constance. She can heal the cuts and bruises," Professor Mia said in a concerned tone. Blood soaked through my sleeves and my elbows felt raw and painful. "You don't need to walk around in agony." A small smile appeared at the corner of her mouth, and I nodded before running to the exit.

Maybe it was all I needed, to see Constance's friendly face again. She somehow made me feel as if I wasn't an outcast. I knocked on the door, and she smiled, nodding for me to enter. "Look who's here," she sang, but her smile disappeared as she saw the agony on my face. "Come here." Her arms were open and she hugged me tightly. Her arms felt so motherly, and she even gave me a soft kiss on my head.

"It's so hard," I said, and my mouth felt parched.

She poured me a glass of water and handed it to me.

"Just look at me." I showed her my elbows.

She took my arms softly and examined me.

She's really beautiful.

"It's going to be okay, Elena. Before you know it, everything is going to make sense and I'm sure with the help of Lucian, you'll not have these anymore." She gestured at my bruises.

"Why didn't you tell me?" I whispered.

She squinted and looked as if she was thinking really hard about what I was asking.

"That you're a dragon."

She giggled as her hands started to glow. I couldn't take my eyes off them.

"At the time you had a lot to cope with." She laid her hands on both my raw elbows and a warm tingling sensation emerged from her palms. It went deep into my skin and felt as if it reached inside of my bones.

"Why didn't you heal me the first time this way?"

She smiled. "Because it would have freaked you out, and Master Longwei suggested that a natural healing process might be the best at that time, considering we were trying to keep you sane." She stroked my elbows as if she tried to wipe away something. "There, I'm sure that feels much better."

I looked at my scrapes and they were gone. Even the blue around them had vanished.

"Wow." I laughed nervously. "Thank you so much." I hugged her without thinking, and she tapped me softly on the back.

"Go, you'll see. It's all going to be fine." She winked and I left feeling mildly better.

~

MONDAY COULDN'T HAVE COME FASTER. I was so not looking forward to spending time with Arianna. But if she was the best at charms and spells then I had no choice. I needed her.

"Elena, you need to concentrate and for crying out loud, learn to speak Latin," she snapped at me, sounding extremely irritated.

"It's not my fault everything is in Latin!" I yelled back, already frustrated.

"Who do you think you are yelling at, missy? I'm royalty and it's 'princess' to you. We used to hang commoners for back-biting. Again, Elena. What do you do when an enemy tries to attack, and you have nothing to defend yourself with?"

"You try to shield yourself," I whispered.

"Show me," she ordered.

"Arianna," I said, and she gave me the eye. "Sorry, Princess Arianna, I don't know the spell that well." I felt how my throat thickened and angry tears started welling up.

"Aw, are we going to cry?"

"I..." Nothing came out. I hated enchantments and knew I would never be able to learn any of it. Maybe I was stupid.

She chanted some things in a different language while

gripping the bridge of her nose. It was the words to the spell and could hear the vibration of the invisible shield taking form around her.

"It's a lot to take in. I don't even know what that means!"

"Maybe if you pay more attention in class and stop daydreaming about guys that are way out of your league, you might learn something. I told Master Longwei teaching a *dragon offspring* was going to be a waste of my time." She spat out the words as if they scorched her tongue.

"You're not really making it any easier for me. You don't even want to be here."

"You got that right."

"I really need your help, Arianna. Why are you so mean?"

"Isn't it obvious? You don't belong here; maybe that's why you don't get it."

"I didn't ask to be here." I was pissed off with her attitude. "You know what? Go to hell!" I was done with her and turned to walk away when she spoke another incantation. My air supply was cut off. My heart felt as if I was busy running the hundred meters. I fell on my knees as I tried to breathe, but there was no air. It was as if my lungs had collapsed and were no longer working.

Water poured out of my mouth as if I had swallowed a gallon. I started to panic as my breath disappeared and began hitting my chest as everything faded.

Far away, I could hear Lucian's voice rambling a couple

of foreign words. I felt his hands on my chest as air filled my lungs and I started coughing violently. "Are you insane? Arianna, you could've killed her."

"Oh, please. I only tried to teach her a lesson," she said, flipping her strawberry curls over her shoulder.

"What's wrong with you?" He sounded pissed off and helped me up. My lungs burned as if they were on fire.

"Come on, Lucian. It's not like you haven't done it before."

"That was different. It was an exam!" he roared. He shook his head and led me away from her. "I'm so sorry, are you okay?" His tone was full of concern, and he held me tightly. It felt good in his arms and I started to cry.

"This is my fault," he whispered. "I promise I'll handle this, Elena. She won't do that ever again."

I was glad there wasn't an audience to witness my tears. It wasn't the first time I played on death's porch, but it didn't mean that I was used to it either. It was weird how in the movies your whole life plays out in slow motion. It was nothing like that.

It felt horrible.

I stumbled up the stairs as if my limbs were made from paper. I felt Lucian's one arm behind my legs, and he lifted me up. Becky's smile vanished the moment we entered the room. Her face turned pale.

"What the f—" she shouted and she helped Lucian get me onto the couch. Not that he needed it. "What happened?"

"Arianna used a moon spell on her."

"She what!" Her eyes turned a shade darker that seemed almost pitch black.

I was glad Sammy wasn't here otherwise the whole fourth floor would have heard that Arianna had almost killed me.

"She'll be fine, I hope. I think I got there in time." Lucian's voice broke a little, like on the night Becky had ascended. He hugged me again.

"We have to tell Master Longwei. Princess or no princess, she's going down," Becky threatened.

"Don't, please," I managed to say. "She's the best at Enchantments, and I need the best to pass my exams."

"Elena, she almost killed you." Lucian's tone was full of disbelief.

"She wasn't going to. I disrespected her. She had the right to do that."

"What, by not calling her princess?" he snapped back.

"Well, she is one."

"I can't believe you fell for that, it's an old trick of hers."

"Oh, come on, Lucian. You know it's not the reason why she used a moon spell on Elena," Becky quipped.

I understood what she was saying. It was because I hadn't backed off from pursuing him.

Becky turned her gaze on me. "You must be really desperate to graduate or really stupid."

"Becky!" Lucian chided.

"Don't, Lucian, please," I whispered. "Becky, I begged Master Longwei to give me a chance. I'm not going to fail. She can use whatever spell she freaking wants and believe me, she's not getting off easily. She hates every minute as much as I do, but I will learn every single one there is, and if Arianna is the best one to teach me, then so be it."

"Elena?" Lucian sounded concerned. I could tell that he didn't like my tone one bit.

"Lucian, I'll be fine. I have a week to learn a spell to protect myself," I said. "You guys think you can help me?"

"Whatever, Elena, you're nuts," Becky snapped, and Lucian just sighed.

"Fine, there's a basic protection spell that might do the trick," he said.

"Thanks."

"However, I'm with Becky. You are nuts." He raised his eyes playfully. The corner of his mouth twitched slightly.

"Oh, do you now," I said, and gave him a hug. "I'll be fine"

The door opened and Sammy entered. She was returning from drama rehearsal and still had paint all over her face. I had no idea what the hell she was supposed to be.

"Oh crap, what happened?" She dropped the costume that she was carrying, and her concern was ten times worse than Becky's.

"Nothing, just that Elena has lost her marbles. Oh, and that Arianna almost killed her with a moon spell." Becky said.

"She did what?"

"That's nothing. Elena wants to face her again next week."

"That biatch. Elena, are you insane?" Sammy said.

"It's not that bad. Becky is a big drama queen," I said, giving Becky a look.

"Sweetheart, you almost died." Lucian was serious again, and Sammy just gawked at me.

"Elena, a moon spell is not to be taken lightly. She can get expelled for that." Sammy's tone was exactly the same as Lucian's.

"Well, that is nice to know." I smiled softly.

Both the girls just looked at me with wide eyes, and Lucian squinted at me. "I'm not the blackmail type, but if I have to use it, I will. I'm sure daddy would just love it if his little princess got expelled."

Lucian finally chuckled. "You are spending way too much time with Becky and Sammy."

"Hey," Becky said, and Sammy threw a pillow at him. He caught it. His reflexes were wicked. Guess the girls weren't the only two who rubbed off on me.

"Well, I've got to go. I'm sure tomorrow will go much better. Cheng is hardly someone that will feel the need to use a moon spell." He kissed me quickly and walked to the door.

"Good bye, Lucian," the girls sang in unison, which made him blush with a super cute smile. I walked with him to the door.

"Thanks for being there," I said, trying to sound as sincere as possible.

"I will always be there, Elena. I want you to know that."

I nodded, letting him know I knew.

"Just be careful next time, please," he begged, and I was in his arms again. He deserved a long, passionate kiss for being my knight in shining armor.

We said goodbye and I went back into the room.

"She really used a moon spell on you?" Sammy asked, and I nodded. "How does it feel?"

"Sucks big time. I thought I was a goner for sure." I shivered as I remembered the suffocating feeling again. "Wait, neither of you has ever gotten hit with a moon spell?"

"They don't work on dragons," Sammy said.

"Moon spells only get covered in the third year," Becky interrupted. "I guess she must be very good if she can cast a moon spell already."

"See, that's why I need her."

"Elena, you have to be careful," she warned.

"She told Lucian that he used to do it too. Do we have to defend ourselves in the exams?"

Sammy nodded. "Lucian cast something similar in his second year. It was in all the magazines. It's called a Riptide, but not as powerful." She still looked worried, or maybe she was wondering how it was possible that I was still alive.

"Can he be more perfect," I said, and fell backward on

my bed just imagining him in his exam last year. I felt sorry for his opponent. Both the girls laughed. "So what is it we have to do for this exam?" I asked after some time.

"You need to know all eleven protection spells and need to cast at least three." Becky sat on the edge of my bed and took one of my pillows.

I sighed. They were right, I was only kidding myself. I needed a miracle to graduate with this year's class.

The conversation changed to Becky and her new classes with George. It all sounded extremely interesting, especially the one that taught her everything about her ability.

George was still the same, though. They were supposed to train together and learn new kinds of magic that was meant for both of them.

During dinner, I tried to ignore Arianna as her group laughed and nodded toward me. Becky and Sammy almost said something.

"Don't. It will only satisfy her more knowing that it bothers us." I put my hand softly on Becky's. She bit hard on her lip, trying not to chirp something over her shoulder, and took a deep breath.

"She's so not worth it." She repeated that a few times softly until she calmed down.

Lucian wasn't there, and I hated that I wasn't going to be able to tell him goodnight.

I went to bed not knowing what to expect with Cheng. He was going to help me make some sense out of Paegeia's history. It was such a boring subject. *Why can't people just leave things in the past?*

That night wasn't any different. As I drifted off to sleep, the lady appeared again, and I was relieved when Becky's alarm went off the next morning.

16

AT THREE, I went to the cafeteria to meet Cheng. Today was my first History lesson, and I was nervous, but not as nervous as I had been when I was going to meet Arianna. Scanning the room, I noticed a group of four boys huddled around one of the tables. Not one of them resembled the description Sammy had given me earlier of Cheng, and I became discouraged. A tall figure appeared from behind a Buddha statue. He wasn't oriental, as I imagined he would be, and looked like he was a true ethnic mix.

"You must be Elena. I'm Cheng," he said, and held out his hand for me to shake. I realized what he was when I noticed the bronze glint in his hair.

"You're a dragon?" I asked.

"Busted." His smile reached his eyes as he held up his hands in mock surrender. I couldn't help but smile back at him. "I hope that it's not going to make you uncomfortable."

I shook my head. I was used to dragons now. Hell, I was sharing a room with one.

"Good, shall we take a walk?" He led the way, taking me along the same route Lucian had last week. We went to the stables and found Ginger standing outside in the pen, lazily eating grass. Cheng took out a handful of sugar cubes from his pocket and started calling her by clicking his tongue. He stroked her gently as she nibbled at the sugar cubes in his palms.

"Horses like dragons?" I asked, shocked at how calmly she behaved.

"Only the Metallic ones," he said in a very soothing tone.

"What is it about horses that you love?"

"They're such graceful creatures, Elena. I do believe that they have a soul too. The way some humans use them to get over their fears tells me that they are teachers just like us, in their own special way," he said as he stroked her mane.

"Yeah, there's something soothing about them," I agreed, and remembered my trip with Lucian.

"I know history can be boring, but you're looking at it the wrong way. Without history, we would not know where we came from or what direction to go," he said. He blew gently into Ginger's mouth. Her lips vibrated and she stomped her feet, neighing.

"What are you doing?" I giggled.

"I'm making her used to my smell. It's a small human trick. The Sioux tribe used to believe that blowing in their faces makes them used to your smell. I hope it's true, otherwise I just looked like an idiot."

I laughed. "So what is it that makes history so exciting?"

"What are they teaching you?"

"Oh, very boring stuff about medieval times."

"You don't like the medieval times?" he asked, as we carried on walking toward the coliseum.

"Not really. They were cruel and saw dragons as the enemy, right?"

"Yes, it was. I'm really lucky to be born during King Albert's time."

"Why were they so afraid of the dragons?"

"It was mostly the Chromatic dragons that gave them reasons to fear us. There was no enchanted wall back then and Paegeia was free for everyone to visit. People passed fluidly through the barrier. The Metallic dragons, like me, were wise to hide. They knew that the humans would never trust dragons, so they disguised themselves as the very creatures who wanted to destroy them. At that stage, it was still a dragon secret. I can just imagine how hard it was for them to watch their kind being slaughtered like monsters. When King Alexander ascended the throne, with the help of a great sorcerer, the wall was erected to protect magic from the humans on the other side who wanted to abuse it."

"A sorcerer?"

"Yes." He chuckled, but it quickly disappeared and was replaced by a sad frown. "I wish he'd died before he could produce an heir," he said.

"Why?" It was a weird thing to say.

"Because the most powerful sorcerer that ever lived descended from his bloodline. His power consumed him, and he betrayed and murdered his best friend."

"Who did he betray?" I was intrigued by Cheng's story. *Why can't they talk about the interesting stuff in class?*

"King Albert."

"His best friend was a sorcerer?"

Cheng's lips twitched while he stared holes into the ground. "It happened about fifteen years ago. The Viden warned King Albert, or so my mother tells me. The Viden said that someone in his kingdom would betray him. He didn't want to believe her because everybody loved him. She planted the seed of doubt, though, said there was a time that he became suspicious of everybody, became really quiet too. Mom was a serving maid in his castle, and she remembered the sadness in his eyes around the dinner table, just looking at his men and wondering who was going to betray him. She told me that it was a look that didn't suit him at all," he said softly.

The story of King Albert had hooked me, and I stumbled over the only rock in the path.

Cheng's reflexes were fast, however, and he caught me before I landed on my face. He chuckled. "I can see why you don't do so well with classes on this side."

I giggled at his sarcasm. "If you think this is bad, you don't want to see me in Enchantments."

We walked past the coliseum toward the edge of Dragonia, while he continued his story. Looking around, he chose a spot on top of a big rock and wanted me to sit with him, but I chose to stay on the grass with my back turned toward the view. My fear of heights had spoiled plenty of breath-taking scenes, and this was no exception.

He told me how King Albert had been the only one who had given Chromatic dragons a chance. He explained how Sir Robert had been evil, but King Albert had been adamant about claiming him. Night Villains weren't very pet-like, he explained, while shrugging, and I laughed at his comment when he said that it was the Metallic dragon's job. I was mesmerized by King Albert's bravery, how he'd claimed the first Chromatic dragon. It had changed Paegeia forever. Cheng told me it was also when he decided to build Drago-nia. It took many sorcerers and strong enchantments to raise the Academy into the air, and keep it aloft. The minute King Albert discovered that humans born with the mark could actually bond with the dragons, he chucked them inside too.

"I don't know why people like that always have to die. The world doesn't have many of them to start with." His tone was soft, and some sadness lined each word.

"So this best friend that betrayed him, is he still around?"

"Goran." "He's the reason Etan is forbidden."

"Yes, Becky told me about the creepers. Is it true that only Blake and his Dragonian can enter?"

He grinned. "I doubt that anyone would be able to claim the Rubicon."

"Why do you think that? King Albert claimed the first Chromatic dragon. How should the Rubicon be any different? There always has to be a first, even if it seems impossible."

He looked at me, surprised. "You've listened."

"Well, your story's interesting," I said..

"It's history, Elena."

I frowned when I realized what he meant.

"Then why's mine so boring?"

He roared with laughter. "Don't tell anyone, but I agree."

We both laughed then he sighed. It was quiet for a while, before he spoke again. "I know you and Lucian have something going on, and don't get me wrong, he's got the makings of a great Dragonian, but I truly don't believe that he'll be able to claim Blake," he said.

"Why not?" His statement intrigued me.

"Easy. The Viden."

"The Viden sucks things out of her thumb." Just thinking about her made me pissed off all over again. Grabbing a rock that was next to my leg, I threw it as far as I could, pretending that it was her crystal ball.

"Yes, most of the time, but when she makes a true fore-telling, it always happens."

"You mean like when the so-called wind blows and her eyes become silver," I joked.

He threw a stone over the edge. "Yes, it freaks me out too."

"It happened when you were with her?" I asked, and he nodded. "What did she say?"

"That's only meant for me, Elena. Foretellings are very personal, and you'll never find anyone that will reveal what the Viden told them, unless they are written in the Book of Shadows for everyone to see," he said.

"Book of Shadows?"

"It's a book that follows the Viden's foretellings. Nobody knows how it came to exist. Every time she makes a foretelling that is of importance to Paegeia, it will magically appear in the Book of Shadows," he said.

"What did it say?" I asked, curious. I was always curious when it came to Blake.

"That the only one who will ever claim Blake is his true Dragonian. His egg hatched three years before King Albert and Queen Catherine were murdered. When she said that the Rubicon would be claimed by a royal, it meant them. When she received a foretelling about King Helmut or King Caleb, she would refer to them as the Knights. My mom said that it was the best news she ever gave them, because she was telling them indirectly that they'd get a child. It was the only thing they ever wanted. My mom told me that before the Viden made the prediction, the queen prayed for a child every single day for at least a hundred and fifty years."

I gasped. "She had the essence of life too?"

"Yes. Their dragons gave them each a piece. King Albert was two hundred and fifty years, and Queen Catherine was about two hundred and forty-five."

Jeez. It sounded so old to try to have children. "Are you

sure it was one of their children? What if the Viden had it wrong just this once?"

He laughed. "Then she wouldn't be the Viden."

"Is it true that all Moon-Bolts can see the future?"

"Depends on how old they are."

"I saw two, before George, I mean."

"Yes, I know. How did it happen?" he asked.

I couldn't believe it when my mouth just opened up and my story started spilling out.

"My dad was a Copper-Horn. I never even knew that he was a dragon. We used to flee from our home every three months. He told me a lot about Paegeia when I was little, but I thought it was just bedtime stories." I didn't tell him I'd forgotten most of it. The pain buried deep inside me slowly emerged to the surface. I missed Dad so much. I told Cheng everything about that night, and when I was finished, I looked away to wipe off a tear before it rolled down my cheek.

"No wonder you don't cope with classes. You've hardly dealt with all of this."

"I just don't know why it happened. What was so important that they felt his life had to be the price? What if he died thinking that I would never forgive him? I can't tell you how many nights I'd prayed for a miracle, a normal life, a life where we didn't have to flee anymore. Now that I've gotten my wish, I feel like such a nobody. The way some of the students look at me as if I don't belong here, the Viden..."

"You're not a nobody, and your dark mark is why you are in Dragonia, Elena, not who or what your father was."

"Then why don't I get anything, Cheng?" I said, tossing my hands in the air.

"Give yourself some time, woman. You'll get there," he said. It was as if he knew something I didn't.

"When?"

"Rome wasn't built in a day, or so I've heard," he joked, and it worked, it made me smile. "You put so much pressure on yourself, why do you do that?"

"It's stupid, you'll laugh," I spoke, turning my face away.

"Try me."

I took a deep breath. I might as well tell him. I had told him everything so far, and I felt as though I could trust him with my life. "I've never felt so alive."

He just looked at me and frowned. "I'll help you with whatever I can, Elena. If it's that important to you not to fail, I'll give it my best."

"Thanks, I really appreciate it. You're really cool," I said, meaning every single word.

"Wow, I don't think I heard that one before. Most of the other students think of me as a geek."

I laughed again and punched him playfully on the leg. "Well, maybe they should try to get to know you."

"So, do you want to know why I believe Lucian won't claim Blake?" He moved from the rock and plopped down on the ground beside me. "It has to do with another foretelling she made a couple of years later. It's also written in the book. She said that only the King of Lion can claim him."

"The King of Lion, like in the sword?" I asked, and he nodded.

"Nobody knows what she meant. Not even her. They still think that using the sword is the answer, but it's also the one thing that can kill Blake, so they don't even consider it."

"You don't believe that?"

"I can give you a lot of theories, Elena. Crown-Tails love theories. If you ask me, I think she didn't mean the sword at all."

"What then?" I said, leaning in so I wouldn't miss a word.

"I think it's has to do with King Albert's bloodline."

17

CHENG'S STORY WAS intriguing, although a bit far-fetched. The King of Lion sword was the only weapon that could defeat evil, and Paegeia had plenty of that!

He told me that once flesh-eating plants had devoured people in their sleep. The only way they could kill them was when King Alexander destroyed them with the King of Lion sword. King Louie had used the sword to vanquish a fog that would dissolve whoever entered it. The sword could defeat every supernatural entity, no matter the form. Cheng believed that the blood of King Albert and his family was special. Not like alien blood or something strange, but that it contained trace amounts of magic, because the sword had been in the possession of Paegeia's true rulers for thousands of years. King William had his arm severed by it, and after the incident, the sword acquired the ability to destroy evil. Whatever the reason for this sword's magic, I felt safe in the knowledge that there was a weapon like it out there. Cheng also said that Goran was still alive, trapped in Etan, and that he had tried to steal the sword through dark magic. As he explained how Goran had harnessed his dark magic through the blood of wyverns and by forcing his own dragon to commit horrifying deeds, my knees trembled and my heart pounded.

Goran wanted to destroy the sword so it wouldn't pose a threat to his dark sorcery. With the only weapon that could kill him gone, he would become invincible if he ever broke out of Etan. The people of Paegeia believed that if Blake succumbed to his evil, Goran's magic would be able to control him. This new information scared the living crap out of me. I shivered involuntarily as if icy fingers were tracing patterns on my spine.

If Cheng's theories were right, Lucian was wasting his time and Arianna had really high hopes.

I now understood why Sammy worried about her brother so much. She believed what Cheng did and knew, deep down in her heart, that her brother would never be claimed. Returning to my room from the meeting with Cheng, I forced myself to think about something else.

Tomorrow was my first session with Lucian, and the butterflies in my stomach started to do a happy dance. I'd never looked forward to Art of War before, but I hoped he would be able to transform me into a warrior, as he had with Becky. I did pause, however, as I wondered if he was really the slave-driving demon she'd accused him of being.

That night I fell into a dreamless sleep as soon as my head touched the pillow. I guess Cheng's information was too much to dream about, even for the mysterious woman who haunted my dreams every night.

∿

THE NEXT MORNING I felt incredibly well rested. I assumed it had something to do with the mysterious woman not appearing to me. *The lady must cause some sort of an emotional drainage while I sleep.*

To sum it up in one word, breakfast was uncomfortable. George had started following Becky around, and he even sat at our table. He completely ignored the other guys' remarks and had a look of admiration on his face whenever Becky spoke.

Sammy gawked at him, forgetting to eat her breakfast, while Becky tried to ignore his unexpected behavior.

My first class of the day was Latin. I didn't understand any of it and every foreign word made me feel as if I was going to explode. Leaving one punishing class for another, after Latin I was rewarded with Arithmetic. I didn't have anyone tutoring me in Arithmetic, so I was basically doomed. Even though I was struggling, I was determined not to ask for help; they might end up having Tabitha tutor me, and believe me, dealing with Arianna was more than enough.

∿

MOVING THROUGH ANOTHER less than excellent day, I was relieved that it was lunch until I realized Becky had another riddle she wanted me to answer. Lucian begged me to give her the answer too, and Sammy simply rolled her eyes while stirring her vegetables.

"Okay, let's hear it," I said.

"There was a green house, inside the green house there was a white house, inside the white house there was a red house, inside the red house there were lots of babies. What is it?"

They all looked at me in anticipation, and my mind wandered back to Dad again. He'd asked me this riddle before.

"It's a watermelon," I said, trying to mask the sadness inside my voice at the memory.

She hopped up from the table and ran off at a breakneck speed, excited to tell the chef her answer.

Lucian stared at me, concerned about my sudden shift in mood. "You okay?"

"My dad asked me that one not so long ago," I said, shrugging in defeat and letting the emotions roll over me.

"Sorry, sweetheart." He gave me a soft kiss on my temple and stroked my back. The bell rang, and he insisted on walking me to my class. I guess he was scared Brian was going to try to steal me away or something.

We didn't talk much as we made our way through the halls and parted with a quick kiss.

THE DAY ENDED with Art of War, which meant I was

going to have a double period if I included Lucian's session too. I barely had the strength to walk to my dorm and take a shower just so I could sweat again. It didn't make much sense.

When I got out of the shower, it was time to meet Lucian. I forced myself out the room with a soaking body vest lumped in my arms. Unfortunately, the vest wouldn't retract into a disk when it was wet.'

"Enjoy," Becky said, without taking her nose out of her book.

I found him inside the dome waiting for me. He was practicing moves that made me stare at him like an idiot. He wore black pants with the body vest I'd only seen in Wetherley's and Co. He wasn't wearing a shirt underneath, and his muscular arms could make any girl's knees tremble. I closed my eyes, thinking how lucky I was to call him mine.

He is so effing hot.

When he turned around I pretended I'd just walked in and hadn't been gawking. "You're late," he said in a harsh tone. He looked away. When he turned to face me again, a smile lurked in the corners of his mouth. "This is going to be hard, isn't it?"

I giggled at his internal struggle. "Can we please just rest for a while, I just finished with a fighting class."

He squinted and contemplated my request. "It's not my fault." A huge teasing grin appeared on his face, and my stomach made another flip. My body vest was still icky and sweaty from my previous class, and I almost gagged when I pulled it over my head.

I picked up the heavy sword from the cupboard and dragged it all the way to where Lucian waited patiently. The screeching of the sword on the floor should've made me cringe, but I was too tired.

"Elena, how heavy is that thing?" He reached out for it, and I gave it to him without answering. My body language said enough.

He laughed softly. "I think I just found your first problem."

"What?"

"This one is way too heavy for you." Lucian went back to the cupboard and replaced it with another one. "Here, this is much lighter."

I took the sword from him and felt the difference immediately. "You want to say my problem this entire time was that I was using the wrong sword?"

"Yes, that's why you have to be early for class so you can choose the right weapon." He smiled again.

"You sure this weapon can protect me? It looks so thin." I examined the blade skeptically and barely saw his sword coming straight for me. My reflexes kicked in, and I blocked it, just the way Professor Mia had shown me in class on my first day. He came for me again, and I blocked that one too. He was so fast I barely saw him move, but he was right about the sword. It was as if I'd found my Excalibur and had become King Arthur.

When he finally stopped, I gasped for air and pressed a hand against my burning side. He laughed as I struggled to take a breath and playfully slapped away the hand I had raised in surrender. Becky was right. He was a slave-driving demon.

"One thing I can say, your reflexes are really good, Elena. I don't recall seeing that before in a first-year."

I gave him the *whatever* look.

He chuckled. "I'm serious, no joke."

"You'll say otherwise when you see me sparring with Collin," I said, wincing at the thought.

"Get here early and you might show him a thing or two," he said and forced me to get ready for another round.

"Don't you ever get tired?"

"I've got plenty of energy left," he said, pounding his fist on his chest and jumping up and down like a boxer.

"Oh, please, you're going to kill me if you say the break is over."

"That's your second problem; you're nowhere near as fit as you need to be. So I suggest a two-mile run every morning."

I grunted.

He gave me a hard slap on the ass that made me shriek. "C'mon, Elena, you'll thank me after a month."

If you live that long, I thought as I narrowed my eyes.

He chuckled seductively, making me forget why I was upset. Then he attacked me again. His blows grew stronger after each swing.

I blocked two of them and landed on my butt. I didn't want to get up, but when he offered me his hand, I had no choice.

"Becky was right, you are a slave-driving maniac," I said, still out of breath.

"You complain on the first day, sweetheart, I see hard times for you," he joked.

I hoped it was a joke.

He only gave me thirty seconds before he attacked me like a samurai lunatic. It didn't look so hot when I was facing him. I blocked five of his blows before my strength got the better of me, and I found myself flat on my back once again.

He pulled me up one more time, not accepting my surrender. It carried on like that for the next hour. When we were finally done, I thought I was going to drop dead right in the dome. I lay on the cold floor, and placed my flushed cheek to the cool surface. He could leave me there, I didn't care.

He came to sit down next to where I'd almost passed out. I heaved like someone who had run for two days straight and my parched throat made me feel like puking. "You're not bad, Elena." He touched my leg.

"I beg to differ."

"I know you don't see it right now, but I wasn't kidding about that run. So I suggest you go to bed early. I took it easy on you today."

I gave him the *excuse me* look.

"Get up and take an afternoon nap. You look like hell."

"I can't."

He shook his head, then a playful grin appeared on his face. He picked me up, threw me over his shoulders with ease. I squealed playfully and laughed as he carried me to my room.

I felt his hands on my legs, pulling me gently off his shoulder. When I reached his waist, he held me in place, and my legs automatically wrapped around him. Our lips found each other, and we kissed for a long time. It turned into a different kind of war, and I finally understood the phrase 'Love is a battle field.'

He grunted and chucked me on the bed.

"I have to go, before I do something we might regret," he said, and I could hear the strain in his voice.

I laughed.

"Am I too much for you, Prince Lucian?" I teased him, looking at him suggestively.

"Sweetheart, you have no idea," he whispered, leaning down to give me another soft kiss before forcing himself out the door.

I couldn't stop smiling, but I was so tired I dozed off a few seconds later.

It felt as if I had only been asleep ten minutes when Becky's alarm clock went off.

"Becky!"

"It's not mine, it's yours," she yelled back.

My eyes flew open. I didn't own an alarm clock.

"Elena, shut that thing off," Sammy growled.

I saw a small digital clock right next to my bed, showing it was 4:45 a.m. The sun hadn't even risen yet and I had to get up. I struggled to climb out of bed. I crawled to the bathroom and manage to take a sniff. I needed a shower badly.

I needed the shower for my aching muscles; the knots made it feel as if I'd carried weights on my shoulders. This guy was really messing up my routine. Usually I took a shower after exercising, not before.

I pulled on some sweatpants and a shirt, hoping it wouldn't be cold. When I got out of the bathroom, it had grown lighter outside. Unfortunately, my joints didn't want to work; my knees didn't want to bend, which made the stairs extra challenging.

I found the slave driver stretching near the cafeteria. He took one look at me and tried to suppress his laughter, but failed miserably. Only when I pointed my finger in his face and gave him the *not now* look did he bite his lip, which made him extra hot. I turned my head away so that I could at least stay mad for a minute.

"You should have stretched yesterday. Sit on the floor. Let's see what we can do."

The moment I tried to bend my knees, I tipped over and he caught me right before I landed flat on my face.

We both laughed as he lowered me to the ground and started to stretch my limbs like a physical therapist. The pain as he pulled my legs to my head brought tears, but when our eyes met, they disappeared. I felt better afterward, but it wasn't what I'd hoped for.

We used the last half hour for a run. His pace was fast and my lungs burned after five minutes. I had to make him stop by the lake so that I could catch my breath.

"I—can't—go—on."

He jogged in the same place. "C'mon, sweetheart, we still need to do some crunches." He chuckled.

"You have got to be kidding me."

"You see how unfit you are?"

I wanted to hit him with my fist in the gut, but I didn't have the energy. Instead, I grunted.

"Can we please go back now?"

"No, Elena, c'mon." He pushed me from behind and forced me to run again. I held my breath, wishing for the pain to disappear.

"We're almost there." Lucian sounded as if he hadn't run at all.

"I would so like to kill you right now," I said through clenched teeth.

"I don't believe that," he said, and it made me giggle.

I followed him to an open area right next to the lake. Seeing an opening in the brush, I collapsed on the ground and lay on my back, heaving. "This feels good."

"You ready for crunches?"

"Urgh! Fine, let's just get this over with."

We had done about a trillion crunches when my stomach

felt as if it was about to tear. I didn't know if I would ever feel anything other than this excruciating pain again.

I was so glad I had tutoring with someone else today. Then I realized it was Latin with Blake, and my throat closed up. If he was the best at it, I'd just have to deal with it like I did with Arianna.

Lucian made sure we stretched afterward, before we walked back toward the dorms. After shower number two, I didn't feel as stiff as before. I was still busy gulping down muesli and yogurt in the cafeteria when the bell rang and I was forced to lumber off to class.

The day flew fast and before I knew it, it was already lunch.

"Elena!" Sammy yelled my name. She and Becky were sitting at a different table today, because the princess wanted to sit at the table where we usually sat. She was such a pain in the ass.

"So anyone get the riddle yet?" I asked, showing Arianna that switching tables didn't bother me.

"No, but I'm getting my saddle," Becky said, bouncing on her pillow.

"Saddle?" I looked at Sammy.

"Dragon saddle." She rolled her eyes.

"George finally let the tailors take his measurements this morning." Becky ignored Sammy's eye roll.

"When a Dragonian claims a dragon, Clifford and Brook's tailor makes your saddle. They were here today to take George's measurements.".

"And why is that exciting?"

"Elena! It means that I'm finally going to feel what it's like to glide with him in the air," she said as she closed her eyes and sighed.

"Well, when you put it like that, getting a saddle sounds pretty cool." I tried to sound excited for her, but the reality of it scared the jeepers out of me. It was definitely the height thing.

"Way cool, it's like a girl's first kiss," Becky said.

"You're finally getting your saddle?" Lucian placed his tray of food on the table and plunged onto the pillow next to me. He gave me a quick peck on the lips then took a bite out of his pizza.

"Going to, next week," she said, launching into the story all over again.

We finished our lunch quickly, forced to listen to Becky going on and on about what kind of leather she'd chosen and the type of buckle and rope she'd picked out for the reins.

When the bell finally rang, I curled up my lip. I wasn't looking forward to class.

18

AFTER SCHOOL, KNOTS twisted violently in my stomach. Sweat beaded on my forehead as I fought the urge to puke, not knowing what to expect with Blake's Latin lesson. He'd told Sammy to have me meet him in the library. I cringed, thinking back to how I had ogled him the first time we met like some star-struck idiot blinded by his unnatural beauty. I was such a dork when it came to things like that.

Taking a deep breath, I braced myself as I entered the large room. I saw him sitting deep in thought and playing with a lighter at one of the tables. What was it with him and fire? *Don't stare, Elena,* blared in my head. Walking up to him, I silently recited my choreographed greeting. Should I say "Hi, Blake" in a chirpy voice, but then he would know that he had some kind of an effect on me. If I said it in a dull tone, he would think I was depressed. When the time came, it was worse than I'd imagined. I was speechless, I couldn't even say hello like a normal person.

"Io, Elena," he started.

Huh? I frowned, trying to think what the hell he'd just said.

He rambled a couple of other strange words, and I realized he was speaking Latin. He'd asked me something, but I had no clue. An awkward silence lingered for a couple of minutes. He stared at me with his smoldering blue eyes as if staring straight into my soul. It made my heart beat extra faster . I didn't like it.

When he spoke again, I shook my head. I assumed it was his way of rebelling against having to tutor me.

"What?" My voice disappeared.

He seemed irritated by my reply and answered in Latin again. His chair made a horrible screeching as he pushed it back. Heads shot up from the noise of the chair. He rose, said something else with a nod, and headed for the door.

"Blake, please," I yelled after him, and he stopped. "I really need your help. I don't want to fail."

He just stood there with his back toward me.

"Please," I begged again, hoping it was working.

He growled and turned back to face me, his top lip curling up. It made him look extra hot, and I could hear a couple of girls nearby sighing.

"Fine," he said. "But if you're going to cry, I'm done." He threw himself hard onto the same chair he'd on which he'd sat in a few moments ago. I cringed as he pulled himself, chair and all, closer to the table. The librarian frowned at him, her glasses resting precariously on her nose.

He started with the easy stuff—the words that were similar to English.

Eventually, we switched over to conjugating verbs and recited words like *confirmare*, which meant to confirm, straight through to *vocare*, which was to call. We recapped pronouns.

When he started to use an example with the word "give", it was beginning to make sense for the first time; however he wasn't kidding about the crying part. He was mean and made me recite each word a million times until I pronounced it correctly. He would flinch if I mispronounced the word as if it was insulting him. I sighed, trying really hard not to scream.

"You struggle with verbs the most. For dragons, it's easy. We are born to speak Latin where humans find it difficult. In Latin, the ending of the verb changes every time. The ending is crucial, as it tells you tense, person, and number," he said, counting with his three fingers to make it easy for me to understand. I had already forgotten what the first finger represented. I was lost in his eyes.

Snap out of it, Elena, the voice inside my head said through gritted teeth.

I forced myself back to the present, while he explained when using singular and plural, you always change the verb. I struggled to keep up and felt guilty when I caught myself staring at his mouth. His lips made me feel like I wanted to grab and kiss him. I felt as if I was already cheating on Lucian and my head ached , lucky for me, he called it a day.

He said goodbye and grumbled for me to meet him at the same place next week.

Until dinnertime, I stayed in the library and pored over my notes. Everything seemed to go back to not making sense now that he had left, and I wished he didn't have this effect on me. I had no idea how the hell I was ever going to be able to speak Latin fluently, the way Blake had this afternoon.

Becky was right though, he was *verautiful*, but such a dickhead, and I didn't feel like meeting him again next week.

During dinner, Sammy and I stared at George as he whispered sweet things to Becky, who was acting mildly amused.

I tried hard not to burst out laughing.

"You're an idiot, go sit with your buddies," Becky said, pushing him off his pillow.

He grunted as he jumped up to go sit with Blake again. Blake was making fun of him and the way he'd suddenly changed toward Becky. George laughed, and I realized Blake was only teasing him and not actually treating him like an outcast.

"He's like a fly circling a piece of crap," Becky whined, and hid her face in the palms of her hands.

"You know you just referred to yourself as a piece of crap, right?" Lucian joked and we all laughed.

"Oh shut up," she snapped, and then joined in our laughter.

We got up after our dinner and I felt dead tired.

"See you at five, my love," Lucian's voice roared from the boys' stairs, and I really wished I had a smart comeback to wipe the excitement out of his tone. I'd never met anyone who looked forward to morning runs.

"I'm a poet and didn't even know it," he said.

Sammy and I laughed hearing how the other guys teased him.

"So how has it been with you and Lucian?" Sammy asked, amused.

"Becky's right, he's a slave-driving demon."

After my shower, I went over the stuff Blake had taught me before I slipped underneath the covers.

The second I closed my eyes, I was faced with the same dream again. I really had no idea who the woman was, and it was starting to freak me out.

My alarm clock went off again at 4:45, and I rolled out of bed to get ready for my two-mile run with Lucian. My abs still hurt like hell from yesterday's training but I pushed through it.

Lucian didn't care about my pain either, and we ran the same path we'd taken yesterday. After the trillionth sit-up, we walked back to the Academy. I was so grateful for that. He wanted to know more about me and asked about my life with Dad. He looked at me with soft eyes as I told him about Dad's paranoia that made us move every three months. When he had questions regarding why Dad had done it, I couldn't answer. The only thing I did know was that it had something to do with the dragons and the conversation he had with Matt right before he died.

I swallowed hard when he empathized with how hard it

must have been to lose my mother to the plague at such a young age. When he saw my look of shock at his statement, he quickly explained that Master Longwei had explained to everyone at the school the unfortunate events of my mom's passing. *If they only knew.* This prompted another thought I hadn't even considered. If Master Longwei had told everyone that she had died, how the hell did the Viden know she had abandoned me? Was she really that good?

The conversation about Dad brought tears to my eyes. Lucian dabbed one softly with his thumb and then kissed me.

"I'm sorry for your loss, Elena. Your dad sounded like an amazing dragon, well, except for the paranoia part," he joked.

"Do you think you're up for a fancy affair at the palace next weekend? It's my mom's birthday, and you would do me such a big favor if you came."

"Lucian, please," I begged. "I'm not ready to meet your parents or go to a fancy party. Sorry."

"It's fine. However, it's something we need to fix. Otherwise it's going to become a huge problem." I had to suppress my smile. "You know, if it was any other girl, they wouldn't hesitate to come."

"I'm not any other girl," I snapped, hating how people always compared me to others.

"That you aren't," he agreed, and I laughed at how formal he sounded. He wrapped his arms around my waist. "That's one of the reasons I'm so crazy about you."

"You're crazy about me now?" My heart started to beat fast as he bit his lower lip. *Crap, that's so hot.*

"You know you make me crazy," he admitted, and I just kissed him. It was a long one, and we were out of breath when we finally parted.

"No running back?" I said hopefully.

"There's still time." He slapped me hard on my ass as he ran away. The chase was really stupid, because he was crazy fast and before I could spell the words 'blink of an eye' he was gone. I found him a few minutes later running in place down the trail.

Switching back to walking, he started to talk about a way to enhance his hearing ability, so he could use it the next time he was going to try to claim Blake.

Cheng's theory popped in my head. "You know Cheng? He helps me with History—"

"He doesn't believe that anybody can claim Blake," he interrupted me. "Just like no one ever believed King Albert could claim any dragon."

"What do you mean?"

He smiled. "He wasn't born with a mark, Elena."

"What?" I was shocked.

"You heard me. Back then, they didn't know about the mark thing. He believed in what was in here." He tapped on his chest. "If your mind and heart are in the same place, you can do whatever you want."

"But didn't you have to be special to claim a dragon with abilities?"

"Or just really smart," he said, and grinned. "Why do you think Master Longwei allows the rich to pay so that their non-gifted kids can attend Dragonia?"

I huffed, remembering Becky's conversation and how she'd complained about that. Had she meant King Albert? "He really claimed a Night Villain?"

He nodded. "He claimed the first Chromatic dragon. He started everything."

"How?"

"It's one of the legends you'll cover soon. Some say that he studied one for years. King Albert was really good with his hands, enhancing equipment was his specialty. He made a shield of the thickest metal that helped him block their acid breath and slobber. They're evil dragons, and why he chose a Night Villain, no one knows."

"What do they look like?" I asked, intrigued.

"Extremely ugly. Their faces look like they have been burnt. It's almost like they aren't immune to the acid themselves. I guess it was one of the reasons King Albert chose the Night Villain."

"So he claimed one of the most evil dragons just by studying them for a long time?" I said, not completely convinced.

He nodded. "That's how I know that deep down inside, I don't have to be the kind of royalty that the Viden foretold about."

"But the Viden said that only the offspring of King Albert and Queen Catherine can claim Blake."

"Elena, didn't you hear anything I just said?" he asked.

"The Viden has never been wrong, Lucian."

"I don't care. She will be with this. I have to claim him."

"Why on earth do you want to claim him?" I was starting to lose my patience. I stopped, but he still carried on for a few steps.

"Because he used to be my best friend," he said as he turned back around to face me. It took some time for that to sink in and I struggled trying to imagine Lucian and Blake walking arm in arm next to each other the way Becky and Sammy always did.

"You used to be best friends!"

"Yes. Both our fathers served in King Albert's court. We used to play outside while they were attending meetings."

"Why are you no longer friends?"

He looked at the ground with a huge crease on his forehead, and he sighed. "It's not his fault, Elena. It's the dark side that starts to take over. He hardly has control over it. I promised him when we were thirteen that I would do anything in my power to try to claim him." He stroked his face hard to hide his emotions, or perhaps he was starting to realize how difficult it was going to be to keep that promise.

"I'm so sorry, Lucian. I didn't know," I said.

He gave me a crooked smile. "No one does, except for Sammy. If I told you we never tried to ditch her ass, I would be lying."

I giggled, imagining them as children, running away

from a small blabbermouth. "So when did you stop being friends?"

"More or less the same time that we arrived here," he said. "My first claim was right after we enrolled. It's against the law to participate in a claim before your sixteenth birthday, and on mine, I tried for the first time. I was down for two weeks," he boasted.

"You mean he almost killed you."

"Trying to claim a dragon that doesn't belong to you does have its risks, but we both know it's not impossible."

"Lucian, why don't you wait till you ascend before you try again," I begged him.

"I might not even ascend, Elena," he said. "You know my mark isn't that dark."

"Then how are you going to use Blake's powers once you have claimed him?" My tone was full of concern mixed with questions and disbelief.

"It's not mine to use, so it becomes his."

I frowned. "I don't understand."

"If someone claims a dragon that doesn't share the same ability, then it becomes the dragon's. Emanuel revealed that little secret to me when I turned seventeen. He also said that it hurt when my father claimed him because they shared the same ability. My dad is a fire wielder too. Emanuel believes that it would've been ten times worse if they were dents."

"Is it true that Blake has many abilities?" I asked.

"He does, but the problem is that they're nothing like the other dragons' abilities. I only know of three," he said.

19

THREE!" I yelled at him. "So he's got more! Lucian, what if you're just wasting your time? I mean, you know of only three abilities. What if he uses another one that might claim your life?" I could feel my voice rising.

"Elena, I have no choice. I promised him!" Lucian threw his hands up in aggravation.

"You were only kids!" I shook my head, trying to understand.

"I can't break my promise and let him become evil. Urgh! Forget it. You're just a girl who knows nothing. You'll never understand."

My hands fisted into balls of fury. I was glad we were close to the main building, because otherwise I would never have found my way back. Shaking, I forced myself not to yell at him for being so stubborn. He was just going to get himself killed.

He left for the weekend without even saying goodbye or hello when he came back on Sunday afternoon.

I didn't go for my morning run with him on Monday so I was surprised to find him close that afternoon as I went to Arianna's Enchantment lesson. She didn't like it one bit that he was hanging around, keeping an eye on her.

Tuesday was Cheng's turn. We spoke about the Rubicon, not just Blake but the previous one as well. There were four they knew of, but the museum in Elm only carried two. The Rubicon before Blake had been killed by King William. The people celebrated for a whole month. The picture that popped into my head was comical. People drank, passed out, woke, drank some more, and for some reason they danced around a roaring bonfire. He led me toward the coliseum today during our walk, and we stopped in front of the two huge stone dragons at the entrance.

"They aren't the same as Grimdoe are they?"

"No," Cheng said. The detail on them had started to fade, and when I softly glided my index finger over the carving, a bit of sand fell to the ground.

"But they will wake up when they are really needed," Cheng said cryptically.

"What?" I yanked my hand back as if I had been burned.

Cheng just chuckled.

"Are you playing with me?" I asked through a huge grin.

"No, they will wake up, but they haven't for a very long time."

The idea of the dragons breaking through stone imprinted on my mind as we talked about them. There were four altogether, and they had something to do with the elements of nature. They weren't anything like Grimdoe.

Just before we said goodbye, Cheng asked me if I wanted to come with him this Saturday to Elm. He really wanted to show me the Museum of Etan; well actually, it was the Museum of Paegeia, but when the creepers consumed Etan, they had changed the name.

Feeling excited about the upcoming trip, I entered the dorm whistling. Sammy and Becky looked at me, puzzled.

"What?" I protested. "I really like spending time with Cheng."

Becky lifted her head from her pedicure. "Elena, he's a geek."

I shrugged. "So, he's the geek that's going to help me pass History."

Rolling her eyes, she went back to painting her toes. "Just don't fall for Cheng. Lucian is already worried about other guys tutoring you."

I huffed. "I don't care what Lucian thinks."

"Are you two still fighting?" Sammy, who was sitting on the couch, asked.

I ignored her question. He was the one who didn't want to speak to me.

I skipped running again with him on Wednesday, and I saw him chatting with Dean at one of the tables at breakfast. He didn't even look my way, but I knew he saw me.

I sighed, realizing today was my Art of War lesson with him, and I knew he wasn't going to show up this afternoon.

I found Becky and Sammy sitting alone at a table outside.

"Elena," Becky said, "You need to speak to him sometime."

""Why must I—"

"Becky, Master Longwei wants to see us in his office." George came out of nowhere.

She jumped up, did a quick happy dance, and ran off with him in the direction of the headmaster's office.

"I think her saddle just arrived," Sammy whispered, and I tried to look happy.

"You really should try to make amends, Elena."

The bell rang before I could tell her to butt out of my business, and I slumped to class.

The day went really fast as I pondered what both of them had said.

Maybe I should try to say I'm sorry. Heaven knows I need his help to master war skills if I want to pass. Not to mention how much I miss him, but then again, why should I be the first to apologize?

When I found Lucian at lunch a part of me wanted to go over and say I was sorry, even though it wasn't my fault, but I couldn't.

I plunged onto the pillow next to Sammy.

I could feel her eyes on me, Becky's too. "Elena, is it so hard to say you are sorry?" Sammy asked.

"Why should I apologize? I wasn't at fault here." I was angry.

"Well, my mom always says that men are way too stubborn for 'I'm sorry,' so even if it wasn't your fault, just suck it up."

"You think I should apologize too."

"No," Becky said but gave me that look. The one I learned quickly there would be a 'but' following soon. "But he is the Prince of Tith, and I doubt that they teach royalty how to master at apologizing."

I shook my head. This was so wrong, but decided to suck it up and say I was sorry for something I really didn't even do.

I pushed myself from the pillow and walked to his table. He was talking to another guy, which only aggravated me more as I knew he saw me out of the corner of his eye.

"Lucian. I'm sorry about what I said," I spoke fast, hoping it would be enough for the Prince of Tith. It was't easy to say those words, especially after I felt as if I'd done nothing wrong. "If King Albert claimed a Night Villain, then you could claim the Rubicon," I said, knowing it was what he wanted to hear.

It was a lie.

I didn't believe that he could, but I didn't want him to think I doubted him.

He smiled. "Sorry too, sweetheart," he said, and pulled me down to sit on the pillow beside him. "I shouldn't have lost my temper like that. I wanted to apologize so many times, but every time I saw you, you looked so upset. It's not very knightly to fight with a damsel in distress."

I giggled. A part of me was still livid with him but when he cupped my face, kissing the tip of my nose, it all disappeared.

"Well hopefully, I won't be one anymore in a month's time," I said.

He smiled. "I still wanted to ask you how your first Latin lesson went."

I curled my lip. "You mean what kind of a teacher your buddy is," I whispered. "He's a maniac when it comes to Latin. He gets a hernia every single time I pronounce one word wrong."

He grinned. "Latin is like sex to Blake. It has to be perfect."

"Way too much information." I blushed and tried to hide my face.

Lucian roared with laughter. "Don't do that. I think I just found my new favorite feature of yours," he teased, and kissed my red cheeks.

"Don't. It's stupid." I giggled as he kept on kissing me playfully.

"So what, you blush every time someone says sex."

I blushed again, which made him laugh even more.

"Stop that," I mumbled.

He rested his chin on my shoulder and looked at me through his thick eyelashes, burning his blue eyes into my soul.

"Blake will warm up to you, Elena. He's not the bad guy here."

"If you tell me he's just confused, I'll kick you," I threatened.

He just chuckled.

"I'm sure I can fail one subject," I said hopefully.

"Latin's not one of those subjects," he said. "You need to speak at least fifty percent by the end of the year."

I wanted to scream but bit my tongue. "I don't want to speak stupid Latin."

"Sweetheart, everything's connected to Latin. I'm afraid you have no choice." He played with a strand of my hair and placed it back behind my ear.

"Whatever." I sulked.

He smiled and shook his head. He looked past me, narrowing his eyes at someone, and I turned to see who had captured his attention.

I giggled as I saw Brian waving at me. He had no sense of self-preservation and didn't even care that he was flirting with me in front of Lucian.

"You're not the only one driving me nuts," he said through gritted teeth.

I gasped. "You have a thing for Brian too?"

"Ha ha, funny," he said, and a smile appeared.

"Why do you worry about Brian?"

"Why do you think, Elena? The guy has a lot to offer, and it's wrong on so many levels for me to think that, not to mention saying it out loud."

I laughed. "You're so cute when you're jealous." I snickered, and he laughed too. Grabbing his jaw, I turned his head to look at me. "I only have eyes for you, Lucian McKenzie." I kissed him softly as the bell rang, but I was a million miles away.

20

W E SAID GOODBYE with a kiss in front of my Arithmetic class. It was a brutal hour, but I raced from the room as fast as I could to make it to Art of War.

I showed up early but couldn't claim my sword, because Tracey was swinging it in her left hand, the way professor Mia had that first day. Collin beat me again, and when I slouched to the cupboard to put my sword back, two small axes pushed to the far back caught my eye. It gave me an idea; I was sure Lucian knew how to fight with any kind of weapon, and now was the time to see just how good he really was.

I patiently waited for him after class.

"Hey, Sweetheart. Jeez, you're early. That anxious to see me?" he teased as he walked in.

"Can I change weapons?" I asked, ignoring his flirting.

"To what?"

I ran to the cupboard and picked up the two axes to show him.

"Where did you find them?"

"They were here," I said, and pointed to the cupboard.

He looked at the engravings and froze.

"Do you know who they belonged to? They were Queen Catherine's."

"Then what are they doing here?"

"I don't know, but can you keep it a secret for now? Just until I find out."

"Sure, anything. Do you know how to fight with them?"

He chuckled. "Do I know how to fight with them? That's an insult." He threw one in the air. It flipped end over end and he caught it by the handle in an outstretched fist. "They're called Frankish Throwing Axes, and *you* have to be careful."

"Just teach me," I said, rolling my eyes.

He juggled with them one last time before handing them to me hilt first. "Why do you want to learn how to fight with them?"

"I like the way they look. They're easy to carry around and the sword looks uncomfortable to travel with." I decided to go with practical.

"You chose them just because they are easy to transport?" he said, and snorted.

"Does it matter?" I asked, smiling. "Just teach me."

"It's not common to fight with them. The queen was only one of a handful of warriors that chose axes. As you can imagine, you have to be close to your enemy to strike, whereas with the sword you are allowed some distance. I guess Master Longwei wasn't wrong about his mark theory."

I rolled my eyes. *For the love of blueberries, not him too?* "Can we just start?"

The corner of his mouth twitched slightly. "With axes, fear of your enemy isn't an option. Close range, like this." He spun around me so fast that I didn't see him and trapped me from behind. He came so close I could feel his breath on my hair. The butterflies in my stomach fluttered wildly, and I felt the urge to kiss him.

"What is nice about them is that you have two, which means you have time for a surprise blow." He spoke with a soft, seductive voice, and I swallowed hard. He moved fast past me again and faced me, while his other hand came out of nowhere and hit me softly on the left ribcage. "That hit could have cost you your life." He gave me a quick smile and kissed me fast on my lips.

I laughed.

"Axe warriors are fierce, they don't hesitate, and they have fast reflexes." His smile disappeared and his tone grew serious. "Now if you just want to knock someone unconscious, you can with the haft or the blunt side of the blade. I bet Collin will think twice after a blow like that, or it can be a weapon to throw." He took a few paces backwards, putting distance between us, and threw the axe in his left hand so fast I didn't even see it properly. It hit the target board on the bull's eye.

"You're really good at this," I said, impressed.

"Thanks, sweetheart. I used to play with a lot of weapons as a kid. My father is one of the best weapon experts in Paegeia. I guess the apple didn't fall far from the tree." He walked to the target board to retrieve the axe.

I pinched my arm quickly. He was such a god, and I had to make sure that this wasn't a dream. He came back and gently handed me both axes.

"Shall we?" He was formal again and bowed in front of me.

"Just go easy, please." I tried to remember what Professor Mia had told me and stood up straight, not taking my gaze away from him.

"Okay." He dropped his sword and picked up a shield. "Tell you what, you just swing away until you get the hang of it."

I blew out a big gush of air and my hands trembled, but I decided to try it. I swung at him with the axe in my right hand and took my eyes off him for one second. He blocked my blow with his shield while stepping forward. With one push of his shield, I fell on my butt.

"Why are you holding back?" He lowered his shield and lent me a helping hand.

"It doesn't feel right; you don't have any weapon to fight back," I complained, and put both axes down on the ground to accept his hand.

He pulled me up. "Would you rather I pick up the sword again? It's hardly a fight, Elena." His smile went straight to his eyes.

"Fine, don't complain if I hurt you."

He shook with laughter, making me feel like an idiot.

"With weapons, not easy," he teased.

I squinted, raising the axe in my right hand, keeping the left back, holding it defensively as I crouched low and approached him. The axes felt good in my hands, much lighter than Excalibur. My quick attacks surprised Lucian, judging by his expression, though my blows rattled off his shield harmlessly.

Somehow, I knew what to do next, as if the axes and I were meant to be together. When the pain grew too unbearable in my side, we stopped.

He didn't speak but stared at me with huge eyes. We burst into laughter.

"That really felt good."

"I think you've found your weapons. You're really good with them, Elena."

I wasn't comfortable with compliments but had to admit it felt great. Becky might be right about this class becoming my favorite. "Beginner's luck."

"There's no beginner's luck in fighting, only in gambling." We started fighting again when the pain in my side faded.

He was better prepared this time and blocked all my blows, except the last one where he tripped over his own feet. "Dammit, Elena! Whoa!"

My stomach did a double somersault.

Damn, this is fun. Who would have thought?

The third time, he didn't fall, but it was a hard and long fight. When we'd had enough, we were both breathless. I couldn't believe it felt so easy now that I'd finally found the right weapons. They were going to be my twins, and we would never be separated, that is if someone didn't take them from me because they used to be Queen Catherine's.

"Do you think Professor Mia knows about them?" I asked Lucian as I put the axes back in the cupboard with the other weapons.

"I have no idea. She should know, but then I've never seen them before, so she might not." He was no longer out of breath, but his skin glistened with sweat.

We walked hand in hand to the main building, chatting about our session. I could tell that he truly enjoyed it, and I couldn't recall a time when I'd seen him this excited.

Satisfaction was a sweet feeling, and it made me feel as if I was finally getting somewhere. I found my second wind, ran up the stairs to my room and reached the fourth floor in no time. A smile ran across my face as I thought about Lucian. I was crazy about him, and I'd never felt anything like this before. Why did he have to be a prince?

I took a shower and couldn't wait to tell Becky and Sammy about the axes.

Sammy came in first after her drama lesson. Her eyes lit up as I told her about my little discovery.

We both fell silent as the door opened and we watched Becky drag a huge saddle into our room.

She smiled from ear to ear and her face looked flushed.

"That. Was. Amazing!" She left the saddle by the door, threw a pair of flying shades that could easily be mistaken for swimming goggles on top of her dresser, and collapsed onto her bed.

"You finally rode George?" Sammy said.

"Yes, and it's the best feeling in the world. I can't explain it." She turned around and rested her head on her one arm to look at us. "Lift-off was really scary. I didn't like the speed at first, and George must have sensed it somehow, because he slowed down until I was ready for more. He took me high above the clouds, and I actually wanted to cry when Master Longwei told us to go back."

"Master Longwei was with you?" I asked. "Flying as a dragon?"

"No, he had a magic carpet with him. Yes, in his dragon form. C'mon, Elena, it's not as if you don't know that he's a dragon," Becky teased.

"I just can't imagine him as one," I admitted.

"Well, he's a beautiful one," she said and went over to the fridge to get a soda.

At dinnertime, Chef had prepared a feast. Roasted beef with gravy and mash, and pork glazed with honey, served with rice—food that made Becky pull up her nose. Sammy and I loved it.

Lucian came in shortly after we'd seated ourselves at our normal table, and took the pillow next to me. We chatted about my skills with the axes and listened to Becky and George telling Lucian about the flying lesson.

After I said goodbye to Lucian, I prepared for my Latin lesson tomorrow but called it a night when my mind felt as if it was going to explode. I didn't dream about anything, and when my alarm clock went off again, I finished getting dressed so fast that I had to wait for Lucian.

The two-mile run turned into three, and right before I wanted to pass out, we reached the lake. He took me on a different route today. We even ran half of the way back, which made me feel pretty good about myself.

Blake called off our tutoring for today. The Viden wanted to see him after school. Sammy tried to help me, but was nowhere near as good as her brother.

The next day went fast, and before I knew, it was Friday afternoon.

21

E LENA, YOU NEED to go to bed early," Becky mumbled with a toothbrush still in her mouth. "We have loads to do tomorrow."

"I've already made plans." I made my way across the room.

"What!"

"Elena, we're going to watch *Doubt of Fire*." Sammy's voice came drifting from the couch.

"I didn't know that you wanted me to come with you guys." A feeling of regret that I'd already said yes to Cheng emerged in my gut.

"Did you think we were just going to leave you here?" Becky said, and the way her eyes widened and her mouth partially parted told me that she wasn't happy about what I'd assumed.

"I don't know? Sorry."

"Can you call it off?" Sammy suggested hopefully.

I shook my head.

"Why not?"

"Cheng already asked me on Tuesday, and I didn't know if Lucian was going to come with you guys or not, so I said yes."

"Does Lucian know?" Becky asked.

"I'm going to tell him before he leaves, which reminds me, I have to go. I just came by to drop off my bag," I said quickly as I made a dash for the door.

If they wanted me to come they should have opened their mouths and not left it till the last minute. I went looking for Lucian and found him sitting at one of the tables outside talking to a redhead I'd never seen before.

I curled my arm around his waist as I slid next to him. "Are you ready?"

"Yes, see you later, Tom," he said, and we got up and started to walk to the lake. "I wish I could stay this weekend. Are you sure you don't want to come with me?"

"As tempting as that sounds, I'm so not ready to meet the king and queen of Tith yet."

"You scared?" he teased, tugging on a strand of my hair playfully.

"Yes. For all I know, they hang commoners just for thinking about speaking to the prince."

He chuckled and swung me around for a kiss. "Then, my dear lady, I will just have to save you. Will you meet me tomorrow?"

I cringed, knowing he was not going to be happy with my new change of plans. "About that. Cheng asked me to go with him to the museum for strictly educational purposes." I said the last part slowly so that he would understand it was not a date.

"Just as long as you promise me that I don't have to kill

a dragon one day because he stole my lady," he said, looking deeply into my eyes.

"Please, Lucian, Cheng doesn't have anywhere near your charisma or charm," I told him, giving him a squeeze so he knew I meant it.

"I could get used to this kind of flattery," he said, and our lips met again. The warm kiss felt good, and I didn't want him to stop. These feelings he stirred up inside me scared the living crap out of me. I didn't know what I was going to do if he ever told me we were finished.

"You can go, but on one condition,' he said, with a smile that told me he was busy conjuring a plan that might get us in trouble.

"Which is?"

"Sunday, you're mine."

I didn't reply, too scared it would involve his parents.

He must have sensed my nervousness, because he said, "Don't worry. It won't be near the castle. I just want to spend some time with you."

"Deal," I said enthusiastically, wrapping my arms around his neck.

He laughed while shaking his head.

"What?"

"You're really that scared of meeting my parents?"

"It's not like they are the neighbors, Lucian. Where I'm from kings and queens don't approve of girls like me, especially a dragon's offspring. It's going to take a miracle for them just to like me." I stared at the ground, not wanting to meet his gaze.

He lifted up my chin gently. "That's your opinion, sweetheart. They're going to love you. But if you're not ready, I can wait."

"So where are we going on Sunday?"

"It's a surprise," he said.

"Fine, I guess I'll just have to wait then."

He looked at his watch and a frown pulled at his face. "I really don't want to go home. I hate not being able to see you every day."

"It's only tomorrow, Lucian. Besides, next weekend you're staying here with me."

"It's not the same."

"You want some cheese with that whine?" I said, rolling my eyes.

"Ha, ha," he said, and kissed me one last time before we went back to the main building.

I said goodbye as he ran up the stairs to get his suitcase. I had to agree that it was hard for me to stay here while he went home.

When I got back to my room, Becky and Sammy at first didn't approve of Lucian's decision to let me go with Cheng, but by that evening, they came around and understood the reason I needed to go. Learning about Paegeia was the only way I was going to pass this year.

I crawled into bed contemplating whether I should ditch Cheng, but he really looked excited when I told him that I would love to go to Elm with him. I didn't want to disappoint him after everything he was doing to help me pass History.

"Don't fall for Cheng, please," Becky pleaded, and I giggled, thinking of how Lucian had also said something along those lines.

"He's so not my type, Becky."

"Goodnight, y'all," Sammy said, mimicking a Southern accent, and gave a huge yawn, effectively ending the conversation.

Becky ran to switch off the light and tripped over something, probably her saddle that was too big to be chucked into her cupboard like all the other things she owned. She cussed like crazy, and her dark silhouette hopped in one spot. Sammy and I tried very hard to suppress our laughter, but failed miserably.

We settled down not long after, and I started to drift away. I dreamed that night about the mysterious woman again. She kept pointing at the forest, and I wished I could ask her what the hell she wanted from me.

THE NEXT MORNING Cheng and I stood in front of a large brick building that had two huge stone dragons framing a gilded door. There was a warning written in big bold red letters demanding that everyone who entered must remain silent right at the entrance.

It looked like any other museum I had ever visited. Thick red carpet lined the path through the building, and a strong antique smell lingered inside. Parents pointed out objects to their children, whose eyes grew wide with wonder.

"Come, this is the starting point," Cheng whispered, and took the path closest to the entrance. The brass plate read VIKINGS in big golden letters. It reminded me a lot of the Madame Tussauds museum Dad had taken me to once.

Vikings carrying huge weapons were trapped behind glass, frozen in time. Most of them were big ogres with long beards and messed-up hair. Pantene would have done wonders in those days. A small description on another brass plate explained the era and the people who lived during the time. The activities they did mostly consisted of gathering food and making weapons to slay dragons.

"The Viking era is quite boring. The only thing they did was drink, eat, sleep, slay dragons, and have plenty of sex."

I giggled and blushed simultaneously.

"C'mon Elena, does the word sex bother you?" He bumped into my left shoulder.

Why does everyone keep bringing it up? I shook my head, feeling like an idiot.

The next exhibit displayed a badass dragon, and I couldn't figure out if we had covered it in Anatomy or not.

It was dark, a mixture between a red and a purple-black. Red eyes were set deep in its sockets and the dragon had huge nostrils that I imagined emitted fire. Thick catfish whiskers covered its whole head like fur, which really made it look like pure evil. Its tail resembled a big tree stump that had been whittled down into a spear end. Webbed feet and huge claws told me it was a swimmer, and wings that looked as if they had been shredded protruded from its back. Pointy, vicious talons were displayed on the edges of each wing and I couldn't make up my mind if it was beautiful, ugly, or just plain deadly.

"His name was Quito," Cheng whispered. "He was the Rubicon before Blake."

"That's the Rubicon?"

"One hell of an ugly bugger, isn't he? Only a mother can love that mutt," he joked. "The total opposite of his human form."

Right next to the dragon, a tiny figure reached up to his knee. The sign read that it was an average human male. Goose bumps made my skin crawl as I realized it was the human-dragon ratio.

"Does Blake look like that too?" I asked, thinking Lucian must be crazy to try to claim him.

"Not quite there yet, but he is the biggest of all the dragons at Dragonia. They grow bigger as they reach their milestones."

Milestones? It must be similar to birthdays.

"Where would I fit on him?"

"Oh, about up to here." He crouched and showed at least half the human figure's size.

"I'm so glad I'm not Lucian."

"Me too, but size isn't everything," he explained.

"Do you have a Dragonian?"

"Yes, his name is Andreas, but he's only ten years old."

"Ten years old?" I looked confused. That seemed too young to have a dragon.

He nodded and a huge smile lit up his eyes.

"How did you know he was your Dragonian?"

"A dragon knows."

We moved on. Knights with jousting sticks and wearing heavy armor came next. They even had Yorkshire and some of the Eastern Europe countries displayed with model dragons soaring through the air breathing fire down on unsuspecting villages.

Cheng sighed. "The Sun-Blast and Moon-Bolt made it really difficult for dragons to be considered tamable in the old world."

"You mean the world before the wall?"

"Ah-uh."

"How long has the wall been up now?"

"Oh, for the last nine hundred years," he explained.

"Did you ever visit the other side?"

"I really want to, but they say it's hard for a Metallic dragon to return. We like humans and feel more appreciated on the other side. It's the reason my mom's scared to give her consent," he explained.

"So your guardian has to give permission?"

He nodded.

"Until when?"

"Forever."

"That sucks," I said, and he chuckled.

"Yes, you humans have things so much easier."

"You humans? That's not nice," I said, teasing him.

"Elena, you know what I mean."

"I'm just joking with you, Cheng, and yes, I do know what you mean." I felt sorry for him, not having a chance to follow his heart without his mom's consent.

"After you." He showed me the way, and we moved to the next exhibition. It was some sort of obstacle course that reminded me of *First Knight*, a movie featuring Richard Gere and Sean Connery. Richard's character had to complete an obstacle course just to get a kiss from the lovely Guinevere. The obstacles were scaled down, and I gawked at the detail of the hammers sliding past one another and huge boulders crashing down. Logs with swinging balls attached to them rotated at very high speeds. Even the surface where the contestant walked to get through the obstacle was moving.

"It was entertainment in the old days," Cheng said.

I imagined me, super tiny, trying to get through in one piece. I was smashed by the two rocks colliding on top of each other.

The next exhibition was a cave. "The Sacred Cavern." The detail they used to display the replicas was amazing.

"What is it?"

"A cavern only the brave or the desperate will enter."

"To do what?"

"To retrieve the most prized possession in all of Paegeia —a millpond so magical that it can show you anything you wish to know. Whether it's past, present, or future, it will reveal all to whomever gazes into its surface."

I looked at him.

"It's not that easy though. The price is high. If you can't face whatever the cave is hiding, then it claims your life."

"Has anyone ever made it out alive?" I asked. I couldn't take my eyes off the detail. The million steps made me think of a Chinese temple. The steps led to huge doors molded into a cave, surrounded by a forest.

"Yes, but only a small number. The funny thing about it is that all of them were women."

I could feel another one of his theories coming, but had too many questions on my mind.

"What's inside?"

"Besides the millpond, no one knows. The five women that did make it out never revealed what they saw or did. No one knows why. It's very mysterious."

"Wow." I was fascinated by his story, but we had to keep moving.

As we moved further into the exhibition we came to a room that explained the sports that the knights used to compete at. Some were jousting on horses and the others were battling one on one. The last one looked like some sort of a team battle.

"It is said that all the soldiers were forced to compete to

keep them fit for war. In those times, the war was between your kind and mine," Cheng narrated.

"Humans can be so horrible," I said, moping. "Was it any different after the wall?"

"No. The only time things changed was when King Albert's father, King Louie, took over. He fell in love with a dragon, but never knew that she was one. They killed her in the end, but it also revealed one of our secrets, that we could take a human form. King Louie knew from then on that Metallic dragons posed no threat. When he became king, he studied the Metallic dragons and learned a lot from us. He discovered another secret, that we could be ridden. My mom said that these were exciting times, but he still killed a lot of the Chromatic dragons. It was only when King Albert claimed his dragon that things really changed for all of the dragons. He taught the others that the Chromatic ones weren't different from the Metallic ones. I know they look a little scarier and are a bit fiercer, but deep down inside, dragon is dragon."

"You guys really loved this king, huh?"

"More than you'll ever know. I wish you could have been here when they ruled. He believed that Chromatic dragons could be rehabilitated by getting the right nurturing. I guess it's why he started Dragonia."

We went through a few more individual exhibits. The first one was a blond guy with the most beautiful green eyes with a shade of blue around the iris. The era was right after the Vikings. I thought they were a bit more civilized, but still needed Pantene.

"King William," he announced. "He was the first blood-line of the royals. The sword he carries is none other than the King of Lion's sword." He smiled. "His queen was the fourth daughter of one of your French rulers." I looked at the woman standing next to him with dark hair. She almost resembled the woman in my dreams, but not entirely. The women before me had larger eyes, higher cheekbones, and thinner lips.

We kept walking and moved past a room featuring all the important figures that had been a part of King William's council. Surnames like McKenzie, Abbott, Johnson, and Smith had been there since the beginning. I wondered if some of them were Becky and Lucian's ancestors.

We exited King William's era and moved to a section that had to do with famous foretellings. The first figure was none other than the beautiful woman living in Rapunzel's tower. They weren't lifelike and some features were way off. The wax doll's eyes in the exhibition were incredibly warm and friendly. Hers weren't.

"Is she really three hundred years old?"

"Yes, still young for a dragon," he said.

"Was she always into foretellings?"

"Those days it was more like fortune-telling or cup-gazing."

"What, no crystal ball?"

He laughed. "I think hers is only used for decoration."

He went back to telling me the story about how humans used to seek out Moon-Bolts to tell them their futures, but that sometimes they didn't like what they heard so Moon-Bolts were killed for no reason.

There was a book on a wooden pedestal right next to her that some young girls were flipping through. I smiled. "Is there really stuff written in that book?" I asked, still skeptical.

"Elena, that book is the real deal."

22

W HEN THE GIRLS left their spot in front of the book, I took their place. On the first page was a single paragraph.

The leaves of change will come at last, when the fate of two hearts' bond is cast. Souls intertwined and hearts no longer torn, through their love Paegeia will once again be reborn.

"This is beautiful," I said after reading the paragraph.

"It's the Viden's very first words that came out of her mouth. We have no idea who it belongs too."

"Wait, it's some sort of a foretelling?"

Cheng nodded. "The most famous. A lot of couples, and lovers want it to be theirs but the words are still black, which means it's a love that hasn't come to existence yet."

"What do you think they will do?"

"Whatever it is, Elena. It's going to be the kind that will bring Paegeia peace for thousands of years to come."

I read it one last time before I started to flip through the pages, reading one foretelling after the other.

"Why are some of the sentences red and others blue?"

"The ones in red have already been fulfilled. The blue ones have expired without being fulfilled. The black ones like the one on the front page, well, they still haven't come to light."

Unbelievable.

My eye caught a red one as I flipped toward the middle. It belonged to a dragon and said that his Dragonian would be struck by lightning.

I showed Cheng and he smiled. "You think it's George's?"

"It's got to be. Becky was hit by lightning, and they forced her to claim George. The only thing is she feels his future isn't important enough and they could've let it slide," I said.

"Nothing written in this book is unimportant. Who knows, maybe a second part of that foretelling will come soon. It sounds as if a part is missing."

I smiled and kept paging through.

I found a foretelling about Blake. It was about his Dragonian. Although the text didn't use the exact words 'spawn of King Albert and Queen Catherine', it sure implied it. I frowned. "Why is this one still black?"

"That's the mystery. No one knows. It's the only thing that gives us hope," he said sadly.

I read further. Many were black and my mouth became dry.

"This one's new," Cheng said, and started reading the lines "A day will come and a day will go, a choice you have to make, otherwise the truth will never be known." He frowned and looked at it through squinted eyes.

"What does it mean?" I tried my best not to let my voice break.

"I have no idea, but if it's in this book, it's important."

I took a deep breath and tried to shake the creepy feeling off. Maybe it had nothing to do with me, and the Viden was seeing the foretelling about her next meeting. I had already been on my way out when she had said those words.

I closed the book and we moved on to the next exhibit.

It was about Master Longwei. The museum had both his forms on display—the human form as I knew him, and his dragon form. His scales were gold, and he had whiskers sprouting from his nose. If dragons smiled, Master Longwei definitely did the day they made this model. He looked beautiful and majestic, just like Dad had that night. It must be a Metallic thing.

The Renaissance era was boring.

King Alexander, King Louie's father, ruled Paegeia with the same cruelty toward dragons.

As I passed another display case, the two axes I'd practiced with a couple of days ago caught my eye.

How is this possible? I found myself in front of the display box as I read what the inscription on the brass plate said. The axes belonged to Queen Catherine and she had fought with them in three separate wars. She entered her first war at the age of eighteen, and the crusade was led by King Louie. I scrolled through the boring stuff. The second war in which she fought was at the age of twenty-three, and the third war she had fought at King Albert's side for the rights of the Chromatic dragons. The information on the brass plate said that it was the most important battle in the history of Paegeia. The war meant that all the dragons, Chromatic and Metallic, were to be seen as equals.

My favorite exhibition was the one that displayed all the dragons and their signs. The last sign belonged to the Rubicon. It looked complicated and in a league of its own. I tried to memorize the design and decided if I could draw it, I might be able to make a buck or two printing them on t-shirts.

"His sign is all the dragon signs combined," Cheng explained.

"Sorry?" I said as he shook me out of my get-rich scheme.

"Blake's sign. It's all the ten species signs combined. Come look here, they break it down for you." I followed him around the corner. "Here is the Fire-tail. The Copper-horn goes in this way. There's the Fin-Tail, and the Swallow Annex." He showed me where everything fit, like a puzzle. Blake carried all of them inside of him, even the Night Villain. I grabbed a leaflet that broke it down beautifully.

"He's really an unbelievable dragon," I said.

"Just a pity there's a time limit to his claim."

"Why is that?"

"His dark side. It's too powerful and you need to remember, Blake is only a carrier. Those powers don't belong to him. Without his Dragonian, it will become too heavy for him to bear." I frowned. If that was the case,

Cheng was right about Lucian not being able to claim Blake. My heart ached. I couldn't believe how emotional I became every time Cheng explained things about Blake I didn't know.

We moved on and found all the different species of the dragons displayed in smaller size models behind glass. Dragon eggs came first and they varied in size. Some looked like egg-shaped rocks that needed to be baked to hot temperatures, like the Sun-Blast and Fire-Tail. Some had little spotted dents that reminded me of a huge egg-shaped golf ball. Then there were eggs of different colors. One was a soft green. Another had a mixture of the rainbow melting into each other. They were all amazing.

As we left the egg room, a model of a full Snow dragon confronted me. It was the purest white I had ever seen. The tail reminded me of a crocodile's with strong hind legs, and its torso was covered with small, white, triangle-shaped scales. The front legs were not as big as the back legs, and the claws reminded me of an eagle's. Two wings sprouted from the back, and the neck arched a little with big scales covering it completely. The face looked like a dinosaur's, with long teeth and a sharp pointy nose.

The Green-Vapor and Sun-Blast I'd met the night Dad died, and I quickly walked by their models.

The Night Villain was the last dragon. It looked skeletal and its feet were webbed like the Rubicon's. Its face and wings were skinny and the flesh looked like it was pulled tightly over the skeleton-like features. Its overall appearance made me shiver right down to my core. It almost looked like it was busy decomposing where it was standing.

The Metallic dragons around another corner were simply magnificent. They all carried a posture with puffed-up chests and raised heads, and shimmery gold, silver, bronze, copper, and brass scales.

The section that explained what their skin could be used for brought a shiver up my spine. Most of the Metallic dragons were harvested for armor, whereas the Chromatic ones were slaughtered for their blood, guts, toes, and scales —the main ingredients for almost all the important potions. Dragon teeth were used for making weapons, but ever since metal had been discovered, the only purpose they held was as trophies.

A more civilized era greeted us in the next room. It began with large paintings of hulking castles. The one in Etan was the most enchanted; it looked as if fireflies made homes on the edges of the walls and rooftops. I stared at it for at least ten minutes, completely entranced.

"It's beautiful, isn't it?" he said.

"Does it still exist?"

"I don't know. I was only five when the creepers consumed Etan. If I did see it with my own eyes, well, but I remember it like it was yesterday." He closed his eyes.

"Such a pity," I spoke.

Etan was his hometown, and his dad was trapped there because his Dragonian had chosen to side with Goran. His father couldn't break their bond, but had made sure Cheng and his mother got out before it was too late. A longing grew in his eyes as he told me his story. It made me feel sad for him.

We moved on to another Night Villain. This one had a human figure right next to it. He had dark hair with honey-colored eyes and was handsome.

"Sir Robert," Cheng whispered.

I read the dragon's name on the brass plate. Right next to it was indicated that he was King Albert's dragon.

"This was *the* Night Villain King Albert claimed?"

"Yes." He smiled.

"Where is the queen's?"

"She had a Green-Vapor that believed she was a Crown-Tail."

I giggled.

"She wasn't into all this limelight stuff, so she didn't give her consent when they asked if they could make a model of her."

"You said "wasn't". Is she dead?"

"No. Her name is Tanya Le Frey. She carries a lot of the queen's secrets with her, and as you can imagine, a lot of people looked for her after the queen's death. Sir Robert went through the same scrutiny. The royal Council tortured him, thinking that he had something to do with the betrayal. They tried to look for her too, but she was already on the other side of the wall for almost a year. When she finally came back, she went into hiding, and even today, nobody knows where she is."

"You think she's still alive?"

"I don't know. She's definitely not on the other side."

"How do you know that, Cheng?"

"Because of what she is. To hide as a human is too difficult for Chromatic dragons. They don't share the same passions as our Metallic ones. I have to give it to her, she did manage to live two years on the other side. I would love to know what her business involved. A lot of people thought that she'd betrayed the queen from the other side of the realm, but even if she was a Chromatic dragon and a Green-Vapor, Tanya would have never betrayed Queen Catherine. They shared a sisterhood."

He spoke until we reached a temple. Cheng lit one of the thousand candles that were outside the two doors. He gestured that I should do the same.

I followed his lead.

"It's to pay respect. Some people come here to pray. Although they know the dead are in the spirit world, they still believe that God is always present where there are people that live by His Son's example. Remove your shoes, Elena."

I toed them off and waited for Cheng to enter first. I followed him and felt everything around me stop. I couldn't stop staring at the two figures sitting on their thrones.

A soft gasp left my mouth.

Cheng looked at me and smiled as he kneeled down to them, as if they were still alive. I did the same and was glad that he misunderstood my gasp. My heart beat inside my throat, which made it hard to swallow. It was the same feeling I experienced when I read that foretelling. When I looked up, she was still there, sitting next to him; the lady from my dreams.

A golden rope was the barrier between them and us. They both sat on their thrones, tall and proud as if they waited for something. She sat upright, very gracefully, and his pride shone in his erect posture. They didn't smile, and they looked unnatural.

"My mother said the crafters got almost everything right, except their faces—the eyes in particular. His were friendly, hers full of compassion," he said quietly. We bowed down once more before exiting.

My head pounded with questions as the tour went on, and Cheng led me through the last part of the museum.

I froze as I found the statue of Blake. It looked nothing like him really, except for his blue peacock eyes. A few teenagers who didn't attend Dragonia took pictures standing next to him, as if he was some sort of idol. I understood now why Blake didn't like the city very much.

More wax figures of kings and queens greeted us in the next room. Cheng told me that the first couple was Lucian's grandparents and the second couple Arianna's. He explained that Paegeia had been too big for King Louie to rule alone. With all the changes he wanted to make, he needed help and solved this by giving Tith and Areeth to his two most loyal knights.

I giggled softly as I saw a statue of Lucian standing

behind the throne of his parents. "The Royal Family of Tith" was printed in big golden letters on a brass plate. Lucian's mom had light brown hair with a tint of red, and his father looked a lot like him, except for the moustache.

"He never liked doing this. I have to give it to him, Elena, he's as knightly as they come. When he ascends, he'll make one heck of a Dragonian." A warm fuzzy feeling warmed my chest as Cheng's words of praise washed over me. "I have a feeling that someday you'll be here too."

"Now why would they put me in here? My brass plate would probably read something like 'The Dragonian with the Dragon Father'," I joked, laughing to myself.

"Or it could read, 'The Girl That Stole the Prince of Tith's Heart'."

I giggled. It was nice to hear that.

Next up was Arianna's figure. A huge smile reflect pearly white teeth. I assumed she hadn't been able to wait to have had a model made of her and had welcomed this opportunity with open arms. Even her family looked happy. She looked so friendly, which was the last thing Arianna, was. *She's capable of evil things.*

The last exhibit was a replica of the King of Lion sword. "The blade of Aegis" was written on the brass plate in front of the glass box that protected the sword. I had seen it in my Mysteries book on my very first day. Many of the kings and queens posed with it and Cheng mentioned that King William had killed the first Rubicon with it. After that he had carried it everywhere he went and so had King Alexander, Louie, and Albert. The sword was always close to them.

"Why isn't there a model of Goran?"

"He doesn't belong in the museum, Elena. He gave up that right when he slaughtered King Albert and Queen Catherine."

"Why do you think he did it?"

"Envy, who knows? He had no reason to be jealous, but he was anyway. I think it was his power that turned him evil. Before Sarafina, his dragon, died, she gave him a part of her essence. I think if a dragon gives you too much of their essence, the human body changes. Goran wanted more and everything after Sarafina died. People say that she gave him a lot of her essence. A couple months later he became consumed with greed, power, basically all the deadly sins there are and he just didn't care anymore."

"I like your theories, Cheng," I complimented him. He chuckled and his face turned red.

We spent the entire morning inside the museum and when we left, the sun was sitting high. I took a lot of leaflets stuffed with information to read later on. I had really enjoyed the tour.

He took me to the beach front where he bought two hot dogs and two sodas from a cart for us to eat.

I felt terrible because I didn't have any money but he just shrugged it off with a short wave of his hand.

We ended up strolling through the market as we ate. A variety of colorful people were offering T-shirts, necklaces, handmade clocks and other artifacts for sale. We stopped at one compartment where they had potions in little bottles for sale. The words "Truth Serum" and "Healing Tonic" grabbed my attention. I looked at the old lady with her long, thin red hair hanging over her shoulders. She looked like a Gypsy. Huge silver hoops dangled from her earlobes. She just kept staring at me so I gave her a small smile, which she returned with a crooked one. Cheng nudged me forward.

"What were you thinking of when we entered King Albert's chamber?" he asked.

"Nothing much," I lied. "I guess because it's the first time I finally got to see them. I didn't know what to expect. I've learned and heard so many great things about them that it was hard to imagine what they would look like, until now. You know there aren't many books in the library with their pictures."

"Yes, they weren't the type to parade in front of cameras. There are a lot of newspapers with articles about them in the library's archives, though. You should page through them if you want to get a clearer picture of what they really looked like."

I made a mental note to look through them once I had more time. "Why did you ask what I was thinking when I saw them?"

"Nothing major, it was just the way you gasped. As if you knew them," he said cryptically.

I smiled. "That's silly, Cheng."

"Yes, it's silly, but you know how much I love my theories."

Did Cheng see through my gasp?

Does he know that I'm dreaming about the queen? Why am I dreaming about her? Of all the women in Paegeia why her? Well I'm not going to tell anyone about that. They'll think that I believe in my mark and that I think I'm special or something because she showed up in my dreams. Whatever the reason, it's bound to start students asking questions that could invariably end up causing a lot more problems than what it's worth. I've had my fair share of dealing with problems too.

"What are you thinking about, Elena?" he said.

"I was just thinking about home, the other side of the wall." It wasn't a lie. I was sort of thinking about it.

"Do you miss it?"

"Except for my dad, no. It's weird how comfortable I feel on this side. I mean I never knew what friendship was before now. Here I have so many people looking out for me. It's nice, but sometimes I miss being alone. Do you know what I mean?"

He smiled knowingly. "If you want to call it a day, Elena, I won't mind."

"I didn't mean it like that, Cheng. I like spending time with you, and I'll put in a good word for you with Master Longwei about making you the new history professor."

He roared with laughter. It was so contagious that I joined in.

"Thanks for the compliment," he said when he finally stopped laughing.

He started asking me questions about New York and the Empire State building and my mind wandered back to my old life. That much I could tell him, because we'd lived everywhere in America. The Golden Gate Bridge was on his list of things to see too.

"Thank you, Cheng. Besides Lucian, you're one of the coolest guys that Master Longwei could've asked to tutor me."

"You're welcome, Elena. I'm happy just as long as you learn something."

On our trip back to the Academy, all the things I had learned started to swirl in my head. The queen was at the forefront. As if dreaming about her wasn't enough.

The nagging bit of information was the foretelling. *How could mine have appeared magically in the book? What was it I had to decide on? How would I know what the Viden mean by "if I don't the truth will never be known?" Could it have been about somebody else that she happened to receive while I was there?*

"What is it, Elena?" he asked as we reached the stairs of the dorms.

"Nothing," I said quickly.

"I can see there's a question burning inside of you."

"There is but it's not important."

He waited patiently for me to speak, crossing his arms so I would know he wasn't going to let it drop. I took a deep breath, knowing that Cheng might be the only person who would ever tell me the truth.

"Does the Viden sometimes make a foretelling that isn't meant for you?"

"What do you mean?"

I cringed and almost stopped, but decided what the heck. "When I met her for the first time, I didn't like her very much, I still don't. She's vain and only has nice things to say to her prodigies, like they're the only ones that matter. It's all a load of bull anyway. When I got up to leave, she said something. Could it have been meant for someone else?"

"Did the wind blow and her eyes light up?"

"You could say that," I said, trying my best not to give away that it was the one he'd read out loud at the museum.

"Yes, Elena. It was meant for you and only you," he said knowingly.

"Thanks, Cheng. That's all I wanted to know." I smiled and we said our goodbyes. I was tired when I reached the room, drained by today's trip and I fell on top of my bed. I was glad Becky and Sammy were still somewhere in Elm. I didn't have the energy to recap my trip with Cheng.

I was so frustrated I didn't have the answers. I wasn't desperate enough to crawl back to that awful hag and beg her to tell me what she'd meant.

I fell asleep only to be awoken by an over-excited Becky, who jumped on top of me.

"Wake up, sleepy head."

I growled into my pillow, but it didn't stop her bouncing.

"I hope your learning about the past is over now."

"Yes, and thank you, my lady, for giving me the time off to roam free," I joked, slowly raising my face from my pillow.

Sammy sat on the couch sucking on licorice and smiling at us.

"I've learned so much today about everything."

"That happens if you mix business with pleasure," Becky said.

"How was your day with George? I assume he was with you since he can't do anything without his Becky," I teased, trying to do an old British butler accent.

Sammy laughed.

"Ha, ha, funny, did a clown swim in your cereal this morning?" she said, glaring in my direction.

"Admit it, Becky, you dig George. You've always had this little crush on him ever since we started attending Dragonia." Sammy teased her too.

"Fine, so I like him. It was bound to happen since I'm forced to spend every single day with him." She crossed her arms in defense.

"There's nothing wrong with liking George, Becky. He has really changed, and hey, I even forgave him for the stupid prank."

"I forgot about that. I fell for a loser," Becky cried, and she fell backward on my bed.

"He's not a loser. I've got a feeling you're going to do great things together." I remembered Cheng's words when we found George's foretelling.

She rested on her one elbow. "You really think that?"

I nodded encouragingly.

"Thanks, Elena, you're so cool. Next time, you're coming with us."

We talked all night long about everything they did in Elm. When the main clock struck twelve, we called it a night and went to sleep. I couldn't wait for tomorrow. Lucian had sent Sammy a message telling me what time I should meet him.

As much as I wanted to put my questions aside and fall asleep, I couldn't. The Viden's words haunted me so much it made my head hurt. Not to mention the queen. Why did she appear in my dreams? I closed my eyes, and before I knew it, I was standing at the top of the hill once again.

23

THE NEXT MORNING I found Lucian waiting by a rented SUV. I ran straight into his arms and gave him the longest kiss ever.

"I hope you're done mixing business with pleasure," he said with his face buried in my nape. He opened the passenger door for me. "So, did you enjoy the museum?"

"Yes, especially the exhibit on you and your family," I teased.

His face turned red. "I hate that stupid thing. It took hours for them to get the measurements right, and they still did a crappy job."

I laughed excitedly. "So where are we going?"

"I told you it's a surprise, although not the one I had planned, but it will have to do." He started the SUV and music blared from the radio.

"I want to play you something, " he said, and took out a disc from a gray CD file and slid it into the player. The song had an upbeat rhythm, and I started bouncing in my seat. The lyrics were deep, and I got lost in them as I listened to the vocalist singing of a girl he hadn't found yet. He sounded lost.

Lucian smiled, and looked at me every five seconds through the corner of his eyes.

"What?" I asked, scared I had something in my hair or worse, my teeth.

"You know who that is?"

"Who? The guy singing?"

He nodded.

I listened again. "No, should I?"

A huge grin appeared on his face.

"C'mon, Elena, guess."

I giggled. "Is it you?"

He roared with contagious laughter. "Hell no. I can't keep a tune."

"Then who?" I knew I'd never heard this voice before.

"It's Blake."

My mouth dropped. "Get out! Really?"

"He has what it takes to make it big, but the council doesn't want to grant him permission to go for it, because he's the Rubicon. It doesn't stop him from doing a couple of gigs, though."

"Wow. Do you think he wrote this song for Tabitha?"

Lucian gave a chuckle I'd never heard before.

"What?"

"Elena, Blake only keeps Tabitha for one thing?"

"He's that shallow," I asked, disgusted.

He smiled again, but this time I could see sadness around the edges. "You still need to learn that Blake only does things for himself, no one else."

"Then who did he write this for?"

Lucian shrugged. "He recorded this about a year ago." His forehead crinkled in thought.

"You really miss him, don't you?"

He wrinkled his nose, not answering, as he gazed out the window on his side.

"So, what song did you play when you faced the big, mighty Rubicon?" I needed to change the topic. A huge grin spread over his face and lit up his eyes. He happily took out another CD.

"Blake once admitted that there was something about this song that scares the living crap out of him." The radio swallowed the CD, and his grin spread wider.

My eyes grew bigger as the song started. "You know AC/DC?"

"Elena, everybody knows AC/DC," he said, rolling his eyes.

I leaned back in my seat and closed my eyes, trying to imagine what Lucian looked like being introduced by "Thunderstruck". It gave me goosebumps.

"Wow." It slipped out as my image of him in gladiator gear exposed his muscular arms.

"What?"

"I can just imagine what it must be like. I'd be scared too if I was Blake."

He laughed and turned into a deserted parking lot. When the SUV stopped, he put on a baseball cap and shades.

"Just a precaution." He smiled and jumped out to open

my door. "You don't know what I had to do to pull off this surprise."

When we walked to the entrance, I saw that it was an art gallery. "You didn't?"

"I had to." He knocked three times on the glass doors.

A woman with a short bob opened the door. She wore a soft gray suit with a white satin blouse completely covering her neck.

"Good morning, your Highness," she greeted Lucian.

I suppressed my giggle.

"Maggie," he muttered.

"You must be Elena. I'm Maggie and this is my art gallery. Welcome."

The gallery was empty, besides us and the masterpieces on the wall.

We followed Maggie from painting to painting as she explained more about the pieces and the artists. Suddenly I missed Dad again. He had promised me that one day we would go to an art gallery, but we had never gotten around to it.

A painting in the corner caught my eye. It was a pencil sketch of a woman sitting against a tree. The artist had done an amazing job. Her face and eyes carried a deep sadness in them that made my heart ache.

"This is a portrait done by Renaldo Aramiz; the woman in the picture is none other than Queen Catherine."

Lucian and I both gasped.

"Are you serious?" he asked, and she nodded.

"It doesn't look anything like her."

"It's not supposed to either. She was merely the inspiration," Maggie said simply.

"Was she really so sad?" he asked.

"It was the year before she died," Maggie said. Cheng's story of Tanya leaving her jumped to my mind. The queen must have struggled with losing her dragon sister.

Lucian touched the lines that formed the queen's face, as if he wanted to wipe away an invisible tear. "How much?"

"It's not for sale, Lucian."

"Are you sure about that?" He smiled.

She grinned back with soft eyes. "That smile won't work on me. I'll never sell it."

"Elena's an artist too." Lucian said.

She looked at me with slightly raised eyebrows and a Julia Roberts smile. "You should show me one day," she said.

"They're not that great." I pointed to the picture of the queen.

Lucian glared at me. Clearly he didn't like the way I sold myself short.

A bright flash reflected on the colors of the next painting as we made our way over to it. It almost made the leaves on the trees come to life. Lucian jolted his head back when more flashes bounced off the walls. He yanked me back behind a pillar, pulled off his leather jacket, and threw it over my head. Maggie froze on one spot, staring with huge eyes at the front door.

My heart beat fast. "What is it?"

Lucian ignored my question. The light overpowered the gallery and people were yelling Lucian's name.

His jaw muscles clenched and his eyes hardened. It almost made him look like a dragon. "Who did you tell, Maggie?"

"Lucian, I promise I didn't say one word." She spoke fast and she sounded just as shocked.

He took a deep breath. "Just wait here okay. I'm so sorry, Elena."

I just nodded, not really knowing what was happening and feeling as if my heart was going to explode with the tempo it beat in my chest.

"I'm going to kill the person that leaked this," Maggie said.

"Are those people from the press?" My voice broke on the last word and I cleared my throat.

"Yes, Elena. He really didn't plan on this."

"Can we wait them out?" Images of them trampling over us to get clear shots jumped inside my head.

She huffed. "If it was another celebrity, maybe, but Lucian McKenzie? No way."

I closed my eyes and wished I could disappear. I wasn't good with handling big crowds, especially ones with cameras. "Is this going to be in the newspapers tomorrow?"

"Sweetheart, it's the prince of Tith. It's going to be in every magazine."

Lucian came back. "I'm so sorry, Elena. Welcome to my world."

I felt sorry for him if this was what his life felt like. "What are we going to do?"

"We can wait it out, but they're not going to leave. By the next hour, the crowd will have multiplied and who knows what it could look like in in three hours. They know that I'm in here with you and will wait until you come out, even if it takes three days."

I swallowed hard while my stomach took a few turns. An image of me hurling in front of cameras jumped into my mind.

"Honey, the way I see it is, give the ones out there what they want and get the hell out before more arrive," Maggie said.

I closed my eyes, not knowing how I would be able to walk out of here. I was nervous.

"Here." Lucian gave me his shades that were way too big for me and pulled the hood of his leather jacket over my head. "We walk out when security arrives. Don't say a word, Elena; we might be able to hide your identity." He glared at Maggie again.

"I won't say anything, Lucian."

"Nobody else knows her name except you. Don't get any ideas, Maggie!" he warned.

She locked her mouth with an imaginary key. Three hard knocks on the door made me jump.

"It's just security. Are you ready?" he croaked.

I nodded.

"Not a word, Elena, and keep your head down."

I did what he said and kept my eyes on the ground, while clinging to his hand.

He opened the door and the first thing I heard was the security men speaking over their radios using codes.

"Prince Lucian, what's her name?" one reporter shouted.

"Are you a couple?" another yelled.

I didn't know what he did, as no sound came from his lips. Everybody yelled questions as security tried to lead us back to the SUV. I allowed Lucian to guide the way as I stared at the ground. My heart bounced with the rhythm of a thousand flashlights. *How could Lucian handle this kind of attention?*

We finally reached the SUV, and he helped me inside.

"Sorry about this," he whispered in my ear. "Just keep your head down."

I smiled as he closed the door.

Don't look up, Elena. I waited for him to get in the driver's seat.

When his door opened, more flashing lights assaulted us. The security men asked the paparazzi to back away from the vehicle, but it didn't look as if it was working.

Lucian revved the engine and reversed out of the parking lot. I was glad the windows were tinted, but the photographers didn't care; they still took pictures like crazy.

"It's fine, you can look now. Are you okay?" he asked, sounding the way I felt.

I lifted up my head to look at him. "Yeah, are those pictures going to be in all the magazines?"

"I'm so sorry, Elena. I should've thought twice about today's trip. I'm so naive when it comes to people keeping their mouths shut," he said through clenched teeth.

"Is it like this every time you go outside?"

He chuckled. "Pretty much. Sometimes I get away with hiding behind my disguise."

Lucian honked for the two bikes in front of us. They saluted him and turned in the opposite direction at the stop sign. He floored the SUV, and we were back at Dragonia in no time. We kissed goodbye at the stairs until someone close by cleared his throat.

It was another student, and he didn't look very happy. "Master Longwei wants to see you in his office."

"Thank you, Stan," Lucian said, and the guy ran off. "Don't worry, he probably wants to know what happened. It's not a scolding. Go take a hot bath and I'll see you at dinner, okay?"

I did what he said and sighed as I slid into a hot bubble bath. When Becky and Sammy returned from their day out, I told them what had happened.

"Are you okay?" Becky asked. We sat on the couches, each having a Coke. The sugar helped as it entered my bloodstream.

"Taking a bath seemed to work." My heart beat at a high tempo as I told them everything.

"Elena?" Sammy put her arm around my shoulder.

"It's going to be in every newspaper and every maga-zine, you guys. I don't want to even think about what his parents are going to say. Not to mention what they will do."

"Well, if Lucian didn't tell his dad about you, I guess they're going to find out the hard way. I'm so glad that I'm not Lucian," Becky said.

"Becky!" Sammy glared at her.

"What?"

Sammy rolled her eyes.

"Will he get into trouble?" I tried to ignore Becky's remark.

"We'll have to wait and see," Becky said, and eyed Sammy again with a huge question in her eyes.

Sammy shook her head. "Remember what you said to me? Everything happens for a reason. We just need a little bit of faith."

"Thanks you guys," I said, feeling a bit better.

We talked about their day and how goofy George acted around Becky, who was gloating.

At six, we went to dinner. I didn't speak much. The images of King Helmut forcing Lucian to break up with me played over in my mind. Lucian kept stroking my back, and every ten minutes or so, he kissed me on my shoulder.

Lucian started to tell them about the gallery and the queen's painting.

"I'm sure it's a first date Elena will never forget," Becky teased.

I couldn't help but smile. "You got that one right."

Around eight, we walked slowly back to our dorms.

"Elena, meet me tonight?" Lucian whispered in my ear. I gave him a frantic look, thinking that we'd had enough drama for one day, not to mention what happened the last time we sneaked out at night.

He chuckled softly. "We won't go to the lake."

"What if we get caught? Master Longwei will chuck my ass out of this place."

He raised one eyebrow. "With a mark as dark as yours, I doubt it. I'll wait for you by the door around twelve." He cocked his head indicating the big wooden one to our left.

"Fine, but if we get caught, I'll blame everything on you."

"It's a blame I'll take with pleasure," he said through a smile. "Goodnight, my Juliet."

I blushed as I climbed the stairs and giggled at how goofy he sounded. Some of the boys teased him about his last line, but he didn't seem to care.

We'd barely made it to the room when the most horrible sound wailed inside my ears.

24

I T WAS A loud siren that had a strong sense of foreboding connected to it. The sound made me clutch my ears as if they were going to fall off. Becky and Sammy looked at each other with huge eyes. That wasn't a good sign.

We ran out of the room as students descended from the stairs around us.

"What's going on?" Becky asked one of the girls.

"We all need to go to the auditorium," a girl with a red prefect badge on her blazer said, and moved with the crowd.

Becky grabbed my wrist and pulled me down the stairs behind her. It felt like it took forever to reach the lobby, not to mention getting to the auditorium.

Students poured through the doors on both sides. Becky led me to a seat in the back row and plopped me down hard. She looked around, frantic, standing on the tips of her toes. Everybody around us had frantic expressions, and some of the girls even cried.

George spun Becky around, and she started to kiss him like crazy.

"Do you know what's happening?" I asked George, who had his arms still wrapped around Becky.

"It's not good, Elena." He spoke in a fast, tight voice.

A cold shiver ran up my spine as I tried to think about the reasons behind that horrible siren.

"The last time they sounded the alarm was the night the king and queen died," Sammy said.

"What?"

Lucian finally reached us, pulled me from my chair and hugged me tightly. I really hoped it didn't have anything to do with his parents. His heart was pounding as I laid my head against his chest.

"Do you know what's going on?" Becky asked.

I looked up to hear his answer, but he just shook his head. His grave expression didn't suit him. He was the bravest guy I knew. It wasn't a good sign if Lucian was scared too.

The auditorium was almost filled with students, and everyone around us wanted to know the same thing. What the heck was going on?

Master Longwei came in, and I didn't like the look on his face. His eyes looked dark and his lips were pressed together in a thin line. He had a huge crease on his forehead. Everyone started to settle down as he ran up the podium's stairs.

"The King of Lion sword has been stolen." Master Longwei blurted over a microphone. Thick silence saturated the auditorium. Then the room filled with noise, as most of the students started to cry out in panic, yelling questions of how, when, and what now?

"This isn't good." Lucian spoke first and rubbed his face

with his free hand.

"How could it be stolen?" Becky asked, fear lacing her tone.

"Silence!" Master Longwei's voice roared and the sound bounced off the walls. "There is no reason to panic yet. Members of the Royal Council are searching for it as we speak. However, we have to keep guard for any sign of danger. Dragonia will be one of the first places they attack if this is war."

"Typical," George uttered.

"Should that news make us feel better?" I asked Lucian as Master Longwei carried on speaking about the plan of action. He just squeezed my hand with a terrified look.

"We will have the groups up in place first thing tomorrow morning," Master Longwei said, and then he called out names I hadn't heard before. Blake and Lucian were the last of the five names, and they were ordered to meet him in his office.

Lucian kissed me goodbye. "I'll tell you what I know, okay?"

I nodded and felt like crying as I watched him disappear through the ocean of students trying to make their way out of the auditorium.

We went to the cafeteria to analyze all of this, finding it difficult to process in all the chaos.

"Who would've stolen it?" I asked harshly, not yet in control of my emotions.

"It could only be one person, Elena." George said. "Goran." He got up to get us each a soda.

"Goran!" I said. "But he's locked up behind Etan."

"It doesn't mean he can't compel someone's mind. He did it before," Becky said.

George came back with four sodas. He handed us each a Coke.

"So the sword is now with him?" I wanted to know, and she lifted her shoulders, not knowing the answer to my question.

Sammy took a big sip of her Coke. "I hope it still exists."

"Exists? You mean he's going to destroy it?" I asked.

She nodded solemnly. Cheng had told me about it during our first History lesson.

"With the sword out of the way, there's no stopping him if he manages to break out of Etan. He'll destroy the wall and Paegeia with it." George took a few gulps from his can, his hand shaking slightly.

My throat tightened as he said the word "destroy" and I struggled to swallow.

"Relax, Elena, they'll find whoever took it," Becky said and squeezed my arm reassuringly.

I waited for Lucian, wishing he would come back. It felt like hours before he plunged onto the pillow next to me.

He gave me a quick kiss on my temple while wrapping his arms tightly around my shoulders. "They stole it some-where between midnight and four a.m. yesterday. The council didn't want to say anything, because they thought they would've retrieved it by now. If they don't find it soon, we're going to be in serious shit. They believe that Goran has found a way to break out of Etan, but won't do it until the sword is destroyed."

"So what, the council's really searching for it?" Becky asked.

"My dad and Arianna's have sent out a small search party."

"We just have to wait?" I was skeptical, just like Becky.

"It's the only thing that we can do, Elena."

"If they destroy that sword, Lucian—"

"Shhh, don't think like that. It won't happen. Master Longwei is with the Viden now to draw up the groups that will guard the school. We'll have to be on watch seven days a week, twenty-four hours a day. Not that it will take that long, I hope."

"Until it's found? Are they crazy?"

"Don't worry, Elena, you won't be alone."

For some reason that didn't make me feel safe. I wanted a better plan.

"You're safe here, you won't be alone," he said again as if I hadn't heard him the first time.

"Will we be together?"

He shrugged. "We don't know which team we'll be divided into. That decision is left up to the Viden."

I jumped from my pillow. "They're relying on a woman that sucks everything out of her thumb?" It angered me that everyone thought so highly of what she had to say.

"Calm down, Elena." Lucian got up too and gave me another hug. "It's going to be fine. I promise nobody will hurt you."

I sighed heavily. I'd never felt so scared in my entire life, and believe me, I had been through some pretty frightening things with Dad, always running away from place to place.

I struggled to fall asleep that night, tossing and turning before finally dozing off around three a.m.

A DOZEN OR SO white sheets were tacked on the announcement board the following morning. Students stormed to the wall in a wave. All the students of Dragonia would be divided into five groups, with two on a team, and about forty teams in a group, if not more. Lucian's explanation was thorough. There had to be guards at all the main entry points of Dragonia, as well as around the school at all times. It sounded scary thinking that we had to watch for any kind of danger. With my luck, I would end up with someone like Tabitha, who would flee at every sound.

One girl glared at me as she stormed off in the direction of the main building. I didn't pay attention to her until some other girls did the same. Some even started to point in my direction. *Oh crap what now?*

I was about to ask Lucian if I was imagining things, but he saw it already.

"What's going on?"

"I don't know. I'll go find out," he said, and ran to the wall. He came back after fifteen minutes.

"Sammy, you're with Dean and in Lionel's group," he said.

She pulled her mouth in a snarl.

"Becky, you and George are in mine." He didn't say anything about me.

"I'm not in yours?" I asked.

"Calm down. You'll be fine. You're in Blake's group."

"With who, Lucian?"

He looked away.

"Lucian, with who?"

"You're with Blake."

We were all speechless for a few seconds as we digested this new information.

"She's with Blake?" Becky asked.

"I can't be with him in a group!"

"Elena, it's not going to help to protest. The Viden makes the decisions. You're wasting your time if you think Master Longwei is going to listen to you."

"I can't be on guard with Blake!" My voice for rising in volume.

"You have no choice. You're safe with him."

"Who's with you?"

"Tabitha," he said through clenched teeth.

"The Snow dragon." I pursed my lips as a picture of the two of them together jumped inside my head.

Lucian chuckled. "Are you jealous?"

"Don't."

"Come here?" He grabbed my shirt and pulled me closer. "Does it help if I told you that I don't even like her?"

It worked and I smiled. "I don't want to be in stupid Blake's group or have him as my guarding partner."

"Well, I don't think it's fair that Tabitha is mine either." He smiled as he pressed his forehead to mine.

"There's something wrong with the Viden, I swear it," I growled.

Master Longwei's voice came through the school's system. We quickly dispersed as he ordered us to go to our rooms and wait for further instructions.

THEY DECLARED SCHOOL was out until further notice. We were all stuck on guard duty until the sword was found.

The ambience around the school changed drastically during the next two days. Lucian's group was first. I was worried sick about him, because they were assigned to guard the main gate during the night. Blake chose the exact same spot when it was our turn on the third night. Lucian explained that Blake was most alert during the night, choosing the best post to guard. As if the enemy was going to attack the main entrance.

I slept most of the day when my turn came up. Lucian came with me. He walked me to the main gate and said goodbye while Master Longwei was talking to Blake, who was already waiting at his post. I hated that spot.

Lucian's watch beeped, and I knew it was nine. I was so not looking forward to this at all. To stay awake for nine hours when you're supposed to be asleep was not cool. Not to mention I had to do it with Blake.

"Just relax. Blake's one of the best dragons in Paegeia, not just Dragonia," Lucian assured me. "And if he transforms, don't freak out."

I'd only seen a Rubicon in the museum, and he was huge. I couldn't imagine what Blake's dragon form looked like for real.

He kissed me as Master Longwei passed. He teased Lucian and me, and I blushed a deep scarlet.

A knot formed in my throat as Lucian winked and let go of my hand. We looked at each other until the door closed. The click of the lock made my heart beat a bit faster, and I sulked to my post where Blake waited.

"Hey," I greeted him.

He didn't say anything, as he stared intently into the night.

I made myself comfortable by a small fire in front of the stone dragons. Cheng had told me in one of his lessons how they would come to life in times of danger. The idea still creeped me out, but at the moment, I didn't care. I felt safer here than on the edge, looking down on the forest and part of Elm.

All sorts of things flew through my mind as I stared into the embers. My biggest concern was what they would do if the sword was destroyed. If its existence could defeat an evil sorcerer like Goran, then that sword was mighty powerful and our only hope of keeping Paegeia peaceful. Skyscrapers burning down and tumbling to the ground, turning Paegeia into ruins, took the sword's place in my mind's eye. The picture wasn't a beautiful one, and I couldn't see myself living in a world like that.

My other concern revolved around Goran's power. Cheng had told me in one of his lectures that his magic was advanced, which made him one of the best sorcerers who had ever lived. What if Becky was right and he knew how to destroy the wall? What would happen then? Humans would know that dragons existed.

That couldn't materialize. Deep down in my heart I was begging for that siren to go off, announcing the sword's safe return.

As I sat there thinking, Blake spoke for the first time. "There's coffee in the flask when you feel tired."

I looked at my watch. It was just after ten. "No thanks, I'm fine." I stared into the night too. A million stars sparkled in the sky above our heads.

"It's the perfect night to watch," he said. "I hope you don't mind me choosing this time."

As if I had a choice.

I lay with my head on my arms. If I didn't know any better, I could've sworn that he tried to make some sort of conversation. I looked at him from underneath my pathetic excuse for eyelashes, and my heart started to beat a little faster. Why did he have to be so beautiful?

"I guess I understand why you chose it." I cleared my throat. "Your senses are most alert at night, right?" I decided to be nice and make the best of the terrible situation.

"Something like that," he mumbled, and smiled. He should smile more. It fell silent, and the stone dragon started to freak me out again. I didn't know if it was just me, but I could swear that I saw them move. "Will they wake?" I asked.

"Who, the stone dragons?" He smiled. "They are not like Grimdoe, and these got no reason to. To be honest, I think it's just an old wives' tale told to get naughty children to go to sleep."

"With the sword missing, they've got all the reason in the world to be awake."

He huffed and shrugged at the same time, as if standing guard or finding the sword wasn't of any importance. He glanced over his shoulder and took a packet out his pocket.

"You smoke!" I said a bit too loud.

"Shhh, Elena," he snapped back, and blew gently over the tip of the cigarette.

I gasped as his breath set it on fire. He took a drag, and the end changed from orange to a burning red coal. He puffed the smoke in my direction. I coughed while fanning the smoke away with my one hand. It smelled disgusting, and I glared at him.

The next few hours were boring. Blake stopped speaking but kept on smoking. I didn't like it, because it made me think about worst-case scenarios. My worries grew as my thoughts kept circling. It was the fourth day, and the sword was still missing. What chance did they have of finding its location? The only excitement I had was around three, as I tried my best to stay awake. My eyes burned painfully, and I felt as if I hadn't slept for two days.

Around six, Master Longwei came with the next shift to relieve us. It was two guys from James's group; at least I thought that was his name. I didn't even say good morning or goodbye, and went straight to my dorm where I crawled into bed.

I slept till about two and went to the cafeteria for lunch. Lucian was waiting for me with a strong cup of coffee. He was so perfect.

"So how was last night?" Concern in his tone made his voice break at the end, and he swallowed hard.

What did he think? That something miraculous would happen, and I would be BFFs with Blake now?

"Nothing much. I now understand the meaning of grave-yard shift, and can tell you that I hated every minute of it. It's so boring."

"I know what you mean. You're lucky you don't have a

nagging partner that wants to flee at every stupid little sound."

I giggled. "Did they find anything while I was asleep?"

"Nothing yet," he said dully.

I sighed as the image of a flaming city jumped into my mind again.

"Hey, come here?" He pulled me closer and hugged me tightly. "I told you nothing will ever happen to you."

"Lucian, what if—"

He put his index finger over my lips, silencing me. "Don't, Elena. Let me worry about the 'what ifs', okay."

I nodded carefully.

He tried so hard to put me at ease but failed miserably. The sword was the only thing I could think of.

The rest of the week went fast. Around the sixth day, they still had no leads as to where the sword might be hidden. It freaked me out. I didn't like how my mind worked when I was nervous, and one thing constantly dwelled on my mind: the Sacred Cavern.

THE ROYAL COUNCIL is never going to find it, Becky," Sammy said in a terrifying tone one morning at breakfast. "They don't even know where to look."

I was glad Lucian had guarded the entrance last night and was still in bed. He didn't like to talk about the 'what ifs'.

The thought of the Sacred Cavern still lingered, but the strange part about it this time was that it didn't scare me anymore. The scary part vanished the minute my foretelling found a way into all this mess.

The Viden did say that I had to make a choice. What if this was that choice? I got a warm fuzzy feeling inside my heart encouraging me, and somehow I knew I was on the right track. This was what she meant. I was sure of it. The only thing that still confused me was the truth part, but something told me it was about my father being a dragon, and that the offspring of a dragon can't be worthy of the Dragonian mark.

Finding the King of Lion sword would prove that, as well as change the Viden's mind about me forever. Not that I wanted anything to do with her anyway. The choice wasn't an easy one to make and I could feel how the corners of my lips twitched slightly as I pondered my choices.

The more I thought about it, the clearer it became. This was my destiny. The only way to find the location of the sword was to go to the Sacred Cavern.

25

I NEED TO FIND *a way to complete whatever obstacles were hiding inside the cavern, to get the reward: a look into the magical mill pond.* Cheng said that it could reveal our innermost wishes and desires, whether present, past, or future. I would find the sword's location, even though I didn't know for certain if it still existed.

I remembered that only five people, mostly women, made it out alive. That part kept me from running straight to the cavern that very instant. Not knowing what hid inside the caves scared the living hell out of me. I knew it wouldn't be easy, but then again, when did I ever have things easy? That wasn't about to change anytime soon. The thing was that nobody else did anything besides guard the Academy.

I thought again about what Goran would do once he broke out of Etan. If he destroyed Paegeia and the wall, the humans would come, and the dragons wouldn't stand a chance. It would end in a war and be the end of my new home. With that thought imprinted on my mind, death didn't sound like such a big sacrifice anymore. I would rather die than watch my biggest fear come to life.

For the next few days, I read up on everything that had to do with the Sacred Cavern. Cheng must have found his information in these books and articles, so I kept looking. Most of the stories said that it was impossible to make it out of the cavern, but the queen and four other women had. Could this be why she'd appeared inside my dreams? Could she have been pointing to the Sacred Cavern?

For some reason, everything was starting to make sense. Why I dreamed about the queen, and what the Viden's words meant. This was my destiny. I was the one meant to find the sword.

I read through the article again, waiting for something else to pop inside my head. The words "young women" caught my eye. Why were there only young women who made it out alive? I researched everything I could find on young women and ended up reading about maidens. In those times, maidens held a different meaning than they did today. Paegeia's dictionary read, "Maiden: a woman with her virtue still intact."

A virgin? For the love of blueberries, the ones that made it out were all virgins!

Something Becky said to me the first time she discovered that I was still intact jumped to my mind. It was about Brian. My fingers flashed across the keys, and I hit the search button the minute the word "Fire-Blast" was typed.

Articles about Fire-Blasts appeared on pages and pages in front of me. It contained everything I needed to know about these dragons. Sites of how bad they really were hit my attention, and I clicked on the link. Pictures of young girls appeared staked against a pole, naked with a Fire-Blast leaning over them; all held fear on their faces. The scene jolted through me and I shivered. I got a funny feeling that a Fire-Blast guarded the millpond. It made sense why others didn't make it out. *That had to be it.* I found a map detailing how to get to the Sacred Cavern on another site. It didn't look that far, but then again, I was no expert when it came to reading maps. My other concern was how to get there. They had bus schedules, but that cost money, money I didn't have.

On the fourteenth day, the night after my third guarding duty, I went back to searching more about the Sacred Cavern. I found a number of really good books, and it took me a few hours to page through all of them.

I took the book that contained the most information about the Sacred Cavern and went back to my room. Cheng really did have good theories. I laid the book over my chest after reading the last paragraph and closed my eyes. There were still some things I needed before I could even think of leaving Dragonia, things I had no idea where to get.

I made up my mind that I would take Ginger. I had ridden her once, well with Lucian on the trails, but how difficult could riding a horse be? It would have to be on a horse. I really needed a few bucks, but who to ask? Master Longwei would want a valid explanation. Lucian was the other source of income, but he would ask exactly the same thing. I didn't know a single person who wouldn't question my intent. I was screwed.

My head pounded as I laid out my plans.

"Elena, what are you doing with that book?" Becky snatched it from my chest. I hadn't even heard the two of them come in. She read from the open pages and her eyes filled with concern.

"Nothing, I just wanted to read up on something," I said as I cleared my throat.

She raised one eyebrow as if she could see right through me.

"The Sacred Cavern? What on earth is going on in that mind of yours? Why are you reading this?"

My upper lip twitched slightly. I really sucked at lying.

She flipped the book closed and her eyes widened. She gasped and froze as understanding washed over her face. "Have you lost your mind?"

"Becky, it's more than two weeks. They haven't found the sword yet. Think about it, the Sacred Cavern holds the only thing that can make us see anything we want to," I said.

"Elena, people disappear in that cave."

"Five didn't." I showed her with my fingers and motioned for her to return the book. "Look." I pointed with my index finger at the five women who had made it out alive.

"These people were raised in Paegeia. No, let the council find the sword!" she yelled.

"Becky, are you blind?" I snapped. "They're not going to find it. They don't even have any clue about where it might be."

"Elena, you're only sixteen, think, please." She was adamant, but so was I.

"No, I've made up my mind."

"What's wrong with you, Elena? Have you really lost your marbles? What are we supposed to do if you don't come back?" Sammy's eyes sparkling with tears.

"What are you afraid of?" I yelled at both of them, shaking my head in disbelief.

"Elena, you don't know how dangerous it is." Becky pleaded this time in a softer voice.

"I don't care, Becky. Something tells me if we don't find the sword, things will get a lot worse."

"Then you don't give me much of a choice," she said, and left. I ran after her, thinking of what a coward she was being by bringing Master Longwei into this, but when she changed her course and headed toward the cafeteria, I frowned.

"Where are you going?"

She ignored my question. I followed her into the library and saw her heading straight to where Lucian sat quietly reading.

I huffed.

She leaned on the table to speak to him softly.

I turned around and left to go back to the room. I didn't care if she told Lucian about my plan, just as long as it wasn't Master Longwei. I got ready to run up the stairs when someone yanked me back and pushed me to the side of the stairs.

"Is this true?" he growled, and looked straight into my eyes.

I looked around me for other students but found none. "Lucian, please, I'm not going to stand here and wait while the sword gets destroyed."

"Elena, the Sacred Cavern? People don't come back," he said through gritted teeth. He sounded the same as Becky had a few minutes ago.

"The queen did, Lucian. There's no other way."

"No," he ordered.

"No?" I said, surprised. *A few kisses and he thinks he owns me.*

"I said no. It's too dangerous, and not to mention how stupid it is."

His words pissed me off even more, and he would learn how much, right now. I was sure about my fore-telling. "You aren't the boss of me, Lucian McKenzie. I'll decide how dangerous it is. Besides, none of you knows what danger really means or what will happen if the sword is destroyed. You think your worst enemy is Goran and what he'll do to you once he frees himself of Etan. Try imagining what will happen once that wall disappears. Your precious dragons won't stand a chance against the other side. The people living on that side don't listen to anyone, and they have the weapons to destroy and incinerate countries like this one. So don't you dare tell me no."

I made sure that every word counted before I pushed him away. Becky and Lucian fell silent, and I hoped I'd left them with something to think about.

When I entered the room again, Sammy was gone. I hadn't seen her with them, but at the moment, it didn't matter if she was with them.

An hour later, the door opened and Lucian, Becky, and Sammy entered.

I pretended to read, trying to prepare myself for my trip. To be honest, the words might have swirled around on the page, because I had no clue what I'd read this past hour.

I knew it scared the living crap out of them, and maybe I should be frightened too, but there wasn't time for that. The humans would destroy every single dragon if the wall was destroyed.

Lucian knelt down in front of me and placed his hand on my knee.

I glared at him for a second and slowly put the book off to the side.

"Elena, please don't do this," he pleaded.

"Lucian, I meant what I said. I can't live my life in fear anymore. If the sword is the only weapon that can protect us from all evil, then we have to get it back. Why am I the only one considering this?" I yelled at all three of them. "Paegeia is your birthplace, for crying out loud!"

Becky and Sammy lowered their eyes and stared at the

floor. Lucian closed his eyes for a moment before taking a deep breath.

"Elena, what you're thinking of doing is suicidal."

"Do you have a better plan, Lucian?"

He shook his head.

"Then the cavern is our only hope," I said.

26

"KAY, FINE, ON one condition, I'm coming with you," Lucian said, crossing his arms over his chest, daring me to argue. My heart flipped. I'd been hoping for that, and now that he'd said it, I was instantly relieved that someone was going to come with me on this crazy quest.

"Lucian, are you insane too? You're supposed to talk her out of this!" Becky shouted, clearly agitated once again.

"She's made up her mind. There's no way to talk her out of this." His one hand stroked his head methodically.

"You're both nuts!" Becky picked up her jacket and headed for the door.

"What're you so afraid of? You of all people should be backing me up, Becky." I could feel my nostrils flare. I was furious that she wouldn't even consider my plan.

She spun around angrily. "What's that supposed to mean?"

"You really think that you're just going to waltz into the Royal Council and tell them, 'Hey, I want to be a member', and they'll give it to you? You have to earn it. This mission will help you live up to that dream. So if you're really serious about that dream of yours, you have to pursue it while you can. If Goran finds a way out of there—"

"I heard you the first time, Elena! He'll destroy us all!" She sounded beyond pissed off. Clearly I had struck a nerve. "Fine, I'm in, but you're all insane."

We flinched as Becky slammed the door behind her.

"I'm in too," Sammy said resolutely.

"Okay." I sighed, not wanting to fight anymore. Fighting was really exhausting.

"So what's the plan? We have to get more than one dragon onboard if we want to pursue this mission." Lucian took a deep breath.

"What? Why?" I asked, confused.

"It's a long trip. The Sacred Cavern is northeast from Tith. It'll take us at least half a day traveling on top of one."

My shoulders slouched in disappointment. I hadn't thought it was that far, and dragons were my last choice when it came to transportation. I couldn't even consider what it would be like on top of one. The image of landscapes flashing by underneath me made my knees tremble.

"George has no choice. He'll follow Becky," Sammy said softly. She looked scared and swallowed hard. This was followed by a couple of deep breaths, and she started to look uncertain.

I didn't care if they doubted my plan. Deep down, I knew it was the right thing to do.

"You told Blake about this?" Lucian's arms were folded. He still looked pissed.

"No, he'll tell Master Longwei," I said, not wanting to involve him for my own sanity.

"Elena, he's the Rubicon, he might offer his assistance." Lucian's jaw muscles clenched.

"We have enough people already, Lucian. We can fly with Sammy." I gave her a look, and she nodded quickly.

"And what if we get into a battle?" he asked.

"Then we fight. You're not a Moon-Bolt, don't try to foresee things," I said, growing frustrated that he kept insisting on bringing Blake along.

"So, take it one step at a time."

I nodded.

He stroked his face and roughly ran his fingers through his hair. "Fine, when do you want to leave?"

"Nightfall at shift change. There's a delay of five minutes," I said confidently.

"Where do we meet?"

I didn't know. I never thought about it, until now.

"There is a tower right behind the cafeteria. Becky and I used to go there in the beginning of the school year until someone told us it was off limits. It's the perfect place, surrounded by trees. No one will see us from there. It will be an easy escape, Lucian." Sammy had come to my rescue but she didn't sound happy about it either.

I wanted to give her a hug, but instead I let out a sigh and hoped her explanation would be enough to stop the pissed-off vibe emanating from him.

He went to the window in our room and turned around with a huge frown dented between his eyebrows. "How long have you been planning this?"

"Since the sixth day," I said.

He huffed and looked at the carpet for a few seconds. "Tonight is Bill's shift." Lucian drew back the curtains and peeked outside. "George and I will meet you there at half-past eight. Don't be late, or we can forget about making a clean break. Elena, there's only one condition: you do exactly as I say."

He didn't give me a chance to argue.

"See you tonight." He grunted, and left.

WE ATE OUR supper in complete silence. Lucian was absent and Becky hadn't said one word to me since I said those awful things that had helped me change her mind. George didn't approve of the idea either, and I could feel his eyes drilling holes into my soul.

We went back to our dorms around seven and prepared for our trip. Sammy grabbed all the sodas in the fridge and fruit from tonight's buffet line. She chucked everything into her backpack along with two sets of clothes. We all did the same, just in case. We shouldn't be gone that long and hopefully we would make it back before anyone knew we had left. If not, Sammy and George could catch fish. Dragons were known to be excellent fishermen.

We dressed in dark sweat suits, grabbed our backpacks, and left our dorms around eight fifteen. We arrived at the tower early, and when we heard George and Lucian coming up the stairs, my heart beat like a jackhammer.

There's no time for fear, I repeated over and over in my head, trying to calm my nerves. Silently I hoped this was what the Viden meant. The three of us froze when Blake, Tabitha, Brian, and Arianna arrived with Lucian and George. Blake carried a huge bag around his left shoulder. The ratio of the bag and his human figure was way out; it didn't look natural.

"Lucian?" I wanted to scold him.

"I had no choice, Elena."

"So, are we going to do this or what?" Blake asked in a pissed-off tone, without looking at me.

"Three more minutes, Blake, then we can be off. You guys should get ready," Lucian said.

I closed my eyes, furious about our new companions. *I'd bargained on five people going on this mission, not nine.*

The four dragons took off their clothes in preparation for their change. Tabitha and Sammy were in their underwear while the boys stripped down to their boxers. They handed their clothes to Arianna, who was chewing gum like a cow, climbed out the tower window, and disappeared. I had to admit, Arianna even knew how to look sexy on a mission. Her hair that used to hang loose in curls framing her face was tied up into a bun. She seemed nervous, though. Lucian put a pair of flying goggles over my head and adjusted the straps so it would fit.

I took another deep breath, trying to calm my anger. "Arianna?" I pulled Lucian back so we could have a private conversation.

"She heard Blake and I talking and wanted a piece of the action."

"It's not a game, Lucian."

"I had no choice."

"Who's going to transport her?" I asked. "The others are Chromatic and Sammy can't take all of us." I jumped as I heard pieces of rock falling.

"Damn it, you guys should be careful," Lucian whispered as loud as he could without risking being heard.

I tried to imagine what I would find outside, but for some reason, my mind was filled with so many other crazy things that no picture appeared. In an attempt to end the conversation, he started to repack some of the backpacks to lighten the load.

"She can ride with me and George," Becky said to Lucian.

She still refused to speak to me as she slid her goggles over her eyes and gestured for Arianna to follow her outside.

"Are you ready?" Lucian peeked down at his watch.

I picked up one of the backpacks and walked to the window. Lucian jumped onto the ledge, and put on his pair of flying goggles. He reached for my hand, clasping it in a firm grip.

I squeezed in front of him and balanced precariously on the thin ledge.

I gasped, staring at the five dragons hanging on the tower's wall by their claws. They were huge, even with their wings still folded in place. Lucian gave the sign to go, and I flinched as three of them took flight. George followed with Becky and Arianna on his back until everyone was airborne except Sammy, who still clung onto the wall.

My hands cramped as I struggled to hold on. Pieces of rock crumbled from under my feet as I took sideways steps. *Please don't fall.*

Lucian jumped on her back and held out his hand for mine. When I grasped it, he swung me onto Sammy's back as she took flight.

I held on tight to his waist. I didn't dare open my eyes and waited for the siren to announce our escape. Nothing happened. *Almost there. Just a few more seconds and then we're free.*

Sammy climbed higher and higher as her wings drummed loudly in my ears with each flap. I felt queasy and didn't like the speed at which we flew. It was crazy fast, like being on a bad rollercoaster that never seems to end. My legs, tucked tightly around her torso to keep my balance, moved as her body expanded. I wanted to see her so badly in her dragon form, but I couldn't gather the courage to open my eyes. I just kept them closed and prayed I would be able to face whatever lay ahead.

I still didn't appreciate all the dragons, and the fact that Arianna had come along with us. Why had Lucian told Blake about this? He made me so mad sometimes, and I didn't want to be angry at him. The fact that he'd brought Brian was the cherry on top of this whole crappy sundae.

As we flew, curiosity dwelled in my mind. How had Lucian convinced Blake to come on this trip? A small part of me was glad the Rubicon was with us, but not enough to forgive Lucian yet. If we did get caught, which was likely to happen, the punishment wouldn't be as severe because of Blake. They would see it as him living up to his expectations, and nobody would suspect it was in fact me behind this crazy adventure.

My legs cramped as I clutched onto Sammy with all my strength. *How far is this stupid place?*

"Are you okay?" Lucian asked.

"Just a cramp," I said, my eyes still closed tightly.

"Where?"

"Left thigh."

He touched my leg and started to rub the cramp away. My eyes flew open, because he was supposed to hold on to Sammy for the both of us.

I gasped as my brain tried to take in my surroundings.

We glided on a bed of clouds. The stars were bright with the moon shining full in all its glory. *Beautiful.*

I looked to my left and saw Becky on top of George. Arianna held on to her, but not the way I clung to Lucian.

They made it look so easy. The other dragons were far out in front. I got a glimpse of Blake, or I assumed it was him, because the dragon was gargantuan with his wings stretched out. I turned my focus onto his massive dragon body and knew when he descended, we'd almost be there.

"You chose a perfect night for this, Elena. If there weren't so many clouds in the sky tonight, we wouldn't have made it," Lucian said.

I nodded, not really processing his words.

He chuckled. "You're afraid of flying?"

"Shhh."

"That's so ironic."

I didn't say anything. He was right about the ironic part. I felt his hand on mine and my eyelids were heavy, but my fear of heights forced my body to stay awake. I held on tighter when Blake started to blur. I kept staring at him until the first ray of sun made its appearance on the horizon.

I noticed instantly when Blake finally started to descend, which meant only one thing—our destination was not much farther. Sammy followed his lead, and I grabbed Lucian tighter. When we exited the roof of clouds, I saw plenty of open land and mountains. My head spun and I closed my eyes again. The cold air helped with the hot flushes, and after a few minutes, I opened my eyes again. In the distance, stood a large castle.

"My dad is so going to kill me," Lucian said as we turned toward the mountains and away from the castle. It was the first part of Paegeia I'd seen, and I couldn't believe none of them wanted to fight for it.

An hour later, Blake landed near the woods on top of a mountain. All the dragons followed him. Sammy landed last and almost fell over.

"That's it, girl, you did great." Lucian tapped her. The other dragons disappeared into the woods. Becky struggled to remove the saddle from George's back as Lucian ran over to help. He kindly lifted her so she could reach the buckle.

Why on earth she had brought the saddle with her? No one knew.

Sammy didn't go into the woods, but asked for a towel. As she stood in the clearing, I was finally able to examine her in her dragon form. She was beautiful, with sweeping wings that lifted from her shoulders and continued down her tail, ending in an elegant flourish. Compared to the other dragons, her lips were lush and full, as defined facial bones highlighted her fiery eyes. Her amber scales glistened in the rising sun, and I could catch all of the colors of a brightly burning ember radiating around her body. She was simply the most magnificent creature I had ever seen.

When she changed, she barely had the strength to cover herself before she fell.

Blake appeared out of nowhere and caught her right before her head slammed into the ground. She must have been really tired.

"Dad's going to kill me for letting you come with us," he scolded.

"Dad's not here, so shut up." She giggled, sounding out of it, too tired for anything else.

The corner of Blake's mouth curved up, and he shook his head. He led her to a tree close by, and she sat down, exhausted.

All the dragons quickly retrieved their clothes from the backpack Arianna carried.

"We need to rest." Blake spoke for all the dragons.

Lucian nodded. "We all have to rest, Blake."

It wasn't long before all the tents Blake carried in his large pack were transformed into a makeshift camp. The boys were really handy, and Brian made a fire in no time. I guess it was easy when he had the ability to breathe on top of a few sticks and they would burst into flames. Arianna and Tabitha went to look for more wood while George went hunting. Becky sat with Sammy. I really wanted to speak to Becky, but she made a point not to even look at me, so I left it for now.

"Elena, you need your rest," Lucian called from inside the tent we shared.

I crawled in, trying to hide that I was concerned about Becky being so upset with me.

For crying out loud, I have too many things on my mind already. Doesn't she care about that? She's so selfish, a spoiled brat. I felt bad the minute I thought it and struggled to fall asleep.

We will go to the Sacred Cavern tonight. So many things

popped in my head as I considered what the cave hid in its inky black depths. *Why hadn't the five women ever revealed what had been inside?* I dozed off with images of bats and dragons hiding inside the cave in my head, and the fear of having to kill each one of them.

27

QUEEN CATHERINE APPEARED in my dreams again, and the woods to which she pointed looked similar to where we were. I knew now why I'd been dreaming about her. She had prepared me for the decision I had to make. The dream changed from her to the Book of Shadows. I saw my foretelling, and the words were red.

The smell of a strong woody and sweet essence filled my nostrils, and I opened my eyes. Lucian just smiled as I looked at him. He looked so beautiful when he woke. Not like me, hair a mess and eyes thick from sleep. The tent was barely lit. When we crawled out, the sun had begun to set. We found four rows of small skinless animals spiked on sticks, roasting over an open fire. I gawked at the amazing survival skills these guys had.

When the meat was done, we all ate in silence. I didn't think they were very happy to be here, but it wasn't for nothing. I needed to know whether the sword still existed, and if so, where it was hidden.

After dinner, Lucian took me to wash up by a nearby river. I grasped his hand to steady myself on the moss-covered rocks that lined the riverbed. Away from the camp-fire light it was difficult to find my way around, and I had to rely only on my sense of touch. When I gathered enough courage to jump into the inky depths, the water felt like a thousand ice cubes, but it was just what I needed.

On our way back to the camp, a dark figure was heading our way.

"We need to talk about what it is we are going to do." Blake spoke right in front of us.

I lost my balance and slipped on the smooth rocks.

"We take it as it comes," Lucian said simply, catching me before I tumbled in again.

"Excuse me?"

"We don't know the rules on this one, Blake. What do you want to go over?" he snapped.

"You bring me here only to tell me we have to wing it?"

"I didn't bring anyone here. You wanted to come," Lucian said as he passed him, shoving his shoulder roughly into Blake's.

Lucian held out his hand for mine. I took it without looking at Blake. Back at camp, we packed the water bottles and snacks we needed for the trip. Lucian's watch beeped, and a small electronic voice said it was eight.

"It's about an hour's walk to the Sacred Cavern. I suggest we get a move on," Blake said, and took a backpack from Tabitha, who glared daggers at me.

"Would Brian do me the honor?" George said, and held out a man-made torch in Brian's direction. Brian blew on it, and the torch caught fire instantly. He lit two more and gave one to Blake, who took the lead.

"Your highness," Brian joked, and handed Lucian one too.

"Ha, ha," Lucian said with a tone drenched in sarcasm.

Brian winked at me then ran to catch up with Blake at the front of the group.

Small animals made noises in the brush as they ran from our heavy footsteps. I jumped every time.

"You're scared of little things in the woods? Unbelievable." Arianna passed us and shook her head.

"Ignore her, Elena. I think what you're doing is pretty brave," Lucian said in a soft tone, rubbing my back gently.

"Why does she have to be here?"

"Why?" Arianna whipped around at my words and looked at me with a ferocious expression. "Because what you are doing, Elena, isn't brave at all." She looked at Lucian. "It's stupid. And if any of us die tonight, it's on your head."

I hadn't thought about that and swallowed hard.

"Arianna, you begged to come with us tonight, so shut your pie-hole," Lucian snapped.

"You guys, enough," Blake yelled. "Nobody was forced into coming tonight, Arianna, but I agree with you, this is a suicide mission. There's nothing we can do about it now, so all of you shut your traps."

The dragons all stood with Blake, except for Sammy. She stood right next to Becky and looked everywhere but in my direction.

She's pissed off with me too?

The rest of the trip felt long. Arianna's words weighed like a ton of bricks on my mind. *What if somebody dies? It will be on my head.*

Sammy whispered something to Becky, and she put her arm around Sammy. It frustrated me so much that I couldn't hear what they were talking about.

Lucian squeezed my hand a little tighter every time I looked at the two of them.

We exited the woods and ended up in front of a towering mountain that had a stone staircase winding up into the fog surrounding it. I'd seen it in small-scale at the museum, but never had I imagined it would be this colossal.

"Welcome to the Sacred Cavern," Blake bellowed in a theatrical tone. Tabitha and Arianna giggled. We reached the stairs, and Lucian let me go first, a true gentleman.

The climb took everything out of me, and my muscles felt as if I'd spent an entire day at the gym doing leg lifts. I was glad Lucian had drilled me every morning, otherwise my lungs would've collapsed, or worse, Lucian would've had to carry me.

"Becky will speak to you again, Elena," Lucian said.

"You sure about that? I said some pretty mean things to her."

"They were the truth. She'll only become part of the Royal Council if she gets a bit more of what you have."

"You make it sound as if I'm not scared at all. I'm shaking in my shoes, literally."

He smiled. "But you're here. Which means you're as much of a knight as any of these guys here with you?"

"A stupid knight."

"Not so stupid to me. I admit, it sounded crazy the first time you explained it, but it makes sense. Once you said those words about the wall coming down, it scared the living crap out of me too. You're right. Goran will get tired after taking over Paegeia, and then he'll do whatever he can to take down the wall. If he's smart enough to find a way to exit Etan, he's powerful enough to find a way to break through to the other side."

"Thank you."

"For what?" He had a questioning look on his face.

"For being the first to join me on this crazy mission," I said. "Do you think that they'll look for us?"

"You mean Master Longwei?" he asked with a mysterious smile, and I nodded. "It will take them about a day to reach us, and you saw how tired the dragons were after a flight like the one we just took. So they won't catch up if that's what you mean. Besides, they don't know which direction we went. Everyone that knows about this is here."

"They could ask Cheng. He's smart and would put two and two together. He's the one that told me about this place." I was afraid of what Master Longwei would do if he found out I was behind this mission.

"Elena, you worry too much about the little things. They must first discover that we are gone."

Gasps came from up ahead on the trail. Something told

me they had reached the top. I heard backpacks falling to the ground, and when Blake came into sight, he was drinking water out of a bottle.

The steps stopped, and I had to hoist myself up the last ledge. My eyes caught Blake's, and his beauty made my stomach feel queasy. He reached down and gave me his hand.

I grabbed it and looked away quickly so he wouldn't see my blush. I didn't like the way he made me feel whenever our eyes met. He lifted me up with one pull and helped Lucian after me.

I inhaled sharply. In front of me were two eighty-feet-tall wooden doors.

"So what's the plan, big shot?" Blake asked as he thrust a water bottle into Lucian's hand.

He took a few gulps and handed it over to me.

"We all go and face whatever comes our way together," Lucian said with more confidence than I felt.

We all looked at one another. Becky still didn't glance my way.

"All of you agree?" Blake asked. We all nodded. Tabitha was the only one who appeared as if she wanted to make a run for it.

"Tabitha?" Blake asked in a sweet tone. She didn't answer or look up. "Babes, are you in?"

There were tears in her eyes. "I can't do this, Blake."

Some of the guys and Arianna sighed heavily.

"Just leave her here, I doubt anything will happen, and if there is any danger she can fly away," Arianna snapped.

"Arianna take a hike." Blake sounded furious, and Lucian stepped in.

"We can't afford to fight. We need Arianna inside. She's the best at enchantments, Blake. Use your head."

"Fine, but you stay as far away from me as possible. Get that."

Arianna shrugged, rolled her eyes and raised her upper lip sarcastically, before turning her back to him.

We took a minute to gather our strength and approached the door. Just as we were about to reach for one of the doors, a huge dragon came out of nowhere, landed with a thud, and stopped us. The spikes on his head looked like a crown and two long whiskers ran down his mouth. His scales were a dark auburn and his snout was long and pointy.

He roared something in Latin that I didn't understand and my knees shook with every syllable.

Blake bowed, and we all followed his example. My heart pounded so fast and loud I struggled to hear what Blake was saying. Some sort of introduction happened, and I only caught the word "Rubicon" and all of our names. I didn't dare look up.

Words like "unseen" and "millpond" were the only ones that I did understand, thanks to Blake's lessons. I hated not being able to speak or understand this stupid language.

The dragon said something, and I listened closely, but it

was no use; I didn't understand enough words to follow the conversation.

"What's he saying?" I whispered to Lucian.

"He said there is no we, only one. Blake's trying to find out what the rules are and how to decide who to choose, but he hasn't answered yet."

The dragon spoke again. "Call me when you have made your choice," Lucian translated, "no dragons."

The dragon flew away, and we got up slowly.

"This was a waste of time, Lucian," Blake snapped.

"We just have to choose one person," Lucian bit back.

"Yeah, who's going to do it? You heard what he said, no dragons." Blake sounded really pissed off.

My heartbeat went up a notch as I remembered my list, my calculations quickly added up of how many of us could enter. Lucian wouldn't make it out, and it was between me, Becky, and Arianna.

"I'll go. There's no other choice," Lucian said.

"You can't." I stopped him with my hand.

"What?" Blake and Lucian asked the same time. The others just stared at me.

"No man has made it back. It was only women," I said.

Blake laughed. "So what you're saying is that men can't do this?"

"Yes," I barked at him, anything just to make that grin on his face disappear. It worked.

"Elena, you don't know that," Sammy said, and her voice trembled a little.

"I did my research. Five made it out. They were all women."

That gave them all something to think about, and it was quiet for a moment. Blake cussed loudly in the silence.

"So you want to tell me it's between Arianna and Becky."

"And me, Lucian."

His face hardened at once. "No, Elena," he said. "I meant to say that you don't have nearly enough training to face anything behind these doors."

"I'll go." Becky stepped forward. George pushed her back and started to speak in Latin.

"Becky, are you still...intact?" I interrupted George, whispering the last part.

"What does that have to do with anything?" She pushed George aside, and gave me a look that almost made me regret I'd asked her.

"Everything. You have to be a maiden." I blurted it out, and all of them froze.

"Becky?" George demanded for her to answer. It was written all over her face. "You got to be kidding me."

My heart pounded as I tried to change the subject. *Just another reason for her to hate me.*

"They were all maidens, which only means somewhere in there is a Sun-Blast," I said.

Brian smiled.

Saying it out loud made me not want to do it anymore. I

looked at Arianna and hoped by some miracle that she might still be a virgin.

"Well, Arianna, that means you are screwed." Blake chuckled with Brian after him.

She flipped them off with a curled up lip.

George still argued with Becky.

"Oh, come on! It was a onetime thing, and a huge mistake," she yelled.

"George, not now," Blake said through a grin. He was a dickhead and probably loved every minute of the two of them fighting.

George grunted.

You would think that he was a Sun-Blast and not a Moon-Bolt.

"So what you're saying is that only you can enter through these doors?" Blake asked me, not sounding hopeful.

"No, we tried. You can't go through those doors." Lucian begged me to listen.

"We can't back out now. We're so close." I was frustrated.

"Elena, I don't know what's behind those doors," he started, speaking fast. "If you don't finish in a certain time, you'll never come back."

"I know that."

"What if there is a dragon that you have to fight? You don't have enough training. This is crazy."

"Please don't start. I need to do this." I wiped off a tear

that had made its way onto my cheek. "If there's a dragon, then I'll fight." I showed him the queen's axes that were safely in a harness tied around my waist.

"Elena! You don't know what you're saying." He had tears in his eyes.

"I'm the only one that has a chance of making it out. Please, have a little faith in me." I cupped his face with my hands as I tried to soothe him.

"I promised that nothing would happen to you," he whispered.

I closed my eyes and tried to stop them from tearing up. "And nothing will."

Blake spoke to him in Latin. I just sighed, as I couldn't make out one word.

"You better come out, you hear me? Otherwise I'll blow this cavern apart," Lucian said with tears in his eyes.

I nodded.

He grabbed me and buried his face in my neck. We stood like that for a long time.

"Come back," he said.

My eyes were starting to sting, but I swallowed it fast and nodded.

It was difficult for both of us to let go. Sammy was next. "Be safe." Tears lurked in the corner of her eyes.

"You're a cool chick, Sammy, I mean, dragon."

She giggled and quickly wiped away the tear that rolled over her cheek.

"Don't change anything and have faith, okay?"

She grabbed me tightly around my neck. "Just come back, please."

"Good luck, Elena." George grunted. He still sounded pissed.

I gave him a soft smile. "Take care of my girl, okay?"

Becky turned her back to me.

"It is going to take a miracle for you to make it out alive," Blake said, and sighed. "But if you do, you'll have my respect."

I was stunned by his words and huffed.

"I guess Brian will see how right Master Longwei was about Elena's mark." Brian chuckled.

I smiled and shook my head.

"You're one crazy chick for doing this, and it's driving Brian nuts," Brian said.

"Brian!" Lucian and Blake scolded him.

"What? It's the truth."

I just stared at him. Guess I would never know how bad he really wanted my virginity.

"Good luck," Tabitha and Arianna said softly.

Blake called the dragon back, and we bowed again as he landed. He boomed in Latin,.

Blake asked him something and the dragon kept quiet for a brief period. Then the strangest thing happened; the next time the dragon spoke, it was in English.

"Did you understand him, Elena?" Blake asked carefully.

I nodded slowly, not sure what was happening.

"Thank you, Great Keeper," Blake said.

Lucian tapped me on the bum, and as I looked at him, he was staring up at the dragon with tears in his eyes. It was my cue to get up.

"What's your name?" the dragon asked me.

"Elena Watkins."

"Elena Watkins, are you ready to face the consequences if you fail to complete what the cavern holds?"

"Yes." A shiver ran up my spine. *I might be stuck in there forever.*

"Good, let the games begin." He flew away.

A big shudder that felt like an earthquake made all of us lose our balance. When it stopped, one of the wooden doors was halfway open.

Lucian hugged me again before he let me go. "Come back to me," he whispered fervently in my ear.

We shared a passionate kiss, and I had to break away, biting my lip to keep tears from cascading down my cheeks.

Well, Elena, you wanted this. So move your ass.

I reached the door in what felt like a heartbeat.

Don't look back.

"Elena, wait!" Becky shouted as I went to slip through the opening.

Her eyes sparkled with tears. "You know I would do this if I could, right?"

I nodded and fresh tears wanted to emerge. *Stay strong.*

She grabbed me around my neck. "You kick some ass, and you come back to us. I'm so sorry about earlier."

"It's okay, Becky. I'm sorry too."

She held on a little longer before letting me go.

I slipped through quickly. "Wait for me for two days, please. If I'm not out by then, go home," I said as the door closed behind me with finality. Lucian yelled something, but I didn't hear what it was.

"Please, just get me through this," I begged out loud in the darkness. I didn't know if it was to God or the queen, but she'd appeared in my dreams, so she'd better be listening too.

Gathering my courage, I opened my eyes and turned around carefully.

Let the games begin.

28

A FAINT BURNING SMELL drifted from the glowing lanterns mounted on the walls. In the front of the cave was a drizzling waterfall that sent a misty spray into the air. The cave rumbled as a square stone hoisted from the floor. I wasn't sure at this point what I was supposed to do.

This was a bad idea. Taking a deep breath, I stepped toward the stone and words magically appeared on the wall to my right. "A challenge you have to complete in fifteen beats." I read the first words out loud, hoping it would help me make sense of them.

They do love their rhymes. The first two sentences disappeared.

"Paegeia is enchanted with dragons, shifts, and nymphs hidden behind a wall. The most important one is not one, but them all."

They have nymphs too.

I frowned, already confused, as the words swirled in my head.

C'mon, Elena, you have to think fast. The most important one? The only thing that I could think of was Blake's words. I would have his respect when I exited those doors.

Not one but them all, Blake! The riddle was about the Rubicon.

I ran to the stone and found a puzzle. It looked ancient, and the blocks I needed to move were huge. This kind of puzzle was my favorite as a little girl, so this should be easy.

Ten square disks stood in front of me, and only one square empty space. I was allowed fifteen moves to get them into the right places. Each square disk had the sign of a different dragon embellished on it. I knew immediately that it was Blake's sign. I closed my eyes, imagining the order, as I'd intended to draw this on t-shirts for extra money but hadn't had enough time. The Fin-Tail was first and then the Copper-Horn; next was the Swallow Annex sign. The Crown-Tail and the Fire-Tail after that. That was the first five Metallic dragon signs. Then came the Chromatic dragons; the Snow dragon followed by the Moon-Bolt, the Sun-Blast and Green-Vapor. Last was the Night Villain. I had the final picture of Blake's sign fresh in my head.

I found the Fin-Tail and reached out for my first move. The square disk was stuck, and I couldn't move it. My heart pounded and sweat formed on my forehead. A picture of Lucian busy laying dynamite popped in my head.

Stop it, Elena, there is no time for negative thoughts. I pushed Lucian out of my mind. *Deep breaths, Elena, you've got this.*

I searched about me and found an hourglass-shaped

object. Something told me that it was the timer, but the amount of sand didn't equal an hour. It was only fifteen minutes. I ran toward the glass and wiped off all the spider webs.

Jeepers! I hate that. A cold shudder ran up my spine as I rubbed the goosebumps from my arms. I took another deep breath and turned it over.

A big clicking sound indicated that I needed to hurry, so I ran back to the puzzle. I didn't have time to think, I just started moving the Fin-Tail into position. I worked out the order of disk movement that would allow all the others to end in their correct location. Every move was critical. The adrenaline must have been making my brain work ten times faster as I shifted the last one in place and closed my eyes.

My heart beats faster. The only thought running through my head was what the consequences would be if I was wrong. I would probably have to stay here forever, until I died.

The cave rumbled again. One of the walls had left an open doorway.

I blew out my breath slowly. I turned around to look at the first door I had entered. Right behind it, Lucian and all my friends waited. I slipped through the wall without saying my goodbyes, and it closed behind me.

It was dark. All I could hear was the sound of my beating heart as it pounded inside my ear.

Come, come, come. My hands trembled. I shook them a few times, hoping it would take off the edge.

A spark right next to me made me jump. Fire ran along the wall all the way down to light up the second cave.

My throat became dry as I faced my next task.

What is this?

My eyes grew wider as I realized what was ahead.

You've got to be shitting me. It was my worst nightmare. In front of me stood a huge obstacle course. It was the same one we'd seen in the museum—the one where I imagined being a tiny human. Yeah, it hadn't worked out so well for my tiny self, who had been crushed. This time, it needed to end differently.

The only thing I could see was two huge upside-down axes, swinging at a slow pace past each other.

Words appeared on the wall again.

"A task you must complete, that only the brave can defeat. One false move and you might be without a heartbeat."

No time limit appeared, and I blew out another breath.

Okay, Elena, you can do this. It's easy. Yeah right. I bounced on one spot as I kept my eyes on the obstacle of death. The movement of the axes started to pick up its pace. I had no choice but to do it now.

I decided to trust my reflexes, but my legs wobbled as I climbed the stairs, not making me feel very confident. The axes parted from each other, and I glimpsed a crusher and something else that looked like it that could slash me in two. There were balls turning at the end with things going up and down. *At least the speed seems manageable.*

As I slipped through the blades, the tip of my shoe bumped up against a piece of bulk that stood out, causing me to fall flat on my stomach. I felt something miss my head by an inch. I jolted up and moved a step forward.

The object that missed me seconds ago came back. I saw that it was a wooden log, and I arched my body forward. Who would have thought my clumsiness would someday save my ass?

My heart pounded so fast, it felt as if it was going to explode out of my chest. I took another few steps and found myself sliding onto something icky. Another blade slashed right past my nose.

Lucian's voice rang inside my head, loud and clear. "Move your ass, Elena, and no matter what, trust your reflexes."

Relying on my clumsy butt was more like it. I'd made a joke. That was a good sign.

I listened to Lucian's words as my voice of reason to survive. The crusher came next. I decided to dive for it. If I lost a leg, I could somehow still manage to finish and get the reward.

As I dusted myself off, I couldn't believe it. I had escaped the crusher and made it three quarters of the way through the obstacles. I didn't have a moment to celebrate because there was no time to waste. I had to get up fast as ankle-height blades were approaching. I ran forward, and my body ducked for no reason. Blades that could split me in two missed me by a hair. I moved forward the minute they parted. Even though I couldn't see the next obstacle, I still managed to jump over it, and I ran a few feet. I heard a deadly noise approaching.

The sound came from all around me, and the solid object hit me directly in my shoulder. The instant I heard a loud snap, I cried out of pain. I bit hard on my jaw, trying to suck it up, and forced myself to move forward. The pain coming from my shoulder triggered my tears, and I wiped them away.

When I looked up there weren't any more obstacles in front of me. I couldn't believe I had somehow managed to survive my worst nightmare.

I grabbed my shoulder with my other arm and ran. I fell over my shoelaces, the ones I knew I had double-tied. *How the hell did they get loose?*

My entire body froze as a blast of fire erupted inches above my head. The heat from the flames baked one side of my face. When the fire stopped, I got on my good arm and knees, lifted my ass, and crawled into the third cave.

Using my good arm, I touched my hair and face. Everything felt fine, except that my skin felt hot, and tight, as if it had shrunk a few centimeters. I wanted to cry when it dawned on me that I was going to be fine. Well, apart from the acute pain in my shoulder.

It was unreal to think that I'd just finished the second task.

Before I could process what was happening, an old

chandelier came to life above my head and illuminated two doors.

Oh, please, I can't handle another obstacle. New words appeared on the wall.

"There are two doors. One leads to the fourth cave, and the other to purgatory. The door that leads to the fourth cave is the one guarded by the old man telling the truth. The other door that leads to purgatory is guarded by his twin that always lies. One exact question you may ask, but be careful for the question can only be a yes or no. Beware they don't know time or space, and your question may not be linked to whether they are related."

I had to ask them the same question. A yes or no answer to find which one was guarding the door that leads to the fourth room?

Questions filled my mind immediately. If I asked the one "are you guarding the door to the fourth chamber," both of them would say yes. I couldn't ask them personal questions either, or the time, because they didn't know what time was. Yes or no answers. My mind suddenly went blank.

For the love of blueberries, this always happens to me.

Come back to me, Elena. I forced myself to concentrate on Lucian's words.

Think, think, think.

If I hid the door to purgatory and lied, what question could I lie about that would give the answer away?

It has to be about the doors; it couldn't be anything about the two men or their relation. *Doors. One is hiding the*

352

fourth cave, the other one hiding purgatory. I knew it was in me somewhere. I could feel it and taste it on the tip of my tongue. *Are you guarding the door of truth? No. Are...both doors?* My body went through an ocean of pins and needles. I might have it.

I ran to the hourglass and saw the sand running really fast. Two small crazy men appeared.

They were skinny, as if they hadn't eaten in weeks, and were missing some teeth. They smelled really bad, and I started to make gagging sounds. Becky would have cracked up if she were here with me. They each had long beards and hair, with only a scruffy rag covering their private parts. When they saw each other, they started to scold one another. Cussing and fighting. How could one of them be capable of telling the truth?

"Do both doors lead to the fourth cave," I asked the first one carefully.

"No," the one on the left answered, and the other one on the right answered, "yes". They started to fight again as they disagreed.

"I choose the door on the left," I yelled, and it opened up.

I slipped past the crazy men, who had started to go mental on each other, and went through the door. It closed immediately after me, and I felt bowled over as I found myself outside. It was a weird place. Mist and fog covered everything. I could barely see through the mist, but I made out the shape of a small wooden rowboat. Plants and trees that grew near the swamp were everywhere. The Night Villain jumped to my mind. What if Lucian was right and I did need to fight a Night Villain?

I ran to the boat and cussed a little when the man inside the boat startled me. He wasn't as old as the two in the third cave, but smelled just as bad nevertheless. He resembled a lazy fisherman, with a hat covering his face.

I bumped the boat with my foot. "Excuse me."

He woke angst-ridden and grabbed the edges for balance.

"Jeewiz, miss, what are you doing here?" he asked in a frantic British accent, but smiled as soon as he realized where he was. "Ah, you have come to take a look at your future, maybe present or past."

I clutched my pounding arm and asked, "What is it I have to do?"

"You got hit?"

I nodded.

"Those balls are a bummer. It was my idea," he boasted.

I felt like kicking him, but was too scared that if I did, he wouldn't help.

"Hop on. I'll take you to your final task."

I climbed into the boat and closed my eyes. I didn't know how long I'd been away.

"So, you want to visit the millpond, hey?" he asked.

"No, I'm here for the pleasure of it."

"Oh, I guess there is always a first for everything," he said. "Have we met?"

"No!" I snapped at him. Idiot.

"Must have mistaken you for someone else then, besides once you enter, you can never leave." He started to fold himself in two at his lame joke, and I just stared at him.

Poor guy must have inhaled too much fog or something.

The trip to the other side felt long. My head started to ache with his non-stop babbling, and I started every time something bumped the boat. Maybe this was the fourth task, trying not to throw myself overboard just to get a bit of peace and quiet.

"Don't worry, miss, it's the lost souls that weren't worthy enough to complete the last task. They won't hurt you," he said in a singsong tone.

My heart rose, and my eyes felt as if they were going to pop out of their sockets.

Dead people. I pulled my gaze away from the water and stared at the idiot.

"What's the fourth task?" I hoped for some sort of a distraction from the dead-people thing.

"You'll get the assignment on the other side," he said, and just kept rowing, starting to whistle as he paddled along.

It felt like hours before we hit something and I managed to see some land through the mist.

"Get out!" he said.

I huffed and almost fell out of the boat.

He pushed the boat back with one of the paddles and started to row back to the other side.

"Wait, what if I need you to get me back?"

He laughed.

Idiot. I turned around and couldn't see anything in front of me because of the fog. I tried to wave it away, but I was only wasting my time. A low growl alerted my senses, and I grabbed one of my axes for protection.

I didn't like this feeling of not knowing what might attack me. Not being able to see meant that I had to rely on my senses. That was going to be interesting since I didn't even trust my senses myself.

Lucian was right. I was not cut out to fight a dragon, especially one that spat acid.

"Good day, Elena Watkins," a deep voice rumbled in front of me.

A strong force pulled me forward. I could feel my feet skimming along the ground, and I was suddenly ankle-deep in yucky mud. "A true maiden." A strong wind blew into my face, almost causing me to fall down on my butt. When I opened my eyes, the fog was gone. In front of me stood a huge dragon, a kind I'd never seen before.

My head started to thump, and I squinted to make sure that they weren't playing tricks on me. Vertical stripes covered his entire body, as if he had stolen a rainbow and made himself a suit.

"Hey." I swallowed hard.

"Here to take a look at my millpond?" His low, honeyed voice made me feel safe, but I didn't dare trust it. "So you can't speak Latin. That's what the Keeper told me. He had to lend you the gift."

"Thank you for that." I remembered Blake's words as he asked me if I understood him.

"Appreciation. It's a rare quality. You'll be one of my most prized possessions," he said, as if I had already failed the final task. "Come in."

I followed him to a massive gate that resembled the one at Dragonia, and tried to kick off the mud that still clung to my shoes. The gate opened and I stepped inside.

The hill was steep. Simply looking at it drained the energy I had left.

When we reached the top, I saw some sort of a castle. It had the most beautiful garden with a giant labyrinth in front. Cupid and dragon statues surrounded by fruit-bearing trees and a beautiful big pond reminded me of the Garden of Eden. The stars shone brightly in the sky. Laughter came from the garden, and I saw young women chasing each other.

So creepy. One wanted to be more beautiful than the other, and they all wore garments that made me think of ancient Greece.

"You know I can take away your pain for a small price," the dragon said.

"What's the price?"

"No, you have to trust me, Elena. First I'll heal, and then I'll ask something in return."

Lucian's voice screamed "Hell no" inside me.

"No, I'll bear it. Thanks for the offer."

"Are you sure? They might have to cut it off the longer you wait."

It was tempting, and I really wanted to give in, but I came here for one thing, and that was to look in the millpond. Temptation might be the final task, not to give in. "No."

"So be it. Here's your final task."

29

"FOR YOUR FINAL task, I need to know the answer before sunrise."

I scratched my head. "Before sunrise?"

He nodded his big purple-and-yellow head.

"*It* is greater than God and more evil than the Devil. The poor have *it*, the rich need *it*, and if you eat *it*, you will die. What is *it*?"

"You're asking me another riddle?" I wanted to pull out my hair. *As if all the other riddles weren't enough.*

"Oh, I love riddles," the dragon said with a smug look. "You have until sunrise. If you don't know the answer to it, you will stay here forever." He began walking toward the castle and disappeared through the big steel door.

I realized what the Sacred Cavern was all about, a cave full of riddles and brainteasers. All these years, the people of Paegeia were afraid of nothing, and I wondered why dragons weren't allowed to enter.

I tried to ponder the answer, but for the moment, fatigue, as well as a throbbing shoulder, made it too difficult to think clearly.

I sat beside a rock and rested my head against the cool stone as I watched the maidens play in the dragon's garden. I started to think about Becky and what would have happened if it had been her and not me that entered those wooden doors. Would he have let her in or eaten her up and chucked her soul in the lake with all the others?

Lucian was next. I had given him my word, but I felt so sleepy. I couldn't think about riddles anymore.

My mind went blank for a long time. When it rebooted, I thought about my mom. All I had was that picture and deep inside me, I knew that I would never find her.

I would never know who she was. Somehow, the Bible and God crept into my thoughts as well. The riddle was linked to Him. What is greater than God?

Could it be a dragon?

A dragon might be more evil than the Devil, but how could the rich need a dragon and the poor have a dragon? The last part didn't make sense. It wasn't a dragon.

I folded my arms around my legs and rested my head on my knees, contemplating everything for hours. I gave up, thinking I would never see Lucian again. If Paegeia was destroyed, would they find all of the maidens and the dragon here?

I must have passed out from sheer exhaustion, and when I woke an hour later, I started to freak out. How could I have fallen asleep, there was so much at stake? *If I don't get this riddle's answer, I will stay here forever, with a rainbow dragon that has a yellow-and-purple head.* My mind rambled and didn't stop for a long time.

I felt as though I had dragged everyone into this for

nothing. I'd given it my all, only to draw a blank now. It wasn't fair.

I saw the maidens again. They weren't so curious about me anymore.

My father jumped into my head, reading from the Bible after he'd tucked me in. Knowing now what he really was made it sound ridiculous. A dragon reading from the Bible. He used to tell me that nothing was greater than God or more evil than the Devil.

My heart felt as if it stopped for an instant. Then it continued beating faster and faster. Could the answer be nothing? The poor have nothing and the rich need nothing, and if you eat nothing, you will die.

I jumped up overwhelmed with a sense of both shock and euphoria as I was sure that nothing was the answer. The maidens in the garden froze as I rejoiced. I looked at them, and then they started screaming hysterically. I spun around with my axe in my hand, but found nothing behind me. Alertness made my heart bounce like crazy and my arm ached, the nerve endings pulsating. I stared at absolutely nothing out of the ordinary. The earth rumbled and I fell down. The dragon appeared inches from me.

"You've got the answer!" he roared.

"Yes," I whimpered.

All the friendliness he'd shown before was gone. "What is *it*?"

"Nothing."

Twin jets of flame twenty feet long shot out of his

nostrils. He looked like a two-year-old throwing a temper tantrum, as I watched as the frustrated dragon screeched and kicked a few boulders around.

I crawled in a fetal position and covered my head with my good arm. When he calmed down, the entire garden was engulfed in flames. I just looked at it, not believing that he'd just scorched everything.

"It has been a long time since anybody has gotten one of my riddles. But a deal is a deal." He grabbed my body with his front talons and started to fly.

I closed my eyes. *I just completed what the cavern holds, and I still don't have the stomach to deal with heights.*

He took me up another mountain and dropped me as he swooped down, before he landed himself. I fell and rolled over a few times before stopping. Was he trying to break my neck?

I lay there for a while, just listening to my heartbeat. Then I lifted my head. Tall trees with a small path to the right greeted me, as I inhaled the smell of the grass. I got to my feet, and watched the dragon fold his paws under his huge body and lie down like a cat. He made a soft purring that made me feel some sort of serenity.

"That path leads to a waterfall," he said in a calm tone. "You have one hour to ask one question. Make it clear, or you might not like what you see. Remember, it can be anything you want to know—past, present, or future."

I nodded and walked straight down the path to which

he'd pointed. It had a mystical ambience. The ground was foggy, but not as much as the lake in front of the dragon's lair. I had never seen anything quite like it before. Trees bearing fruit were growing everywhere. It looked so delicious, but I didn't dare to eat anything. I didn't want to be stuck there because of my grumbling belly.

I followed the drizzle of the waterfall, and when it came into view, a feeling of tranquility swept over me.

So beautiful.

I crouched and rested up on my knees. The reflection in the pond didn't look anything like me. Her face held all questions. *Will my friends still be waiting if I get outside?* I started to think about my question. I needed to make it clear. Today's date was Friday the eleventh. I would ask where the sword is tonight, Friday the eleventh of May. If it showed me nothing, I'd know it didn't exist anymore and we could go home.

I sighed. *Please exist.*

"Where is the King of Lion sword on Friday evening, the eleventh of May, tonight?" I said

At first nothing happened, but then the water rippled and turned into a movie screen. My heart leaped as I saw it tied up in a cloth and bound with string. It zoomed out after a few seconds, showing the inside of a jacket. Three seconds later, it showed me a man in his forties with a crooked nose, as if it had been broken way too many times. He had gray streaks mixed in with his dark brown hair. The sun was starting to set. He flew on top of a dragon, a Sun-Blast. I saw the scenery from the sky above, and I knew it wasn't the way we'd come. They landed carefully on top of another mountain. When his dragon let him slide off his wing, he took a small rocky path surrounded by bushes and trees.

He carried on walking toward the volcano. Nothing made sense until I saw that he was in a trance. Cheng mentioned that Goran liked to compel his subjects, and I could easily make the connection. He entered the volcano and didn't seem to mind that his skin had started to melt off his body.

My stomach turned at the sight, and I covered my mouth. I saw his hand as it pushed away his jacket and took out the parcel. He untied the strings. The flesh on his hands and face bubbled from the heat. His face held no emotion and the scene made my skin crawl. The strings and garment wrapped around the sword turned into ash before they hit the floor. The sword was next, and I watched while it disappeared into the lava. Last, it was the Dragonian who melted away into a pool of goo.

The vision stopped, I had gotten what I came for. I reached the rainbow dragon who was cleaning his huge claws with his teeth.

He froze in midair, with his talon still in his mouth, and yanked them out. He tucked them back under his body. "Sorry," he mumbled. "We need to talk, Elena."

"Sure," I said, trying my best not to smile at his little moment. A jolt of pain jabbed through my shoulder again.

"Are you sure I can't fix that for you?" he asked.

I shook my head.

"As you wish. I will take you back to the entrance. I am sorry about my behavior earlier. It's rare that I get a maiden that is worthy of the fourth task. I don't part easily with maidens, so you can imagine how hard it is for me to part ways with you." He spoke to me as if I was the love of his life. *Creepy.*

"You will sign a book. The Keeper carries it with him. Look at it as a treaty. You must never tell anyone what you saw in here, otherwise, I will claim your first born. Your name in the book seals the deal. You may tell others what it is you have seen in the pond, if that is your wish, but nothing more. What you've seen in the Sacred Cavern must stay with you until the day you die."

"I promise." I understood now why not one of the women who made it out alive ever broke it, especially the queen.

"You can't tell them about the treaty either. Nothing, Elena." "Not even hints. I can use the pond at any time and will know when you have broken the treaty."

I nodded.

He got up and stretched. I couldn't hold back my laughter when he arched his back like a cat. I could swear he grinned, but I didn't know what a grinning dragon looked like. His wings unfolded, and he grabbed me the same way he had earlier. It was so embarrassing to be carried that way, and I was glad that I couldn't say anything about what happened here to anyone.

He took me back the same way I'd come. Wind blew my hair back and I struggled to breathe. I waited for him to hit something, but he never did. He landed gently and put me down. "You sure you don't want me to heal that shoulder of yours?"

I shook my head, as I took huge breaths to calm my beating heart.

Lucian.

Suddenly, he turned into a man—a really beautiful man with a glint of the rainbow in his eyes and auburn hair. His body was to die for. He asked me the same question in a seductive voice, making me swallow hard as I looked down.

I shook my head one last time.

"Well then. Farewell, my fair maiden," he said, and bowed his head. The cave rumbled again and the door opened. I hoped everyone was still waiting for me outside.

Tears filled my eyes as I knew in just a few seconds I would see Lucian's face again. It was only a crack in width, and I huffed.

Really. He wasn't kidding about parting ways. I squeezed myself through the opening, crying out in pain as my shoulder felt worse. The first person that grabbed me was Becky.

I yelled, and she let go as if I was a hot potato.

"What happened?" She looked at me with huge brown eyes.

"My shoulder."

"You got hurt?"

I nodded.

"And they let you out?" she asked, surprised, and pulled me away from the doors. All of them froze and stared at me with huge eyes.

"No! I had to finish."

What the hell is going on here?

"You finished?"

"Elena, you just went in a minute ago." Blake found his voice next.

"What?" It was still night time.

Lucian got himself free from whatever held him to the ground and grabbed me just as Becky had done.

"Ouch!" I cried again.

A minute? I hadn't been in there for a minute. I saw the freaking sun come up.

"You dislocated your shoulder, how?"

I shook my head.

He sighed and started to kiss me all over my face. "We must push your shoulder back."

"Wait, you said you finished?" Arianna asked.

"Yes, I know where to find the sword."

"It still exists?" half of the crowd asked in unison.

"You really finished?" Lucian asked with a glint of a smile, and I nodded.

The wind started to blow hard and it was followed by a loud thud. The Keeper came back, and we all bowed again. He stopped me with one of his front paws. "Not you." He bowed his head. He stayed like that for a short moment and got back up. "Well done, Elena Watkins."

A book appeared out of nowhere, and he held it out to me. I swallowed hard, knowing what that book was, because the rainbow dragon had explained it so beautifully. I took it from him, forcing myself to let go of my other arm.

It wasn't a big or thick book; it looked really ordinary. I opened the page and saw the five names of the women who had made it out. I hit my pockets, searching for a pen.

"Does anyone have a pen?" I asked.

We all chuckled as none of us had brought a stupid pen.

"You don't need a pen, Elena," the Keeper said. "Give me your hand."

It was shaking a little in his big claw which felt like ice. He slashed open my wrist. Blood oozed from the cut, and I thought that this was it. There was no way I would survive this. The blood squirted on the blank pages, destroying the other five names, and he closed the book. He took my wrist and sealed my wound with something that looked like a small laser burning out of his claw. It left a small scar, but it didn't burn at all. I looked at it a long time and knew that it was some sort of magic. He showed me the book one more time, and the stain my blood should have made was gone. In its place stood my name, Elena Watkins, and the date written in small beautiful red letters.

I saw the one above mine.

Catherine Squire and the date was 1768. He shut the

book and bowed one more time before he took off into the night.

Lucian was the first one to reach me and gave me a long kiss. He then looked at my wrist and stroked my scar with gentle fingers.

"We need to move," Blake said quickly.

"She's hurt, Blake," Lucian and Becky said at the same time. I was glad she was back in my corner again.

"We have to get it now or this will all be for nothing."

Lucian was really pissed at his tone, and the two of them were instantly in each other's personal space.

"Don't fight, it's no use," I yelled at both of them. *They always fight, I'm so sick of it.*

"What do you mean, it's no use?" Blake asked.

"I don't know where it is right now," I snapped.

"Then when, Elena?" His stern expression made my blood sizzle.

I held my ground. "Tomorrow night."

"We have to wait a whole night!" He turned around with arms flapping in the air.

"Deal with it," Lucian growled, and lifted me in his arms. He carried me down the steps.

We reached camp in no time, and the others helped make a fire and brew coffee. Lucian and George tried to push my shoulder back into place. He gave me his belt to bite on. It hurt like hell with his hand on my shoulder pushing hard, and I screamed and my eyes began to water.

Then I felt the click. Lucian put my arm in a sling he'd made out of his leather belt and pulled me on top of his lap.

I'd never felt so safe and so exhausted all at the same time.

It dawned on me what had transpired tonight. I'd accomplished something only five women had before me and I was the only one alive who knew what happened behind those doors. I'd promised on the life of my first born not to reveal any of it to anyone else.

I fell asleep as Lucian's rocking started to become more than just soothing. I could feel myself being moved as he took me inside the tent and laid me down on the sleeping bag.

Then everything fell into blissful silence.

30

I WOKE UP, drenched in sweat. It was quiet except for the sound of a fire dying, and water babbling in a nearby stream.

A faint light emerged from an electric lamp inside the tent. Lucian slept next to me. He looked so peaceful, and I reached out to stroke his cheek.

A deep growl emerged from my stomach, telling me I desperately needed food. I tried to slide out from beneath Lucian's grasp, but when he flinched, I stopped. He went back to sleep, and I waited another five minutes. Crickets chirped like crazy and the singing sound rang in my ears. I decided to make another attempt to get free. This time I managed and made sure that the pillow I slept on was tucked underneath his arm, just in case.

I just needed some time alone, without his constant worrying.

The *zip* noise sounded as if it would wake the entire campsite, but once I was out of the tent, I realized it was still quiet. I stared at the glowing coals that must have been a huge fire a few hours ago. There was no food left.

Not one bite? I picked up a log and chucked it in the fire. Orange coal dust rose into the sky. I jumped when I saw Blake leaning against a tree in the distance. My heart beat fast, and I took deep breaths to calm my nerves.

Blake guarded the entrance of the campsite and the moon lit up his face, making him look extra mysterious.

I swallowed hard.

Crap! Why do I feel like this around him? I shook my head. *Every girl feels like this in Blake's presence.*

He was writing in a small journal but stopped. I stared at Blake. He looked up as if he was searching for something in the sky then went back to writing in the journal. I assumed by the cloudless night, he was stargazing.

He didn't look at me when I reached him, but he buried his journal under his ass.

"Do you mind?"

"Sure, whatever," he mumbled.

His promise jumped into my mind—the one where he would give me his respect if I made it out alive. *It's so not going to happen, Elena.*

I sat opposite him, resting my back against one of the trees.

I don't think Blake likes anyone much, except his precious Tabitha.

"It was really brave what you did tonight," he said.

What? Is that a compliment?

"I guess anyone in my position would have tried their best," I said.

He huffed, and the corner of his mouth twitched. "How's the arm?"

"Hurts like hell."

He gave a lopsided smile and stared into the night again. *What does he hear?*

The crickets started to work on my nerves again. I sighed and decided that maybe it was time to go back to the tent.

"You're wrong about everyone being able to do what you did."

"Blake, please. I did what I said I would do." I didn't want to talk about it. It might be his way of trying to find out what I saw inside the cave.

I can't break my promise.

It was already hard enough not being able to tell them anything. I was dying to know a number of things myself. Like, who were those ladies playing in the dragon's garden?

"That's exactly my point. What people say they'll do and what they actually do are two different things, Elena. I learned that the hard way."

I felt sorry for him again, but knew exactly what he meant. Dad also said things and instead did the opposite so many times. "I always do what I say I will."

"You don't get it." He chuckled. "You could have asked to see anything."

"And your point is?"

"You have no idea why your dad died? Or why that dragon was after you? The pond would've even shown you where your mom is?" He looked away the minute he'd mentioned Mom.

How?

"How do you know about her?" My voice broke at the end.

"Just forget what I said."

I swallowed hard and felt angry; no one was supposed to know she might still be alive. The witch must've told him. After all, he was the highlight of her week.

He was right; I could have asked to see where my mom was or why those dragons attacked Dad that night. But what good would it have been? "It doesn't matter. The past isn't going to save us from any of this. I went in that cave to find out about the sword, and I did." I tried to hide the fact that I'd lost the only chance of ever knowing if my mom was still alive. Maybe I wouldn't even like what it would've shown me, and then what?

I made the right choice.

"It's brave of you to have given up that opportunity."

Whatever. I wanted to say it out loud, but knew if I did, I would probably say more things I would regret later on. I had to admit, a part of me would always regret not asking the pond where my mom was instead.

I pushed it from my mind and focused my full attention on the guy in front of me. "You guys were brave for coming with me."

"We're dragons, Elena. What kind of a Rubicon would I be if I chickened out?" Blake said with a soft smile.

"Still, it was very brave."

He sighed. "You have much to learn."

"So everyone tells me. Thanks for asking that dragon to give me the gift to understand Latin. I would never have been able to go through it, if it wasn't for that."

"Tell me about it," he mumbled, and I gave him a sarcastic smile.

"So, you guys really don't understand English when you're in your other form?" I asked. It sounded so stupid. Why didn't I just say dragon?

"No, dragon is what I am. My true colors show when he comes out. I don't have to hide the way I feel." He lifted up the left side of his butt and took out his packet of smokes. I started to cough as he lit one.

"So you know every time you end up hurting someone, during a claim?"

He nodded.

"You don't care?"

"It's not who I am." He released a deep breath. "I don't know how to explain it to you. A part of this form doesn't want to be a dragon and it clashes when I'm one. It's hard to explain."

"Dr. Jekyll and Mr. Hyde," I thought out loud.

"Exactly. The only thing that we've ever agreed on is this mission."

"Is it why you and Lucian are no longer friends?"

He glared at the tent where Lucian slept. His jaw muscles tensed.

Me and my big mouth.

"I knew he would tell you about us." He grunted.

"You didn't answer my question," I probed.

"Yes, Elena. The older I get, the more I want to be a dragon. The more I'm a dragon, the less I will stay human, which means I'll end up losing this." He gestured at his human form. "Believe me, I did Lucian a big favor."

"How can you say that, Blake? It's selfish to make that kind of a decision on his behalf."

"Elena, it's not that easy," he growled. "I know Cheng gave you the breakdown of what I'll turn into if I'm not claimed by a certain date. That part of me grows stronger every single day. My human form can't fight this. It's just too much, and you have no idea how much it hurts when I'm forcing myself to do the opposite of what *he* wants." He sounded defeated, as if the dragon in him had already won.

"Will it change if Lucian claims you?"

He started to laugh. "He will never claim me."

"He could, Blake."

"You live in a dream world. I'll become evil, and it's something I struggle to make peace with, but sooner or later, I'll have no choice."

"You don't have to," I said. "You have to fight it, Blake, don't give up."

"You think I'm not trying. I'm seeing the Viden on a daily basis just for one ounce of hope. Just so you know, I haven't found it yet, and to be honest, every time I leave that tower, I become happier. That's not a normal reaction," he snapped with a few cuss words in between.

"She did predict your true Dragonian being born."

He narrowed his eyes. "My Dragonian didn't get a chance to take a single breath. Goran made sure of it the night he killed them."

"You don't know that. What if he's born and no one knows about it? Like maybe not with Queen Catherine."

He looked at me with disgust. "Are you implying that the king committed adultery? The king loved the queen; he would never do that."

"How do you know that?"

"Because his dragon would have known." He was starting to get annoyed with me, but I didn't care.

"Oh, and you know Sir Robert?"

"Yes, he's my father."

I stared at him for a short while. *Sir Robert is Blake's father.* The wax doll of him at the museum jumped into my head. His eyes were the same as Sammy's. I should have seen it. "Your father's *the* Night Villain King Albert claimed?"

"My dad knew everything about them. He would've told me if that kind of hope existed. There is none, Elena. I've got no Dragonian."

For a second, I felt his pain and tasted his bitter defeat. It seemed there was no hope, and Blake would eventually become evil.

"Just try to give Lucian a chance to claim you, Blake."

His jaw muscles tightened again. "I can't. I'm already giving everything in me not to kill him." He got up while flicking his cigarette butt away.

I listened to him zipping down his tent with force. He was angry, and it was my fault.

I started to feel bad. I was insulting—not only to him, but to his father and the king. I sighed. He was right, there was no hope. If the dragon in him was already stronger, he would kill Lucian in the end.

My eyes stung, as I considered how this mission might end up being worthless. If Blake turned evil, we didn't need to worry about Goran destroying Paegeia. Blake would.

My stomach growled as I walked to the tent, and I crawled back inside to snuggle up next to Lucian again.

As I struggled to fall asleep, I silently wished that Constance was here to heal my shoulder. Heck, I would even welcome Julia with her drip. Then my mind shifted from the pain and began dwelling on Sir Robert. I couldn't believe he was Blake's father. How had he escaped that night, leaving his Dragonian alone? Night Villains were not known to be cowardly.

A series of scenarios played in my head. In some of them, I did see the Night Villain escaping, leaving the king and queen to fight for themselves. Maybe the Royal Council was right. Maybe the dragons had sided with Goran and his evil plan to destroy the king and queen.

Then an opposite scenario appeared.

What if King Albert ordered Sir Robert away, because he was Blake's father? Goosebumps ran down my entire body. Yeah, it sounded like something the king would do.

My eyelids started to feel heavy, and I drifted away.

~

I WOKE TO the smell of fish roasting over a fire. Lucian's place was empty, and I crawled out of the tent.

"Good morning, sleeping beauty." His voice came from the fire pit.

I smiled. "You know that story too?"

"We know all kinds of fairy tales. They have been told here for centuries," he joked. "How's your arm?"

"Much better," I lied. I would get it fixed once we were back at Dragonia.

"I'm glad to hear that. Are you hungry?"

I nodded without taking my eyes off the fish.

"It's almost done."

"I've never had fish for breakfast, but I don't care. It smells too good."

"Fish for breakfast?" Becky said in a singsong tone.

"Hey, I can only do so much," he said, shrugging.

"Where's Blake?" Becky asked as Tabitha crawled out of their tent.

My heart tightened at her words. "Is he gone?"

"He'll be back. He just needed some time alone," Lucian said and tasted a piece of fish.

I almost burst out laughing when he discovered that it was too hot. It was comical as he jumped around, spitting it out and frantically trying to cool his mouth.

"He better be. I'm not waiting for his brawny ass,"

Becky said as she disappeared back into her tent. "Wake up, George."

We chuckled softly when we heard "oomph", and I imagined her kicking a sleeping George.

She came back out with two bottles of water. "The food supply is getting low."

"It's only for tonight, then we'll go home. Right, Elena?"

I nodded. The dragon said that I was only allowed to tell them what I saw in the vision.

"Where's it we have to go?" Becky asked, curious.

"A mountains with a volcano. You guys know where it is?"

"The Mountain of Ekwador?" Arianna shouted.

I jumped a little. I hadn't even seen her walk up.

"Yes, it's where he's going to take the sword to destroy it."

"He wants to destroy it?" Lucian's eyes narrowed. He had so many of Blake's habits in him. "Who is it?"

"I don't know. He was old with dark brown hair that had started to turn gray. His dragon is a Sun-Blast."

"You saw him destroying the sword tonight?" Becky asked.

I nodded.

"We need to hurry up then," Lucian said. "Ekwador is a push from here."

"Which way?" I hated the fact that I was going to be

astride a dragon again, even if that dragon was Sammy. *Where is Sammy?*

"It's northwest of Areeth," he said. "Brian, see if you can find Blake. We have to pack up soon."

"Got it." Brian yanked off his jeans and exploded into his dragon form. His wings made such a thunderous noise that we all covered our ears with our hands. I unfortunately could only use one hand.

It was weird how everyone else went back to what they were doing, pretending that they hadn't just witnessed a human transforming into a dragon. I still watched Brian flying in the distance. I guess I needed to get used to the idea that it was normal to see dragons sharing the sky with birds.

Master Longwei was right about how easily someone like me could lose her mind.

As I stood thinking, Sammy emerged from the surrounding woods. Her hair was soaked, and she had a towel in her hand, which I assumed meant she had gone for an early morning swim in the river. She came over to me, and gave me a small hug.

We all dug in when the fish was ready. Lucian must have woken early to catch all of them. I didn't know if I should tell him about my conversation with Blake last night.

Brian came back and morphed the minute he landed with Blake not far behind him. I looked away as both of them pulled on their clothes. They hungrily took the plates Tabitha dished up for them.

Blake glared in my direction, and our eyes met for only a second.

I felt bad about last night, and I knew I shouldn't have said those horrible things. He was right—I had a lot to learn —and I hoped he could forgive me for what I'd said.

We finished breaking down the campsite after breakfast.

"So where do we go?" Blake asked.

"Ekwador, he's going to destroy the sword tonight in the volcano." Lucian while breaking down our tent.

"Who is it?"

"Don't know, Blake, Elena had never seen him before." Lucian sounded irritated.

"Let me guess, we *wing* this one too."

I rolled my eyes behind Lucian's back.

"Yeah, and if you got a problem with that, you're free to leave."

"Lucian?", and he just looked at me. I begged him with my eyes.

They had been best friends, for crying out loud.

"I hope you're right about this, Elena," Blake snapped at me, and closed the bag he carried with him.

The five dragons started to take off their clothes again, and I looked away. The people of Paegeia were so at ease with naked bodies. It was something I still needed to get used to. I listened to them changing and then the beating of their wings as they flew away, except Sammy and George.

I took a deep breath as Lucian helped me onto Sammy's

back. I really didn't like flying and held on to Lucian again. I shut my eyes and yelped as Sammy took off.

I didn't open them, but concentrated instead on her breathing. Her body expanded every three seconds and the sound coming from her wings made me wish that I had an iPod like Becky.

The trip wasn't as far as the one to the Sacred Cavern, but it was a stretch, as Lucian had said. He tapped my leg and I opened my eyes. In front of us was the picture I'd seen in the millpond. It was Ekwador.

31

SAMMY START SLOWING down beneath me, following the other dragons as they made their descent. I held Lucian's chest as tightly as I could with my good arm, and buried my face between his shoulder blades. I'd kept my eyes shut, trying to soothe my rolling stomach.

We landed with a hard thud, although I knew Sammy did try to make her landing as graceful as possible. She transformed back into a human after we'd slid off her left wing and were back on solid ground.

The dragons dressed quickly while the rest of us spent time discussing a plan of action. This mission was getting more dangerous by the minute, but the thought of returning home with the sword somehow made everything seem worth it. Blake and the others joined in the discussion once they had all dressed.

"Elena, what side is he coming from and when?" Blake started asking important questions.

I looked around and compared our surroundings with those I had seen in the Sacred Cavern. "It showed nightfall, we're in the exact right spot."

"Are you sure?" Arianna asked. She had that set to her jaw that told me she didn't trust me one bit.

"Yeah, positive. If I'm not mistaken, the volcano is just ahead about two miles." I pointed into the direction, and Brian sprinted down the path. He was the only dragon able to get close to a volcano.

"Okay, we have to corner the Dragonian here. We can't let him get past the PONR," Blake said.

"What is PONR?" I whispered to Lucian.

"Point of no return."

"Where's the sword, Elena?" Blake asked quickly.

"He was carrying it close to him. It was covered with some sort of fabric bound with string."

Pondering this information, Blake gave us our first goal. "So we have to find a way to snatch it from him. I doubt that he'll be compelled—"

"You're wrong," I interrupted, and Blake's expression changed from being sure about his plan to a huge frown.

He gazed at the ground for a minute. "Are you sure?" His voice broke, and he cleared his throat with a cough.

"Walking to the volcano, melting away to accomplish the task. I would say he's compelled."

Melting away? Becky mouthed, and I nodded. She shivered.

"What is it, Blake?" Lucian asked.

"It's not good." He started to pace around, clutching his hair. "If Goran controls him, he'll see everything, including us." There was a sense of alarm in his tone. A frown creased his forehead, and I could tell Blake was thinking really hard to come up with plan B.

"Is that bad?" I asked.

"It's very bad, you crazy lunatic," Tabitha yelled. "You've led us to our deaths."

"Tabitha, back off!" Becky jumped in, and Sammy uttered something that sounded like a swearword.

I didn't like Tabitha's tone one bit, but had to admit, she was really brave for sticking with us this long. Usually Snow dragons disappeared at any sign of danger.

"Tabitha's got a point, but we've made a choice," Blake said. "We can't transform, Lucian. We have to fight in our human form. Elena, to get back to your question, yes, the mission just turned into something suicidal. If Goran does compel the Dragonian, we are going to fight him indirectly. None of us are ready or trained for that."

We all fell silent. Fighting Goran wasn't on the agenda and running seemed like the only option.

"Blake, I will change!" Sammy sounded terrified.

"Sammy, if Goran controls the Dragonian, he'll see through his eyes. If he knows that we're dragons, he'll use magic. We will all die. We have to stay hidden, let him think that we're humans."

"I can't control it yet!" she shouted frantically.

"You can't change, Samantha!"

Tears rolled down her cheeks. "I really suck in Transformation class. I always turn when it gets too scary."

"Try," he pleaded with his sister.

She nodded, and Becky's arm curled around her shoulder.

"I can't fight Goran, Blake." Arianna had tears in her eyes too.

He walked over to Arianna and cupped her face in his hands. For a second I thought he was going to kiss her. "Don't think of it like that. You're the best with chants and spells. We need you, Arianna." Blake's tone was soft and sweet. He'd taken charge of this whole mission, and the worst part was that Lucian let him.

Lucian finally opened his mouth. "He's right, Arianna. Don't do anything stupid. If Goran knows that you can do counter and reversal spells already, he'll take you out first."

Arianna started to panic.

"You have to stay calm," Blake ordered her with her face still cupped in his hands.

Does he have the ability to compel someone?

"We'll have to hide, wait for him until he's surrounded. We can trap him, and if we need to fight, so be it," Blake said.

"Blake, who will get the sword?" George asked.

"Elena has already proven herself ready for something like this. Lucian said that you have crazy reflexes?"

I just looked at him with huge, unblinking eyes.

"Urgh! For crying out loud, what is it?" he asked.

"I can't do this, Blake," I said through gritted teeth.

"Elena? You're the only one that knows where the sword—"

"It's not that! My arm is killing me. I won't succeed with only one arm."

He looked at me with a glare, turned sideways, and cussed softly.

Why does he hate me so much?

"Fine!" He leaped toward me with huge steps. I retreated a bit, scared that he was going to cup my face too.

"Just relax!" He grabbed my arm and pulled me closer to him. He was inches away from me. I could feel heat radiating off his body.

He uncovered my shoulder and unbuckled the belt strap that had started to cut into my neck.

What is he doing?

"Don't look at me," he grunted.

I looked at Lucian, who was now glaring at Blake. My heart bounced as Blake touched my shoulder. I tried not to make a sound, but it was painful as a warm heat burned my skin.

What the hell? I wanted to see. As I analyzed the burning sensation, it reminded me of the time Constance healed my elbows after Art of War, but it was nowhere near this excruciating pain.

"I said don't look!" he yelled again.

My head snapped back to Lucian again and the warmth grew hotter. I bit hard on my lower lip as images of a burned patch on my shoulder popped inside my head.

A tear rolled down my cheek. Lucian dabbed it away with his thumb, and mouthed, *It's okay.*

It felt as if my shoulder was on fire, and I screamed out of pain as the heat reached a boiling point.

"Blake, that's enough!" Lucian yelled, and pushed him away from me. I looked at Blake, who knelt on the ground.

"What the hell did you just do?" I shouted.

"I'm sorry. I'm still learning how to control it," he said with a sting in his tone.

"How do you feel?" Lucian asked.

"I'm fine," I said.

"Do you think you'll be able to get the sword now?" Blake asked again.

I rolled my shoulder around. The pain was gone. I nodded and took a deep breath. It shouldn't be that difficult. *Then why does it feel as if I am going to fail miserably?*

"Why didn't you heal her arm earlier?" Lucian lashed out.

Blake turned around with his index finger inches from Lucian's face. "Don't start with me."

George and Brian stepped in between them and spoke softly to Lucian and Blake.

"Lucian, just drop it," Arianna said. "Her arm is healed. So please, can we just get back to the mission? I really want to go home, and we need a solid plan."

Lucian's jaw was set; he was angry and just glared at Blake. "You stay away from me," he said to Blake, who laughed.

"Blake?" Arianna said, and gestured for him to carry on.

"Fine, once Elena gets the sword, Sammy, you morph and get Elena the hell away from here. The rest of us will take care of the Dragonian."

ADRIENNE WOODS

"Okay," Sammy said in a faint whisper.

"Please, just try not to blow your cover," Blake begged his sister.

"I said I will try."

"It might work," Lucian said after a long silence.

"Of course it will," Blake said. The conversation changed over to who would be teaming up with whom after Sammy and I had fled with the sword.

"What if his Sun-Blast comes after us, Blake?" I asked.

He kept quiet.

"Don't worry about that, Elena." Brian winked at me. "Brian's got it covered."

"Brian, he might be fully grown," Blake said.

"Brian doesn't care. He's going to struggle to get past Brian."

Blake started to chuckle and the two high-fived each other.

"Idiot," Becky said in a singsong tone and rolled her eyes.

"That's good, Elena," Lucian whispered.

"What?"

"You're starting to think like a Dragonian in battle." He smiled reassuringly.

The corners of my smile pulled a little upward, but I still felt unsure about me being the one who got the sword.

"Don't worry, Elena, I'm really fast. I'll get us to safety, even if it's the last thing I do." Sammy misunderstood my unsure expression.

"I know." I decided to try to hide my fear. They were just as scared as I was. I would give anything for one of the council members or even Master Longwei to find us right about now. Becky said that Fin-Tail dragons were champions against all evil, and Master Longwei would fight with us. This really wasn't a task for teenage wannabe Dragonians.

We waited patiently for the Dragonian and his dragon to land, as Blake guarded the entrance.

I stared at him the entire time, thinking that he didn't seem to be scared of anything.

He was brave. I was glad Lucian had told him about the mission. I did feel safer with all of them here. What would I have done if it was only me?

"You know that he can see just as far in his human form," Lucian spoke into my ear. "His night vision is crazy good. When we were children, we used to play hide and seek at night. It was his favorite game, and he loved it when he was it. It didn't take him too long to spot us in our hiding places." Lucian's grin was satisfied as he told me memories of their friendship. He really missed the way it used to be between them.

I looked back at where Blake stood as he watched and waited for the Dragonian.

I noticed him sprinting down the path. That was the sign, and he dove for his hiding place behind a bush. There was no turning back now.

Becky was with Sammy trying to keep her calm, and I

prayed she would stay strong. I couldn't bear to think about what would happen if she transformed.

I put my hand in front of my mouth, trying to silence my breath, as the Dragonian and his dragon landed.

The Dragonian I saw in the millpond jumped off his Sun-Blast and landed perfectly in a crouched position. When he stood straight, I could see that he was still in a trance. Goran was his puppet master and he led the Dragonian straight to the volcano.

He waved in an unnatural position over his shoulder for his dragon to leave. I could hear how its wings flapped hard as it disappeared into the distance. That was what I was afraid of.

Sammy moved, and it sounded so loud in the cool silence. It made him stop and look around.

He started to run fast as he made his way closer to the volcano. When he was right in the middle of the trap, we acted, confidently jumping out of our hiding places. His back was to me as he looked at the others who were distracting him from the front. I didn't waste any time and went for the sword. I saw how I was going to push away his jacket with my one hand and grab the sword with my other, before I rolled into Sammy's path, who would be waiting for me. I reached out my arm, and the strangest thing happened.

He turned around a second too soon, saw me, and I froze.

32

I COULDN'T MOVE. I realized after a few seconds that it wasn't coming from me. The Dragonian had made it impossible for me to come any closer. The hoody of my blazer had fallen over my head from the instant stop, and I heard a horrible screeching. At first, I thought it was Sammy transforming out of fear, but the sound didn't come from her direction. His Sun-Blast swept low over our heads, and the Dragonian tossed the sword up to him.

Brian was the closest to the path that led to the volcano, and he morphed immediately. Everything happened so fast. When I looked again, Brian wasn't in his spot anymore. Arianna recited a spell, but the Dragonian shouted something that sounded like a counter spell, and she fell motionless.

Lucian grunted next to me. I couldn't see him, and when I tried to turn in his direction, my head felt as if it was going to explode.

Becky and George both stood in awkward frozen positions. They must have received the same spell that had me immobilized.

Blake charged toward the Dragonian. As his arm went for the Dragonian's neck, he got blasted back ten paces.

I didn't know if he was okay. It was all so unreal. I couldn't believe any of this was happening.

Sammy couldn't hold back any longer and transformed out of sheer fear. Vines and tree roots sprouted out of the ground, forming hands that grabbed her. They pulled her so tight that I thought she was going to burst in half. She squirmed and tried to wiggle herself out of them, but the more she tried, the thicker the roots became. I could hear a soft hum from the Dragonian, as he recited the words to his spells in rapid succession.

Sammy finally gave up and crashed to the ground. I looked around and noticed Tabitha had disappeared. She'd finally fled like the coward she was. Blake came dashing past me again. Soft hums came from him too, but he stuck to the plan and didn't morph.

The Dragonian shouted a spell with his one arm stretched out in Blake's direction. Blake fell hard, inches from me and Lucian. Our eyes met for one second and he looked away in defeat. A chill ran up my spine and my stomach turned.

We are going to die.

The Dragonian started to laugh and crouched next to Blake menacingly. "You really think you could stop me, boy?"

Blake grunted.

I hoped the Dragonian wasn't hurting him. It was hard for me to understand how strong magic was, and to be honest, it scared the living crap out of me.

"I'll kill you one day," Blake said through clenched teeth. "If it's the last thing I do!"

The Dragonian laughed. He stopped and looked at Blake's arm as he lifted Blake's sleeve with his thumb and forefinger.

"My, my, my, how exciting," the Dragonian said in a flat tone, but the laughter was real. It made my skin crawl. "The Rubicon tried to save the day. It doesn't suit you, Blake Leaf."

Blake growled again, and I could just imagine how defeated he must feel right now. There was nothing else he could have done.

"You're so full of anger," the Dragonian whispered to him. "I revel in the knowledge that deep down inside I know that you like it too." Even though he spoke softly to Blake, I still was able to hear the last part. "You won't kill me, boy. You want to know why? Because when you turn, you'll be mine." He laughed again, as if this was his favorite game. "Just think what we'll be able to do together. No one will ever get in our way."

"I'll kill myself before that happens," Blake roared like a lion being captured. Somewhere deep inside, I knew that Blake was fighting against that, while the Rubicon rejoiced.

"Wanna bet," the Dragonian mocked him, and stood up from his crouching position. "However, you'll hate me now because I'm going to kill all your friends one by one," Goran spoke through the Dragonian. "We can't have brave young teenagers running riot when I finally break free from that disgusting hellhole you love so much. Which one should I kill first?"

Blake cussed.

"Blake!" Lucian scolded through gritted teeth too.

"Eeney, Meaney, Miney, Mo." He counted us down one by one.

My heart thumped louder as he stopped in front of me.

Lucian roared like an insane person.

"Leave her alone, you freak!" Lucian didn't appear to care anymore what he said. The Dragonian ignored Lucian and walked straight over to me. He never took his eyes from me once. I swallowed hard and imagined how a gazelle felt right before the predator's kill. The only difference was that I had lost my ability to run.

My heart beat faster as he slithered nearer. Lucian was swearing worse than Blake, but the Dragonian didn't pay him any attention. He stopped in front of me and took a deep sniff. He reminded me of the rainbow dragon.

"Not a dragon," he said, and he slid my hoody off. His face froze. He just stared at me. He didn't make one peep, but our eyes were locked. I could see Goran's evil coiling from behind this man's soft gray eyes. I didn't know how long we stood there staring at each other. It was terrifying that he had so much mockery for Blake, but for me, he had none.

I was probably not worthy enough. Lucian was still ranting like a crazy beast.

The Dragonian's face unfroze, and darkness transformed his eyes from gray to black. I didn't think in a million years that he would do it, but when I felt the blade pushing into my stomach, I knew I wasn't going to live long enough to apologize for bringing everyone into this mess.

His blade thrust more than once in my stomach, each time a different entrance, twisting through my flesh viciously. He held me tightly while the laughter coming from his lips told me he enjoyed every single thrust.

"No!" Lucian's voice cried out the loudest, it didn't even sound like him. My whole body felt as if it was on fire. The last stab he kept the blade in and whispered something into my ear. It wasn't clear, and I only heard part of the words, like "woman" and "condolences."

I was concentrating too much on the mountain that was home to a blazing volcano. I could feel my sight slowly starting to disappear, but I couldn't tear my eyes away from the mountain. In the sky soared my last bit of hope. Not for me, but for my friends. I saw a Sun-Blast diving with the speed of light.

He came so close I could see the yellow of his eyes and the vertical pupil inside a pair of dark red irises. He picked up me and the Dragonian with his talons, and with one jolt, I was free.

Lucian caught me, but the pain was so intense it almost made me feel numb.

"Fight, Elena," he yelled as tears streamed down his face. It sounded as if he was speaking into a tin can. Becky pulled off her blazer and gave it to Lucian. His lips were moving, but this time there was no sound.

I could feel a thud, vibrating through the ground and saw Becky and Lucian jump. Becky disappeared. Lucian lifted me and carried me to safety. I drifted away into the deep darkness with the smell of his cologne lingering in my nose.

WHEN I OPENED my eyes, I saw the same familiar fan spinning above me.

I'm still alive?

I felt as if I was going to lose my mind and wanted to get up, but my fragile body wouldn't let me.

Constance was right by my bedside.

Is this for real? Am I alive? How can it be? Where are my friends? What happened?

My eyes must have told her I was freaking out.

"Relax, Elena," Constance begged, while she fidgeted with the drip. I felt drowsy and everything faded out again.

When I opened my eyes the second time, I found Master Longwei right next to me, sleeping.

I'm alive.

I could tell it was dark by the dimmed lights and the silence around me. My throat was dry, and my restlessness must have woken him.

"Easy, Elena."

"Water." It came out as a hoarse whisper. He poured me a glass, and I took a few sips.

"How do you feel?"

"Like I got stabbed with a knife."

He huffed and looked really pissed off. He had all the reason in the world to be. I bet if I wasn't lying here, he would have morphed into his dragon form and fried my ass on the spot.

"Did you get that while picking a fight with the Sacred Cavern's Keeper?" he asked, pointing to my wrist.

I frowned. *Why is he asking me that? Doesn't he know?*

An alarm went off in my head, which shook my entire body. All I could think about was what could have possibly happened to my friends.

I can't be the only survivor. I'll never be able to live with the burden.

"What happened?" I tried to get up.

"Relax, the others are fine."

"Swear!" I demanded.

"By my dragon's oath, I promise you, they are fine. Now calm down."

I nodded and lay back into the soft pillows. "Why don't you know what happened then?"

"They took a vow of silence." His tone indicated that he

was frustrated, and the way he was grasping the bridge of his nose with his index finger and thumb confirmed it. He sounded tired too.

"What?" I couldn't believe my ears. "Why?"

"They don't want to talk until you're awake."

"How did I get here?"

He swallowed hard and closed his eyes.

"We'd just found out that the nine of you were missing. A couple of us were going to search for you when Cheng spotted Blake coming in really fast. He missed the entrance and crashed through one of the walls. Constance was scared that his heart was going to explode. There was so much blood. She wanted to treat him, and that's when we found you, clutched between his front paws."

I struggled to swallow. *Blake saved my life.*

"I never thought in a million years that Constance would be able to save you, Elena. You had lost a serious amount of blood, but here you are."

"Is Blake—" I couldn't say the word.

"He's alright. He was down for two days, but now you would think that nothing serious ever happened."

I couldn't believe he'd actually carried me, flying so fast that his heart could have exploded.

"The other council members have been breathing down my neck asking me for answers, which I don't have. King Helmut tried to force it out of Lucian, not to mention the way Sir Robert threatened Blake and Samantha. The only thing they did deliver was a new King of Lion weapon. The queen's axes you had." He frowned. "Cheng's theory turned out to be more than just an overactive imagination. You can be glad that it carried some of King Albert's blood, Elena, otherwise none of you would have been here. Now please, enlighten me on all the details. I think I've waited long enough." He didn't sound pissed off, but there was something in his tone that told me he was done waiting and playing stupid teenage games.

I shivered just thinking about having to relive what had happened.

"It's my fault."

"What is?" he asked with a softer tone.

"This mission. It was crazy, but for some reason I was more terrified of what would happen if the wall was destroyed."

He took a huge breath.

"Cheng told me about the Sacred Cavern and the prize at the end when you finished."

His head jolted up. "You went inside the cavern?" Disbelief mixed with shock was all over his face.

"Yeah," I said.

"Elena, you're telling me that you are the sixth person that made it out alive?"

I nodded again and didn't understand why it was so hard for him to believe this. He always said the darker your mark, the more you will accomplish.

"I have the scar," I said, unsure. I mean, he was an ancient, and he should know what the scar looked like.

"I didn't think that you would have made it out alive. Do you know what could have happened if you didn't?" He raised his voice again.

My lower lip quivered.

He sighed deeply.

I swallowed my tears and carried on. "I had to know where the sword was. The council didn't make any progress, and at first, I was going to do it alone, but then Becky told Lucian and Lucian told Blake. It got out of hand, and where I was planning on a one-man mission, it became nine."

"Which only eight returned back alive from."

"What!" My heart skipped a few beats before it started to drum inside my ear.

"Brian..." He couldn't finish his sentence and just shook his head.

33

BRIAN'S DEATH WOULD be on my conscience for as long as I lived. It was my fault he was gone, and no amount of tears would bring him back.

This mission had been a pretty dumb mistake. I should never have gone after that stupid sword in the first place.

No matter how brave Master Longwei thought I was in the end, I felt like a failure. I hadn't saved Brian, and it should've been me instead of him.

I told Constance I didn't want to receive any visitors yet, and she respected my wishes.

Around eight, she dropped off a tray of food for me. I hadn't eaten anything during the past three days.

"Elena, you need to eat something, please?" She sat on the edge of my bed.

"That whole mission was for nothing," I said as new tears formed in my eyes. *I'm so angry.*

"It wasn't for nothing, Sweetheart. Brian didn't die for nothing. He died a hero, protecting his friends from pure evil. It's the code of the Metallic dragons and one King Albert believed with all his heart that the Chromatic carry too. This mission proved that, Elena."

The truth portion of my foretelling jumped into my head. At first, I thought it had been about the King of Lion sword and Cheng's theory, but it could be this. That dragon was dragon, no matter the breed.

"It's still my fault he's dead."

"No, Elena, it's Goran's fault. You guys weren't prepared to fight a sorcerer like him. To be honest, it's a wonder that most of you came back alive. What you did for Paegeia last week, it shows the kind of courage that doesn't exist anymore; it's what makes a true Dragonian. But for your friends to follow you all the way on this mission that seemed crazy, that's what makes kings and queens."

Pins and needles ran over my body as she said those words.

"You need to get out of this bed and carry on with your life. Your friends need to see you, and you need them now more than ever. Don't push them away. Brian wouldn't have wanted this for you." She gave me a soft kiss on my head and left.

I ate the beef stew Chef had made and drank the glass of milk on my tray. I felt so tired and decided to worry about facing life again tomorrow.

I found Lucian on a chair right next to me the following morning. He rested his head on my bed, and his eyes were closed.

A new tear rolled down my cheek. *Why does he have to be so beautiful? I don't deserve him. After what I have done, I don't deserve any of them.*

"Hey," he whispered, and brought me back to reality. He

came closer and closed his eyes while mumbling a couple of words that sounded like a soft prayer. "How do you feel?"

"Better now that you are here," I croaked.

He took a deep breath and leaned closer. "Don't ever scare me like that again. I thought when he thrust that blade inside of you again and again..." His face looked as if he was torn but at the same time relieved. Everything was so messed up and felt wrong.

"What happened, Lucian? How did Brian die?"

"It happened so fast. One minute we were statues and the next I could move. We only realized that it was Brian that had scooped you up when the other Sun-Blast came back for his rider. After Brian released you and the Dragonian, the two of them got into a fight. Brian was no match against a full-grown Sun-Blast. They collapsed near one of the sites. Set an entire forest on fire, or so George told us." His eyes sparkled with fresh tears as he closed them, trying to stem the flow. Strain appeared on his face, making it look as if Lucian experienced some sort of inner turmoil.

"Hey, it's okay. I'm fine now."

He shook his head. "When the Dragonian got up from the fall, I knew we weren't going to make it. Only when Blake picked up one of your axes and threw it at the Dragonian, did we realize what you had. The sword's ability causes its victims to explode. Queen Catherine's axes make them turn into dust. They took them away, Sweetheart, I'm so sorry."

Of course they took away my axes.

"Did Blake really save my life?"

He nodded.

"I owe him my life."

"You don't owe him anything, Elena. Blake's back to the egoistic son-of-a-bitch he always is."

I smiled and closed my eyes. It was silent for a while.

"Thanks for fighting to live," Lucian whispered in my ear.

"Why didn't you tell Master Longwei what happened?"

"It's not our story to tell."

"But your father—"

He put his index finger on my mouth. "Shhh, he'll get over it." He gave me one of Blake's lopsided smiles, and it vanished just as fast. Something wasn't right.

"What happened?"

"Nothing unexpected." His smile returned.

"Tell me."

"You've been through enough, Elena. I'm not going to burden you with a stupid story."

I huffed as I quickly put two and two together. "It's your dad, isn't it?"

His gaze fell to the floor.

"Is he forcing you to break up with me?" My voice broke.

Lucian's head jolted up. "No, Elena, I don't care what my father wants. You're my choice."

"Lucian, your father is the king of Tith."

"He could be the pope for all I care. We're not living in the sixteenth century anymore. I'll choose whom to love."

"You really think that it will be that easy. If your father disowns you, you will have nothing."

"I don't care!" he said, sounding like a spoiled brat.

"You have no idea what it is to have nothing. So don't tell me that you'll be okay with it. When you do discover ten years from now that you don't love me, you'll blame me for everything," I yelled, and grabbed my stomach where the Dragonian had stabbed me. It wasn't healed properly, and I should've given it more time.

Lucian was at my side and helped me to lie back on my pillow.

"Just take it easy. That will never happen. How can you even think that?" He sat on my bed and looked at me with gentle eyes. "I've never felt the way I do with anyone. Don't worry about my father. He'll never disown me. He'll come around once he gets to know you better."

I wasn't so sure about that. I knew the king would only see a troublemaker who didn't think before she acted. He would see me as a person who would get his son killed, because Lucian would always follow me.

I didn't tell him that. "You really love me," I whispered.

"With all my heart."

~

RECOVERY WAS HARD, but I got there. Becky,

Sammy, and Lucian visited me every second they could. Becky was a tough girl, but Sammy... She cried so much when she saw that I was okay that Constance had to give her something to calm her down. The way they acted, you would think that Becky was the dragon and Sammy the human. Still, they were the best friends a girl could ask for.

I was another four days in the infirmary, and all I could think of was my foretelling. It felt good knowing that I had fulfilled it. It was the choice I had to make. One, dangerous enough, that found its way scrawled into the Book of Shadows.

I realized that the truth prophesied was actually multiple things—one, that a dragon offspring could become a Dragonian; two, to learn that any sword or weapon could be turned into the King of Lion, you just needed blood from the true royals who didn't exist anymore; and last, that King Albert's theory about the Chromatic dragons was true. I couldn't wait to see the ink of my foretelling turn red. Only then, could I breathe again and carry on with my life without interference.

Life at Dragonia went back to normal. It spread instantly that I was the sixth person who had made it out of the cavern. The status was cool for a while, but the moment the Viden wanted to see me again, I hated everything about it.

Classes went back to normal, but not for me. Most of them still sounded like Greek. My tutoring lessons also carried on, and Latin became my worst nightmare once again.

They hadn't been kidding when they said that Blake had gone back to his old arrogant self. He was mean whenever I pronounced the words wrong. The one thing I did love was that we didn't talk about the mission at all. It was in the past and like me, I think Blake wanted to keep it in the past too. But I felt that I needed to do one more thing before I buried it completely.

"Thank you," I said during one of our lessons. He ignored my statement and carried on explaining the rules of grammar.

"Thank you, Blake," I said again.

He just looked at me with no humor on his face, stared at me for a while, then carried on.

I sighed, frustrated. I gave it another ten minutes and said thank you again.

"Stop it, Elena. There's nothing to thank me for, okay. I would've done it for anybody in that group." He sounded mean.

"What happened to 'you've got all my respect when you get out of there?'"

He huffed. "To be honest, I didn't think you would get out of there. So, I lied. Sue me."

"I thought dragons lived by their oaths," I snapped back.

"Those rules don't apply to me," he said.

I was so angry I kicked his shin, got up, and left.

"Elena!" He was down rubbing and complaining. I didn't care if it hurt, he was an asshole, and it was our last tutoring lesson anyway. My choice.

The following week, Cheng struggled to teach me history as he kept becoming sidetracked and begged me to tell him what was inside the cavern. At a stage he even tried to guess, which was really tempting, but I didn't break my promise.

Lucian's class was another story.

He wasn't the slave-driving demon anymore, and I dubbed his session as "making out time."

All I know was that I would never leave him, so I hoped he meant every single word when he said he loved me.

The tabloids were full of Blake, Arianna, Lucian, and Brian. With headings like; "Long Live the Chromatic" and "Axes Turning Evil to Dust." They didn't want to stop.

The rest of the tutoring ended when Master Longwei called the eight of us to his office. He told us we were too emotional to study for the exams and that the board was going to let us pass.

It was Tabitha's idea, and I couldn't believe that Brian's death was the miracle I needed to pass first year. It wasn't right.

THE LAST DAY of school came fast. I was going to spend half the summer with Becky and the other half with Sammy. Yeah, I didn't look forward to that other half.

Now that I knew Sammy's father was *the* Night Villain, I was actually a little scared but found some relief that her mother was a Swallow Annex like Constance. I spent the night before with Lucian up in the tower from which we'd started our mission.

"If my father finally comes to his senses, will you come and visit me at the palace?"

"Of course I will." I turned around to look at him. "I don't know how I'm going to spend this whole vacation without you."

He laughed. "Becky and Sammy live in Tith too, Elena. You will see me every day, I promise," he said.

His lips were warm on the tip of my nose. I lifted my chin and we found each other's lips in no time. It was a long, feverish kiss that left us both out of breath.

We stayed there until the sun came up. The morning flew by fast, and before I knew it, it was time to say goodbye to Lucian. It was so hard. His dad waited for him outside with Emmanuel and the royal carriage, so we had to say our "see you later" in the reception area.

He thrust a wrapped package with a beautiful bow in my hands. A girl had clearly helped him with this.

"What is this?" I yelled, as he reached the main door.

"Becky will explain, I'll speak to you tonight," he shouted back. "I love you, Elena Watkins."

The other students in the reception made fun of his last line, but he waved it away. He didn't even wait for an 'I love you' back.

As I went back to my room to pack my bag, I opened

the wrapping and couldn't believe my eyes as I looked down at the Cam-phone nestled in my hand.

"You got your first Cammy," Sammy said. "This is so awesome."

"May I?" Becky held out her hand, and I gave it to her with a new feeling of excitement deep inside my core.

"It is the new Raindrop 5. It must have cost a fortune."

"Please, Lucian doesn't know what that word means." Sammy rolled her eyes and took it from Becky. She slid it open and yanked hers from her backside pocket. She spoke her name into the device and repeated it a few times before lining up the two phones next to each other. When she had a satisfied grin, she put hers away.

"Sammy Leaf," she spoke for the last time into the speaker of my Cammy, and her phone started to ring. It had a techno beat to it, and she jumped up and down in the same spot, pleased with herself. "Whenever you want to call me, just say my name. I'm the second in your contact box."

I can guess who the first is.

"I promise I'll phone you at least once a day, Sammy Leaf."

"You guys?" she cried animatedly. "I'm going to miss sharing a room with you."

"I'm going to miss that too, Sammy," Becky said. "Don't forget, twelve o'clock my house tomorrow afternoon, and don't be late."

"What, no George?" Sammy joked.

"He's gone for three weeks in Acapulco, and I don't know what I'm going to do with myself."

"George is going to the other side?"

"Yeah, he's so excited about it. It was a big surprise. His mom and dad wanted him to keep it a secret. I wish I could go with him."

"Stupid wall," I said, sulking. There were so many places I wanted to visit myself. We helped Sammy with her luggage and loaded it on one of the carriages Tabitha and Blake already occupied.

"These three weeks are really going to suck," she whispered.

We giggled, and I gave her a big hug before she climbed into the carriage and left.

Becky's mom picked us up at three. She waited near the forest, next to a silver Audi. Becky ran to her and jumped into her arms. Her mom was really beautiful. She had big dark eyes and brown hair, just like Becky. The only problem was she seemed too young to be a mother. I also noticed that they shared the same eye for fashion, and she wore a nice top with jeans and knee-high boots.

She kissed Becky's face fiercely, and I giggled when Becky complained, wiping her face with her hand.

"I have missed you so much," her mother said.

"Missed you more."

"You've got to tell me everything about this mission, Becky." Her eyes were full of excitement.

"Oh crap, Elena." Becky suddenly realized that I was there too. "Mom, this is Elena. Elena, the perfect mom."

"She's such a drama queen, but she's right about the perfect mom," she said.

I reached out my hand for her to shake.

"Oh please, come here." She pulled me in a long warm hug. A beautiful smile appeared on her face as she let go. She looked over at Becky. "Get in the car. We still have a long drive back home."

She started the car, and the stereo boomed the same stupid song about a miracle. I thought I would never listen to it ever again, remembering what had happened the last time I'd heard it. Becky and her mom sang out loud with the lead vocalist, as she turned down the road. Their relationship reminded me so much of the one I'd had with Dad; when we didn't have to flee for our lives and things actually felt normal. They were best friends.

I glared out the back window, and sighed as trees passed by. I thought about Brian and about Dad. Both had died while protecting me. Buildings started to rush by. Somehow, I had got my miracle, even if it wasn't the way I truly wanted it. To my surprise, I started to smile.

THUNDERLIGHT

ADRIENNE WOODS

AMAZON
UNIVERSAL LINK

1

CASTLE IN ETAN
GORAN

ANGER, BETRAYAL, AND hate turned my stomach to acid. It consumed my mind and I watched as bottles, papers and books flew off the desk and crashed to the floor.

A maid rushed to my side. She didn't say anything, but her eyes reflected fear in their watery depths. The dustpan in her hand trembled as she started to sweep up the jagged shards of glass. Rising, she began to straighten the books that had fallen to the floor in a heap. Every few seconds her eyes darted in my direction as if a mere breath would make me lash out at her with my outstretched hand.

I touched her face gently until my hand reached her soft, shapely neck, squeezing slowly as my anger began to rise once again. My grip tightened as I lifted her from her position at my feet until her face was level with mine. Listening carefully, I heard her heart fluttering like a bird trapped inside a cage.

"How did I become this way?" I spoke.

She just stared at me with round, brown unblinking eyes sunk deep into the surface of her face; her cheek bones were sharply defined.

Looking at her sullen expression made me feel worse. I lifted my other hand and struck the woman hard across her cheek.

A cry left her mouth and I threw her from me as if she weighed nothing. She skidded across the floor, landing in a heap against a wall of cold, unforgiving stone. *If I was a dragon I would blast fire, reduce this wretched place to a pile of insignificant ashes.*

Two other maids, hearing the startled cry, rushed into the room. Their eyes were wide as they took in the state of the room and the immobile heap near the far wall. "Sorry, m'lord," the older one said, her voice trembling. "She's new, we will train her better."

They picked up the maid who had come to and was sobbing. She clutched the side of her face, covering the huge, red handprint where I'd struck her.

I nodded. The old maid knew her place well, although I still didn't care for her name, she knew where she stood.

I threw myself down onto the chair and closed my eyes. A silent roar growled inside of me, lighting a fire of rage deep in my core.

The girl had made it.

The Rubicon had saved her life, so a part of him was still fighting me. I could still see her eyes searching mine. They bore into my soul, seeking answers. *How was this possible! The wall wouldn't allow any human to go to the other side.*

Albert's laughter echoed inside the castle—a startling

reminder that good would always win. He would pay dearly for this. I would find a way, and I promised myself she wouldn't live much longer.

I pushed myself up from the chair and rubbed my face, hard. The anger escaped my lips making a sickening sound. Rage that emanated from deep within me overpowered the haunting laughter and echoed throughout the entire castle.

"Master," Cain's voice interrupted my thoughts.

"Speak, my loyal servant," I said. "What is the news?"

"Everything is in place. We won't fail you," his voice said in my head.

I closed my eyes, took a deep breath and let it out hard. "We'll see."

TITH
ELENA

S

UMMER WAS ALMOST over, but everyone's spirits were high as Sammy searched for something in her room. I had recently arrived at the Leafs after spending the first weeks of my vacation with Becky. Sammy was in rare form this evening as she bounced off the walls of with barely contained excitement.

"Elena, cheer up! We're going to the Warbel games and I know it sucks that Lucian won't be there, but I promise, you're going to enjoy it, okay?" Sammy spoke fast as I moved out of the way of one of her shirts sailing toward me.

"Sammy, it's not like I'm trying to be like this, I just really miss him..." My lips puffed out a breath. "Tell me again why the Warbel games are so mind-blowing." I tried to change the subject away from Lucian. He was still away on a hunting trip with his father, and the girls had decided the best way to brighten my mood was a sport that basically sounded like Greek warfare. I still had no clue what the Warbel games were about even after Sammy tried to explain it to me while searching for the jersey of her favorite team. It sounded exciting as words like soldiers, attackers and scorers made it into her lengthy description.

"Because it's the Warbel games," she said.

The only thing I retained was that Warbel was some sort of dragon and human sport that they loved to play on this side of the wall. She also said that Dragonia had a similar game at the beginning of each school year, but it wasn't as dangerous as the real one. I became even more confused when she started talking about raiders and incantations and couldn't figure out how all of it came together.

Guess I'll have to see it before I can really understand what it's all about.

"The one thing you need to understand is that the game we are going to tonight is really dangerous," she added as she continued to tear apart her closet, "and that the humans who participate are extremely well developed magic wielders, for their own safety as much as for winning the game."

I still had no clue what the Warbel games were about. *Okay, awesome.*

Sir Robert had gotten five tickets for all of us from a friend who couldn't make tonight's game.

Lucille, Becky's mom, had also gotten tickets for her, Becky and George, so we were all going to the game together.

I had spent the first three weeks of my vacation with Becky and Lucille. Lucille was not a typical mother, but was the most selfless person I'd ever met. She also seemed way too young to be Becky's mom and looked more like Becky's older sister. She hated it when I called her Mam or Mrs. Johnson, and insisted that I called her by her first name. She was a lot like Becky in a sense; they shared the same type of fashion choices and clever comments, but she also had a love of art, which Becky didn't. That part connected with me one hundred percent.

Becky and her mother lived in the totally opposite neighborhood to the Leafs, and they had more money than I could even dream of. I guessed it was why Becky was a bit of a brat. Staying with them made me realize what type of a person she could be sometimes. Having all that money made Becky bossy and turned her into someone I never thought I would be friends with. But the thought of not having her around to give me her two cent comments, especially when I didn't ask for them, was unthinkable. She was also one of the bravest and fiercest girls I knew, and the best friend, apart from Sammy, a girl could ask for.

As we continued to look for the jerseys and get ready Isabel came up to give us a five-minute warning. Blake had vanished around five, simply saying that he would meet us there. Sir Robert had given him his ticket before he disappeared so he would be able to find us.

Ever since that night at camp when he got wasted and put me under some sort of hypnotizing spell which almost made us kiss, which was seriously ridiculous as he despised me, he'd been acting like his old self: arrogant and a total dick. Something about Blake always wanting me when he was wasted made me wonder about the things he was hiding, and if maybe those things only came out when he was drunk.

I shook my head and the thoughts of Blake washed away as I grabbed my bag and followed Sammy to Sir Robert's old sedan.

The drive wasn't that long and I gasped when Sir Robert pulled into the parking area in front of a giant mountain. There were at least a million cars already parked in neat rows and the noise coming from inside the mountain told me that it must be where the Warbel games took place.

Crowds of people wearing different colored jerseys, caps and scarves huddled around. Some even carried flags, and I saw a yellow one with a huge hornet on top of what looked like a raider.

Raiders were flying objects that made me think of an enhanced skateboard.

Everywhere in Paegeia's parks, and ports, people flew

on them. You needed a special license for one and I tried so hard to suppress my laughter when Becky told me that her next try would be her fiftieth or so attempt to get hers.

Becky wasn't one of the safest drivers out there. I still wondered every time I was her passenger if the inspector who had given her her driving license hadn't been smoking weed or something.

We climbed out of the car and a feeling of excitement rose inside my chest as I followed the Leafs into the opening at the bottom of the mountain. It was dark, as the only light came from tiny globes mounted in the wall. It took a while for my eyes to adjust to the soft glow of the lights as we piled into another tunnel.

People pushed and shoved us as we tried to make our way to our seats. The pace we moved was reasonable for such a big crowd, but it was still too dark and too cramped for my liking. We finally stopped when the people in front of us didn't move. I hated every second we had to wait for whatever held up the crowd to pass. I was feeling jumpy and took huge breaths as the heaviness on my chest came back, mixed with a shot of adrenaline.

"Are you okay?" Sammy asked softly and I realized that I was squeezing her hand tightly.

"Sorry, just crowded. What's happening at the front?"

"It's normal, we are close to the check-in point."

I flinched as a huge horn blew right behind me. It echoed off the wall and sounded like an archangel announcing doomsday.

The crowd barely moved now, and I felt like punching the guy when he blew on it a second and third time. The other people thought it was funny, and I wished I felt the same spirit inside of me, but this dark passageway was starting to seriously creep me out.

After a few minutes, I could finally see the outline of what looked like five cubicles and people moving into rows. We took the one closest to us and waited until it was time to present our tickets. Ours had blue dots on them and I still had no idea what I was going to find tonight.

It took a few seconds for my eyes to adjust as we entered a lighter room. Six black elevators, three to a side opposite one another, made my heart jump a bit faster.

In Paegeia, an elevator wasn't just an elevator. It was how the people of Paegeia traveled around the world, if you were a dragon, and inside Paegeia, if you were human. I hadn't experienced one myself and had only seen them once inside their funny-looking tubes when we went to fetch George at the Wall when he'd come back from the other side.

"Are these the same elevators they have at the Wall?" I spoke softly.

Sammy laughed at the small shake in my voice. "No, Elena. They are normal elevators."

People surged forward again as they maxed the elevator's weight limit and I saw Sir Robert pushing the blue button. He wore a black t-shirt with a pair of jeans and a baseball cap. Wrapped around his neck was a green and black striped scarf.

Sir Robert Leaf was Sammy and Blake's father and, The Greatest King That Ever Lived, King Albert's dragon. He looked nothing like the figure inside the museum of Etan, and he was nothing like I'd imagined. He was kind, always friendly and no matter how much Blake pissed him off, he would give me a soft look and a friendly smile. It was hard to imagine that he was Chromatic, a Night Villain, and one of the vilest dragons that roamed this world. The people of Paegeia didn't address him as Sir Robert anymore. Some of them even thought that he'd had something to do with betraying the king, but I knew better. He missed his rider every single day; he missed his Dragonian.

His wife, Isabel, stood next to him with her arm wrapped in his. She wore a parka with a green-and-black striped beanie. A huge smile, along with pure excitement, was written all over her face. She was the spitting image of her twin sister: the first time I saw her I'd thought for a second that Constance, the doctor at the Infirmary, was Sammy and Blake's mom.

Sammy had doubled over with laughter when she saw my expression. She was a Swallow Annex, just like Constance, and I was sure if you put them together you wouldn't be able to tell them apart just by looking at them. She was also just as kind as her twin and made me feel at home the first moment I stepped inside their house.

The elevator screamed as we ascended into the peak of

the mountain. It felt like forever and a million things that could go wrong filled my head. The door finally opened and we all had to get out so a couple at the back could exit.

When the door opened for about the fifth time, we spilled out.

We took a sharp left and walked into a stadium that was located at the very top of the mountain.

Hot flushes rolled through my body I really hated my fear of heights.

The crevice at the top of the mountain was wide open and a million stars shone in the sky. Bright lights blinded me for a second and when my vision came back Millions of seats were stacked in rows, mounted against the wall. It resembled a normal football stadium, except there were no poles and as far as I could tell no floor either.

VIP boxes were located at the very top of the mountain and I couldn't recall ever seeing so many people in my entire life.

Two huge bells elevated in the air were stationed in opposite directions and flags of all colors were flapping around the crowd. Blue, red, black, yellow, light blue and green holographic flags hung in the air and huge screens were located on all sides just below the VIP boxes. Somehow Sir Robert spotted Becky and George in the crowd and pointed in their direction. Lucille saw us and waved excitedly.

Blake was still nowhere to be found and I guessed he'd

probably snuck inside one of the boxes with someone. After all, he was a famous dragon.

When we finally reached them, Lucille gave me a warm hug while Isabel and Sir Robert greeted her with two kisses on each side of her face.

The vibe coming from the people in the crowd was overpowering. Some had dyed their hair the same color as the team they were rooting for, while some simply had scarves and jerseys on. It was so consuming that I didn't know where to look.

I saw the instrument that had made the horrible racket from half an hour ago. Every other person in the crowd had one, and I finally saw the humor in them as I watched George blowing on one too. It made a hollow, low sound and I had to cover my ears as George's breath lasted for at least two minutes.

The people around us applauded him when he finally ran out of breath and Sir Robert slapped him on the back. Becky and George both had a green beetle painted on their left cheeks.

"Ladies and Gentlemen, boys and girls... Oh and dragons," a loud voice said over the sound system and the crowd went crazy. "Welcome to the two-hundred-and-fifth annual opening of the Warbel games!"

Fireworks went off and glittered in enormous star-bursts in the sky. I gaped at the display as it lingered for a few minutes before the sparks descended. People yelled and cheered with their flags flapping in the air as horns blew.

The voice continued to speak about sponsors and the people who'd made all of this possible. It was followed by a small show I'd only seen on TV. It was a display of Chinese dragon puppets twirling in the air. Fire erupted from the puppets and the crowd cheered again. After the show, the voice came back.

"Now the moment everyone has been waiting for. I'm honored to present this year's teams. The Sapphires!"

A team of humans flying on their raiders and dragons flew out of a huge door that opened on the opposite side of the arena.

The players all wore white-and-light blue uniforms, with flying goggles over their eyes and vests for protection. The man who led them did a somersault in the air and landed on his board once again; everyone just soaked up his performance and screamed for more.

"That is Luke. It's a shame he plays for the Sapphire team, he is so frawesome," Sammy yelled and I laughed at her made up word, putting freaking and awesome together. It was something she and Becky were really good at. A close-up of Luke appeared on the big screen. He grinned with his goggles now resting on top of his head, and waved at the crowd. I knew his face from the poster on Sammy's bedroom wall.

"Which team are we supporting?"

"Duh!" She pointed to Becky and George's green shirts. The name "Green Masquerades" stretched across the front and back with the outline of a dragon's head.

"Go Masquerades," I said weakly.

Sammy laughed at my pathetic attempt at a cheer.

The voice over the speaker introduced all the players on the team. There were four humans gliding on their raiders. Four dragons, a Copper-Horn, a Fire-Tail, a Moon-Bolt and a Night Villain, flew out from an opening in the cave wall and hovered in the air below their human team members.

The next team, the Yellow Hornets, flew in from above our heads and the crowds painted and dressed in yellow blew on their horns. Around me yellow flags flapped in the wind created by the beating of the dragons' wings.

They came to a halt opposite the Sapphires and the voice introduced all of the players. One dragon blew a fire bolt into the crowd as a cheer rose, but an invisible wall blocked it before it could do any damage. The crowd rooted as the Sun-Blast dug in and dove into the air.

Another team, this time wearing blue and black uniforms was introduced as The Blue Raiders. I noticed as each team received their introduction that the dragons all had abilities and almost every team had a fire-breather and a Swallow Annex.

Two more teams, the Red Crusaders and Black Leapers were introduced to roaring cheers from the crowd. Last was the Green Masquerades and I was excited that it was finally our turn to cheer.

Four humans dived out on their boards to a roar of applause. The one in front made a loop on the raider and was followed by a couple more.

"That's Blaze, she's so amazing on that raider of hers!" Sammy yelled into my ear.

"That's a girl?" I yelled back.

Sammy's dimples dented deep into her cheeks. "It's not just men participating. She's been the captain of her team for the past four years," she yelled. "She's tried every year to get Blake on the team but the council doesn't want to budge. He can't even participate in his human form."

"Why not?"

"Multiple abilities, who knows."

That is so unfair. He's not allowed to do anything. No fun. No wonder he messed things up.

The booming voice introduced the four humans. Blaze Trulip was the captain just as Sammy had said. She wasn't afraid of anything, and she played the role of soldier, which meant that she could be everywhere, score, defend, attack and help keep the other team from scoring. The guy next to her was Wilson DJ, who was introduced as the keeper. Richard, the diver, was one of the scorers with Baba Johnson. He bowed on his board which made the crowd cheer the loudest. The four dragons were Kyle, the Snow Dragon, Peter, the Sun-Blast, Dez, the Copper-Horn and Fick, the Green Vapor. They were the four attackers.

Once the team introductions were made the five referees were introduced. They wore black pants with boots and white-and-black striped shirts. They each had flying goggles and a baseball cap on their heads.

Sir Robert and George growled at the same time when

Peter McIntosh was introduced as one of the referees this year. "He's a cheat," George yelled.

Clearly half the crowd didn't like this Peter McIntosh dude, but he handled it well. The crowd booed when he bowed as deep as he could.

"The Yellow Hornets are going to win this year for sure," Sammy said. "He used to be their coach."

I shook my head. I'd never been into sports, for exactly that reason. Dad hated it when they cheated at football. This would have been a game we could have enjoyed together. I could just imagine how he would've explained this one to me. I smiled as I imagined him babbling excitedly about scorers and attackers, the words coming from his mouth fast while he crouched on the couch, like he did whenever he got excited when his favorite football team was about to score.

He must have missed this, I thought painfully. Knowing my father, this was definitely his sport. He used to yell at what patsies the quarterbacks and football players were whenever he used to watch the Sunday games. I still didn't know what a patsy was, but the way he used it, it had to be something lame.

I cheered along with Sammy and everyone else when the teams left the arena. The Yellow Hornets and Sapphires stayed behind for tonight's game.

The players each took their places on the field, if you could call it that. The two keepers stood in front of the two bells and we were in the perfect spot as each bell faced us on opposite sides. The rest of the players stood in a row in front of the keepers. They looked so small, but the big screens captured each of their faces in turn.

One of the referees, not the McIntosh dude, was chosen as the main ref for this game. The other four stood on the sidelines. When the whistle blew, the four dragons dove down with the scorer and the two soldiers. Their main target was a huge axe that dangled in the air a few yards below them.

Fire, frost, and acid balls flew through the air in rapid succession. All of them bounced off the invisible shield that protected the crowd and everyone cheered again as one of the humans on the yellow team got to the axe first. His goal was to hit the huge bell on the opposite side. He ducked and dove on his board, and missed a number of fire bolts, as a frost ball smashed into snowflakes right behind him.

The crowd hailed and it turned into what I knew as a wave. It was so fun to participate as it came our way.

When the man with the axe realized he was trapped, he threw it through the air to one of his teammates.

Seeing an opportunity, one scorer from the Sapphire team went for it, and grabbed the axe before the other yellow scorer caught it. The Sapphire crowd jumped up in their seats and yelled with fists pumping in the air.

By the sound of Sammy's rooting, I knew we were cheering for the Sapphires tonight.

The scorer, whom I assumed was Luke, twirled around on his board, ducking and diving through a couple of bolts and with a loud 'gong', he hit the bell with the axe. An animation of a dragon jumping up and down with a huge '3' flickering behind him appeared on all the big screens.

Everyone I'd come with tonight whistled and yelled wildly.

Luke's human team members congratulated him with high fives, slaps and everything you could think of to say well done.

I laughed as one of them bumped him with their head.

After the celebration was over, the players went back to their positions and the whistle blew once again.

The Yellow Hornets scored next and then the Sapphires were on fire, scoring three times in a row. Each time that animated dragon would come back, announcing the total points of the team who'd just scored. I now understood why Sammy was so crazy about Luke; he was really fast and always had a smile on his face.

As the game progressed, the crowd drew in a collective breath as a fire bolt headed for one of the human players. It was too late to block it and the fire bolt struck the player. One of his teammates caught him as his board came smashing against the shield protecting us from the action. His teammate dropped him off at a Swallow Annex standing off to the side, who I assumed was there for medical reasons.

"This is why this game is really dangerous. You've got to pay attention," Sammy said without taking her eyes off the commotion.

The crowd cheered when the player got up, but he was way too disoriented to carry on and they had to make do without him.

The game started again when the Yellow Hornets scored another point.

Dragons flew in all kinds of directions, using their abilities on one another, while the scorers tried to gain extra points.

Suddenly, the crowd went completely silent as all the dragons in the arena froze in mid-air. As if on strings, they all turned their heads in unison in our direction and came charging at us with a venomous look in their fiery eyes.

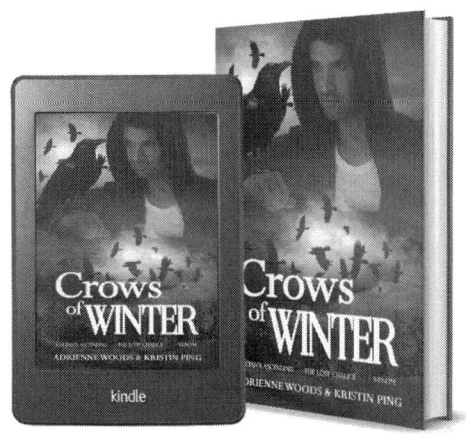

Enjoyed Firebolt. Here is another Free Book written exclusively by Adrienne Woods and USA Today best selling author Kristin Ping.

Ethan Sutcliff seems like a normal seventeen-year-old—at least that's what he's trying to portray. In a secret society run by the Supernaturals, Ethan is what witches call a Bender. Benders are Witches' Guardians, who are able to control a witches' ability, bend it, or move it away from harming humans. In Ethan's case, he is able to bend the Earth element. But at the age of fifteen, he lost all connection to it, and the reasons behind it could only mean one of two things: His Wielder is either dead, or hiding out somewhere.

Alex Burgendorf has been living in her aunt's locket for the past sixteen years with her mother—a Fire Wielder, and her father—a Water Wielder. For sixteen years, her parents vowed to protect her, and they have, as she is the last Earth wielding witch. However, time is running out. Alex must find her Bender, or the fate of the Supernaturals might be at stake.

Get Hinder Now

ABOUT THE AUTHOR

Adrienne Woods was born and raised in South Africa, where she still lives with her husband and two beautiful little girls. She always knew she was going to be a writer, but it only started to really happen about eight years ago. In her free time—if she gets any because moms don't really have free time—she loves to spend it with friends, whether it's a girls night out, or just watching a movie. She's a very chilled person. Her writing career started with *Firebolt*, book one in the *Dragonian* series. Her other series, *Dream Casters*.

SUBSCRIBE TO NEWSLETTER

For more information please visit:

www.adriennewoodsbooks.com

Printed in Great Britain
by Amazon